SEER'S CHOICE

Jennifer Sanders

and

Christen Stovall

Printed in the United States of America

First Printing, 2022

ISBN: 978-1-7362662-3-6

for Carrie and Jay

Contents

Acknowledgements

Cover design by Sabrina Watts, Enchanted Ink Studio. Our thanks to everyone who took the time to read our drafts and bring this story to completion.

A note from the authors

Any 'clan traditions' or ceremonies referred to in this work exist only in our imaginations and should not be confused with anything resembling fact—we just thought they would be fun. Our thanks (and apologies) go to the Maclaren and Stewart clans.

Chapter One

An Awkward Beginning

To find one's attention wandering in social situations is invariably awkward; doubly and triply so when said situation is a ball on the eve of the London Season's most prestigious wedding. On this particular summer evening, Ione Brentwood found herself in this unenviable condition—for the wedding was hers, and she had lately discovered that she wanted no part of it.

"Oh, my dear, I do congratulate you. Such an excellent match!"

Ione blinked and focused on the powdered cheek being presented to her, belatedly realizing she was being spoken to. "Thank you, Lady Whiteworthy," she murmured, and pressed her own cheek to the elderly woman's, the movement more reflex than genuine embrace. "And thank you for coming this evening."

Lady Whiteworthy waved a lacy handkerchief in the air. "Nonsense, child. Your engagement to my

1

great-nephew is the talk of the Season!" She huffed out a laugh. "Never thought he would amount to much, that boy, but your accepting him has quite elevated his standing in... certain circles, shall we say?" The old woman tapped the side of her nose with a gnarled finger. "Your bloodline—your gifts—can only enhance the Gibson name. And your dowry, of course—though we needn't speak of that." She lightly patted her bony chest and sighed wistfully. "I am so very pleased with you both. Do you know, I am considering altering my will in Theodore's favor? And," she paused magnanimously, "I shall certainly do so if there is a child who inherits its mother's gifts. There!"

"Thank you," Ione repeated automatically, though internally she was trying not to take umbrage at Lady Whiteworthy's assessment of her value. Her father, she knew, viewed things in much the same light—as did many members of the secretive community to which her family belonged. Ione had had several offers, John Brentwood had held out for the plum: Theodore Gibson, son of a wealthy, Fae-touched, magical family, much like Ione's own. Ione's desires had hardly entered into it at all.

By the door she could see her parents greeting guests as well: Papa, handsome and imposing, and Mama, her elegant beauty faded not one whit by the passage of time. Ione looked about the glittering ballroom, decorated to the rafters in celebration of her wedding on the morrow. Imposingly tall vases overflowed with pink and white roses; candelabra with strings of crystal teardrops lent sparkle everywhere one looked. Music floated through the air, inviting guests to the dance floor. It was dazzling, beautiful, everything anyone could want; but the magnificent trappings left Ione feeling chilled, the weight of her predicament growing heavier with every handshake and congratulation. Her stomach churned with anxiety that twisted into guilt-fueled misery.

Ione turned to study the gentleman at her side. Theodore Gibson, the man of the hour, winner of Ione's hand, was hardly the strapping hero she'd spent her youth dreaming about. He was a slight figure, with perfectly groomed chestnut hair and mustache. The man was adequately kind, though with a pompous tendency to override any opinion that did not align with his own. She would never want for anything material as a member of his family, and while his Fae-touched talents were simply ordinary, the rarity and prestige of her own more than made up for that. In short, he was exactly what a young lady of breeding hoped for at the beginning of her first season. Their courtship had been a blur of elegant parties, social gatherings, and ill-disguised glee from her father: a whirlwind that had swept Ione up and dropped her at the doorstep of a marriage that held no promise of true happiness.

Ione didn't dislike her fiancé, exactly. In truth, she felt nothing for him at all—only a numbness where affection ought to exist. There was no thrill when he walked in the door, no flutter of anticipation when she thought of building a life with him. Instead, the prospect of her future left Ione feeling empty, and that was at the heart of her current misery. She was living a lie, with no end in sight.

Ione's attention was once again pulled from her anxious musings when a pair of gloved hands wrapped around hers. To her delight the hands belonged to her beloved cousin, Lady Tamsin Claremont.

"Ione!" The blonde beauty kissed her on both cheeks. "You are in excellent looks as always, my dear! May I offer my congratulations, to you and your intended?"

"Tamsin! Oh, I am *so* happy you're able to attend," Ione replied, unable to keep her voice from wobbling. She pulled her cousin into a tight hug, holding onto her for a moment longer than intended. Tamsin had a way of making situations that felt wildly out-of-control seem manageable. It was something Ione envied and admired about her. After another second of desperation, Ione finally released her cousin and attempted to smile as she introduced her soon-to-be husband. "And this, Theodore, is my very dear cousin, Lady Tamsin Claremont."

Theodore looked her cousin up and down, before offering a slight dip of the head—an indication that he found her adequate. "Yes, of course. So happy to meet you, Lady Tamsin."

"And you, sir. I wish you both much happiness in your future lives."

"Thank you," he replied courteously, but his gaze seemed to have drifted over her head to another guest. He raised his brows in response before turning back to Ione's cousin. "Do forgive me, Lady Tamsin—I am being summoned," he added with a smile (*that should be charming*, Ione thought—*why isn't it charming?*). Lady Tamsin inclined her head, and Theodore slipped around her to go deal with whatever it was he'd noticed; Ione wasn't sure what, she was only glad for the distance it offered.

Tamsin's attention returned to Ione. "And you? Are you excited for tomorrow?"

"Well, I—I suppose I feel as any bride must on the evening before her wedding." Ione looked down at her hands. The lie made the knots in her stomach tighten and her cheeks go hot. Ione forced a smile and quickly tried to steer the conversation away from herself. "Did Tav come with you, or is he still recovering from his injuries?" Ione was referring to her cousin's twin brother, Lord Thomas—known as Tav, for his middle name, Octavius.

Lady Tamsin laughed, showing brilliant white teeth. "Oh, he is quite recovered. But you must know it is *death* to one's reputation to be seen escorting one's sister! I've no doubt that he'll be along shortly. He would not miss toasting one of his two favorite cousins." Her blue eyes sparkled.

"Of course." Ione offered her cousin a half-hearted laugh before she looped her arm through Tamsin's. "Come, dearest—I simply must hear of your time abroad, and I must share all the news of the season." Tamsin's brows rose a bit as Ione began half-dragging her through the crowded ballroom, something that took far longer than usual. As the bride-to-be, Ione could hardly take a step without being waylaid by guests spouting about the romance of it all, or the perfection of the evening.

When they were finally sequestered in a small parlor, Ione leaned against the door as if the barrier was the only thing keeping an enemy at bay.

Tamsin studied her cousin. "You're not happy." It wasn't a question.

In the quiet and peace of the parlor, with only her cousin to bear witness, Ione let the words she'd been holding back tumble free. "Oh Tamsin, I hardly know where to begin, or even how I came to be here." She pushed away from the door and sank into a nearby chair. "Theodore is kind enough, but..."

Heedless of her heavy silk dress, Tamsin knelt by Ione's chair. "But?"

"I do not love him. I can barely claim to like him," Ione finished miserably, covering her face with her fingers. She took a deep, steadying breath and tried to continue with more composure. "His family is respected and well-connected. Papa is delighted by the

5

match. Theodore is... everything we are told to look for in a husband. I should be delighted as well. But..." She nibbled her lip. "We have so little in common. All his attention is upon his career in Parliament and—and he's so *dull*. I thought it might be shyness, or... or respect for the rules of society, but it is not. There is nothing to the man but politeness and business."

Tamsin's slim brows drew together. "Ione... you cannot marry a man to please your father, and you cannot marry his family. What on earth made you accept him?"

Ione lifted her hands helplessly and let them drop back into her lap. "He has always treated me well, and by all accounts is what I ought to seek in a suitable match. At the time I thought that was enough." Ione folded her hands together. "But as the wedding drew nearer, I began to doubt that. I kept telling myself that I was clinging to childish notions of romance, or that it was simply nerves, that such doubts and feelings were to be expected. But it's more than that, and now I fear it's too late to reconsider."

"Nonsense," replied her cousin briskly. "You are not wed yet."

"But how can I withdraw when the wedding is tomorrow, when Papa has spent so much money?" Ione took a shuddering breath. "And though I do not wish to wed Theodore, I have no desire to hurt him. What if I call it off and find that it was a terrible mistake to do so? Perhaps I *am* clinging to childish notions of romance." She grew silent again, her mind spiraling with every scenario, every action she might take, and every disaster each choice might lead to. It was overwhelming. "I am an oracle—capable of looking into the future, and yet I cannot see what I should do with my own life. Oh, Tamsin, I feel like such a fool."

"My uncle would recover from the financial hardship with little trouble. For the rest... I confess I do not know how to help you. Tav would happily call him out, but I hardly think that would serve in the circumstances." She frowned, thinking. "Have you looked at his future?"

Ione nodded. "I tried, but as his fate is currently tied to mine, I could see nothing. As you know I cannot read myself." She pressed her lips together. "It is, as always, most inconvenient."

It was Tamsin's turn to nod. "Of course, I ought to have realized. Is there no way to delay the event while you try to work it out?"

Ione considered her cousin's words. Would a delay truly change anything?

No. If she put aside her concerns and was wholly honest with herself, the answer was a simple one: She did not wish to marry Theodore now, and no matter how long the wedding was put off, that was not going to change. She shook her head. "I think the most honorable thing to do would be to tell Theodore that I cannot marry him. I hate that it will cause him grief, but it will be less painful if I do it now, rather than offer him hope with a delay."

"Then do it," Tamsin agreed, "and the sooner the better. You may be assured I will stand by you if the need arises."

"Thank you, Tamsin. I could not think what I would do without your wise counsel. I apologize for thrusting all of this on you as soon as you set foot through the door." Ione took a deep breath, then gave a determined nod. "If I am to do this, I had better do it now, or I shall lose the courage entirely and find myself married to the man. I will speak to Theodore alone; he deserves no less." Ione straightened her shoulders. "After that I will face Papa."

Lady Tamsin slipped off her glove, whispered something over it, and put it back on as it glowed softly. "Here, dearest." She touched Ione's face with bright fingertips; the glow transferred to Ione's face briefly, fading from view after a moment. "Now you look ready for anything." She grasped her cousin's hands and gave them a reassuring squeeze before rustling from the room, chin high.

Ione took a few minutes to brace herself for the conversation to come. Having Tamsin's support gave her the courage to admit that her instincts were correct, but it made the prospect of speaking to Theodore no easier to face. She checked herself in the mirror: Tamsin's charm had erased the lines of strain in her expression and left her looking fresh and content. Ready for anything, indeed. Even so, it took a few anxious turns around the room before Ione rallied enough courage to speak to her intended. It was now or never, and so—stomach still churning—she went in search of Theodore.

She returned to the ballroom and spotted her fiancé chatting with Lord and Lady Markham. Another deep breath and she hurried over to where he stood. Ione offered her guests a polite curtsy before turning her attention to her intended target. "Forgive me for interrupting. Theodore, I must speak with you."

Lady Markham fluttered and disclaimed volubly, her eyebrows capering madly up her forehead, saying something about "the caprices of Cupid must be served", which made Ione wince internally.

Theodore's expression was benign. "Of course, my dear." He waited.

"I would prefer to discuss the matter in private." Ione said in a hushed tone, unable to keep her voice entirely steady.

He frowned. "My dear, I hardly think—oh, very well," he acquiesced after a pleading look from Ione. "Do excuse me, please," he said to Lord and Lady Markham.

Ione led him back to the same parlor where she'd spoken with Tamsin, hoping that the resolve and courage the earlier conversation had granted would somehow still linger within its walls. Once alone, she gestured to one of the chairs. "Perhaps you ought to sit."

"I'm quite all right, Ione, I assure you," Theodore replied. He looked at her quizzically. "Now, what is this matter that is so pressing it cannot wait until our guests have gone? It's hardly appropriate for the two of us to be unchaperoned and ignoring a gathering in our honor."

"Theodore, I..." Ione's voice trailed off. Now that she was standing here with him, the speech she'd composed in her head felt very cold and unfeeling indeed. She took a deep breath and tried again, straight to the heart of the matter this time. "Theodore, I fear that I cannot marry you." She blinked against the tears that were gathering in the corners of her eyes. "I am so very sorry. You must know that it was never my intention to cause you pain, or to mislead you. But I would be doing you a great disservice to enter into marriage with you when I do not love you as a wife should."

Her fiancé looked her up and down, in much the same way he had done Lady Tamsin, though with far less approval. "My dear girl, you can't possibly mean such a thing. You're overwrought—I understand that it happens to delicate maidens in these sorts of situations. Let me find you some cologne."

"It is not a matter of girlish sensitivity, Theodore." Ione laid a gentle hand on his shoulder to stop him. She tamped down her irritation at his immediate dismissal, and tried to continue with patience and understanding. "I have given this a great deal of thought. I should have spoken to you sooner, but I hoped that my feelings would change. Like you, I thought they might have been the natural misgivings of a bride. After a great deal of consideration I am certain they are not, and that proceeding with the wedding would be a terrible mistake on both our parts."

He searched her face, thunder gathering in his expression. "Ione, are you—are you serious? You would break off our engagement on the eve of our wedding?"

"I cannot tell you how much I regret the pain this must cause you, Theodore." Ione looked to the floor, feeling her cheeks go hot with contrition, though she was steadfast in her decision. "I would not do so if I did not believe it was the right thing to do."

He drew himself up, looking at her scathingly. "Very well, Miss Brentwood, if that is your choice, I must abide by it. I must thank you—you have, I believe, saved me from lifelong regret." He stormed out, slamming the door with such force that a crystal vase wobbled on a nearby table.

Ione flinched at the intensity of his departure, but remained rooted in place. Theodore had never displayed such outrage in her presence, and though she couldn't blame him for doing so now, she was still taken aback. She started to tremble with a myriad of conflicting emotions: shock, guilt, sadness, and relief.

Ione eased herself into a chair and made a futile attempt to prepare herself for what was certain to be a difficult evening. Theodore's wrathful departure would not have gone unnoticed; gossip would be quick to follow. She did not need her magic to predict that the conversation with her former fiancé would be the first of many uncomfortable encounters before the night was through.

"You WHAT?" A tall, slightly vain man with a magnificent head of snowy hair, John Brentwood rarely raised his voice; Ione felt sure the very crystal drops on the chandelier all the way in the ballroom were trembling at the sudden crescendo of his baritone. He paced in front of the fireplace in his study, looking rather like a frustrated lion in a cage. "Describe it to me again, Ione, for I feel sure you cannot just have told me that you have broken off your engagement on the eve of your wedding!"

"Papa, I..." Ione stood before her father like a child being chastised. And though her voice faltered, her resolve did not. She'd rarely been on the receiving end of her father's ire, and though it shook her to the core, it could not make her believe that her decision had been wrong—poorly timed, but not wrong. She clasped her hands behind her back to hide the nervous shaking. "It was folly that I accepted his proposal at all. I should have spoken sooner, but I cannot marry Mr. Gibson. It would lead to nothing but unhappiness."

"Nonsense! And why can you not marry him, pray?"

Ione nibbled her lower lip, trying to form a response that would satisfy the family patriarch. There was little she could offer, so she chose to speak the truth. "I do not love him. As I spent time with him, I realized I do not enjoy his company at all."

"Love him?" Ione's father threw up his hands. "What romantic idiocy is this? D'you think your mother and I were in love when we wed? Do not," he pointed at her, eyes narrowed, "answer that." He shook his head. "Clearly, I have been far too lenient with you, my girl. Love, indeed. Have you any idea of the scandal this will cause? Of the effect it will have on your sister's reputation? Not to mention my pocketbook, though I should never stoop to concern myself with anything so petty. No, it's the principle of the thing. You have wounded me *here*, Ione." He thumped his own chest with one fist, his other hand upon the mantel, the picture of paternal sorrow. "I have been too tender with you. No more."

"I am sorry, Papa." Ione replied honestly. She looked to the floor, fighting back tears. To think of the pain and hardship her actions would cause her family made her heartsick. Yet she was certain calling off the wedding was the honorable course. "I deeply regret the pain this causes you, but I did what I felt right."

He bowed his leonine head, staring morosely into the fire. "Go, then; the hour grows late and I have little left to say. *I* shall not rest tonight, but do not let me keep you from your repose. After all, what are the feelings of a mere father? What matters is your future— a future I believed I had secured. Ah, well." His voice broke a little at the end.

Any other night Ione would have given her father a kiss on the cheek before retiring for the evening, but she felt certain such humble affections would be unappreciated. "Goodnight, Papa," she whispered, before stepping out of the room and closing the door as quietly as she could, desperate to avoid any further confrontation.

She trudged heavily up the stairs as her conscience twisted itself back into knots. Had she done the right thing after all? Perhaps she was merely being naive and childish? She hadn't considered how this would impact Elsie's reputation. Suddenly, Ione felt every bit as alone and conflicted as she had before calling off her engagement.

Despite her loneliness, Ione dismissed the maid when she reached her bedroom. She changed into a nightrail and dressing gown on her own, then went to say goodnight to her mother before putting an end to what had been an utterly wretched day.

The light was on in her mother's room; peeking in, she could see Elizabeth Brentwood sitting by the fire in her dressing gown. "Come in, my darling. What is this your father tells me?"

Ione all but ran to her. She'd been holding back tears; but now, free of Mr. Gibson, reeling from her father's anger, and safe in the quiet comfort of her mother's room, the tears cascaded down her cheeks. She recounted her misery over the past weeks and the conversations with Theodore and her father, hiccupping loudly when she was finished. "Mama, I am a terrible and ungrateful creature. I have made such a mess of things for Papa, for Elsie, for all of us."

Elizabeth gathered her daughter close, just as she used to do when Ione would suffer some small hurt. "Your Papa will recover, my love; for what is a small scandal when weighed against your future happiness? If you really cannot love Mr. Gibson, then better not to try." Soft lips kissed Ione's dark hair. "Was he ungallant in any way, my darling?"

"He was not. He was unhappy with my decision, but I cannot fault him for that." Ione laid her head on her mother's shoulder. She sniffled a little, fresh tears trickling down her cheeks as her mind drifted back to her father. He'd never been so angry with her before. "Papa will never forgive this."

Elizabeth stroked her hair. "Oh, my love, of course he will. You are the brightest star in his firmament. Of course he is angry, but it will pass, I promise you. He really does want to see you happy. It was just such a surprise to him, I am sure."

"But what of Elsie?" Ione pulled away from her mother with an expression of wide-eyed concern. She appreciated the soothing words, but could not ignore the feeling that her poor judgement was being too easily excused. There would be consequences for her actions, and not all of them would be hers to bear. "He is correct, it will ruin her season."

"I doubt anyone will notice," came a voice from the door as Elsie padded into the room in her dressing gown, her ruddy hair braided for bed. "My season has been decidedly lackluster, I assure you. I would be just as happy to end it now. Besides, the Little Season comes soon enough, and I am just eighteen. This will all blow over by next spring, I make no doubt." She perched on the edge of the bed. "Are you all right?"

That was the limit of what Ione could take. Elsie had played no part in this debacle, but society would care little for that fact, likely painting her with the same harsh brush. They might both be labelled jilts—or worse, women of questionable moral character, and her sister was completely blameless in the matter. Yet Elsie's concern was for Ione alone. A fresh batch of tears erupted. "You are far too good a sister to me, Elsie." Ione wrapped her younger sister in a tight hug. "How have you managed to be so calm?"

"One of us has to be," her sister pointed out with a soft laugh, "and it's unlikely to be you, given the circumstances. But I shall not disabuse you of the notion; indeed, I am far too good a sister to you. Mind you do not forget it." Elsie kissed Ione on the cheek.

"Would you like something to help you sleep? I asked Tamsin to charm your father's brandy snifter, and your hairbrush just in case this evening was too exciting," Mama told them, a twinkle in her eyes. "I feel sure Finagle will be helping Papa to bed shortly."

"Oh, Mama." Ione dashed at her cheeks, actually managing a slight laugh. "Bless you and your good sense. Yes, I most definitely would like help finding my own rest tonight."

"Then come along and I shall brush your hair." Mama held out her hand to her eldest daughter.

The following morning dawned as bright and beautiful as any could hope for a wedding. It seemed a bit of proverbial salt in the wound, and something that would do little to improve her father's mood, Ione thought. She was in no hurry to face him at the breakfast table, and fussed with her dress and hair long after the maid had left the room. Ione glanced at her reflection, blue eyes shadowed by anxiety. Was it her imagination, or was she paler than usual? Perhaps it would be better to stay abed and rest?

No. Ione shook her head: without a true illness to plead indisposition, her absence would only aggravate Papa's mood. With a heavy sigh, she pushed away from the dressing table and made for the door. There was no sense in prolonging the inevitable.

Much to her relief, the dining room was rather full. Her cousins had apparently come for an early visit from their London townhouse and were already seated at the table next to Elsie, chatting quietly. Ione chanced a glance at her father's face: his expression was dour. Oh dear, that did not bode well for the rest of the day. She walked to her seat without announcing her presence and sat down, feeling very much at a loss for words.

"I have come to a decision," her father proclaimed, frowning direfully.

Ione was reaching for her spoon but stopped when he spoke, looking up with a growing sense of trepidation. "Yes, Papa?"

"Scotland."

Tav looked around the room. "Beg pardon, Uncle, but that's not so much a decision as it is a country."

Mr. Brentwood shot his nephew a look. "I mean, of course, that Ione will repair to Scotland immediately, to consider recent events. The remainder of the season is lost to her in any case, and perhaps she will learn a lesson about hasty decisions."

"You... wish to send me away?" Ione kept her tone level, though she could hardly believe what she was hearing. It was true that the rest of the season was likely ruined, but to be sent away to Scotland? To be exiled?

"What I wish became irrelevant yesterday evening. You shall go to Scotland, to recover your health and hopefully your senses. That is my decision."

"As you say, Father." Ione replied stiffly. She had made her bed and now she had to lie in it. Still, if it was between exile and marrying Theodore Gibson, she would spend the rest of the season in Scotland, and be happy to do it.

Tamsin buttered her toast. "How fortuitous," she said mildly, "that Tav and I were planning to do that very thing. We can accompany you, Ione. Then you need not travel alone."

Ione turned to Tamsin, smiling at her cousin's casual brilliance. "Fortuitous indeed! Your company will make the whole thing a marvelous holiday. We have not had the pleasure of an extended visit since we were children, and as I said last night, I should very much enjoy hearing about your time abroad."

Tav looked rather as though he'd been punched in the stomach, but was nodding manfully. "Yes, Scotland, looking forward to it," he mumbled.

Mr. Brentwood glowered. "Unfortunately, I have made arrangements for Ione to leave tomorrow. I know that you and Thomas had planned to remain in London for at least another week."

Tamsin lifted a shoulder. "Plans can be changed." Tav made a squeaking sound.

"That they can, and often for the better," Ione agreed carefully, looking from one cousin to the other. She knew perfectly well that her cousins had no such plans—Tav's reaction was evidence of that, though he was doing his best to go along, poor man. It was clear to her that Tamsin had concocted this fable so that she could accompany Ione herself. Ione began to pick at her breakfast, her appetite creeping back. Perhaps it would not be so bad after all—in fact, Scotland was sure to be more pleasant than facing the scorn of London's upper crust. "Having you and Tav at my side would do much to ease any concern my family might have about my traveling with only Miss Stern for companion."

"Yes, indeed," Ione's mother agreed, placidly unfolding her napkin.

The aforementioned Tav was practically choking on his porridge. Having achieved her objective, Tamsin grinned and let her brother off the hook. "Only me for now, I'm afraid. Tav has pressing business that will keep him in town for a few days. Possibly longer." Her brother sighed with ill-concealed relief.

"Then the matter is settled! Time away from the city, and in the care of my beloved cousin is just the thing to put all to rights." Ione smiled, allowing herself a small amount of satisfaction in seeing her father's plans for punishment foiled. She finished off her porridge and set her spoon aside before turning to address her father again. "May I be excused? If I am to leave tomorrow there's much I need to attend to before I depart."

Her father nodded gruffly. "You may. And you, Tamsin, before you ask."

His niece dimpled and got up from the table, following Ione up the stairs and to her room. Hardly had the door closed behind them when the blonde said, "Scotland! Good heavens!"

"I knew he was displeased, but the reaction seems a bit extreme." Ione sat down on the edge of the bed and began to fiddle with the tassel on the cord around her bedcurtains. "Thank you for volunteering to join me. I did not mean for you to be sentenced to banishment as well."

Tamsin grinned. "It will be an adventure; do not you agree?"

"I did say Mr. Gibson was boring. I suppose adventure is what I wanted." Ione returned her cousin's grin and moved to her vanity to begin sorting through her favorite combs and hairpins. "I hardly know what to bring, though I am determined to make a show of enjoying this holiday. Let Papa and the pillars of society make of that what they will!"

"I know what we shall not bring," Tamsin returned. "I insist that we not inconvenience 'Old Ironsides'." Thus she referred to Ione's rather severe governess-turned-companion with a merry smile.

Ione sputtered with laughter. "Miss Stern, you mean? Someday she will hear of that awful nickname, and then you will be in for it."

"Melt me with a glare, I feel sure," Tamsin agreed. "Which is why I believe we can dispense with her services. For you know she will live up to her name and be forever reading you sermons about how you ought to have sacrificed yourself upon the altar of

Society's good opinion. No, indeed—I am to be your companion, for I am the elder cousin."

Ione rolled her eyes, still laughing. "Oh, yes, so very much older. Nearly three whole years, you gnarled and wizened crone."

"It isn't the years, it's the experience, my child." Tamsin's blue eyes were sparkling. "My Rose will be lady's maid for both of us, and you will escape the censure of your household entirely. And we can take my coach instead of one of those dreadful trains, so that our clothes won't smell like coal and I shan't have cinders in my hair." To that Ione agreed with alacrity, for she felt she had suffered enough censure already, and the public nature of a departure by train would, she felt, be mortifying. "That's the spirit. I suppose I'd best get packing too." Tamsin kissed her on the cheek and went to call for her carriage.

After an afternoon of hurried packing and a night of deeper sleep than Ione had experienced in weeks, everything was made ready for the journey in Scotland. By half-past nine in the morning, Ione was waiting patiently in the vestibule with Tamsin as the latter's coach was brought around.

The air of tense upheaval that seemed to have settled over the household since the night of the ball filled Ione with remorse for her part in it. She could hardly take it back, and so could not wait to climb into the coach and leave the gossip and judgment of London Society—and her father—far behind. Avoiding Theodore was no small part of that. She had sent the engagement ring back to him right after the momentous breakfast the day before, feeling a great sense of relief as soon as it had left her possession.

It was another few minutes before a servant announced the carriage, and Ione turned to bid her family farewell. She waited until the last to speak with her father, hoping that his mood had softened a little after another night of rest, and with the distance her departure would bring. "I will write if you wish, Papa. It saddens me greatly that my actions have disappointed you so very much."

Mr. Brentwood cleared his throat comprehensively. "Of course you should write, child. This will all blow over soon," he said, not unkindly, and patted her hand before turning to his niece. "Tamsin, my girl—thank you."

She smiled at her uncle. "You're quite welcome, sir."

The efficiency of the household staff was a blessing. It took mere minutes for Ione's things to be loaded, and after a final round of goodbyes, the cousins were comfortably situated and on their way.

Chapter Two

Exile

At the start of their venture, Ione's mood was as bleak as the busy London streets on a foggy morning. The coach bumped and jostled them along at a pace that felt relentless. She tried to put the wedding and her father's fury from her mind, but it was of little use. No matter how hard she tried to imagine this was to be nothing more than a jolly holiday in the highlands, she continued to fret and worry over the turmoil she was leaving in her wake. Eventually, she gave up and simply stared out the window as the bustling city streets gave way to country roads that wound through grassy fields and lush forests.

Yet as they approached the Scottish border, Ione felt a weight lifting from her shoulders—and from her heart. When they finally crossed into Scotland some days later, she was feeling more herself than she had in months, and thought that perhaps her father's prescription was not so dreadful as it seemed before.

"It's quite lovely," Ione commented, gesturing to the passing landscape before turning back to her companions. "Have either of you been before?"

Tamsin's maid Rose, a pretty girl of just twenty, with brown curls and a ready smile, was nearly vibrating with excitement. "No, miss," she said shyly, "I've never been outside of England. Will we see the blue savages?" She shivered in anticipation.

For her part, Tamsin was all smiles. "I don't believe the clans paint themselves blue anymore, Rose. All the same, it's rather exciting, is it not?" she asked Ione, bouncing in her seat a little. "Such a change from the weariness of the London Season—to be on such an adventure! Even if I don't know where—" she consulted the address on the introduction her uncle had given them— "Brudhach a Chladdaich is. Or how to say it." She considered the envelope again. "That seems like an excess of 'h's, doesn't it?"

Ione reached across the carriage to take the paper. "Oh my," she murmured, giving the complicated name a double-take. "It certainly does. I suspect you managed the pronunciation better than I would have." She passed the paper back to her cousin, who promptly tucked it inside its envelope. "To think, by this time I was supposed to have been a wife, and now I find myself in quite a different situation."

Tamsin's eyes, blue as Ione's own, narrowed. "Regrets?"

"Only that I did not find the courage to end my engagement sooner," Ione smoothed her skirt and tried to look as confident and collected as her cousin. "Though I doubt we'd find ourselves on the road now if I had."

"Almost certainly not," the pretty blonde agreed. "And I believe that one way and another, you and I will find some way to entertain ourselves. Still," Tamsin picked up her fan and employed it, curly tendrils wafting gently in the slight breeze, "I infinitely prefer my own method of escaping the dreariness of a midsummer engagement."

Ione laughed at that, shaking her head as she turned to gaze once more at the countryside. "And what method do you employ? I may need guidance after all of this."

Her cousin's smile grew impish. "Why—never to become engaged at all, of course." She leaned forward and peered out the carriage window too, squinting at the setting sun. "It must be nearing suppertime, surely. I wonder when we shall arrive at the next post inn?"

Ione reached over her shoulder to tap on the back wall of the carriage. "Master William, how much further are we to travel today?"

The tiger answered cheerfully, pitching his voice above the rattle of the carriage wheels. "Nearing Thornhill, miss. Only another half an hour at most, I'd say."

"There you have it, and not a moment too soon," Ione said, returning her attention to Tamsin and Rose. The statement was punctuated by an insistent growl from her stomach. "I shall be glad to settle in for the evening with a hot meal and a comfortable bed." She sighed. "Travel does make one appreciate the simple things."

The post inn at Thornhill was surprisingly busy, but luck was on their side and they engaged the last two rooms available for the night, plus one in the servants' wing for Rose. It was delightful to be free of the confines of the coach, luxurious as it was, and the girls wasted no time in rinsing the dust of travel from their faces and hands.

Refreshed and rejuvenated, Ione opened the door and nearly trampled poor Tamsin, who was standing with her hand raised to knock. A meal, Ione declared, was next upon the agenda. "Shall we embrace our adventure in earnest and take our meal in the common room?" she asked, still laughing at their near-miss.

Tamsin's expression was one of pleased surprise. "Finally! I was beginning to think we would eat in our rooms at every post inn along the way."

Ione looped her arm through her cousin's. "I'm sorry for that; but I'm feeling much more the thing now that we're out of England." She gave Tamsin's arm a squeeze.

Without further ado, they made their way down to the bustling common room. They wove through tables, jostling past other patrons to settle at a table that was quiet enough to allow for comfortable conversation but not so out of the way as to feel isolated.

A bit of a ruckus erupted in the taproom mere minutes later. "What do you mean, ye're full up?" cried a male voice with a thick Scottish brogue. "Have ye no idea who graces yer establishment? 'Tis the Maclaren himself, God rest the Maclaren that was!" Another voice chimed in, much more modulated and therefore unintelligible, and the first voice replied, still at full volume. "But Geordie—I mean Maclaren, sir—"

Ione exchanged a glance with Tamsin, who rested her chin on her fist and sent her cousin a merry look as they eavesdropped. Ione playfully wiggled her brows in response, as she craned her neck to see if she could catch a glimpse of the action in the mirror behind the taps. Unfortunately, and much to her frustration, the reflection was obscured by the innkeeper's head.

Ione frowned thoughtfully. There was something about the name 'Maclaren' that seemed familiar. She leaned back in her seat, trying to recall where she'd heard the name before. Then it struck her: a memory of her parents speaking in hushed voices, rumors of a violent end, and a discussion that was brought to an immediate halt when she made her presence known.

"All right, then," cried the exasperated voice. "A meal it is, an' we'll find another inn—but woe betide the day you turned the Maclaren from yer door!"

A tall gentleman—tall enough to have to duck the door a bit—came into the room, his cheeks a vivid red. "Honestly, Angus," he protested, a lighter Scottish lilt in his husky baritone, "behaving like a comic-opera Scot will get us nowhere. If they haven't got a room, they haven't got one. D'you expect them to build one on while we eat?"

"No, Maclaren. But I did think they might empty a room for ye, considerin'." His companion was smaller, stouter, swathed in the same tartan as the taller man.

"And do what, throw their guests with better foresight than you or I into the street?" As he took his seat at the next table, Ione could see the Maclaren much more clearly than just his reflection in the mirror behind the taps. He was broad through chest and shoulder, narrow in the waist, his national dress only emphasizing the fact. His hair was ruddy, but not sister Elsie's deep red; more of a tawny blonde, a sunset gold. It was thick and wavy, longer than was strictly fashionable and brushed back from a well-shaped forehead. He was clean-shaven, showing a strongly defined jaw; his mouth was exceptionally well-cut, his nose straight and patrician, and his eyes a stormy grey which was startlingly at odds with his gold-tipped lashes and tawny brows. With an unencumbered view of the fellow, Ione was certain she'd seen his face before.

Lady Tamsin's own brows rose at the sight of him, and she sent her cousin a meaningful look.

Ione felt her cheeks warming as she studied the man. This Maclaren looked the very image of the Scottish heroes she'd imagined when her father read the country's history to her as a child. "Our first day out and it seems we already have a story to tell," she murmured quietly to her cousin.

Without warning or consulting Ione, Tamsin leaned forward and spoke directly to the younger man. "Forgive my impertinence, sir. Did I hear you say you were in need of a room for the night? My cousin and I would be glad to share, and that would free up one room, if it would help."

The man turned, and those stormy eyes, which had started out so forbidding, softened to the color of summer mist. "I'd be most grateful, Miss...?"

"Lady Tamsin Claremont, and this is my cousin, Miss Ione Brentwood."

He stood, and bowed. "George Maclaren, ladies. A pleasure indeed."

By his side, Angus tsked. "Lord George Maclaren, Viscount Kirkleith," he clarified. "Chief of Clan Maclaren, Laird of Balmaclaren." The viscount went red at this recital.

With a smile for Lord Kirkleith and a grin for her cousin, Tamsin went to speak to the landlord and make the arrangements.

"A pleasure to meet you, my lord." Ione smiled pleasantly at the handsome viscount, hoping her traitorous cheeks had settled and weren't the color of ripe cherries. She had seen his face before, of that Ione was certain. Perhaps that was why the name seemed familiar, and had nothing at all to do with the rumor mill. Amid all the gruesome murders in Whitechapel of late, it was easy enough to let one's imagination get the better of them. Still—best to have out with it, or she'd be puzzling over the connection all evening. "Forgive me, sir, but have we met before? In London, perhaps?"

His smile was one of extraordinary sweetness, and Ione was immediately seized with the notion that it was tempered with sadness. "I am flattered to know that you remember me, Miss Brentwood. We were indeed introduced by Lady Seddon at her ball, this April past. It was a sad crush, I fear, but I recall our introduction with gratification." He hesitated. "May I offer my congratulations—I seem to recall an announcement in the papers?"

Ione's smile faded at the mention of her former engagement, and her gaze dropped to the ring finger on her left hand. Well-meaning as his statement had been, it was an uncomfortable reminder, just when she was beginning to feel free of the disastrous affair. "Thank you, my lord," she managed quietly. She tucked a curl behind her ear and tried to find a polite way to steer the conversation in a different direction. "I do hope the remainder of your evening will prove more pleasant, now that you have accommodation for the night."

"Thanks to you and your cousin, I am sure it will," was his courteous reply. "Will you do us the favor of dining with us? Perhaps in the private parlor?"

"Oh, that's very kind." Unsure about the propriety of such a thing so far away from London, she shied away from committing to an answer one way or another. Thankfully, her cousin had impeccable timing. Ione rose to her feet as Tamsin returned. "Dearest, we have been invited to take our meal with Lord Kirkleith in the private dining parlor."

"What a kind invitation! We'd be delighted to join you." Tamsin graced them with her most charming smile, the one that made most men look like they'd been clubbed over the head. But though the smile Lord

Kirkleith returned seemed genuine enough, Ione could not help but notice that his regard kept straying back to her. She wondered briefly whether she had a smudge on her face, or a leaf in her hair that drew his attention so. She glanced at her cousin, whose smile took on a distinctly mischievous cast as they followed the two men to the private room.

Dinner with a viscount was certainly an unexpected turn of events, Ione mused as they stepped out of the noisy common area and into the small and simply adorned private dining room. A small knot of anxiety twisted through her. Was it wise for her to accept this invitation when she had so recently called off her engagement? But there was little chance anyone back in London would hear about it, and it was a single dinner, offered out of gratitude. At any rate, it was likely she would never see the viscount again, and Tamsin had raised no objection, so surely there was no harm in enjoying his company for one evening. Ione's fretting eased as she took the seat Lord Kirkleith offered her, his smile warm and charming.

The meal was delicious; the landlord was utterly beside himself with delight at having 'the Maclaren' at his table, along with the titled Lady Tamsin. He spared nothing in his attention to their small party. Plates laden with roast meats, cheeses, and freshly baked bread were brought into the room in absurd quantities for a table of four. The finest bottle of wine in the house was uncorked and poured into goblets that the landlord assured them were reserved for special occasions. Ione was certain that the Queen herself would not have received greater care.

By the end of the final course, she was full to the brim and in high spirits. "That was simply superb," Ione said as she dabbed at the corner of her mouth. "And with such wonderful company as well." She smiled and turned her attention to Lord Kirkleith, mentally noting how the candlelight danced on his hair and brought out the gold amid the red. "Lady Tamsin and I are on our way to Brudhach a Chladdaich." She mangled her way through the unfamiliar language. "Perhaps you can recommend suitable entertainment while we're there?"

The Maclaren chuckled; the irrepressible Angus laughed aloud. "Och, ma ears!"

The viscount's grey eyes were twinkling. "'Tis Bruichladdich ye mean," and he pronounced it 'Brookladdie'.

"Ah, yes," Ione replied, adding an embarrassed giggle of her own to the levity. She considered the handsome Scotsman, wondering idly what it was about her that seemed to fascinate him. It was tempting to summon her magic and see what reading his past and future might reveal. But that went against every boundary she'd been taught to respect. She would not invade the viscount's privacy, regardless of her curiosity or the special attention he seemed to pay her. "That certainly has a better sound to it than my pronunciation," she added, still smiling at her own pitiful attempt.

"I should hope so," the Maclaren replied teasingly. "As to entertainment, um... are you much of a walker?"

"I do enjoy a stroll, particularly if the scenery is appealing. From what I have seen of Scotland that seems to be the case." Ione answered. "I take it Bruichladdich is located in a rather remote part of the country?"

"Just a bit," chuckled Angus, wiping a merry tear from his eye. "Entertainment, she says." He went off laughing again.

"Oh, dear," murmured Tamsin.

"It seems my father gave his plan more thought than we credited him for." Ione turned an apologetic look to her cousin. "I am sorry if this has spoiled the rest of the season for you, dearest."

"Not at all," her cousin replied stoutly. "We shall simply make our own entertainment."

"Indeed." Ione had no doubt that between the two of them they could come up with interesting ways to pass their time, but she still regretted that Tamsin had likely sacrificed more exciting plans to join her in exile. She turned her attention back to their companions. "And you, my lord? Where do you go?"

"A gatherin' of the Clan, at Balmaclaren," Angus furnished. "'Tis the wake for the Maclaren that was, and the swearin' of the Maclaren that is." He nodded to George, who was blushing again.

"I'm sorry for your loss," Ione murmured gently, feeling confirmed in her conjecture about the Whitechapel connection, but regretting that her question had turned the conversation to sad tidings. "Where is Balmaclaren?" She did her best to match the word to the way Angus had pronounced it. "Is it a long journey from here?"

The Maclaren shrugged. "A few days to the northeast. Nowhere near Bruichladdich, I'm sorry to say, or you'd be welcome at the festivities."

Tamsin graced each man with a smile. "How kind of you to say so. For now, I fear the hour grows late, and we must leave early on the morrow. Our thanks, my lord, for the excellent meal, and the diverting company. I hope we shall someday have the pleasure of meeting again."

The viscount got to his feet and bowed. "Your servant, Lady Tamsin, Miss Brentwood."

Ione had to work to hide her disappointment, but her cousin was correct about the hour. She wished the viscount and Angus a pleasant night, casting a final glance at the Maclaren before she followed Tamsin out of the parlor and up to the bedroom they would be sharing for the night.

When the door was closed behind them, she turned to Tamsin. "Well, that was exciting. At least if we are to be banished to the country, we'll have an interesting story to recount from the journey."

Tamsin sat at the writing desk and rummaged for paper and ink. "Banished indeed. Plans, as I told my uncle, can be changed."

"What are you doing?" Ione stopped fluffing her pillow and peeked over her cousin's shoulder.

"Canceling our scheduled arrival at Brook— bro—that horrible place," she pulled out another sheet of paper, "and letting Tav know we can be reached in Balmaclaren."

Ione's eyes went wide and her mouth dropped open. It never occurred to her that they might take matters into their own hands. She'd simply resigned herself to the doldrums of her father's punishment and accepted that that was to be the way of it. But then Tamsin was so much bolder. She seemed fearless at times.

A slow, approving smile spread across Ione's face. She'd always wanted to be as courageous as her cousin, and life, it seemed, was giving her the opportunity to do exactly that. "A good thing too, for I fear I did not bring a single pair of shoes appropriate for long walks." Tamsin looked up and flashed Ione a merry grin.

"What's got you gloomin'?" Angus wanted to know as he levered off Geordie's boots in the room that had once belonged to Miss Brentwood. "I know there's nae shortage of sadness, wi' your father's death an' all, but you seemed cheery enough at sup." He sat back on his heels and regarded Geordie, before asking gently, "Can I help, laddie?"

Geordie shook himself and gave Angus a thin smile. "I'm well enough, Angus, but it's kind of you to ask. I'm done with grieving, at least for now." He shifted in his chair and bid the other man sit with him before the fire. "Brandy?"

"I won't say no to a tipple before bed," Angus acknowledged, settling into his seat. "Open your budget, then, lad. I can see somethin's amiss wi' you."

That thin smile turned to a chuckle as Geordie handed him a snifter. "You're determined to take care of me, aren't you?"

"Och, well." Angus sipped the liquor. "I've done it since you were but wee—it's a sort of habit I've acquired." He tilted his head. "Out wi' it, then, and let's have a look."

Geordie leaned forward, propping his elbow on the arm of his chair as he wiped a hand over his mouth. "Miss Brentwood—I've met her before."

"Aye, you said as much." Angus acknowledged, and Geordie could practically feel the older man's gaze sharpen. "More than just a meetin'?"

"Not on her part." Geordie shook his tawny head. "I'd seen her at other parties and so forth, of course. Angled for an introduction, and finally got one—but a few days later it was announced that she's engaged to be wed."

Angus nodded. "And so?"

Geordie shrugged. "I tried to put her from my mind. The loveliest creature I ever beheld, but there's more to life than beauty. But then—" He ran his fingers through his hair. "I'd gone to the opera, as one does, and in the box next to mine there was a bit of a fracas— one young lady being unkind to another in that sharp, simpering way they sometimes have. Seems the girl had been jilted by some fool, and the other one lorded it over her—never mind the girl's heart was clearly in pieces over the man, whoever he was. The poor child began to weep, and all at once a Fury descends in the person of Miss Brentwood." He smiled at the memory. "She'd been in the box on the other side, I believe, and had heard much of the same as I; without making a fuss or alerting anyone else, she proceeded to tear a strip off the girl's tormentor and defend the poor child. I'd never heard the like." His smile became a grin. "I chanced a peek and she'd run the other girl off—from her own box, as far as I could tell—and was holding the poor lass close, speakin' kindnesses and dryin' tears." His accent thickened as he spoke. "Her kindness—it struck me, stayed with me all the rest of the evening."

Angus thought for a bit. "Was that the same night—?"

"Aye, it was—the very night my father was killed." Geordie had to take a moment to gather himself. "When we heard the news in the wee hours... there was no comfort to be found for me, not anywhere. But then—och, you'll think me a fool." At Angus' indignant demur, Geordie went on. "I remembered Miss Brentwood's words of comfort to that girl, but it was as though she spoke to me. And I clung to them, in all the days that followed. I never thought to see her again—but here she is, and it's like..." He cleared his throat. "It's like my father is reaching out t'me, to tell me all will be well."

A somber but somehow companionable silence descended over the two men. Geordie watched the flames in the small hearth flicker, conscious that Angus was wiping at his eyes. "Your father," the older man said at last, his voice rough, "was nothin' if not determined. If there's a way for him t'reach out t'you, why, he'll do it. So... maybe you have the right of it, Geordie lad."

Geordie looked up with a small smile. "I'd like to think so." He cleared his throat again. "I expect Asher and Quinn are already at the castle—I cabled them when we heard, and Ross said he did too. Mama will be glad for the company, I know—she and Ailsa left London straight after the memorial service at St. Paul's, and the castle can be wretchedly lonely."

Angus nodded. "Aye, she regards those rascals as her own kin—and so they are, in a way. What of Dr. Ross himself? I know we saw him at the inquest—will he be comin' north for the investiture as well?"

The smile that tipped Geordie's lips was a genuine one. "A chance to show off his skill with a sword? You don't think he'd miss something like that, do you?"

Angus chuckled. "Nay—not after I spent all these years tutorin' all four of you, he'd best not, for when else he'd have a chance I dinnae ken. The Maclaren investiture is unique among the clans, and I knew you'd need your friends to second you someday, though I never thought it'd be so soon." He paused, sipping the last of his brandy. "I'm glad for you, Geordie, to have such friends. A man needs to build a family as well as be born to one."

The newly christened Maclaren nodded, pouring himself a second tot and silently offering the bottle to Angus.

Chapter Three

Dreams and Detours

𝕳 strange clanging sound rent the air, and was accompanied by an angry shout. Ione stood in the center of some sort of paddock—or no, it was some sort of arena? She frowned and turned a slow circle to gain her bearings. Suddenly she had the undeniable sense of eyes tracking her movements. Ione looked beyond the field and found that a crowd surrounded her. But even as she scanned the faces of those around her, she realized that theirs were not the eyes that tracked her. The mysterious scrutiny made her feel isolated and desperate. It was like being hunted by something—or someone—lurking just beyond her vision.

She wanted to turn and run away, but the sound of clashing metal intensified, drawing her attention back to her surroundings. It was then that the source of the clanging metal became apparent. A pair of men circled one another in the center of the *field. They were too far for Ione to distinguish their faces, but there could be little doubt that the fight between them was deadly. They charged one another, with broadswords raised high. The impact was spectacular, and the sound of it rang through the air ominously. The two men strained against one another, struggling with weapons locked at the hilt. Anger and loathing seemed to permeate the air around them, spreading out across the field of combat.*

Ione a took a step toward them, trying to make sense of what was happening. The combatants twisted and she saw one of them pull a dagger from his belt. The blade flashed red, then was driven deep into the side of the other man. He gasped, dropping his sword as his hand drifted up to clutch the ghastly wound. Panic and pain flooded through Ione as she watched the wounded man sink to the ground. He was dying and there was nothing she could do to help him.

The air grew heavier with vitriol. Ione fell to her knees, coughing and struggling to draw a full breath. She wrapped her arms around herself and doubled over with agony, as if her heart was shattering. A pair of boots appeared in front of her, and blood dripped from above, spattering the brown leather. Ione tried to look up, but all she could see was a pair of hands clutching a crimson hat, drenched in gore.

A scream of horror rose from deep within Ione's chest and burst from her lips.

"Shh, shh," Tamsin's voice filtered through the dimly lit room. Ione felt a gentle hand stroking her face. "It's all right, darling. You're safe, it was only a dream."

Ione sat up shaking. Her heart was racing, and tears were streaming down her cheeks. "No, it was more than that, I know it was. I saw death, and—and blood." Ione felt her cousin's fingers wrap around hers. "It was a vision, Tamsin. It was a vision, and someone is in terrible danger." For response, her cousin pulled Ione into a warm embrace and rocked her gently until the shaking stopped.

Ione was too disturbed by the images of her prophetic nightmare to try to sleep again. To Tamsin's credit, she didn't utter a word of complaint when Ione climbed out of bed and began shuffling about the room. Her cousin merely rubbed her eyes and stifled a yawn as she threw the blankets aside and reached for her dressing gown and the bell to call for Rose.

Rose was there in minutes, bustling about from one trunk to the other, and by the time they were dressed Ione had managed to regain enough composure to take breakfast downstairs. They were among the first in the taproom, which was something of a relief to Ione's mind.

The hearty breakfast and quiet helped her to reorder her thoughts. These unbidden visions were never easy to endure, but without more details there was little that could be done—she didn't even know whom the vision revealed. Perhaps it hadn't been a vision at all, but the result of all the stress she'd been under, and her own sense of guilt over what happened. So much had happened in so short a time; she could hardly be blamed for being rattled by it all.

Satisfied with this explanation—for the time being, at least—Ione pushed her empty plate away with a nod. She'd done the right thing in ending her engagement, and she was resolved to silence her overactive conscience and embrace the spontaneity of their adventure. After all, doing what was expected of her hadn't served her all that well.

The carriage was loaded and ready to depart by the time they finished their morning repast. Ione climbed inside, feeling hopeful and unburdened. They were away from England, and embarking on an adventure of their own choosing. It was a heady sort of freedom, and one that Ione thought she could grow quite fond of.

As they'd started the day early, the girls decided to enjoy an early stop as well. They stopped at a quaint town with a comfortable inn and a lovely provincial atmosphere. The decision proved to be a practical one as well, for the innkeeper's wife informed them that the next town along their route was quite some miles away, and would have seen them arriving late that night.

With extra time on their hands before dinner, Ione and Tamsin decided a stroll was in order. Comfortable as their transport was, it still felt cramped after several long and bumpy hours on the road. So the girls found themselves with a few idle hours to while away before they went inside to dress for dinner.

"You are truly brilliant to have thought of this adventure, cousin," Ione declared, adjusting the ribbon at her collar, as she waited for Rose to finish helping Tamsin dress for dinner. "Father could hardly complain. We were practically invited to the swearing in of the new Maclaren."

"My uncle may complain all he wishes," Tamsin grinned over her shoulder. "Unless he's willing to come up here and get us, I hardly see that it signifies."

Ione laughed heartily; she couldn't help it. The afternoon had been pleasantly lazy and filled with speculation about the investiture they were to attend. Ione hadn't been this excited since the eve of her first ball of the Season. Perhaps Tamsin had the right of it, with her disinterest in marriage. This could be the first in many holidays the two of them might share. Would a life of travel and adventure be so terrible, if the prospect of a good marriage was no longer available to her?

That thought dimmed her spirits a little. Ione's smile faded and she stifled a sigh, knowing the truth was not so simple. Much as she loved and admired Tamsin, wandering was not the life Ione truly longed for. She'd always envisioned herself managing a household and having children with a man she loved; now it seemed as though that door had closed to her forever. But perhaps another would open somewhere, and she only needed the courage to step through it.

Once again, they decided on taking their evening repast in the public dining room, rather than their own rooms. It did not take long, however, for Ione to begin to wish they had not. The large dining room was overcrowded, and so noisy that she could scarcely hear Tamsin without leaning close. After such an early morning the volume of the place was enough to make her head ache.

"You know, Tamsin," Ione began as they situated themselves at a table near the door, hoping conversation would distract from the headache-inducing buzz of activity, "I am even more convinced now that calling off the wedding was the right decision. Theodore hasn't even put up a fight for me. If he truly did care to marry me, he would not have given up on the notion so easily."

Tamsin nodded. "I agree. The man who will not fight for you is an unworthy suitor."

"Speaking of suitors, you must have quite a few of your own." Ione grinned playfully. "Tell me, are there any dashing gentlemen after your hand? Surely there are those who would try to win your affections, despite your resolve to remain unwed."

"No, indeed," the pretty blonde laughed. "My fortune either scares them off or is their true desire. *I* do not seem to enter the equation at all."

"I have a hard time believing that." Ione cast her cousin a sideways glance as she unfolded her napkin and placed it in her lap. There was something in her cousin's expression, careful though it was, that gave Ione a sense of sadness. She frowned thoughtfully, then leaned in to murmur under her breath. "I could look for you, see what the future holds."

Tamsin shook her head, smiling. "No, thank you. I'd rather be surprised, I think."

"Very wise of you. Knowing the future is far less interesting than people might suppose." Ione was relieved. Her offer was genuine, but sifting through the morass of all that was to come could be tempestuous and draining. She often approached her magic in the same cautious way she would approach an untamed and willful horse. More than once, she wished she'd been born with a more common gift. "Although I suppose if I were a card player it would be quite useful."

"True enough," her cousin replied lightly. "Something to keep in mind, should you ever become a card sharp."

"Perhaps that's a future I should consider. I doubt many of the London gentlemen will be calling anytime soon. I could further scandalize society by making my way in the world at the card tables," Ione remarked dryly, her attention drawn to the door as it swung open.

George Maclaren strode in authoritatively and nearly tripped at the sight of the two women, a smile spreading across his face. He came over, his hands out in greeting. "Never say your plans have changed?"

"It seems they have." Ione replied, stifling a chuckle. Thoughts of her magical struggles and London society were immediately replaced with absolute delight at his approach. "Tamsin and I decided that Bruichladdich could wait. I am sure the quiet will still be there if we delay our arrival for a few days."

Tamsin gave him a friendly smile. "You mentioned festivities. It seemed too good an opportunity to miss."

"Indeed, it is not every day that one is presented with the opportunity to attend the swearing in of a new Maclaren." Ione beamed up at him.

He grinned. "I am delighted, ladies, absolutely delighted! You will, of course, be my guests at the castle for the duration."

Ione exchanged a quick look with her cousin before graciously declining this invitation—though she wished she could say yes. It was truly a flattering offer, but hardly one suitable for a pair of young, unmarried ladies to accept. They were already pushing the limits of propriety—and her father's patience—by going to the investiture.

Ione glanced around the room as she considered inviting the viscount to join them for the evening. But crowded as the place was, she didn't think he'd enjoy taking his meal in the midst of the hubbub. She returned her attention to Lord Kirkleith, appreciating the broadness of his shoulders, and the way a few errant locks of wavy red-gold hair seemed determined to lie across his forehead in a pleasant, windswept sort of way. She could easily imagine the man astride a magnificent steed, galloping through the countryside.

Tamsin pressed her Ione's hand softly. "We are pleased to see you indeed, Lord Kirkleith. As we are traveling in the same direction, I expect we shall do so again, along the way. I hope you rest well this evening, sir—a very good night to you." She curtseyed and all but dragged Ione away.

Ione followed Tamsin toward the door, stifling her disappointment, and a small amount of annoyance. Another dinner with Lord Kirkleith would have been a merry way to end the day, yet her cousin had all but run from the prospect. She cast a final glance at the man and sighed as they stepped into the hallway. "I take it we will be dining in our rooms, then?" She fixed a questioning look on her cousin, even as they made their way up the stairs. "Why did you rush us out of there?"

"Because, my dearest, your face was reflecting exactly what you were thinking, and no gentleman needs that much encouragement. Besides, you are only a few days from a rather spectacularly broken engagement, which he may hear about at some point, and I will not have him think you fickle." Tamsin patted her arm. "You will see him again, never fear. But caution, I think, is our watchword. We know very little of him, after all."

"I have no intention of hurrying into another courtship, even supposing the gentleman was interested," Ione insisted, attempting to sound dignified and practical. They stopped at the door to her room and Ione felt her shoulders slumping. Upon seeing the viscount she'd almost forgotten that this sojourn to Scotland was the result of her father's disappointment with recent actions on her part. "I suppose it's the weariness of travel and the freedom of being away from London society. Thank you for looking out for me. The past few months have felt like a cage that was growing ever smaller. I suppose my newfound freedom is somewhat intoxicating, and I shall have to be mindful of things."

"I do understand, better than you might think." Tamsin wrapped an arm around Ione and gave her a reassuring squeeze. "And I will always look out for you."

Ione returned the embrace, but the tone of her cousin's statement gave her pause. *"Better than you might think?"* Tamsin had always struck Ione as a free spirit. After all, she traveled often and insisted she had no interest in marriage. There had never been any breath of rumor about any such entanglement. And yet, there was definitely something there–but Ione knew her cousin well enough to know that there was little point in asking. She pulled back and offered Tamsin a bright smile. "Well, we're both free now, and we've all the excitement of an investiture to look forward to."

Chapter Four

Band of Brothers

As he got closer to home, the new Lord Kirkleith found that impatience overtook him, so where prudence might have argued that they take another night on the road, Geordie and Angus chose to push through as much as the horses would allow, the better to arrive in Balmaclaren all the sooner.

It was nearing dinner when Geordie strode through the imposing front doors of Maclaren castle, slapping his riding gloves against his thigh. "Hello, the house! Is anyone here?"

"My lord!" cried Pickett, Geordie's English butler, clearly scandalized at Geordie's freewheeling ways. "We did not expect you this evening—the family have gathered in the blue salon. I'll announce you at once!"

However, the sudden clatter of approaching footsteps contradicted him. "Like hell you will," cried Quinn Rutherford, thus completing the butler's demoralization. "There you are, you great oaf—what took you so long?"

Geordie laughed as he hugged his friend. "I'm glad to see you too, you rascal. I hope the fleshpots and gambling hells will be able to do without you for a bit."

"They'll have to lump it," Quinn replied with a chuckle. "I may not have much going on up here," he indicated his temple, "but I do have my priorities firmly in place." His voice gentled. "I'd be nowhere else right now, Geordie."

By his side, quiet, scholarly Asher Burton reached out to greet his friend. "It's good to see you, Geordie. I'm—we're both so sorry about—"

Geordie shook his head. "Don't, please. Thank you—I got your telegrams. But this is a time for celebration—I know my father wouldn't have wanted us weighed with sorrow. Grief is a capricious mistress, and it's best not to let her have her way all the time." He wrapped Asher in a bear hug, dislodging his friend's spectacles. "How are things at Oxford?"

"Oh, well." Asher emerged from the embrace pink but gratified. "Research goes apace, you know. I've made a change to my thesis—"

"What, again?" Amused, Geordie shook his head. "You'll never graduate at this rate, my son."

Asher snorted. "Perhaps that's my plan."

The other two laughed. "And Ross—has he arrived yet?" Geordie asked.

Quinn rolled his eyes, even as he let out a brief snort. "You know Ross, always the last to arrive—if one can get him to show up at all these days."

Geordie chuckled. "Oh, he's coming—I had a cable from him right before I left London." He looked up to see an older woman of regal bearing and a young woman with a head of vivid auburn hair approaching from the direction of the aforementioned blue parlor.

"Hello, Mama, Ailsa. I hope these rascals haven't put you out too much?"

Caroline Maclaren, the dowager Lady Kirkleith, smiled. "Surely you cannot be speaking of my other boys in such a disrespectful manner!" Geordie took his mother's outstretched hands and kissed her on both cheeks. "I hope your journey wasn't too fatiguing," she went on, studying his face.

"It was fine—I had Angus to keep me company. He's taken the carriage 'round to the stables and will be in to pay his respects later." Geordie turned his attention to his younger sister, gentling his tone. "How are you, Ailsa?"

She rushed forward, wrapping her arms around his middle, pressing her face to his waistcoat. "I'm glad you're home," was all Geordie could make out, muffled as she was against the fabric. He rubbed her back as she sniffled a bit before pulling away, biting her lips hard— to keep from crying, he thought. He couldn't blame her—he felt rather like it himself.

"I'm glad t'be home," he murmured. "Run along if you need a moment to yourself, hm?" Ailsa nodded and hurried up the grand stairway toward the family bedchambers.

"Poor child," Lady Kirkleith said softly when her youngest child disappeared from view. She turned back to Geordie, and he could see the lines of grief had deepened. "We're all feeling it keenly, I'm afraid."

Geordie kissed his mother's forehead and offered her his arm to escort her back to the parlor. However, before they'd made it more than a few steps, Pickett—evidently determined not to be caught unawares again—flung open the door to reveal the last of the arrivals.

"Dr. Ross McInerny," the butler announced as Geordie's oft-late friend was revealed frozen in place, hand upraised to ring the bell, his expression that of a man nonplussed by the vehemence of Pickett's greeting. "Shall I take your coat, doctor?"

"Um—oh, yes, of course," Ross stammered a bit, the Irish lilt in his speech unmoderated, further evidence of his surprise. "Am I so late he had you watching the front step?"

"No need, sir," Picket replied primly, acquiring Ross' coat, hat, and gloves. With that cryptic reply he glided from view.

"You made it!" cried Quinn, clapping Ross on the back, while Asher beamed.

The Irishman shot Quinn a look. "What is that supposed to mean? Of course I made it." He ran a hand through unruly dark hair, which immediately flopped back into his eyes. "It's not every day a man is asked to stand as a second for one of his oldest friends."

Geordie excused himself to his mother and rejoined his friends to give Ross a welcoming hug. "Thank you," he said, voice rough. "For this—but for all of it, for bein' the one to tell me about Father, and for lookin' after me when I had to identify..." He glanced at his mother and broke off. "I'm glad you're here."

The doctor's face turned a bit red, his eyes a little shadowed. "After I saw what was—" Ross stopped and put a hand on Geordie's shoulder. "I couldn't let you hear it from a stranger." After another beat, he shook his head and looked around the room. His expression grew brighter in an instant. "Asher! I should have known you'd beat me here. Where have you been off to lately? I had to bribe your housekeeper to let me in so I could pinch a bottle of brandy."

Asher rolled his eyes. "A short trip to Paris to confirm some research. I thought I gave you a key."

"You did, and I put it somewhere safe." Ross confirmed, then followed it with a shrug. "A little too safe, apparently: hidden even from myself."

That made Geordie laugh. "Did you think I wouldn't have any brandy?"

"I was toasting something and I needed it then and there. Besides, I could have used the money I gave his housekeeper to buy my own brandy, but it tastes better if it's pilfered from Asher's stock," Ross informed him with a grin.

"Toasting what?" Asher slung his arm around his friend's shoulders as Geordie returned to his mother and led the group to the blue salon.

They were all seated comfortably and Lady Kirkleith had rung for tea before Ross answered Asher's question. "Work-related. Plenty of time to talk about it later," he explained, settling into his seat. He looked at Geordie. "So, what sort of excitement awaits us as your seconds?"

There was a pause as Ailsa stepped into the room, red-eyed but otherwise composed, and took a seat next to her mother. Lady Kirkleith leaned forward and placed her hand on Geordie's. "We need not stick with tradition, my son. No one would argue, in the circumstances."

Geordie shook his head. "The clan expects it, Mama. Father would want it. And I... need to mark this transition, somehow. Otherwise it won't seem quite real." She nodded and sat back, slipping an arm around her daughter, and he went on to answer his friend. "It's by way of being a wake for the chief that has died, and a celebration for the new chief claiming his place. Happens over several days—there's feasting, and dancing, and the challenges, which is what I need you lot for."

Ross squirmed in his seat, expression turning worried. "I'm going to need to practice a bit before that. I'll not have you lose your clan because I parried when I ought to have thrust."

"It's only for show," Geordie reminded him good-naturedly. "But Angus'll have you back in form in no time."

Ross winced. "Angus is going to tear a strip out of me when he sees how rusty I've let myself get."

"This is what happens when I let you out of my sight for more than a few days," Quinn jumped in, never missing a chance for a bit of playful ribbing. "You get complacent and forgetful."

Ross rolled his eyes and turned to the other man. "I'm only rusty because some of us have important work to occupy us. We can't all be traveling the continent on holiday all the time."

"Lads," came an admonishing voice from the doorway, "no squabbling in front of her Ladyship, please. Take it outside if y'must." Angus grinned as the three friends got up and went to greet him with affection. He gave each of the boys a brief hug, then went to bow in front of Lady Kirkleith. "My lady." The Scotsman's voice was rough. "'Twas a fine service at St. Paul's. I hope your return home wasnae too tirin'?"

Caroline Maclaren took both the old retainer's hands in hers. "Not at all, Angus. I'm quite well. Thank you for your care of my son these last few weeks. I know it can't have been easy."

Angus shook his head. "'Twas the least I could do, my lady. I only wish I could do more."

She rose gracefully. "You can, my old friend. Escort me to supper?" Lady Kirkleith appropriated his arm while Angus chuckled, and they led the rest to the dining room.

Supper was perforce less sumptuous than some of the meals Castle Maclaren had seen, but it was appropriate to a family in mourning, Geordie thought: warm, filling, comforting. Conversation was subdued, but not pained; there was no boisterous laughter, but nor was laughter absent entirely. Impossible not to laugh around his old friends, Geordie thought affectionately. Irrepressible Quinn, clever Ross, good-humored Asher... Despite the differences in station and occupation, they'd all dropped everything and come to support him, and he would never be done being grateful for these friendships.

Geordie's mother and sister retired shortly after dinner, as did Angus, leaving the boys to their own devices. The mood fluctuated between somber and jovial as they each recounted their memories of Geordie's father, or laughed over stories of their school days. It was rare for the four of them to be in the same space anymore, and yet when they were, time had a way of turning backward.

At last Geordie sighed, knowing he was putting off yet something else uncomfortable. "I need," he said, "to get my bearings in Father's study—well, my study now, I suppose. I'll need to know where to find various papers and ledgers and things, but Lord, it seems strange. He was always such a private man." He let out another breath, then straightened his shoulders. "I should get this first time over with. You lads needn't join me, though I'd be grateful if you would."

Ross put a hand on his shoulder. "In for a penny, in for pound, Geordie."

"He's right—we're here to do more than clean out your wine cellar," Quinn added, his tone unusually business-like.

Geordie nodded. "Come along, then. I need to get used to this sort of thing so I don't feel like I'm encroaching." He led them to his father's study and paused with his hand on the knob. "I remember the first time I was invited in here—Father brought me on my eighteenth birthday for a toast, just him and me." The memory brought with it a small smile, and Geordie pushed the door open with a sense of reverence. "Seems right to toast him here tonight."

They filed into the room one by one, heads swiveling from back and forth as they filled the space. Asher wandered to the bookshelf and ran a finger along the spines of the books, Quinn gravitated toward the sword that the former Lord Kirkleith had kept mounted on the wall near the fireplace, and Ross fiddled with the small collection of odds and ends that Geordie's father kept on a table in the corner.

After picking up a pipe and setting it back down for the second time, the young doctor broke the silence that filled the room. "I half-expect him to come in and tell us off for messing about with his things."

Asher spoke up. "He wouldn't have—just a gentle but firm reminder that he expected better from young gentlemen." He huffed out a laugh as he turned away from the shelf. "I only came in for that treatment once, and once was enough. Made you want to live up to his expectations—and feel like a rotter for not having done it."

Quinn was busy excavating glasses and Scotch from a cabinet shaped like a globe. "He was a good man, your father. An exceptional man—with an exceptional son." He poured out four short tumblers and passed them around. "To the Maclaren that was." He raised his glass. "And the Maclaren that is, God bless him."

"The Maclaren that was, and the Maclaren that is," the others echoed, and drank.

Geordie's eyes prickled, and he blinked rapidly to dispel the sensation. "To old friends," he toasted, and drank again. "I've no clear idea what I'd be doing without you three to look out for me."

The lads raised their glasses again. Quinn downed the rest of his and put the empty tumbler aside before clapping his hands together. He looked to Asher, raising a brow before turning back to Geordie. "There's a bit more to our being here than sentiment, I'm afraid."

Geordie frowned. "What do you mean?"

It was Asher who spoke up. "First, a bit of a confession: I'm not an Oxford research fellow—with which assessment my advisor would heartily agree." He grinned. "I do live there, but the rest is just... fiction."

Quinn took up the tale as Geordie's frown deepened. "Nor am I the roguish, carefree man-about-town with no discernible source of income that I appear to be."

Ross' expression was almost comical. He looked from Asher to Quinn, then back at Asher. "Fiction? What exactly does that mean?" He waved his glass between the pair of them. "What is fact?"

The two exchanged glances. "First—it's important that you know, Geordie, that Quinn and I would be here now regardless. But the circumstances of your father's death are of concern to... our employer; and so, given the long-standing friendship between us, Quinn and I have been—um—assigned to you for the duration."

"Assigned?" Geordie had no idea what his friend was talking about, but he didn't much like the sound of it. "What 'duration'? Who's this employer of yours, and what does he have to do with me or my father?"

"Technically, she," Quinn corrected him. "We are agents in Her Majesty's service, under the aegis of William Melville. Melville is concerned that you may be targeted by whoever murdered—I'm sorry," he held up his hand, "I know it's a horrific term, but it must be faced. He is concerned that whoever murdered your father may well take aim at you. Since Ash and I made it clear we were coming here anyway, we're to keep you safe until the criminal is brought to justice."

This rocked Geordie back on his heels entirely. "You—and Asher—?"

Asher's tone was apologetic. "I'm afraid so. We'd've told you before this, but it's a new branch, and rather a secret."

Ross looked rather pale, eyes fixed on the floor. He downed what little remained in his glass and took a deep breath before speaking. "And there's reason to believe that whoever..." A haunted gaze landed on Geordie's face. "That he might try to do the same to Geordie?"

Asher put a hand on Ross' shoulder. "I know," he said quietly. "I've seen the photographs of the crime scene. Horrific—but we're confident that this was someone copying the Ripper murders, to try and escape detection, not the Ripper himself. Melville's concern is more about the Maclaren challenges— whether someone might take advantage of them in some way." He shook his head, and returned his regard to Geordie. "Please believe me—it's unlikely at best, but Melville is unwilling to take any risk—and since we're your seconds anyway..."

"...if we detect anything of concern, Ash or I can take your place, with no one the wiser," Quinn concluded with a nod.

"So I'm to—to hide behind my closest friends, let you be murdered in my stead?" Geordie exploded. "Not bloody likely."

"No," Quinn replied in measured tones. "If the murderer is trying to get to you and we act as your seconds, he'll stand down unless he's a complete idiot. Killing one of us at that juncture would be tantamount to signing a confession. Believe me, Geordie, it's not the risk it seems."

"What of his mother and sister? Are they in danger as well?" Ross broke in with a thoughtful expression on his face. "It seems to me there are three people to protect and only two of you to do it. Unless my arithmetic is wrong, you'll need another man. I may not be a... special agent, or whatever it is you call yourselves, but I'm here and I'm willing to accept the post."

"Good," Asher replied, "because that's exactly what we were going to ask you to do. There'd be little point in harming the dowager or Lady Ailsa; and I doubt this person, whoever he is, will run to anything like kidnapping—ransom doesn't seem to be what he's after. But at the same time, it's best to be on our guard as much as possible."

"Good God," muttered Geordie, and poured himself another drink. "And what am I t'do, exactly?"

"Live your life," was Quinn's philosophical answer. "As Ash said, it's unlikely that the murderer would have followed you up here. For one thing, we'd notice any newcomers in Balmaclaren. This is all just precaution."

Geordie glowered at his friends. "D'you swear to that?"

Asher held up his hand. "On my honor—and on Quinn's, if he's got any."

Quinn's expression of outrage made Geordie snort. He rolled his shoulders and let himself relax a little. "Very well. But if that changes—"

"You'll be the first to know."

Chapter Five

Balmaclaren

For Ione and Tamsin, the remainder of the journey to Balmaclaren passed without incident. They spent another night at a post inn, and by midday the following day, their destination was in sight. Everyone in the carriage was happy to put an end to days of travel, pleasant as the company and countryside had been.

As they hove to a stop in front of the local inn, Ione and Tamsin breathed a sigh of relief—and of pleasure. Even were they not road-weary, the town could not have been a more welcoming sight. A winding river bordered one side, opening into the sea not far away. A wooden bridge stretched across the river from the main thoroughfare to whatever lay beyond. The sandstone buildings that lined the street were darkened with age, but the structures themselves were immaculately maintained. In short, Balmaclaren was as enchanting a place as any might hope to spend their holiday in.

The inn itself, run by a Mr. and Mrs. Murray, was a two-story building of stone and plaster, with old-fashioned diamond-paned windows and a large stable behind. The door was painted the same bright blue as the Scottish flag, and a half-barrel of late flowers sat cheerily on either side.

They ate a light lunch in the private parlor before ascending to their rooms to wash and rest from the journey. Tamsin's maid Rose set to unpacking for her lady, while Ione insisted upon unpacking her own belongings. It was a task she always preferred to do herself. Putting everything in its place helped her to settle into her surroundings and make them her own.

Her room wasn't particularly spacious, but it was comfortable. The patchwork quilt on her bed was several shades of green, with sections of pink floral fabric worked in—a far cry from the luxury of the blankets that dressed her bed back home, but a testament to hours of skilled needlework and care. Apart from the bed and clothes press, there was only a washtable with a ceramic basin and pitcher, a simple vanity and mirror, and a rocking chair placed by the window from which Ione could see the ocean.

Many of the people Ione knew back in London would have scoffed at the accommodations, but Ione rather liked the peaceful simplicity and warmth of it. There was a sense of quiet here that made it easier for her to reflect on the events of the last few days. Had she married Mr. Gibson, she would have been on her honeymoon by now, an idea that made her stomach churn with distaste. It now escaped her entirely why she'd ever accepted his attentions in the first place. She didn't want a life shackled to someone like Theodore Gibson. Ione huffed out a sigh as she laid her hairbrush and hand mirror on the vanity. The vision of what she didn't want was clear, but the image of what she wanted was frustratingly murky.

A soft knock came on her door; a moment later a curly blonde head peeked around the doorjamb. "I came to see how you were feeling," said Tamsin.

"Refreshed and glad to be out of that carriage. I do believe it felt more cramped with every hour we were on the road." Ione answered with a smile. "Are you rested?"

"Yes, thank you." Tamsin came into the room and contemplated her cousin. "Do you need some help? I can charm something for you."

"No, thank you. Now that I've had a chance to rinse the road from my face, I feel quite myself again." Ione reached for the shawl she'd laid out on the bed. "In fact, I was going to propose a walk. I should very much like to stretch my legs. I thought we might explore Balmaclaren, or perhaps take in a bit of the countryside before tea."

Her cousin smiled and shook her head. "Not for me, I think; but you go ahead. I understand there is a magnificent view of the castle from the high road; it will be light for some time yet. I think I'll read for a bit— that carriage very nearly shook my teeth loose and I feel a need to let myself settle, in the hope that I stop vibrating."

"Poor Tamsin, that last stretch of road was rather rough." Ione gave her cousin a gentle pat on the shoulder. "Take your rest; I'll leave the castle viewing for when you're feeling better. In the meantime, I shall scout the town and see what entertainment it has to offer during our stay." She moved toward the door, her cousin following along.

"Tell me all when you return." Tamsin yawned. "Will you need Rose, do you think? I fear she's still a bit ill from the rocking of the carriage, but likely the sea air will do her good if you feel you want someone with you."

Ione considered her cousin's offer. Mama would insist she have a companion, and she could practically feel her Papa's disapproval at the idea of her walking alone... But Balmaclaren was hardly London, and she needed to be out in the open air. "No, let Rose rest. I shan't go far, and I doubt there's much danger in a small town such as this." She offered Tamsin a conspiratorial smile. "Besides, we've set our minds to adventure, and I rather like the idea of enjoying my newfound independence."

Tamsin leaned forward to give her a kiss on the cheek. "There—you have my blessing. Fly and be free, little sparrow—at least until time for tea." With a parting smile she went into her room and closed the door.

Ione chuckled to herself as she made her way downstairs. She wandered out the door and stopped on the step, looking first one way then the other before deciding on her course. After a moment of consideration, she turned to the right and headed back in the direction of the few shops they'd seen from the carriage window. It was the first time that Ione could remember having control over how and where she spent her time. The experience was exciting—and a little intimidating as well.

She nodded politely at the few people who offered her greetings on the street. No one seemed shocked or horrified to see her walking on her own, and emboldened by this, Ione decided to pay a visit to the small general store. She pushed open the door to the sound of a small bell tinkling, that added a sense of charm to her little adventure. Though Ione had little use for most of the wares, she spent time studying each of them. After a few minutes she found a small collection of combs and hairpins that were surprisingly lovely, and she set to the task of sorting through the different options.

The bell tinkled again, followed by the sound of booted feet crossing the floor. "I think the one with tiny shells would be most becoming," said a familiar voice behind her.

Ione startled slightly, having been focused on the task of picking out a gift to bring back to Elsie. She looked up and dropped the hairpin she was holding into its velvet-lined tray. "Lord Kirkleith! I did not expect to see you before the investiture." She started laughing at herself as she picked the pin back up. "I was looking for a gift for my sister."

He smiled. "Have you found anything you like?"

Ione reached for a pair of combs she'd set aside. They were adorned with little pearls and tiny white roses. "I thought these would suit her quite nicely. Elsie has the loveliest auburn curls." She held the combs out for him to inspect. "I was just trying to decide on whether or not I should get her some hairpins to match."

Lord Kirkleith inspected the display. "My own sister has red hair too—no surprise, I suppose," he added with a laugh. "Those will look very well, I should think."

Footsteps heralded the arrival of another gentleman: this one with nearly-black hair that brushed his collar, and eyes almost as dark. "Ah—let me introduce my friend, Dr. Ross McInerny," Lord Kirkleith supplied. "Ross, allow me to present Miss Ione Brentwood."

"A pleasure to meet you, Miss Brentwood," The doctor replied, with a broad and genuine smile.

"And you, Dr. McInerny," Ione returned his greeting with a smile of her own. "Lord Kirkleith was graciously offering me his input on a set of combs for my sister."

"Was he now?" Dr. McInerny looked at the combs with polite interest. Then to Lord Kirkleith, "And were you able to help her settle on anything?"

The Scotsman chuckled. "I cannot believe that Miss Brentwood truly needs my opinion on so delicate a matter—she has excellent taste without my galumphing about."

"I'm gratified to hear you think so," Ione said, blushing with delight. Others had complimented her taste before, but it felt more genuine coming from Lord Kirkleith, though he probably thought the whole thing dull. Theodore had never been interested in such details. She sighed, and put the tray of hairpins back in order. "It's kind of you to take time out of what must be a very busy day to discuss such trifles with me."

Dr. McInerny nodded slightly, his regard moving from Ione to his friend. "Well, Geordie is quite gallant like that. No detail too small for his attention."

"'Tisn't gallantry at all, you great knob," was what Ione thought she heard Lord Kirkleith mutter, but surely she'd heard wrong. He cleared his throat and spoke more loudly. "Ross, if you'll go speak with the farrier, I'd like to show Miss Brentwood what little there is of Balmaclaren. It's the Maclaren's duty to welcome every guest, after all."

Ross' brows came together. He studied his friend thoughtfully. "I did give certain parties my word that I'd keep an eye on things in town." He glanced at Ione before continuing. "But I would hate to stand in the way of the Maclaren's duty." He wiped a hand over his chin, obviously conflicted, though Ione could not imagine why. "Fine, but I want your solemn oath that our friends will not know I spoke to the farrier without you."

"So sworn. And I'll go farther and promise not to leave the high street, will that do?"

"Very well, then," the doctor replied before turning to Ione. "Miss Brentwood, I wish you a good day. Perhaps we'll see more of you." He turned to leave, but stopped at the viscount's shoulder and Ione could have sworn she heard him telling Lord Kirkleith to be careful. After a nod of reassurance from his friend, the Irishman left.

The Maclaren smiled at Ione. "I don't mean to take you from your shopping."

"Oh, not at all. I was out for a walk and just stopped in on a whim. After such a long journey, I felt the need to move about freely," Ione replied, pleased by the idea that Lord Kirkleith was willing to make time for her. She smiled and took her selections to the counter. Once everything was settled with the clerk, Ione turned back to her unexpected companion. He was a striking figure: tall, muscular, and yet there was a gentleness and warmth to him that put Ione at ease. "A bit of an adventure, if you will. Though I suppose buying combs is quite a dull sort of adventure."

"Not at all," he demurred. "In these things it's best to begin small and build up slowly. To that end," he went on with a smile, "might I extend your adventure by escorting you to tea at Mrs. Clark's? It's a small tearoom, just down the way a bit."

Ione nibbled at her lower lip and glanced in the direction of the inn. What would Mama say, were she to accept the invitation? And yet, Mama and Papa had both been thrilled at how she'd conducted herself through the Season, and look how that had turned out. She turned back to Lord Kirkleith with a resolute nod.

"Shopping can be thirsty work, and I'm told one must look to their health during an adventure."

"Yes, indeed," he replied seriously, and offered her his arm.

She slipped her fingers into the crook of his elbow and allowed him to lead her down the high street, lined with homes and shops and offices of one kind and another, each quaint and inviting. The tearoom (Clark's, the painted sign above the door proclaimed) was surprisingly elegant. Even glancing through the window, Ione could see lace tablecloths and vases filled with the vibrant purple heather that grew wild along the roads and in the hills surrounding the town. She made a silent note to come back with Tamsin before their visit was through.

A slight woman of indeterminate years, presumably the eponymous Mrs. Clark, happily seated them at a pretty table in a wide bay window at the back of the shop, overlooking the beach and the sea beyond. "So good of you to come, my lord," she gushed at Lord Kirkleith. "And to bring your friends as well. So kind. What may I get for you?"

"Your best cream tea, if you will," was his Lordship's reply, and he held Ione's seat for her. Mrs. Clark curtseyed and scurried kitchenward.

Ione leaned forward to sniff the heather before she settled in her seat. "Delightful. Such a fine, fresh scent after spending months in London." She traced a finger along the patterned lace in front of her, suddenly worried she'd have nothing of interest to say to a man like this. "Thank you for the tea, and for the informative conversation about our original destination. Balmaclaren already seems the better choice."

He grinned, settling in the seat across from her. "I'm delighted to know you think so. And I agree—the pleasant diversions of London are many, but the odor of the place is not one of them. Though I will not claim any regrets for my time there this summer, as it brought me an introduction to you." His stormy gaze clouded over a bit, and then he blinked and the impression was gone.

"I'm surprised we did not meet earlier," Ione mused with a twinge of regret. She cleared her throat and tilted her head. "We must have passed one another like two ships in the night. A pity, my lord." She blushed and looked away.

He shook his head. "I was there to work as a sort of secretary to my father for that session of Parliament; I had little enough time for parties and the like, though he insisted I attend when I could." The sadness was back in his gaze, and Ione thought she understood its origin. "'Twas experience I'm glad for now."

She would have reached out to touch his hand and offer that small comfort, but they were too newly acquainted. "Then I suppose we have something in common, for Mama insisted that I was there for work as well: 'The work of finding a suitable match, dear daughter, is of the utmost importance in the life of a lady of breeding.'" Ione straightened her shoulders and primped her hair, impersonating her mother, hoping to cheer him up. She relaxed and leaned in slightly. "And believe me, anyone who has spent enough time in a room full of debutantes would likely find themselves prepared to face even the most heated meetings of Parliament."

Her words had the desired effect: George Maclaren threw back his head and laughed. "I'll take your word for it—it all looks effortless t'me. A job it may seem at times, but the result surely is worth it, when the reward is a lifetime of happiness—which I do most heartily wish t'you and your fiancé."

Ione's smile faded and her eyes fell to her lap. "That is very kind of you to say." She tried to find a polite way to tell Lord Kirkleith that, though kind, the well-wishing was for naught. She finally worked up the courage to look up again. "But whatever happiness Mr. Gibson and I might find, it will not be in one another's company." Ione sighed, knowing it would be better to have out with the whole thing. "Lord Kirkleith, you have been kind and generous with your time, and as such I feel I must tell you that my visit to Scotland is not a simple holiday. Mr. Gibson and I have called off our engagement. My Papa thought it better that I was away from London while the dust settles."

A fierce blush rose in his cheeks, but he nodded, his expression serious. "One should not marry where there is no congeniality." A pause. "I am sorry if I have somehow made you feel you must speak of such a private matter t'me. I had no idea, and no intention to pry."

"No, my lord, you were only being polite," Ione replied quietly. She would have offered a better reassurance, but Mrs. Clark arrived just then with a loaded tray. Ione refrained from speaking further until the woman was finished fussing over the tea. When she finally left, Ione returned her attention to Lord Kirkleith. "You were not prying at all, but I've no wish to return your thoughtfulness with dishonesty. I hope it has not lowered your opinion of me, but I would rather you hear of it from me, than through gossip."

He reached across the table and took both her hands in his. "I am glad you hold my esteem in such regard that you told me yourself. It can't have been easy. As to my good opinion of you... it has only increased, in the face of your steadfast resolve to do what was right." The corner of his mouth quirked upward. "I will not pretend that I am anything but glad that you are free of any such... encumbrance. Thank you for telling me." A pause. "May I ask something of you in return?"

"You may," Ione answered, delighted by his acceptance of her confession, and curious as to what he might request of her.

His lean cheeks were still pink, but he went on. "My given name is George—I'm called Geordie by my friends, and I'd like to count you among them. You may not wish to say it before others, lest it be misunderstood in some way, but—" He chuckled. "I'd count myself a happy man to never hear 'my lord' from your lips again."

And now Ione was certain her cheeks must be as pink as his. "You would like to count me among your friends?" The idea of it pleased her—more than it ought to, probably—and she was just as certain that the smile on her lips made that far too clear. "I am honored, my—Geordie."

She caught a glimpse of his smile as he dropped his gaze to the table and stirred his tea. "That's settled, then."

Ione reached for a scone and spread a bit of clotted cream on a piece before speaking again, though she had not the courage to look at Geordie when she did. "And I suppose, if we are friends, then you may call me Ione." She glanced up briefly. "Fair is fair."

"Aye, Ione." His voice was low. "Fair is fair."

Ione's eyes lifted then, and locked on the man across the table, her mouth going inexplicably dry. She swallowed and reached for her teacup again, taking a long—and what her mother would consider an unladylike—gulp. She coughed a little. "Oh, that's rather hot."

"Are you well?" His grey gaze held concern.

"Yes, perfectly," Ione muttered, dabbing at her mouth. "Delicious as the tea is, there's no excuse for me to gulp at it like a fish thrown back into the pond." She took a moment to put herself in order. "Must be all the dust and weariness of travel."

"Och, and here I am, keeping you from your rest, great oaf that I am." Geordie shook his head.

"Not an 'oaf' at all. I did say I wanted an adventure." Ione started to laugh at herself. "Half-drowning in a cup of tea could qualify. Very chivalrous of you to oblige my whim for excitement."

He chuckled. "Would you like a second cup?"

"So I can finish the job?" Ione laughed again, genuinely enjoying herself, scalded tongue aside. She'd known the approach of her wedding day had been an unhappy thing, but until now she hadn't realized how weighed down she'd been by it. In all the parties and pomp, there'd been little authentic joy.

Geordie shrugged, eyes sparkling. "Not at all—I thought you might like a bath before dinner, is all."

Ione almost snorted, and was preparing to respond when a tapping at the window caused her to look around. Geordie's friend, Dr. McInerny, was standing outside, a quizzical look on his face. Ione turned back to her new friend. "Oh dear, we've left poor Dr. McInerny to do all the work while we've been lazing about with tea and treats."

"It's good for him—builds character," was Geordie's assessment even as he beckoned his friend to join them.

The doctor came inside without a moment of hesitation. He greeted them both and settled into one of the empty chairs as Mrs. Clark hurried forward to provide a third cup and saucer for the newcomer. Dr. McInerny paid little attention to the tea, instead reaching for a scone and the jam. If he thought anything of Ione and Geordie sharing tea together, he said nothing to that effect, though Ione thought she caught him sending a small grin in Geordie's direction.

But alas, all good things have their end, and the impromptu tea was no exception. The clock on the wall struck the hour as they polished off the last of the tea. Ione glanced up and winced. "Oh dear, my cousin must be wondering where I've gotten to, and I've kept the two of you here, listening to me prattle on the entire afternoon."

Not at all, Ione," replied Geordie courteously, and the doctor echoed him, though his brows were raised. "'Tis I've kept you here when you must be longing for a rest after your journey." He rose, spoke to Mrs. Clark briefly—settling the bill, Ione assumed—and then offered her his arm again. "We'll take you back to the inn and leave you in peace."

Ione tucked her shawl tighter and accepted his arm as she thanked Mrs. Clark and complimented the service.

It was nearing sunset when they approached the inn and parted ways. Ione waved and watched the two of them head off. After a few paces, the doctor nudged Geordie, and though Ione could not hear what he said, the resulting blush on the viscount's cheeks was visible from a distance.

Chapter Six

His Father's Son

"You can shut it now, thanks," Geordie told Ross shortly as they rode toward the castle bluff. "Miss Brentwood is an acquaintance from London. People do have those, you know. There's nothing for you to gossip about, Mother Hen."

"I'm not 'gossiping', I'm inquiring. There's a difference," Ross replied, with a look of mock insult on his face. "And I am not a mother hen. I was told to keep an eye out for anyone of interest. Miss Brentwood seemed of interest to you."

Geordie felt like growling. "I'll thank you to keep your eyes off Miss Brentwood. You know perfectly well what Quinn and Asher meant." He thought he heard his friend chuckle, but the good doctor had the good sense to cover it with a cough.

When Ross spoke again, his tone was gentler. "You seemed to be enjoying yourself, is all. It was good to see."

"I was enjoying myself," Geordie allowed. He contemplated the sunset. How he wanted to explain to his friend that there was something about Ione—her words of comfort to the young woman at the opera; her ability to uplift him, make him laugh in spite of his grief—something that set her apart from other young ladies of his acquaintance. Something he *needed*. But he hadn't the skill with words to make Ross understand, and this was nothing he wanted bandied about between the other three, to be pulled apart and made foolish in the light of day. "Too soon, you think?"

Ross frowned and grew quiet for a few moments, revealing the more serious and thoughtful aspect that he so often hid behind playfulness. "Society has all manner of rules about grief and how we ought to work our way through it, but it's more complex than a black band around your arm. I don't think your father would want you to turn away from happiness at a time like this." The horse he sat astride snorted, as if in agreement.

Geordie side-eyed his friend. "Seems t'me you're attaching an awful lot to a simple cream tea, Ross."

"Not really," the other man said with a shrug. "You have a great deal on your plate right now, and that 'simple cream tea' seemed to give you a bit of a reprieve from your cares. I'm a doctor; when I see something that relieves pain, I take note." He quirked a grin at Geordie. "So you see, it's all very professional. I'm not suggesting you want to marry the girl, you buffoon."

Geordie chanced a glance at his friend but said nothing more.

Later, alone in his rooms, Geordie stood by the window contemplating the sea as the setting sun turned it to stained glass. Ross saw more than he let on, Geordie knew, and he wondered what it was his friend had seen in him. *I'm not suggesting you want to marry the girl.*

It was an absurd idea to go courting now, barely a month after his father's death. Nothing of the kind had entered Geordie's head when he'd sought out Miss Brentwood—Ione, he corrected himself, and the use of her name made him smile a little. It was only that the idea of her had become so intertwined with what little solace he could find in the midst of his sorrow. His heart felt lighter when he saw her face; he stood taller, somehow, in her presence. And the very thought of her carried with it a whisper of his father's voice, telling him that all would, in the end, be well.

Likely he was making it all up from whole cloth. Grief was, as he'd pointed out to his friends, a capricious thing. But Ione Brentwood gave him comfort—the whys and wherefores mattered little, in the end. No one would begrudge him this small comfort just now, least of all his father.

He considered what Asher and Quinn had said about his father's murderer. Neither seemed to feel that the madman, whoever he was, would be fool enough to follow him to Balmaclaren. If there was the slightest chance that Ione or her cousin might be exposed to danger of any kind through association with him... but that would more likely have been the case back in London, to judge from what his friends had said. This was his home, his refuge. He was lord now; chief of his clan. Nowhere could he be so safe as here.

Geordie crossed the room and poured himself a tot of whiskey from the decanter on his dressing-table, sipping it thoughtfully. Yes, he'd known Miss—Ione would likely arrive today, and yes, that was why he'd decided to ride to town. He'd hoped to pass a word or two, merely to hear her voice; taking her to tea had been an unlooked-for pleasure, and one he had enjoyed far more than he'd anticipated. More than beautiful, more than kind, Ione Brentwood was clever, witty, good-humored... Geordie recalled her comments about drowning in her tea and chuckled to himself. She was honest, too, and forthright, telling him directly about her broken engagement, a painful subject at best.

But what a fool her erstwhile fiancé must be! She'd given no particulars, so Geordie couldn't be sure what had gone wrong; but to secure the affections of a woman like that and then to *lose* them? The man must be a pigeon-livered idiot, a foolhardy, unworthy gump, and she was well rid of him.

The idea of Ione Brentwood unencumbered was an enticing one, and one best left unexamined—at least for now—though Geordie's mind kept drifting back to their conversation to offer tidbits of observation. She didn't seem bereft by her broken engagement, for example; she'd kept calling him chivalrous, for another. And—

The bell rang for supper and Geordie suddenly realized that he hadn't changed yet. With a muttered epithet he skinned off his clothes, sponged off, and readied himself to meet his mother's inspection, and that flurry of activity put paid to any further musings in regards to Miss Ione Brentwood.

Arranged around the breakfast table the following morning, Geordie's friends laid out plans for an afternoon of riding the Maclaren lands. "For the day is temperate, the view magnificent, and both I and Icarus need to stretch our legs," concluded Asher. "Come, join us, Geordie—we'll make a day of it if you like."

The idea was tempting: to roam the bluffs, the beach, the forest at will, just as they had when schoolboys; but conscious of his new duties, Geordie regretfully shook his head. "You lads enjoy yourselves. I've got to hear clan grievances today; God help us all."

Quinn poured himself another cup of coffee. "Perhaps brandies and billiards afterward, then? I suspect you'll want the drink at the very least."

"Anything we can pick up in town for you?" Ross asked as he finished off one sweet roll and reached for a second, his fondness for sweets never satisfied. "May as well make ourselves useful if we're to leave you to that headache."

Geordie considered sending a message to Ione; but after all, what would he say? He shook his head. "There's naught I need, but thank you. I'll see you at dinner, then."

His friends changed the conversation after that, and seemed at pains to keep the mood light as they polished off the last morsels of food. Though no one said it, they all knew that this was another time of change. Geordie was taking his place as the head of the clan, and the carefree days of their youth were another step further away.

An hour later found him seated behind his father's leather-topped desk, facing Archie Thomson and Donal Burns, two of his tenant farmers whose lands bordered one another. Geordie steepled his fingers and appraised the pair: Archie, dour and red-faced, his iron-grey hair wild, as though stirred to a frenzy by his temper; and Donal, older, calmer, his blue gaze guileless, his knotted and gnarled hands holding his hat in his lap. "What may I do for you, gentlemen?"

"Donal intentionally flooded one of my best grazing pastures, Maclaren." Archie pointed at the other man, using his entire arm for the gesture. "He knows well how to divert a stream properly, and he knows I depend on that land to feed my cattle." He turned his angry regard to the accused. "You've ne'er stopped expecting me to pay for yer mistake with the cow."

Donal was shaking his head mildly. "I dinnae flood your field by design. Such an act would do naught but waste working hours." He cast a sideways glance at the other man. "I let the matter with the cow rest last spring. 'Tis you who will not forget the thing."

"Cow?" Geordie frowned. "What's this about a cow?"

Donal opened his mouth to answer, but his explanation was cut off by a snort from Archie. "The man sold me three cows early last spring. They were past their prime and my only interest was in the beef." He crossed his arms and lifted his chin. "A price was agreed upon, paid in full, and one of his lads delivered the cows."

"Except that my lad took a fine young milk cow, instead of one the older cows that Archie purchased," Donal explained tone free of anger or accusation. The man looked apologetic, as if embarrassed that the matter was even brought before Geordie. "When I realized the mistake, I went to Archie with the correct cow and tried to exchange the beasts. He informed me the other cow was already dead and gracing the smokehouse."

Geordie studied the two men. "And you think Donal flooded your field as a sort of revenge?" he asked Archie, who was bristling visibly.

"Aye," Archie replied with a glare for the other man. "Wasnae my fault he hadn't the sense to make sure his boy brought the right animals, but he thought I ought to pay for his mistake all the same."

"The mistake was mine, yes, but any man of honor would have offered up the difference in the cows' worth. I would have accepted a cut of the beef and been done with it if money was scarce for you," Donal replied. His tone was not as patient now. "But you refused, and I could do nothing but suffer the loss."

Archie snorted again. "Until you saw the chance to cause hardship." He rolled his shoulders and looked down his nose at Donal. "I ought to have known a man who'd be so careless with such a fine beast would not hesitate to ruin perfectly good grazing land. The cow is better off with me."

Geordie narrowed his eyes. "Is it, now?" He watched as Archie grew impossibly redder, clearly realizing his mistake. "My father always said you were an excellent judge of cattle, Archie. I find it very difficult to believe that you yourself didn't recognize the worth of Donal's cow—and t'judge from your own words just now, and the look on your face, I'm tempted to send one of my own men up to your barn, to see whether that cow might have survived the trip to the butcher."

"And you dare to drag my good name through the mud! I dinnae flood your field, but now I almost wish I had!" Donal's fingers were clenched so tightly around the brim of his hat that the knuckles were white. "That's why you refused to settle up with meat— because ye only had two cows butchered." He shook his head in disgust. "And here our families have worked neighboring farms for years."

Archie's earlier display of indignation was replaced by obvious shame. He bent his gaze to the floor, and while he did not give voice to his guilt, the evidence of it was clear enough in his demeanor.

"Ye took food from the mouths of my children, Archie," Donal added when no apology came. "We near lost our little Maggie, and would have, were it not for the kindness of the Maclaren that was, God rest his soul, and the doctor he paid to see our girl through it."

Geordie pursed his lips. "Seems mistakes were made more than once," he observed mildly. "You'll return the cow today, Archie, and no more talk of Donal flooding your fields on purpose. You can bring your cattle to the castle pastures for the week, until your own drains." He turned to the older man. "How long did Archie have your cow, Donal?"

Donal took a moment to answer, mopping at his forehead and casting another look of disbelief in Archie's direction. "The sale was made early last spring, Maclaren. I'd say a year and a few months, give or take a week."

"And how much coin d'you conjecture you lost in that time, from sales of dairy and cheeses and so forth?" The old farmer thought for another moment and named a fair sum; Geordie took that for what it was worth and doubled it, writing out a cheque and handing it to him. "Now: I'll have no more nonsense like this between you. Archie, if your stock is past its prime and you need new blood, come t'me and we'll see about it. Donal, if you need help with simple tasks like properly diverting a stream, I'll send along a man or two." He paused. "I know it's been hard without my father these past weeks. I intend to try and be as good a steward of the land as he was, and t'do that I need to be able to count on my clan." He studied the two men and took a chance. "Will you shake and say pax?"

The mood of the room seemed to shift a bit. Donal and Archie looked to Geordie and nodded solemnly. Archie made his peace with his neighbor, thanking Geordie and promising that the cow would be returned with all haste. Donal lingered and when the other man was gone, he turned to Geordie. "You're as fair-minded as your father, my laird. I believe you've made him proud today, if ye don't mind my saying so."

Geordie came around the desk, a broad smile on his face, and clapped the old man on the shoulder. "I don't mind in the least, Donal. I'm glad to've been of service to you both." He shook the farmer's hand. "Don't hold it against Archie if you can help it, hm? But—come straight t'me if such a thing happens again."

Donal reassured Geordie that he'd do just that, adding that he doubted Archie would have the nerve to try something like that again. He wished Geordie well and parted, head high and shoulders straight.

Geordie moved back around the desk and settled in his father's chair, casting a quick glance at the whiskey decanter on the bookshelf and then laughing quietly at himself. "Get used to it, Geordie, lad," he muttered, and rang for the next grievance to be shown in.

The next claimant upon his time was a kinsman, Hamish Maclaren. Geordie greeted him cordially and invited him to sit down. "What can I help you with, Hamish?" he asked.

"I've come to see where things stand now that you're the chief of Clan Maclaren," Hamish cut straight to the point, hard eyes studying Geordie. He wasn't known for his warmth, but could hardly be blamed when one considered all the hardships he'd faced: an unhappy marriage with a wife who'd gone mad, lands that struggled year after year, and no children to carry on after him. "We are not all so blessed as you here at the castle."

Geordie shifted in his seat and contemplated the man across his father's desk. "Just as you like. What things, specifically?"

"Your father had some modern ideas that I do not hold with. You are young to be filling this post, and it is understandable that you might think your father's way is the only way," Hamish answered calmly.

Geordie's brows drew together. "Post", as though he'd answered an advertisement for employment? Still—best to give the man the benefit of the doubt. "I'd've happily waited decades to inherit my title," he replied mildly, "but some London madman took the choice from me, so if you've some doubt about my suitability, take it up with him." He paused. "I agree with my father on most issues. Is there something in particular that concerns you?"

Hamish offered a small smile, an expression that lacked any sort of charm or warmth. "Scotland concerns me, boy. The well-being of the Maclaren clan. I have lived my life for those causes. Is it wrong for me to come take the measure of the man who will be making decisions that impact so many?" He leaned back in the chair he occupied and studied Geordie. "As I've said you are young, but youth need not be a hindrance if you have the counsel of those with more experience to rely on."

That "boy" stung. "I see. And you're volunteering for the position, are you?"

"I'm offering to be a sounding board if you need one—to help navigate the complicated issues that a holding this size presents," he replied in what Geordie thought was an attempt at a fatherly tone; it was difficult to say with Hamish. "I'll not pretend your father and I were the greatest of friends, but we understood one another. You need not face the trials of running the clan on your own. Knowing when to listen to the words of another is the mark of wisdom."

Geordie reined in his temper with an effort. "I appreciate your offer, Hamish, and I'll take it under advisement. Fortunately, there's nothing currently on the docket about which I have any doubts on my position, but if something comes up for which you might have insight, I'll be sure to ask."

A muscle in the older man's jaw twitched, his eyes narrowed and turned steely. "There *are* matters on the docket which I consider pressing. I tried speaking to your father before he left for London to vote on the Crofter's Act, but he'd hear none of it." Hamish crossed his arms and met Geordie's gaze. "You ought to consider that not everyone can afford the handouts the crofters are asking for. A generous spirit is all well and good, but you cannae afford to take on the burdens of all."

"I take it you do not side with the crofters on this issue." Geordie frowned. An odd stance for a working man to take. Still—he shrugged. "Whether I agree with you or not, it's no longer on the docket. It's been passed." He considered the man across from him. "For what it's worth, I don't agree with you. But it's out of my hands. Was there anything else?"

Hamish's eyes narrowed further, his jaw clenched and his face turned almost purple. He rose from his seat to pace back and forth, reminding Geordie of a frustrated and angry beast that might strike. "Fools, the lot of ye!" he growled. "The consequences of this will be on your head, mark my words, pup!" He turned on his heel and stomped out of the room, slamming the door before Geordie could respond.

The young viscount stared after him. "Charming," he muttered to himself after a moment, and rang for the next grievance.

The rest of the morning passed in a succession of complaints that were brought before Geordie; most were handled easily enough. A farmer who had lost a plow horse to an unfortunate accident during the last storm sought aid in replacing the animal; the local blacksmith complained that several customers had grown lax in paying their bills over the past months; a few other minor disagreements required the authority of the clan chief to settle. It was not as trying as some of the days Geordie's father had dealt with, but the decanter of whiskey only looked more appealing as the day wore on.

To Geordie's surprise, the next man who strode through the door was none other than Harris MacRainey, an old family friend. He paused a few paces past the threshold and studied Geordie. "You fill that seat well, Maclaren. Morag believed you would. Always been a fine judge of character, my daughter." He moved closer to the desk. "Though it saddens us to see her proven right so soon."

Cursing the uncomfortable blush that rose to his face at the mention of Morag MacRainey, Geordie gestured to a chair. "Thank you, Harris, and welcome. I hope the family's well?"

The older man situated himself, nodding. "As well as can be expected at such times as these. Be assured my family is at your service should any need arise." He shifted slightly. "My daughter has been quite concerned for you, knowing the burdens you must bear on your own now."

"That's very kind of her." In truth, "kind" was one of the last ways he'd describe Morag, which was why though he'd courted her after a fashion, Geordie had never offered for her. "How can I help you today, Harris?"

"In truth, I'd hope my family might be of help to you," Harris answered slowly. It did not escape Geordie's notice that the man was turning red from his neck to his ears. It was a sure sign his daughter had a hand in today's visit. "A man should not face the difficult changes of life on his own. The Lord God himself said, 'It is not good for man to be alone.' A sentiment with which I agree."

A sense of foreboding settled around Geordie. "Oh aye?" he replied, folding his arms across his chest.

Harris faltered, shifting again. No doubt the man was debating whether he'd rather face Geordie's ire or Morag's; it was a decision worthy of pity. He finally settled and spoke again. "I would wish for your happiness as fervently as for one of my own children. Perhaps it is one and the same?" He cleared his throat. "My dear, sweet Morag speaks of you often, and fondly, Maclaren."

"Very kind of her," Geordie repeated, and decided to cut to the chase. "Am I to gather that your motive in seeing me today is to promote a match between Morag and me?" He shook his head. "I appreciate your care, Harris; but surely you know that door was closed long ago. Morag and I... do not suit."

"But Geordie..." he began; then his mouth snapped shut. Harris MacRainey slumped in his seat, and never so defeated a man had Geordie seen. "Forgive me, Maclaren. I speak with the love of a father. I wish only to see my daughter with a man who would think of her happiness as carefully as I do. I ask only that you do not dismiss the idea entirely."

"Harris..." Geordie sighed and came around to face the man directly. "I'm sorry, old friend. I think you know my answer; I wish, for your sake and the sake of our families' long friendship, it could be otherwise. But I am not the man to make your Morag happy, and she is not the wife for me. If I can help with introductions, should you choose to do the London season, I'm more than happy to do so. More than that I cannot promise."

Harris nodded. "It was good of you to hear me out, Maclaren. I know you have plenty of matters to attend." He put his hands on his knees and stood up heavily. "My Morag will be saddened, but I will extend your offer for introductions."

Geordie winced as the man left the room, fervently hoping that Morag would not require introductions, as he'd prefer to keep the friends he had, and no one would thank him for introducing that virago. It was a pity, for he liked the father well enough; but the daughter took after her mother, a woman of entitled disposition and a permanent sense of injury. Morag was pretty enough, and her manners were generally all that one could desire upon first meeting, but she did not hold up upon closer inspection, and Geordie was relieved that he'd escaped that particular noose. The clock on the mantle announced the noon hour, and a reprieve from business for a time.

To his surprise, Quinn was at luncheon. "Had to compose a quick letter," was his cautious explanation at the table, from which Geordie deduced that he'd had to send a report to a superior or something and was loath to say so in front of the dowager and Lady Ailsa. "Asher and Ross took luncheon in town, but I expect they'll be along sooner or later."

"I've a better idea," Geordie replied, bolting his food, much to his mother's expressed disapproval. "This last grievance," and this time it was his turn to choose his words in front of his mother, "was enough for any man to deal with in a single day. There may be a dispute or two left, but I'll deal with them, and then you and I can ride out to find the others." He rose and tossed his napkin on his seat. "Tell the grooms to saddle Goliath and whichever horse you want; I'll finish up and meet with you in an hour, hm?"

Quinn considered the plan and nodded. "And if we miss them on the road? They could as easily head back here while we're on our way out."

"Then you and I will take tea in town without them." And if Miss Brentwood and her cousin were free... but further refinements to the plan could wait.

Geordie gave Quinn a nod and headed to his father's—
no, his—study.

Fortunately, the remaining concerns of the clan
were easily enough dealt with, and just as he'd said an
hour later found Geordie striding toward the stables,
riding gloves in hand. He'd dispatched his duty and
could now join his friends without (much) guilt. Quinn
greeted him with a grin, and together the two set out to
find their friends.

Deep in the surrounding woods and nearing
teatime, they were forced to admit that they'd probably
missed the other two, and Asher and Ross were likely
back at the castle by now. Quinn chuckled. "You owe
me a cream tea at Mrs. Clark's, I believe."

Geordie wheeled Goliath onto the path that led
back toward the village, flashing his friend a grin. "Aye,
I promised. And if the lads are mad about it, then next
time they should be easier to fi—"

A loud report caught him by surprise;
something buffeted him hard in the shoulder, nearly
knocking him from his mount and Goliath bucked
hard, whinnying in terror. Geordie lost his grip and hit
the ground, pain jarring him hard, winding him for a
moment.

Quinn shouted and slipped from his saddle,
pulling a pistol from the back of his waistband as he
landed by the stricken man. "Show yourselves!" he
cried.

Geordie rolled to his feet—with far more
difficulty than he usually had—and staggered toward
his friend. "What—" he began, and something buzzed
by his head. Both horses took off at a gallop, stranding
the men.

Quinn let loose with a string of multilingual
epithets, took aim, and fired into the trees to the left.

He was answered by a cut-off cry. "One," he grunted, and then, "Get down, idiot!" to Geordie.

Geordie ignored him as he began to realize the enormity of what had just happened. He'd been shot— someone had shot him— His vision swam red and he let out a roar. "COWARDS!" he cried, doubling his fists, ignoring the flare of agony in his shoulder. "Come on, then—face me like men!" Something rustled a short distance away, and Geordie headed in that direction, loping toward his attackers. "COME ON!"

Behind him, Quinn cursed volubly. "Geordie, stop! You've been shot!"

Chapter Seven

The Unmistakable Sound of a Gunshot

That day found Tamsin much recovered, and true to her word, Ione showed her all the small wonders Balmaclaren had to offer. But as charming as the town was, they exhausted this activity by the early afternoon. "I'm given to understand," Tamsin said with a merry expression, "that there is a charming view of the castle from atop the forested bluff, just there." She pointed to a pretty stand of trees some distance away.

Ione nodded. "A castle viewing seems a lovely way to end our outing for the day. By the time we've walked there and back, it ought to just be time for tea." And so saying, the girls took off down the road at a leisurely pace.

Castle Maclaren came into view well before they'd reached the top of the bluff. "Good heavens," Tamsin murmured, and Ione found she was entirely in agreement. Even from this distance, the scope of the place was impressive. A sprawling Georgian home, turreted and crenellated: the golden sandstone of its walls caught the sunlight, and paired with the many windows the castle seemed to sparkle. It was beautiful and formidable, and Ione wondered if it was equally magnificent on the inside. She imagined so.

"Nearly as spectacular as the view of the man himself," her cousin observed cheekily.

Ione's gaze darted from the castle to her cousin. "He is a striking figure, to be sure," she agreed, and opened her mouth to tell her cousin of the cream tea, but all at once the unmistakable sound of a gunshot rang out from the woods. A second was quick to follow, and two terrified horses burst from the forest, barreling past them toward the castle.

The women exchanged wide-eyed looks; the crack of a third shot made Tamsin flinch, while Ione nearly jumped out of her skin at the sound.

Heart racing, she closed her eyes and summoned her magic. She forced herself beyond the fear and the surprise, clearing her mind of everything but the power that flowed through her. The vision manifested itself and sped toward the source of the shot. Ione could see the smoking barrel of the pistol, hear the pounding of running footsteps. Her eyes flew open and she pointed toward the break in the trees. "They're coming this way."

Seconds later two men—one holding a smoking pistol—came bursting from the treeline, heading straight toward the two women. "Hostages!" one of them shouted, pointing.

"I think not," muttered Tamsin, and bent to quickly scoop up a handful of rocks, her lips forming a silent incantation. The rocks glowed briefly and then she threw them at the approaching assailants, who stopped and staggered about as though disoriented.

Ione turned her gaze to the future again and grasped her cousin's arm, pulling her out of the way as one of the men came careening in her direction. Tamsin nodded her thanks just as another shot echoed from the treeline, felling the assailant nearest her. He collapsed on the ground with a howl, clutching his knee as it began spurting gore.

"Bloody hell!" roared the last one, wild-eyed. Whatever Tamsin had charmed those pebbles with seemed to have worn off, for he suddenly ran at them and grasped Ione's wrist, trying to get behind her.

Ione jerked her arm back, struggling with every ounce of strength she possessed. She clutched at his arm, digging at his skin with her nails. All at once something snapped and fell from her attacker's wrist; he cursed volubly and sprinted away, leaving her holding a broken leather string, which she promptly dropped. She took a breath and closed her eyes, trying to concentrate, but more running footsteps pulled her from her trance.

From the woods came a roar, and another voice. "Geordie, stop, you've been shot!"

The Maclaren came crashing through the woods like a wounded bear on a rampage. He was nearly unrecognizable, as all of his elegant address was gone, his shirt was torn and heavily stained with blood, and he was in a towering fury.

Even in his fit of rage, Ione could see the man's color waning. The women picked up their skirts and hastened toward the viscount, who was weaving a bit, still roaring after his assailants. Another man burst through the brush to join the fray; there was blood on his coat too. He sprinted toward Geordie, calling his name, and got there just in time to catch the wounded man as he fell over.

The ruffian on the ground nearby was still gripping his knee and moaning loudly, but Ione paid him little heed. All her focus was on Geordie, her heart pounding so wildly she feared it might burst. She rushed to her new friend, yanking her lightweight shawl off as she knelt at his side. It would be worthless as a bandage, but perhaps it would protect his head from the ground, she thought distractedly. Despite her best efforts to remain calm and composed, Ione's hands shook as she folded the garment and placed it under his head. She had never seen so much blood, and the pallor of his skin filled her with dread. There was little she could offer in the way of healing, but the urge to help him was a powerful one.

Desperate to be of use, she took his hand and squeezed it gently. "Look at me, Geordie. Take deep breaths and stay with me." The Maclaren's fingers curled around hers, and he offered a weak nod. Ione tried to smile reassuringly. "That's it, dear friend. Hold tight and try to remain still."

Tamsin stripped off her gloves and began to peel the gory shirt from the Maclaren's shoulder, welling red with blood. Her expression was calm but resolute, and Ione had the strangest impression that this situation was far from extraordinary for her cousin.

Geordie's companion felt the viscount's forehead, chafed his wrists. "Quinn Rutherford, at your service, ladies. I see you know something of medicine," he added. "How can I help?"

Tamsin was focused on examining the injured shoulder. "We must bind the wound and clean it with something. Have you any whiskey or other spirits on your person? Anything we can tear into bandages?"

For answer the gentleman nodded, doffing his riding jacket and waistcoat and tugging his shirt over his head, revealing a lean, well-muscled torso. "There is a flask in my coat pocket, Miss," he said to Ione, and began to tear his shirt into wide strips.

Ione released Geordie's hand and grabbed the discarded clothing, rifling through the pockets until she found the flask. She twisted the cap off and passed the flask to Tamsin.

Knowing her cousin would do everything in her power to help Lord Kirkleith, Ione slowed her breathing and tried to still her mind. She might not know much about healing, but she could still be of use. She reached into the future yet again to be certain no one else was lurking to launch a second attack. Much to her relief, the only people nearby were those running toward them from the town below. There was no sign that the attackers were returning, nor of any danger from others. "Help is on the way," she assured Tamsin under her breath.

Nodding, Tamsin tipped a bit of the alcohol into the wound and a good deal more into Geordie's mouth. She took the strips from Mr. Rutherford and began to efficiently bandage the Maclaren's shoulder. "Still with us, my lord?"

He gave a jerky nod, his teeth chattering. "Could use a bit more of that brandy," he replied roughly, wincing as Tamsin tied off the bandage. She gave it to him with a thin smile and turned to Mr. Rutherford. "We must get him to... somewhere—and the other man, of course. What's closest?"

He ran a hand through his dark hair, scanning the landscape. "Got a bit turned around when those thugs burst out of the underbrush," he muttered. "Horses bolted, so we'll have to take him on foot; probably to the high street. I can carry him, but we'll have to do something about that fool," he jerked his chin toward the injured assailant, "and I felled another, in the forest. He'll need to be collected as well."

Sounds of consternation and running feet reached them as several men from the town—Ione recognized two of them as grooms from the inn, and another as Murray the innkeeper's son—came hurrying up the path that connected with the high street. "Reinforcements. Excellent," observed Mr. Rutherford. He consulted with the new arrivals briefly, describing the location of the unfortunate attacker in the woods and debating what to do with the man with the wounded knee. Ione stepped away from the group as they debated the best course of action.

She glanced back in the direction her would-be kidnapper had fled. *Where have you gone, you brute?* Her jaw tightened, fingers clenching. Now that there was help, anger was quick to replace fear. She stared down the road and tried to summon a clear image of the man, but all the noise and commotion was too distracting, and she had nothing to tether her magic to her quarry. Ione rubbed at her temple and replayed the encounter in her mind.

The leather string! It had come from her assailant—some kind of bracelet, perhaps? She scanned the ground and almost let out a triumphant cry when she found the broken cord on the road, a strange stone bead threaded on it. Ione snatched it up and smiled. "I've got you now," she whispered under breath as she shoved the rough bracelet into her handbag. *Heaven help the fool who tries to hide from an oracle.*

She returned to Tamsin's side and waited for the others to organize their efforts. They sorted themselves, and two of the men lifted the injured assailant while a small group went to the woods and one young Hermes lit out for the castle.

Quinn held out a hand to his friend. "Come on, old thing, up you go." Geordie got weakly to his feet with a good deal of assistance; Rutherford pulled his good arm across his shoulders, bent, and hoisted the larger man onto his back. "If you'd be so good as to lead the way," he asked Ione with a grunt.

"Of course." Ione snatched up her shawl, uncaring that it was now stained with blood, and jumped to her feet. Geordie needed help, and she was eager to be away from this place and to see him settled safely. She glanced back at the viscount—so pale, his grey eyes clouded with pain—it caused a dull ache to see him brought to such a state. The trees that lined the lane seemed ominously shadowed now, and was it her imagination or was the walk back to the inn twice as long as when they left? The sun was dipping lower in the sky; it had to be well past teatime.

"We're nearly back, Geordie," Ione reassured the Maclaren when she finally saw the inn. He was alarmingly pale, and she worried that the trek back had undone Tamsin's quick care. Certainly the bandage was no longer pristine, but crimson and dripping sluggishly. "I'll alert Mr. Murray, and see that fresh bandages are made ready." She ran ahead to open the door, calling out for help as soon as her feet crossed over the threshold.

The innkeeper was out the door in a trice, and ushering them inside. They took the stricken man into the private parlor and laid him out on a settee barely long enough to accommodate his height. "Have you a telephone I could use?" Quinn asked Murray, who shook his head.

"'Tis one for use at the telegraph office," he supplied helpfully.

Geordie's friend nodded. "An extra shirt, by any chance?" The innkeeper hurried back toward the door and beckoned for him to follow. "I'll return shortly,"

Rutherford assured the women, and left to see to business.

"Just as well," Tamsin muttered, and grasped the pillow under Geordie's head. "Sleep, my lord," she murmured, and the pillow brightened and dulled as the viscount's eyes fluttered closed.

"How bad is the wound?" Ione asked, reaching for a blanket that was folded in the seat of one of the chairs. She draped it across Geordie's legs and tucked it in close. The action would do little to treat the injury, but it helped Ione feel that she was contributing to his care.

Tamsin inspected his shoulder carefully. "The ball is still inside. I'm going to create a first-aid charm, to keep him from bleeding so much while we wait for a doctor to see to him." She suited action to words, choosing her own glove for the talisman, and pressed it to the bloody bandages as she whispered over it.

Ione pulled a stool up to the settee and sat at Geordie's side, taking his hand as she settled in. Now that they were safe and away from the curiosity of others, she could do more than summon brief glimpses. She focused on the details of the attack, knowing her vision would be more accurate if she took care in recalling the encounter before using her magic. Starting at the moment the ruffians burst from the trees, Ione tried to picture their faces and anything other minute detail that might be of use. They'd worn rough clothes, and one who escaped bore a striking black beard. It wasn't much, but perhaps enough for her magic to provide the answers that would ensure justice would be served.

Reasonably confident that she had enough to go on, Ione pulled the leather cord with its odd stone bead from her handbag and turned her attention to the flickering flame of a nearby candle. She cradled the object in her free palm, concentrating on the hypnotic movement of the flame. The parlor faded into shadows, giving way to the images of her trance. The scene of the encounter materialized through Ione's magic. Her perspective changed to that of an observer and the attack played out before her eyes at a slower pace. She saw the men run toward them, saw the one who'd tried to take her as a hostage, only to flee when she refused to be meekly taken. Concentrating on the escapee, she followed his movements to a barn—not far at all, for the castle was visible behind the dilapidated building. This was the information she needed.

"Fool," Ione muttered, blinking a few times and breathing slowly to disperse the vision. "He's only gone as far as an abandoned farm," she told Tamsin. "It can't be much more than a mile from where the attack happened. He's hiding in the barn like a frightened dog."

"Easy enough to find, then," Tamsin agreed, tossing her head slightly to shake a wayward curl from her forehead. "You'll have to figure out how to tell them."

Ione nibbled her lower lip thoughtfully. "He did try to take me hostage. I can claim to have heard it when he laid hands on me." She glanced down at Geordie's shoulder, then turned her attention to the doorway, willing help to arrive quickly.

As if in answer to her thoughts the door opened, but it was merely Rutherford returning. He wore a fresh shirt, though it seemed a little large on him. "How is he?"

"Stable," Tamsin returned, slipping the bloodied glove out of sight. "Best not to move him until help comes."

Ione gently placed Geordie's hand on his chest and moved away from the settee. She had entirely forgotten she was holding his hand, and felt uncomfortably exposed in front of his companion. Ridiculous really, for few were likely to see it as anything but an attempt to offer comfort in the face of suffering. "One of them got away, I know. Are the other two in custody?" she asked, setting aside her embarrassment to focus on the practical.

Rutherford nodded, then winced. "One is; I'm afraid the other didn't make it. Someone from the commissioner's office will be along soon to take a statement from you, I expect. Thank you," he added to Tamsin, nodding toward where she kept pressure on the wound. "My thanks to both of you, actually. May I know your names?"

"This is my cousin, Lady Tamsin Claremont, and I am Miss Ione Brentwood, sir." Ione supplied, as Tamsin's efforts were still focused on Lord Kirkleith.

He bowed. "My lady, Miss Brentwood, we are in your debt. I have heard Geordie speak of you—recent acquaintances, I believe?"

"Yes, quite recent. We met in London, some weeks ago." Ione inclined her head a little in Mr. Rutherford's direction, but her regard shifted to Geordie's face. "Do you think it will take the commissioner's men long to arrive? I have information which I hope might aid them in their pursuit. The one who escaped tried to take me as his hostage. I heard him say something about a barn. I think he may be hiding there." Now she openly returned her attention to the stricken man, resolved as ever to see that his pain was paid for. "I should like to see these men brought to justice for the suffering they've caused."

Mr. Rutherford raised his brows. "He spoke of a barn? Perhaps they are in collusion with someone in the neighborhood."

"I didn't get the impression that he knew the farmer," Ione replied quickly, horrified by the idea that she might have implicated some innocent person in her haste to be of service. "In fact, as my nerves settle, I seem to recall hearing something about an abandoned farm."

"I see—" The clatter of hoofs on cobbles interrupted whatever Quinn was going to say. "That must be the authorities now. I'll go speak to them." He excused himself again.

Ione moved through the room impatiently, finally settling near the door. Had she given Mr. Rutherford enough information? Should she hand over the beaded bracelet she'd pulled from her attacker? She considered opening her mind again, but decided against it. There were only so many details she could share without raising suspicion. She'd offered what she could and would have to trust in the competence of others to put it to use.

The ladies possessed themselves in silence, waiting for help to arrive as the minutes ticked by. After what seemed like hours, but was likely not, they heard a commotion in the front room. Two men burst into the room, followed hard by Rutherford. Ione recognized the first as Dr. McInerny, a doctor's bag in hand, and she heaved a sigh of relief. "Bloody hell!" he muttered, and interposed himself as Tamsin moved out of the way. The second man carried a small valise, and was more temperate, with dark wavy hair and brilliant blue eyes that were largely obscured by a pair of spectacles and a deeply worried air.

He spoke first. "Asher Burton," he introduced himself, "and this is Dr. Ross McInerny. Quinn tells us we have you to thank for our friend's life."

Tamsin wiped her hands with a towel. "Your friend exaggerates," she replied courteously, "but of course we were glad to offer whatever succor we could. Lady Tamsin Claremont," she added, "and my cousin, Miss Ione Brentwood."

"Miss Brentwood and I have met," said the doctor absently from his place at Geordie's side, his focus on unwrapping Tamsin's handiwork.

Mr. Burton nodded. "Lady Tamsin, Miss Brentwood. You have our deepest gratitude."

Ione offered Mr. Burton a small smile, breathed another sigh of relief and turned to watch the doctor at his work. "Will he recover?"

"He'll do, once I get the ball out," Dr. McInerny replied, focus never leaving his patient. "Ash, Quinn, come hold him down." His friends arranged themselves as per Dr. McInerny's instructions. "Thank you, lads. This is likely to cause enough pain to bring him around, and I'll not have him make it worse by thrashing about." The doctor reached into his bag and produced a pair of forceps. With a quick nod to his companions, he leaned close to Lord Kirkleith's shoulder and began to work. The second the instrument made contact, the young viscount's eyes flew open. He gritted his teeth, rasping out a sound that was something between a groan and a growl, that ended in a curse.

"Easy, Geordie, you don't want me to cause any further damage. Hold steady and it will be done before you know it," Dr. McInerny's voice was calm and confident. His wrist twisted slightly, and he pulled the forceps back, red with blood and clamped down on a metal ball. "And that's it. Stubborn little bugger, it was." A fresh gout of blood welled from the injury.

Ione swallowed against a wave of nausea and looked away quickly. The gore alone wasn't enough to upset her—it was the sound of Geordie's pain. She lowered herself into a nearby chair and fought to retain some sense of composure. A fainting fit would be the last thing anyone needed just now. Despite her discomfort, Ione's gaze shifted back to the doctor's work, curiosity overwhelming distress.

One of Dr. McInerny's hands obscured her view of the wound, and the other was busy with a needle and thread. The worst of it seemed to be over with. At the very least Geordie was quiet now, though she could see his right hand fisted into the blanket across his legs, knuckles white as the doilies that adorned the table.

"All over with," Dr. McInerny said, finally stepping away to rinse his hands in the water basin before he returned to bandage Geordie's shoulder. "Not so bad after all. The ball wasn't terribly deep. You'll be right as rain after a bit of rest. But you bled like a stuck pig, Geordie."

"Ross, laddie," muttered the stricken viscount after a bit, "if I didna' love you as a brother, I'd clean your clock for you just about now." He paused, shifting tentatively. "My thanks."

The doctor dried his hands and flashed his friend a quick smile. "Why do you think I had the boys hold you down? I've seen your right hook and have no wish to be on the receiving end of it."

The Maclaren chuckled, the sound giving way to a groan. His stormy gaze scanned the room, lighting upon Ione. "My apologies, Miss Brentwood. And my thanks, to you and to Lady Tamsin." Tamsin smiled at him and gave a nod.

"It is enough for me to know that you will recover. I hope those brutes receive the justice they deserve," Ione replied, conviction in her voice. He'd been so warm and welcoming at each of their meetings, it galled her to see him suffer an attack of this kind. "Why anyone would behave in such an uncivilized and cruel manner is utterly beyond me."

Quinn stepped away from the settee and moved to glance out the nearest window. "I can think of a reason or two." After a beat he pulled the curtains shut and turned to address the doctor. "Ross, is he well enough to travel? He'll be safer at the castle."

"Aye, he'll do," Dr. McInerny replied with a nod. "He can ride if there's nothing for it, but I'd be happier if a carriage can be arranged. I'll put his arm in a sling to keep it still until he's had some rest." He looked at the Maclaren. "If you do not overtax it, you should have full use of it tomorrow."

Lady Tamsin's expression was speculative, but she untucked her fichu and held it out. "This might perhaps serve as a sling, at least for the trip back to the castle."

"My thanks for this as well," Lord Kirkleith replied as Asher helped him to sit up. He glanced down at himself and then at Ione, cheeks pink. Asher wordlessly handed him a shirt, and after some finagling, the three men were able to get the Maclaren roughly two-thirds into his shirt, the other third snug against his chest, secured with Tamsin's fichu.

"That'll do to be going on with," pronounced Quinn. "Let's get him home and we can figure out the rest there."

Ione bit her lower lip, worrying over the color of Geordie's skin, and wondering if her tip about the barn was enough to see the criminal brought in. The entire incident had her nerves on edge. She couldn't shake the feeling that there was more afoot than an encounter with highwaymen. "I do hope what I heard about the barn offers some help in apprehending him. If I recall anything else I will be certain to report it immediately." In that moment she decided to keep the strange leather cord, so that she could use it to find out more about Lord Kirkleith's attacker.

Quinn bowed while Asher and Ross helped the Maclaren to his feet and held him steady. "Ladies, we are all in your debt. I feel sure we will meet again—"

"Of course we shall," Geordie broke in and turned to the two women. "May we have the honor of your presence at dinner? My mother and sister would be very glad to welcome you."

Dr. McInerny cleared his throat and leaned closer to the Maclaren. He spoke quietly, but there was an underlying note of authority. "You lost a fair amount of blood. You need a night of rest at least, Geordie."

Ione herself would have accepted immediately, were it not for the doctor's orders for rest. But attending a public event like the investiture was one thing. An invitation to dinner in Lord Kirkleith's home was a different matter entirely. She glanced at her cousin questioningly.

"How kind of you to ask us, my lord," Tamsin replied with what Ione recognized as her most beguiling smile. Asher, Ross, even Quinn looked a bit dazed. "But I think your mother would prefer to welcome us when you are feeling more the thing."

The viscount managed a chuckle. "I daresay you've the right of it, Lady Tamsin. But perhaps you would join us in a day or two?" He slanted a look at Ross, who gave an almost imperceptible nod. "I have it on good authority that I'll be right as rain tomorrow. I'll have Mama send 'round an invitation."

The prospect of an evening in the magnificent Castle Maclaren they'd was an enticing one, and not something Ione was willing to pass up. She glanced at her cousin before turning back to Geordie with a smile she hoped was as charming as Tamsin's. "In that case, we would be happy to accept."

Another quarter-hour saw Ione and Tamsin on the front step of the inn as a carriage departed for the castle, with the viscount and his friends aboard. "Interesting," Tamsin murmured, watching it go. "Interesting indeed." She looped her arm through Ione's.

Ione gave a small snort of disbelief. "We bear witness to a violent attack, and 'interesting' is all you have to say?" She shook her head slightly. "My, but you must live a far more exciting life than I do. What, in particular, did you find interesting?"

Tamsin laughed. "All of it, though I was thinking of Dr. McInerny in particular."

"Oh?" Ione replied playfully. "Do I detect potential romance? He is rather attractive, and there is something to be said for the dashing doctor, swooping into the rescue."

"You do not. They were *all* attractive," Tamsin pointed out, "and you know perfectly well I've no intention of marrying anyone at all. Certainly not a mendacious doctor."

"Very well then, my dear, independent cousin." Ione laughed and gave Tamsin a gentle nudge before sobering again. "Why do you distrust Dr. McInerny? He seems genuine enough to me."

"Oh, I've no doubt at all that he's a skilled physician." Tamsin offered her cousin a smile. "Whether he's skilled enough to dig a bullet from a man's shoulder and pronounce him healed the following day, however—that would indeed be something extraordinary."

Ione cast a glance over her shoulder, frowning slightly. "I admit, that did surprise me, but I assumed the injury must not have been as severe as it first appeared. Though truthfully I know nothing of medicine." She paused to watch the carriage turn 'round the bend. Geordie's friends, while obviously concerned for him, did not seem as surprised as one might expect under such circumstances. "There does seem to be more at work here. Perhaps I should not have been so quick to accept Lord Kirkleith's invitation."

Tamsin squeezed her arm as they stepped back inside and made for the stairs. "Nonsense, dearest. For why else are we here if not for adventure?" She chuckled. "All the same, I shall be very interested to see how Lord Kirkleith fares when next we see him."

Chapter Eight

Castle Maclaren

Tamsin and Ione did indeed receive an invitation to dinner at Castle Maclaren, two days hence. There was a charming note tucked into the card from the dowager Lady Kirkleith herself, expressing gratitude and a gentle reminder that this was not to be a formal affair, as the house was still in mourning, but a meal shared between family and friends. Both cousins were touched by the friendliness and delicate consideration thus conveyed, and as Tamsin was still curious to see how well Lord Kirkleith had recovered from his wound, they accepted with pleasure.

They spent the intervening days exploring the delights of Balmaclaren, of which there were many, if one were inclined to an enjoyment of bucolic pleasures. The general store held some interest, as well as a curiosity shop run by an elderly man who styled himself 'auld Gregor' and seemed to carry a broad spectrum of goods. Mrs. Clark's tearoom was another favored destination, and the girls whiled away hours chatting over hot tea and a delicious assortment of tiny sandwiches and biscuits and cakes.

At last the day arrived, and that afternoon found them preparing for their dinner at the castle. With only one maid between the two of them, Ione waited patiently in Tamsin's room, happy to exchange excited chatter with her cousin until Rose could help her dress.

"Which do you think, the peacock or the copper?" the blonde asked Ione, regarding the two dresses in question as Rose held them up.

Ione considered the gowns from her perch atop Tamsin's bed. "I plan on wearing pale blue," she informed her cousin. The silk gown Ione had in mind was one of her favorites. She'd already worn it to a dinner party in London, but no one at the castle would be the wiser. "I think the copper will be a nice contrast to that shade and will make your eyes stand out."

Tamsin nodded. "The copper it is. Rose?" Her maid put the peacock gown back in the press and began preparing the other for the evening.

"I'm quite eager to see the interior of the castle." Ione smiled softly. Truth be told, the castle wasn't the only thing she was eager to see; Lord Kirkleith's recovery had preoccupied her the entire day. She'd never seen an injury like that, and he'd been in such pain. But surely he was well enough, if his mother had invited them to dine.

Ione shook herself from her daydreams and focused on present company. Her cousin seemed to be distracted, submitting to Rose's attentions almost automatically.

"Is everything alright?" Ione studied Tamsin, concern clouding the sunny atmosphere.

"Hmm? Oh, of course. It's only—do be careful, Ione. I've a feeling of... I don't know. Something's not quite what it seems."

"I agree; the shooting incident has been weighing heavily on my mind." Ione answered slowly, thinking back on the details of the attack. Geordie and his friends had been distressed certainly, but had shown little sign of shock in the face of such violence. "To be honest, I'm half-tempted to attempt a scrying to look into things more deeply."

Tamsin grew thoughtful. "I believe I would advise against it," she cautioned. "I know I seem a madcap, but even I am given pause at the nature of the Maclaren's recent... er... *contretemps*. Dinner is one thing, but we know little of the situation, and I think any information you might glean could be easily misinterpreted."

Ione opened her mouth to argue, but she decided to let the topic rest. There was no real reason to push the matter, and Tamsin wasn't likely to be convinced by hollow justifications. Ione sighed, and stifled her curiosity in favor of focusing on the pleasantries of the present. Whatever the mystery, it wasn't for her to solve, and she was determined to enjoy the evening out. "I suppose you're correct. I shall leave you to finish getting ready. Rose, do come help me when you're done with Tamsin. I can undress myself, but I shall be hard-pressed to fasten my own gown."

"Of course, Miss," Rose curtsied slightly, though she continued with Tamsin's hair. "I shall only be another moment or two."

"No need for haste, dear Rose. There is yet plenty of time before the carriage departs," Ione assured the maid before wandering back to her room across the way.

Undressing herself turned out to be a slightly more complicated proposition than anticipated. In the end, it took a bit of ingenuity, but Ione eventually managed to unlace her day dress and wiggle out of it on her own. When she finished, she moved to the dressing table and rifled through the small collection of hairpins and combs she'd brought from home, in search of one that would go nicely with her dinner gown. She tried not to dwell on the questions surrounding their host for the evening, but her curiosity continued to nag for answers.

She had all but convinced herself to delve into the future when the door opened and Rose bustled in, apologizing for taking longer than expected. Ione nearly jumped out of her skin at the sudden intrusion. She turned an innocent smile on the girl and hoped she didn't look as guilty as she felt. "Not at all. I only just finished undressing. Have you any plans for the evening?"

"Oh, yes, miss!" Rose was busy pulling Ione's dress from the press and fretting over wrinkles Ione barely noticed. "Lady Tamsin gave me two gold and said I was to have as good a dinner as ever I liked, only not to get too tiddly on the ale!" She giggled.

Ione gave her an approving smile. She reached for her coin purse and pulled out another two coins. "You've nearly run yourself ragged attending the two of us. Such devotion deserves every appreciation. My contribution to your evening's plans."

Rose's eyes went wide. "Oh, Miss Brentwood, I could not possibly. Four gold is far more than I need for a meal."

"Nonsense, it's just enough for a fine meal and a souvenir to commemorate the occasion." Ione pressed the coins into her hand. "Enjoy your evening out, and buy yourself something to remember your time in Scotland. I insist on it."

The maid dithered for a second more before she settled enough to help Ione with her dress and hair. Thanks to Rose's skilled attention, both ladies were dressed and perfectly arranged by the time the carriage was called to take them to Castle Maclaren.

They arrived at the castle promptly and if Ione thought the outside of Castle Maclaren was magnificent, she was utterly astounded by the elegance of the interior. The foyer, though the term 'great hall' would have been more fitting, was enormous, dominated by a glittering, crystal chandelier that hung from the high-vaulted ceiling. Beyond that an impressive staircase—marble with mahogany banisters—rose up at the far end of the hall, splitting in opposite directions at a landing, above which hung the Kirkleith coat of arms, draped with the Maclaren tartan. That same insignia was inlaid in wood on the floor beneath their feet, polished to a high gloss. Ione had visited stately homes before, but none sparked her imagination as Castle Maclaren did.

She was still reeling from the magnitude and beauty of the place when they were escorted into an equally lovely parlor by an extraordinarily dignified butler. "Lady Tamsin Claremont, Miss Brentwood," he intoned as they entered.

The Maclaren was on his feet in an instant, and crossing to them with outstretched hands. "Here they are, my saviors. Allow me to give a proper introduction: ladies, make known to you my friends Quinn Rutherford, Asher Burton, and Ross McInerny."

"Good evening, gentlemen," Ione said, a bit astounded by Lord Kirkleith's introduction. The term 'savior' seemed a bit extreme, at least in the case of her own actions. Still, he was their host and she was delighted that his vigor seemed to have returned. "I'm happy to see you so recovered from your ordeal." Tamsin gave the company a nod.

"Oh, yes," Geordie agreed heartily. "Hardly a scratch, really—just a few stitches. Sorry to make such a production over the matter." Ruddy-cheeked, he led them to a trio of ladies sitting in the corner. "Mama, these are Miss Brentwood and Lady Tamsin Claremont, of whom I told you," he introduced them. "My mother, Lady Kirkleith; my sister Lady Ailsa Maclaren; and her companion, Miss Anderson."

"My lady, it's a pleasure to meet you." Ione dipped in a polite, but not overly grandiose curtsy, as did her cousin. The dowager had expressed that the dinner was to be a casual one between friends, and Ione had no wish to start the night by disregarding her expressed wishes. "Thank you so much for having us this evening, especially when you have so much to attend to before the investiture."

"I must thank you for your good offices on behalf of my son," murmured Lady Kirkleith earnestly. "I am so very grateful you were there to help him."

"Oh, yes," echoed the companion, Miss Anderson, with a shudder. "How could you be so brave? I know I would have fainted dead away."

"I suppose we were both too surprised by the whole thing to be afraid," Ione demurred, looking at her cousin for confirmation. "Thankfully, Tamsin was there, for I know little of such things. Even so, I do not know what we might have done if Mr. Rutherford had not been present. I don't think we could have managed to get his lordship back to the inn on our own." Wishing to steer the conversation away from the attack, Ione turned her attention to Lord Kirkleith's sister—a young woman of sixteen or so with a wealth of ruddy hair.

"I've a younger sister myself. Her name is Elsie, and she has hair the same lovely red as yours."

"Thank you, Miss Brentwood." Lady Ailsa replied. "Perhaps I shall have the pleasure of meeting her one day."

"If you're ever in London we shall have to make arrangements for just that," Ione insisted happily, hoping that the invitation would ease what must be a trying time for one so young. The smile Ailsa gave in return was strikingly similar to her brother's.

With the introductions out of the way, Ione turned a curious look to Geordie. "May I hear more of this tradition of yours? I'm not familiar with the customs associated with a clan investiture."

"Well," he began, rubbing the back of his neck, "there's an unnecessary lot of speeches—"

His sister broke in, her grey eyes alight. "Don't be so dull, Geordie. They want to know about the christening of the claymores."

"Indeed we do," Tamsin agreed. "What is it?"

Quinn sidled up next to Ione. "Very manly—kilts and ghillies, and the Maclaren has to fend off any challengers with his trusty claymore. That's why we're all here: we're his seconds."

"That sounds quite exciting!" Ione's expression lit up and her lips quirked playfully. "Is that before or after the 'unnecessary lot of speeches?'"

"Oh, after," Dr. McInerny supplied. "There'll be some ceremonial warmups or what have you, and then any challenger will try to take us on with three of his best." He chuckled a little. "Smarter to take Geordie down one-on-one, but the Scots like a good show."

The Maclaren's expression was growing sterner.

"Wait," said Tamsin. "Is that who—" She broke off abruptly.

Ione lifted a brow in her cousin's direction. Tamsin's question was delving into a topic that she'd cautioned against examining. Not that she could be blamed—had Rose been a few minutes later at the inn, Ione would have sought answers in her own unique way. Still, if a conversation about clan traditions provided some insight into other matters, Ione could not be accused of prying. "Is there any danger involved in the challenges, or are they merely to satisfy clan tradition?"

"Generally speaking, a matter of tradition," came the husky baritone belonging to Asher Burton.

She wanted to ask what would happen should a challenger win, but from the look on the Maclaren's face Ione was not sure the inquiry would be appreciated. *Could the attack be connected to the challenges in some way?*

Dinner was announced, forestalling any further conversation. The Maclaren offered his mother his arm. Ross McInerny tucked Lady Ailsa's hand into the crook of his elbow, causing the younger girl to turn a vivid pink, and offered Miss Anderson an escort on his other side. It was Asher Burton who presented his arm to Ione, and she accepted with a happy smile. "Thank you, Mr. Burton." This left Quinn to offer for Tamsin, which he did with élan, much to her amusement.

Mere minutes later, Ione found herself settled at a grandly appointed table with Asher Burton on one side and Lord Kirkleith on the other. Considering that her father had deemed the season ruined, she couldn't help but feel a little vindicated by the present company. "Tell me, Mr. Burton," Ione addressed the dark-haired man to her left, "How do you know the Maclaren?"

He smiled—a charming smile, shy though it was—and adjusted his tortoiseshell spectacles. "A friend of many years' standing. So are we all, the four of us. We shared a dormitory at Farrington, became great friends from our earliest school days. And you, miss?"

"Lord Kirkleith and I were introduced in London, though it was a brief encounter. Recently we had the good fortune of meeting him on our way to," she decided not to risk the name, "another destination. The inn was filled, so Tamsin and I offered to share with one another in order to free a room for Lord Kirkleith. In return he was kind enough to dine with us that evening, and spoke of the upcoming festivities. He made it sound so exciting that we decided we could not pass up the opportunity to attend."

"How lucky for him," Asher replied politely, darting a quick glance at the pretty blonde across the table before returning his gaze to Ione. "And you and Lady Tamsin are cousins, are you not?"

"Yes, we are. Our mothers are sisters," Ione returned. "Quite fond of travel, Tamsin offered to join me for my holiday here in Scotland."

"I see. Well, I hope you will enjoy it. Will you be here for an extended visit?"

Ione wasn't sure how to answer that question. The length of her stay depended on how long it took for her father's temper to cool and society to find a new topic to whisper about. "We have not yet decided. How long do you plan to stay after you've fulfilled your duty as second?" She turned the focus back to her dinner partner with a charming grin.

Mr. Burton smiled again. "Oh, as long as I'm wanted, I expect. It's all a bit sudden, this; but we're happy to do it, for Geordie's sake."

"He is a lucky man to have such loyal friends." Ione replied gently, chancing a glance at the Maclaren himself before continuing. "And where you will be returning to?"

"Oxford, actually. I've a fellowship waiting for me there. Though I will confess," he added in a confidential tone, "that having experienced a bit of life outside the scholastic cloister, I'm no longer certain that I wish to return to it."

"I must admit," Ione began, her tone just as confidential, "that I am finding myself less and less interested in returning to the life I left behind in London. In the brief time we've been here it's already proven much more interesting than the luncheons and gossip back home." She deftly left out her strong desire to avoid run-ins with former fiancés.

Faint color touched his cheeks. "I am delighted to hear it, Miss Brentwood. Of course, the Maclaren cannot run to balls or any such entertainments until his mourning is over, but I am given to understand that as serious a ceremony as the investiture must be, there is also merriment in store. Will you attend the public dance, or the village picnic?"

"This is the first I've heard of them." Ione was quick to latch on to the opportunity for fun. She glanced at Tamsin, certain that her cousin would be game for it. "I will have to discuss it with my cousin, but that sounds too good to be missed." She paused to sip her wine. "When will they be taking place?"

"Oh! The picnic and public dance are this Friday night, if the weather is fine. If it is not, I believe we are to gather in the church hall."

"Are you planning on attending yourself?" Ione made a mental note to perform a bit of scrying to check into Friday's weather. They'd chosen to come to Balmaclaren for this sort of thing, and with forewarning they could be prepared for rain or sun.

He gave her another one of those shy smiles. "Yes, indeed, we all are. We've come to be Geordie's seconds, and we intend to give a good showing."

"Of course, how silly of me," she remarked, gently dabbing at the corner of her mouth with her napkin. "I assume you and your friends have quite a few duties to fulfill as second to an incoming clan chief. I've read a bit on Scotland's history, but I've not read anything on the custom."

He finished his sip of wine. "It's unique to this clan, as I understand it. I gather the tradition began when the Maclaren was something of a warlord, proving his ability to fight and to lead. He chooses three loyal followers, not born of his clan, and they agree to defend him against all challengers."

Ione frowned a little. Recent events seemed to indicate that there may be some with genuine malice, and a willingness to step outside the bounds of tradition to see their goals met. She leaned slightly closer and lowered her voice. "I don't mean to be indelicate, but considering what happened the other day, do you suppose it possible that there are those who might truly oppose Lord Kirkleith, and issue a challenge in earnest?"

He glanced quickly at Lady Kirkleith, and at Ailsa, before speaking under his breath. "The thought had crossed my mind, yes. Perhaps we could speak at another time."

"Of course, Mr. Burton. Hardly a topic to be discussed over the soup." Ione studied the faces around the table. Though newly acquainted, she hated to think of any further harm befalling these people, especially when the household was already marred by grief. "Back to sunnier topics. I have only seen a small part of the countryside, but what I have seen is breathtaking. It makes me wish I had a horse for riding."

Asher finished his spoonful of soup and cleared his throat. "You should apply to Geordie. He has quite the stable here. I'm certain he would have something to suit your skill and taste, and would be more than willing to lend you a mount for the duration of your stay."

"The idea is an enticing one to be sure, but he has so much to attend to," Ione replied, reaching for her goblet. Riding was one of her greatest joys and something she excelled at. There was a simplicity to being atop a fiery steed that gave her a sense of control that so many other parts of her life lacked. "But if the opportunity arises, I'll be certain to ask for a tour. Do you enjoy riding?"

"I? Oh, I'm not much of a horseman," he demurred. "I can stick to a saddle when required to do so, but that, I fear, is the extent of my skill. I am certainly not as accomplished as Rutherford, or McInerny." Asher gave her an admiring look. "I gather, from your obvious love for it, that you are a formidable rider."

"My father used to take me for long rides when I was a girl." Ione sighed, thinking of those pleasant and easy times in her life. She laughed a little. "I'm certain my mother wishes I was not so fond of the activity. I have yet to find a jump that I could resist having a go at." She considered the man at her side, a scholar who was tempted by life outside academics. "If you are not much of a horseman, what do you enjoy doing? When you are not acting as second to the Maclaren, that is."

"Reading, of course. I shouldn't be much of a Fellow without a great love for the classics." He sipped his wine. "As to more physical pursuits, I enjoy a good game of cricket. Fishing, boxing, fencing. Nothing out of the ordinary, as you see."

Ione might have replied to that but for the arrival of the second course; Mr. Burton gave her a nod. "My thanks for the scintillating conversation, Miss

Brentwood." With that he turned his attention to Ailsa Maclaren, seated on his other side.

Ione smiled and shifted her focus to the man at her right, Lord Kirkleith himself. She awkwardly pushed a curl behind her ear and tried to consider an appropriate topic of conversation. Their acquaintance had been an eventful one, despite its brevity, and yet she found herself at a complete loss for words now that she faced him in the comfort of his own home. It was absurd that shyness should strike now. After all, they'd shared a meal before, and she had seen him at what must have been close to his worst.

Lord Kirkleith smiled down at her, his grey eyes alight with pleasure. "At last! I was beginning to think we would dawdle over the soup forever!"

"Well, it was very good soup, worthy of savoring." Ione chuckled nervously. Much to her frustration, she felt her cheeks going hot, and knew she was blushing, yet again. Ridiculous and that Geordie should affect her so. Yet, here she was, as bashful as a girl on her first outing of the Season. There was no excuse for it, and if she didn't begin to conduct herself with more maturity, he would think her nothing but a feather-headed ninny, an idea which bothered Ione more than she cared to admit. "I must compliment your kitchen staff on such a well-prepared meal."

"I shall be sure to tell the cook. It gives me very great pleasure to have you and Lady Tamsin here. I still cannot quite believe my luck, that your plans should take such a miraculous turn. I feel a bit as though I should light a candle in thanks." His grin was boyishly infectious. "I had thought this would be a very somber affair, but how can it be, with such company?"

"You are far too gracious." Ione replied, taking a sip of wine to gather her wits. Geordie was not making it any easier with his earnest compliments. But Ione was determined not to make a fool of herself, simply because the man's smile was one of the sweetest she'd ever seen. She cleared her throat and attempted to sound dignified and ladylike in her response. "I'm pleased that we can ease what must be a difficult time for your family."

His expression clouded over. "One is never fully prepared for this sort of thing," he acknowledged. "The kindness of one's friends—both old and new—is a bulwark in the tides of grief."

"I'm so very sorry, I didn't intend to remind you of painful subjects," Ione replied softly. His smile might have been disarming, but his pain was heartbreaking. The man before her was so solid, and strong, and yet, his face so often reflected great depth and caring. "You are very lucky to have so many loyal and true friends by your side."

He looked around the table, gaze settling on each of his friends in turn before responding. "I am indeed," and he returned his regard to her. "I'm pleased to be able to count you among that number."

"The honor is mine, I assure you." Ione answered, her voice far more breathless than she had intended. She couldn't help it. Geordie's manner was so genuine, his tone free of empty flattery. "I shall take our new friendship as a good omen that the remainder of my time in Scotland will be as pleasant as this evening's dinner. The journey thus far has hardly passed as expected when I set out from London."

"No?" He gave a soft laugh. "I know you have diverted from your original destination to come to Balmaclaren. Surely our little corner of Scotland pales in comparison to the wonders of the London season— and I feel sure society is the poorer for your absence from it."

"And I feel sure society will be taking full advantage of my absence," Ione replied dryly, following it up with a laugh of her own. No doubt her absence was the source of many a conversation in the parlors of London socialites. She could allow the fact to spoil her evening, or simply accept it for what it was, and enjoy the distance Balmaclaren offered. "No, I'm quite happy to enjoy the peace and quiet of the countryside. Though it seems there has been rather less of that than anticipated."

Color crept up his high cheekbones. "And now 'tis I who've brought up a painful topic. Though I cannot say I regret the reason for your absence, not when the results have so signally benefitted me," he began, his voice very soft. "But I hope you were not overset by the... debacle. I would never want you to feel so."

"Oh, you need not worry for that," Ione assured him gently. She relaxed a little. "My father is quite fascinated with Scottish history. He used to read accounts of various battles and clashes in the Highlands to me," she leaned toward him with a playfully conspiratorial tone, "much to my mother's dismay, of course." That elicited another smile from Lord Kirkleith, as warm as the glow from the candles. "The history of your homeland has always fascinated me. It seems that education served me well the other day. I know that pride is a sin, but I must admit to it, for as startling as our last meeting was, I did not swoon, or scream, or even grow queasy. At any rate, you had the worst of it, and seem to be doing quite well."

"As to that, Ross is a most skilled physician; and he informs me that the injury was not so terrible as it seemed at first." He was still blushing. "And you enjoyed the history of our clans?"

"I did, and still do, in fact. Of course, my knowledge of Scottish clans is likely quite limited compared to yours," Ione admitted. "My mother eventually convinced my father that it was better for a young lady to be educated in needlepoint and the running of a proper household, rather than the details of bloody conflicts long past. Sadly, I have not had the opportunity to study the subject further. Spending the evening in a castle such as this is like catching a glimpse of those bygone times."

"Perhaps after the meal you and Lady Tamsin would like to tour the castle, then." He gave that boyish grin again. "I can show you the oubliette, if you like."

Ione nearly clapped with excitement at the idea but managed to contain her enthusiasm. Though she couldn't keep from laughing a little when she imagined how some of her friends in London would respond to such an invitation. "Nothing to help the digestion like viewing an oubliette after the dessert has been served."

The Maclaren laughed with her. "And what else would you enjoy? As you are my guests," his glance at Tamsin included her in that statement, "I have every intention of seeing that you take the very best memories of Balmaclaren when you return to London."

"You have set a challenge for yourself, Lord Kirkleith. For how is one to surpass touring an oubliette?" Ione teased, grinning as she lifted her glass to her lips. "Though there is still the christening of the claymores, and all the excitement of an investiture to look forward to." She paused, not wishing to add to shoulders already burdened. "But surely you have more important matters than our entertainment?"

"Not to say more important," he insisted, "but in that I shall have my hands quite full, you have the right of it. However, that will not prevent me from spending what time I may with you and Lady Tamsin, or seeing to it that you have access to any other diversion you may wish for." He lifted his goblet to his lips, grey eyes twinkling over the rim of his cup.

"Your efforts as host will not be taken for granted, my lord." Ione dimpled at him. Amid all the parties and dinners of the Season, Ione could not think of one that she'd enjoyed this much. Geordie put her at ease, in a way she'd never felt with any of the gentlemen in London. There was no need to pretend to be fascinated or flattered. His only concern seemed to be her delight, and for her part, Ione was happy to oblige. They chatted amiably for the remainder of the meal, and retired to the parlor after.

Ione situated herself in a seat near the fireplace and settled comfortably for whatever entertainment followed. She was content simply to enjoy the evening, and the pleasure of being herself in the company of others. It was something that had become more and more rare as her anxiety over her nuptials grew. *No, it started long before I even met Theodore Gibson.* From the moment her magic manifested and her parents realized how rare and prestigious her abilities were, Ione had felt trapped in a world of others' expectations.

The Maclaren came over as soon as he'd settled his mother at the whist table with Miss Anderson, Ross McInerny, and Asher Burton. "Would you like that tour now?" he asked, bowing.

"Very much, although..." Ione's attention shifted to Tamsin; her cousin would likely not appreciate being asked to navigate a dark dungeon in one of her finer dinner dresses. "My cousin and I are hardly dressed for an oubliette. Perhaps we should save the tour for another time."

"Of course," he agreed immediately, though Ione thought she might have detected a hint of disappointment. "Whenever you like—you've only to ask."

Mr. Rutherford approached, a smile on his face. Over the course of the evening, Ione had noted that he was far less serious than he seemed to be upon their first meeting. "I hope you are finding the local inn to your liking, Miss Brentwood? Your amiable cousin assures me they are taking good care of you in the village."

"Yes, they are," Ione agreed. Though small and simple compared to the grand hotels in London, there could be no complaint of the hospitality they'd been shown. "I've enjoyed my time in Balmaclaren as a whole. It offers as much in the way of comfort as it does charm, and there is no small measure of either." She tucked an errant lock of hair behind her ear. "As I told Mr. Burton, the only regret I have is that they do not have any horses to be lent out."

"You shall have the pick of my stables," Geordie was quick to offer, and if the smile Ione gave him in response was too warm, then so be it, she decided.

"And I shall be happy to escort you as you ride, whenever you like," chimed in Rutherford. "I am at a bit more liberty than the Maclaren, at the moment."

"I fear that's true," acknowledged the laird, broad shoulders drooping.

"It's a pity you are kept so busy. I imagine you could tell me a great deal about the area, as I understand it has been in the care of your family for some time." And the idea of seeing him astride some magnificent charger was one Ione rather enjoyed— perhaps a bit too much. She felt the color rising to her cheeks again and quickly turned to Mr. Rutherford, lest her thoughts be too clearly written on her face. "Not to seem overeager, but I should like to set a time for that ride before the evening is through."

"Then we shall have to arrange it as soon as possible. I have some business tomorrow, but I'm free the day after. Would you be available in the afternoon?" he offered. "Perhaps Lady Tamsin would like to join us."

Ione considered the suggestion. "I don't think we have any plans for that afternoon." She turned to ask her cousin, but she seemed to be getting on quite well with Asher Burton, and Ione decided there was no need to interrupt when they could easily discuss the ride on the way home. She shifted her attention to Lord Kirkleith instead. "I know that I've said so before, but it bears repeating: I cannot tell you how much I appreciate your kindness."

"It is the very least I can do, in repayment for your service to me earlier. And it is something I would do for any of my friends." His gaze was warm above a sweet and gentle smile.

"Indeed," Mr. Rutherford agreed readily. "Your fortitude in a very trying situation made all the difference. And you have been instrumental in apprehending the last of the blackguards."

"They did find him then?" Ione sat up in her chair, eager for any details that might be provided. "And it was as I said? He was hiding in a barn?"

"Indeed, we had word from the commissioner just before you arrived. We are to go to the gaol in the morning to identify him," Geordie supplied.

"Thank goodness!" Ione breathed a sigh of relief, and her fingers tightened round the fan she was holding. "I could not bear the idea of that man running free after the harm he caused you, Geordie." It hardly registered to Ione that she'd used his name in front of his friends and family.

"Well, there is nothing for you to worry about, my dear Miss Brentwood," Quinn smiled, eyes sliding from Ione to his friend, though he made no comment on the familiar address. "You have done a yeoman's job, and we are all very grateful for it."

"I simply relayed what I heard." Ione insisted. If she had been with her family, she could have given a great deal more information, but the crisis was past, and all involved were well. A better outcome could not have been asked for, even if she had been able to use her magic openly. Pleased, Ione looked about happily, her gaze lighting on the piano. "That is a beautiful piano. Do either of you play?"

"My sister plays quite well. What a very good idea—my father loved to hear her, and I'm sure she would play for us now, if it would give you pleasure." Geordie bowed and went to speak with Ailsa before Ione could respond.

She chuckled quietly at his eagerness to volunteer his sister to entertain the room. "And am I correct in assuming that there is a harp, there in the corner?" Ione leaned toward Mr. Rutherford and gestured to a blanketed object near the piano. She glanced in her cousin's direction, lowering her voice so as not to be overheard. "Tamsin is a rather talented harpist."

Quinn raised his brows, looking at Ione's cousin. "Do you think she would play for us?"

"I think she would, if asked," Ione replied, knowing her cousin would never volunteer.

Geordie had returned in time to hear this last. "Lady Tamsin," he said with a smile at Ione, "I've just been informed of your talent with the harp. Would you be willing to grace us with a song or two?"

"I—of course," her cousin agreed, giving Ione a look of gentle reproach as she rose from her seat. Ailsa was already seated at the piano and began to lightly run scales while her brother uncovered the harp.

"I haven't had the pleasure of hearing my cousin play in a very long time." Ione informed Mr. Rutherford as the other two women decided upon a song to play together. "I could not let the opportunity pass me by now."

Tamsin raised a brow at her. "You never know what you can do until you try, Ione."

Ione chuckled quietly. Her cousin rarely played outside the family, but in Ione's considered opinion the experience was good for her. A moment later Ailsa began the introduction and Tamsin put her fingers upon the strings, closed her eyes, and soon was lost in the music.

The Maclaren rejoined Ione and Quinn. "It's a pity we cannot dance," the laird said apologetically.

"It is, but dark days always turn to lighter ones, and perhaps another time will present itself in the future." Ione offered him an understanding smile.

His grey eyes lit, like the sun breaking over the sea. "I can think of nothing I'd like more." He turned toward the musicians. "How exquisitely your cousin plays."

"She does, indeed." Ione agreed. She studied the laird covertly as he watched the musicians. She had seen him in times of peace, and in strife. He did not seem to be a person of false pretense, and yet Ione suspected there were depths to the man that only those closest were ever privileged to see. She wondered if she'd ever be one to whom that honor was granted.

The idle thought caught her by surprise and suddenly sitting in silence next to him seemed terribly intimate, though they were far from alone. She spoke up, needing to fill the space between them with polite conversation. "Your sister is just as talented; they're well-partnered."

Geordie sent her an amused look. "You are very kind." The song ended to much applause. Tamsin smiled and nodded her thanks, but did not immediately offer to play a second song.

Mr. Rutherford was quick to approach and offer congratulations. "You play excessively well, Lady Tamsin." He bent over her fingers with a smile. She thanked him prettily, then whispered something else. He looked around at Ione with an air of discovery. "Really?" Tamsin nodded.

"Tamsin, what have you told Mr. Rutherford?" Ione's shoulders tightened as she eyed her cousin suspiciously. The sense of intimacy she'd felt moments before evaporated and was replaced by the equally uncomfortable sense that the room's attention was shifting to her.

He came toward her, a charming smile on his face. "I have it on reliable authority that you sing, Miss Brentwood. Would you grace us with a song?"

"I... I suppose it is the least I can do, considering how gracious our hosts have been this evening." Ione stammered. She leaned to the side and cast a playfully annoyed look in her cousin's direction.

Tamsin fluttered her lashes at her cousin and glanced at the Maclaren before responding. "I will accompany you, if you like." She laid her fingers upon the harp and waited for Ione to join her.

"Very well then." Ione said, pushing out of her chair. She flipped through the sheets of music available and settled on a folk song that her father was fond of. As Tamsin began to play, Ione could feel her cheeks flush crimson, knowing she had no one but herself to blame for being put on the spot. However, once she began, her nerves quickly faded and she allowed herself to relax into the song.

Conversation ceased; the whist players put down their cards and turned to listen. Lady Kirkleith dabbed at her eyes with the corner of her handkerchief. Quinn, Asher, and Ross sat up straighter to listen; as for Geordie, he looked like a man who'd just beheld the dawn for the first time.

Ione's gaze met his briefly when she sang the final notes of the last verse. She looked down just as quickly when the music faded, but could feel his eyes on her still. The urge to meet his gaze again was a powerful one, but the side of her still reeling from those last nights in London urged caution. It was caution that won out.

The clock upon the mantel chimed ten, breaking the silence that lingered after the song. "Heavens, is it so late?" Tamsin got up at once. "Forgive us, my lady—yours is a house of mourning. Thank you very much for your hospitality."

"Yes indeed. It was very considerate for you to have us," Ione echoed her cousin mildly. She summoned the courage to glance at Geordie, but he had turned his attention from her and was looking up at the clock with an oddly sad expression on his face.

The dowager wished them a good night and thanked them once more before the girls gathered their wraps and were escorted to the door. Outside there were curtseys and bows all around. "I shall send word to the inn, to finalize plans for our riding, Miss Brentwood," said Quinn Rutherford, kissing her fingers. "I look forward to it."

Asher Burton was speaking in a low tone to Tamsin, his color high. She took a smiling leave of him and he helped her into the carriage.

At last it was just the Maclaren left to help Ione in after her cousin. "I have much to thank you for, Ione," he said softly. "May I hope to see you soon?"

"I should like that very much," Ione answered in a voice as soft as his. "I hope that tonight is a turn toward happier times for you, Geordie." Suddenly afraid that her remark was too intimate, she turned to step into the carriage.

Ione settled next to Tamsin with an almost inaudible sigh as the carriage began moving. They bumped down the road in companionable silence for a time, almost as if speaking might break the enchantment that seemed to have fallen over the evening.

Ione's mind drifted back to the delights of their dinner, and the conversation that followed after. "Oh!" she exclaimed, remembering Geordie's offer. "Lord Kirkleith has promised the use of his stables, and Mr. Rutherford has volunteered to take us riding, the day after tomorrow."

Tamsin was not precisely transported with delight. "Riding?"

"I take it you have not grown any fonder of the activity than you were as a girl." The corner of Ione's mouth turned in a sympathetic smile. "If you really do not wish to go, I won't force it."

"Oh, I'll not let you down. And if your preference leans toward the handsome young laird, then riding alone with Mr. Rutherford will do you no favors." Ione kissed Tamsin's cheek and thanked her profusely, ignoring the remark about her preferences.

Chapter Nine

Seaside Revelations

The day after their dinner together Geordie found he could settle to nothing. He paced the parlor, prowled the halls of the castle and generally drove his mother to the brink, at which point she firmly suggested that he should go for a ride. She needed a new pair of gloves, having burst a finger the evening before, and would be obliged if he would procure a pair at the small shop in town.

As Balmaclaren was where his thoughts currently lay, Geordie accepted the commission with alacrity and it was no more than a quarter-hour before he and Asher were cantering down the road.

The sea breeze was fresh and clean as it came over the bluff, and Geordie found himself chuckling aloud. He'd forsworn a hat—the sun was not so bright that he would burn, and the wind was pleasant in his hair.

Asher glanced over at him. "Something amusing?" he asked, though his own smile was broad.

Geordie shook his head. "Not amusing—pleasing. 'Tis a lovely day."

"It is, at that," Asher agreed, and they rode on, Geordie's mood growing ever brighter the closer they came to town.

They slowed their mounts to a walk as Balmaclaren came into view and entered the town far more sedately than they'd traveled to it. First things first: Asher gave the horses to the ostler at the inn, and the two men strolled to the shop where Geordie acquired a pair of gloves, tucking them into his coat pocket. "It's nearly luncheon," he observed, trying to be nonchalant. "Shall we see if there's a table to be had at the inn?"

"Bit early," Asher replied, studying his friend's face, eyes glinting with amusement behind his spectacles. "But I suppose we can just see if they'll hold a table for us in half an hour or so."

"Capital idea!" Geordie exclaimed, and strode to the inn, leaving Asher to follow as he would.

The table was thus secured (and if the proprietor was a little bemused at the request, he said nothing of it). The two men made for the door, but at the last moment, Geordie turned back. "Oh," he said, as if he'd only just thought of it, "I meant to ask—how is Miss Brentwood today? And Lady Tamsin, of course," he added, and longed to kick Asher when the latter snorted audibly.

"Ah," replied Mr. Murray, scratching his chin, "I understand her ladyship is attending to her correspondence; but Miss Brentwood, I believe, is in the back garden, just over th—" but Geordie was already at the garden door.

Geordie heard Ione before he saw her. A soft, sweet hum drifted across the rock-lined beds of herbs and flowers. She was sitting on a wooden bench in the far corner, surrounded by a profusion of brightly-colored flowers. Her gown was pale pink, simpler than the one she'd worn to dinner the night before, but elegant in its simplicity. There was an air of gentle quietness to her, a soft smile on her lips. A small pile of heather rested in the folds of her skirt, her fingers deftly fashioning the stems into a crown.

Geordie was almost loath to disturb her peace, but she looked up at the sound of the door. "Miss Brentwood," he said, aware that Asher was hovering somewhere about.

Ione's smile broadened—warmed—and her eyes seemed to light up. "Geordie," she answered sweetly. "I did not think to see you today, but I'm glad to have been wrong. It seems your recovery is complete."

He went to her, feeling a bit like a moth drawn to a flame. "I feel perfectly well—better now than ever," he added. "And you? You rested well, I hope?"

"Indeed I did," Ione laughed. She finished with her crown and held it out for Geordie to inspect. "I thought Tamsin and I might wear flower crowns to the picnic. I've never made them with heather, and thought it wise to practice before putting the idea to my cousin."

"A charming idea," Geordie pronounced. "I've no doubt my sister will want one as well, and likely my mother too. You and Lady Tamsin will no doubt set a fashion." He tucked his hands behind his back and bent to examine the floral headpiece. "Given my years of expertise in the subject, that looks like a prime example of a flower crown." He nodded sagely.

Her cheeks colored ever so slightly, blue eyes full of merriment. "Years of expertise? Had I known I was friends with a master of the trade I would have sought your input sooner."

"Oh, aye." He twinkled at her. "It's one of the things they teach in viscount school, you know. Can't be a peer of the realm without it."

That got a hearty laugh from her. "Oh, I can hardly breathe for imagining a room full of peers adorned with blossoming hats." She shook her head, dabbing at tears of laughter. She passed the completed crown to Geordie. "My gift to you, good sir. May it serve you well the next time Parliament is in session."

He plopped it on his head and grinned at her.

"Quite—" she pressed her lips together, clearly trying to keep from busting into another fit of laughter. "Quite dignified and..." She put a hand over her mouth giggling. "Oh, you really must take it off, or I shall never be able to get myself under control."

He laughed with her, feeling lighter than he had in weeks, and obligingly removing the flower crown, though he kept hold of it. "I wonder, Ione, if you'd consent to walk with me a little?" Asher, he thought ruthlessly, could lump it.

She hesitated before answering, glancing up at one of the windows on the second floor. Then she plucked up one of the unused stems of heather and tucked it behind her ear. "I believe I'd enjoy that. Perhaps along the beach? I wanted to go earlier, but Tamsin and I decided to pick flowers instead."

Geordie rose and offered her his arm, hooking the circle of flowers over the other one. "As you wish," he replied gently.

Her small hand slipped into the crook of his elbow and rested gently there, feather-light and warm, even through the sleeve of his jacket. They passed Asher, who was leaning against the wall near the garden door; Geordie entirely ignored the way his friend's brows rose as they went by, or the way he pushed off from the wall and followed at a reasonably discreet distance.

Ione was quiet as they walked away from the inn and made for the nearest stretch of beach. She inhaled deeply when they set foot on the shore, then turned to Geordie with a blissful expression on her face. "There is nothing quite like the smell of the wind coming off the waves, is there?"

"Not t'my mind—indeed, I was thinking the very thing on my way here." He smiled down at her. "Do you like the sea?"

Ione's eye grew distant and serious; the sound of the sea ebbing and flowing filled the brief silence that fell over them. "I suppose, though not as much as my sister." She looked out over the churning waves. "It seems like freedom, and yet it is controlled by the currents and the tides."

"We're all controlled by something," Geordie replied after a moment. "Society, parental expectations, tradition..." He shrugged. "I suppose the trick is to find your freedom where you can."

"That is something I'm beginning to learn," Ione replied, voice soft. They walked on for a few paces before she spoke again. "I'm afraid I've made quite a messy start. Though I told you of my broken engagement... I ended it on the eve of my wedding, during an event to celebrate the occasion." Her fingers flexed on his coat sleeve. "I should have demonstrated better judgment and refused Mr. Gibson from the start. But I was a silly girl, with nothing but romantic stories in my head."

Geordie stopped and turned her to face him, taking both her hands in his. "No more of that, now. 'Tis a waste of regret, to worry about something you're better off without." A small smile curved his lips. "For myself I'm grateful for your promise to the man, for 'tis through the breakin' of it that you came here, that you're here now; and I'd have you nowhere else, Ione. I sometimes think it's the only thing that'll see me through this." He paused, studying those blue eyes, bright and warm as the summer sky. "You'll think I've run mad, I know, but it's you—your words, your kindness to another—that got me this far." Geordie touched her cheek softly. "D'you remember a night at the opera, a month ago or so—a young woman in the next box to yours had been jilted, and another was making sport of her for her heartbreak?"

Ione nodded slowly, and a puzzled frown creased her brow. "But how could you know about that?"

"I was in the box on the other side, you see; and I heard every word you said to the poor lass—comforting her, letting her know that while there would be pain for a time, her heart would heal, and all would be well." He took a deep breath. "'Twas that same night we heard my father had been—had died, and I remembered your words, and took them for myself. So many times since, I've felt near t'breakin'," his brogue broadened a bit, "and then I hear your voice in my head tellin' me 'twill hurt for a time, but not forever—that someday all will be well again." He gave her hand a squeeze and then tucked it back into the crook of his arm, continuing to stroll down the beach. "I know your words weren't meant for me. But the comfort they have given me is beyond measuring." He patted her fingers and smiled at her. "Doesnae seem so silly t'me."

She let out a little breath, and Geordie saw her blink several times. "I—I don't think anyone has ever made me feel so... so..." Ione shook her head. "I'm not even certain what the word is. Real, perhaps—or important? I had no idea you were there, but to know that my words have helped in such a profound way..." and now she was the one to stop, forcing Geordie to turn to her. "Perhaps it was providence that you were in that box, that I felt compelled to speak for the girl. But whatever the reason, I am glad I could offer comfort to you, for you have offered the same to me today, George Maclaren."

His smile widened a little. "I'm only giving as I've received, Ione Brentwood." They walked on a bit further, picking their way along the pebbly shoreline. "Part of me still can't quite believe you're here," he admitted.

Ione laughed a bit. "If you'd been privy to my father's speech when I told him there would be no wedding, you'd wonder why he did not send me further." She nudged his arm a bit, her expression turning playful. "Perhaps if he'd known of your oubliette, he would have sent me directly to Castle Maclaren."

That made Geordie chuckle. "As I recall he did try to send you all the way to Bruichladdich," he pointed out. "But I can spruce up the oubliette a bit if you like."

"The very spirit of generosity, you are," Ione teased as he guided them around a large grey stone. She sobered a little, looking at him thoughtfully. "I'm glad we met on the road. You've turned what was meant to be exile into a lovely holiday." She looked down, blushing. "It's a pity you won't be joining us for our ride tomorrow. I will miss your company."

Geordie studied her for a long moment. He was sorely, sorely tempted, but the duties of his clan were not a small thing. "We must find a time to ride together," was what he said, spying Asher on the road above the shore, who waved at him and held up his pocket-watch. "And I must bring you back to Lady Tamsin—she must be wondering where you've gone."

Ione's eyes went wide, and her mood seemed to shift in the blink of an eye. "Oh, Tamsin! I should have left word before we went walking! We were to meet in the dining room for luncheon." She turned on her heel suddenly, half-dragging Geordie back toward the path that led back toward the inn.

"As it happens, Asher and I were planning much the same thing—and here he is." They crested the top of the shoreline; Geordie laughed at the exasperation clear on his friend's face. "Are we late? My apologies."

"Miss Brentwood," Asher gave her a courteous half-bow, then turned his attention back to Geordie "Yes, a quarter of an hour," he answered Geordie. "Mr. Murray likely thinks his Lordship has gone completely 'round the bend after that kerfluffle this morning."

"Oh dear, Tamsin is likely already waiting for me." Ione winced a little before offering Asher a quick greeting. "But since we are all to dine at the inn, perhaps we can spare Mr. Murray a table and share one instead. And if I might prevail upon you good gentlemen to make my case to my cousin, I'm certain she'll forgive my tardiness."

Geordie assured Ione he'd do all in his power to see that all was forgiven. Asher confirmed that he would back the cause as well, and the three of them made for the inn with all haste. Just as Ione said might be the case, her cousin was waiting.

"*There* you are," exclaimed Tamsin as they hurried into the public dining room, and then her gaze lit on Geordie, and she dropped a curtsey with a broad grin. "Lord Kirkleith, how very fortuitous that you and Mr. Burton are here, for I am inclined to forgive Ione immediately."

Ione sent a quick grin in Geordie's direction before she released his arm and moved to kiss Tamsin's cheek. "I'm terribly sorry for leaving without a word. I promise it will not happen again." And so the matter was settled, and the conversation turned to pleasantries as they were led to one of Mr. Murray's finest tables.

Luncheon was delightful, in Geordie's view; possibly one of the best in his recollection. And though they dawdled over dessert, all too soon he and Asher were riding back to the castle, a wreath of flowers looped about the viscount's pommel.

"So," said Geordie's friend.

"So," replied Geordie.

"Miss Brentwood," Asher went on.

Geordie nodded. "Yes, that was who that was."

"Geordie..."

"And that is who I am. Well done!"

Asher laughed. "All right, all right—if you won't tell me, you won't."

"Asher, my friend," Geordie glanced at him, "that's three you've got right in a row. Best stop while you're ahead."

After luncheon, Ione and Tamsin went to their rooms to freshen up. Ione took a little time sponging away the salt spray from the beach, and when she had finished drying her face she found her cousin inexplicably in her room, sitting on the bed with an expectant look on her face.

"So?" The blonde wiggled gracefully arched eyebrows at her.

"So what?" Ione replied, feeling the blood rush to her cheeks traitorously. She turned away from her cousin and pretended to tidy the dressing table. "It was a lovely day and we simply enjoyed a walk on the beach."

Tamsin chuckled. "You know what. He seems very smitten."

"Perhaps he looks at all ladies that way." Ione offered lamely, then smiled despite herself. Whenever Geordie looked at her, Ione felt like the only person in the room, like she was really and truly being seen for the person she was. "He is very sweet, and has a rather endearing smile."

Tamsin adjusted her ruffles. "Speaking as a lady myself, I can verify that he did not look at me that way, thus rendering your hypothesis moot." She laughed. "I hope you like Scotland, Ione. It seems you may be seeing plenty of it."

"I do, as a matter of fact." Ione replied, her smile turning impish. She saw her chance to turn the tables and seized upon it, plopping down on the bed beside Tamsin. "But if I'm not mistaken, George Maclaren did not seem to be the only one smitten. Mr. Burton was quite taken with you, I think. He blushes almost as easily as I do."

"Don't be silly," Tamsin replied quickly. "I am not in the market for a husband—I am perfectly happy as I am. And you shall not deter me so easily." She nudged Ione a little. "Tell me: how do you feel about the Maclaren?

"I hardly know the man." Ione replied with a shrug, trying to keep her voice and demeanor casual. Tamsin lifted a brow and crossed her arms. Ione sighed and gave up on the pretense. "But since I can see you are not going to let the matter rest, I will admit that I enjoy his company." She paused, her blush deepening. "He is the very image of the dashing hero... but I only just ended my engagement to Theodore. I must be sensible if there is anything of my reputation to be salvaged."

"Oh, *Theodore*." Thus did Tamsin dispose of the man. "A mistake from the first, clearly. He never looked at you like as the viscount does, did he?"

"No, he never looked at *anything* like that," Ione admitted, laughing a little despite herself. The closest Theodore ever came to a look of adoration was when his attention settled on the trappings of wealth and prestige. She sobered, a sense of anxiety slipping in to darken the afternoon'. "But there's more to it than that." She pulled one of the pillows close to her chest, hugging it tightly as she tried to find the words to explain her concern.

"What troubles you, dearest?" Tamsin asked. The playfulness she'd displayed earlier was tempered by gentle concern.

"It's all so much. The castle, the lands. I cannot even imagine what such a life would be like. The idea of having so many depending on you. The demands one would feel, running a household like that. It would be dizzying on even the most ordinary of days. Were I faced with that, I believe I'd weep, to have so many decisions placed on my shoulders. I haven't the knack for decisiveness that you do, Tamsin."

"I?" Tamsin met Ione's gaze, brows lifting nearly to her golden hairline. "I have never managed such a home, and likely never will. What can you mean?"

"I know your resolve to avoid marriage is steadfast, but I also know that if you were to run such a home, you would do it with far more skill than I." Ione twisted the corner of the pillowcase, carefully avoiding Tamsin's gaze. "Every decision I make leads to disaster. You, on the other hand, have travelled the world. You set your course and do so with such confidence." She finally met her cousin's gaze. "I have always admired that about you."

Tamsin gently pulled the pillow from Ione and took her hands, giving them a tender but firm squeeze. "What is this all about? I assure you, dearest, there is very little to admire in what you are pleased to call my 'decisiveness'. I am far too impulsive, and stubborn into the bargain, and it has led to trouble as often as not."

Ione shook her head. "At least it did not lead to your own father banishing you from the household. I have the ability to look into the future, and yet I have managed to make a spectacular mess of mine." She offered her cousin a rueful smile. "Were it not for you, our time in Scotland would be spent in an isolated corner of the country with none but cows to keep us company. It was entirely due to your skill at making quick decisions that led us to this lovely place, dining in magnificent castles." Ione took a deep breath, and straightened her shoulders, hoping to look more confident than she felt. "Therefore I have decided that I shall begin following your example."

Tamsin seemed to pale a bit. "You'll do nothing of the kind, thank you very much—that *would* put the fox among the hens. Ione, my darling," she regarded Ione, "you ought not blame yourself for what others decide to do. I love my uncle, as you must know; but he sent you away because he himself is embarrassed, or ought to be, that he very nearly pressured his beloved oldest daughter into an untenable match." She reached up to stroke a loose curl away from Ione's face. "The shame would have been in your unhappiness, and he knows it. As to why your choices seem to go awry?" Tamsin frowned. "It is my firm belief that that is because you have never really been allowed to make any, not until you were presented with the one that was crucial to your future life—and even then you were told what you *ought* to do. For my part, Tav and I have been left to raise ourselves, more or less, and so I have more practice in making decisions for myself, for good or for ill."

"You should have been the one born with my abilities," Ione replied, shaking her head a little. "It seems your upbringing was more suited to it. I am simply expected to know the best course." Ione gave her cousin's fingers a little squeeze, whether for her own sake or to offer her cousin affection she wasn't altogether sure. "But despite what you say, I still believe you to be a fine example. You, dear Tamsin, are one of the bravest souls I have ever met. You do not give yourself enough credit."

The pretty blonde began to laugh. "Oh, Ione, do you hear yourself? *I* do not give *myself* enough credit? Which of us refused to countenance an unhappy future? Which of us had the presence of mind to gather the information needed to bring a would-be murderer to justice? Which of us is renowned, not just for her beauty, but for her kindness?" Tamsin laughed again. "Which made a peer trip over his own feet?" She patted Ione's hands. "My love, if you wish a pattern to imitate, I beg you will look in the mirror, for you will see there the person *I* would emulate, if I could."

"Me? You wish to emulate me?" Ione's eyebrows lifted so high on her forehead she had to credit Tamsin for not laughing at what must have been a truly ridiculous expression. She opened her mouth to argue, but Geordie's words on the beach seemed to rise up in her mind, to join her cousin's. She pulled Tamsin into a tight hug. "Thank you, my darling. I am not sure I deserve such high praise, but you are the second person to say such things today."

Her cousin wrapped her arms around Ione. "Then how can it be doubted? Listen to what your heart is telling you."

But Ione continued to fret, despite her best effort not to. "Even so, it is not as simple as all that," she insisted. "I cannot go directly from a broken engagement to a new courtship. I don't want Geordie to think me a light or fickle woman."

"A valid concern." Tamsin nodded decisively. "You must be very careful, Ione dearest. There are a number of attractive men about. You must not seem to prefer one over another unless you truly do. As the Maclaren is our host, you have some leeway there; but you must take great care, all the same."

Ione nibbled her lower lip. She did not mean to show Geordie extra attention, but George Maclaren wasn't like any of the men she'd met before—he wasn't like any of the men she'd met since arriving at Balmaclaren. She exhaled slowly and turned to her cousin. "I am not trying to show any of them extra favor. I know I must be careful, and I will not do anything to further embarrass myself. But when I am with Lord Kirkleith I do not feel unsure of every step to be taken, every decision to be made. I feel... comfortable with myself."

"I see." Tamsin was grinning now, the expression an irrepressible one. "When do you see him again?"

"I don't know. He isn't free for the ride tomorrow. Although," and here Ione returned her cousin's grin with one of her own, "he did say that we must ride together some time." She pressed her hands to her cheeks. "I know I shouldn't be so delighted by the prospect, but after everything that happened back home, it feels *good* to enjoy myself again."

Tamsin shook her head emphatically, her perfect curls bouncing. "You've had enough of 'should'—it's time for 'would', now." She paused. "That was rather a long walk for 'we must ride together sometime'. The strong, silent type, is he?"

"He is strong, in character as well as body," Ione agreed thoughtfully. Her mind wandered back to the conversation on the beach. She hadn't given the incident at the opera much thought; someone had been hurting and she'd simply done what she could to help. Yet her words had meant so much more to Geordie, and that meant the world to her. She'd never thought herself as particularly wise or helpful, but in what must have been one of Geordie's darkest hours he'd heard her. "Tamsin, Geordie told me that *I* helped him when his father died. He'd overheard me comforting someone that very evening, and those words eased his burden." Ione looked at her cousin. "He values what I have to say, and he trusts it. I did not know how much I needed to hear that until he said it."

Her cousin's puckish expression sobered; she was quiet for a moment. "Ione, if that's the way of things... if he values you, trusts you..." Tamsin turned to look out the window at the sea across the way. "Try not to lose that, for if you do, you'll regret it forever."

Chapter Ten

From Delight to Disaster

Ione woke early on the day set for their ride. Though she'd hardly slept, she felt happy and invigorated as she waited for Tamsin to finish getting ready for the day. Much of the night was spent thinking of the conversation she'd shared with Geordie as they walked along the beach. Ione could hardly believe that she'd had such an impact on him—or that he had such an impact on her. He valued what she said, trusted it.

Any remaining self-doubt after that conversation had been staunchly refuted by Tamsin only a few short hours later. Now, for the first time in her life, Ione didn't doubt every decision she made. She held up the two riding hats she'd brought and picked one without debate or anxiety—the navy velvet would go nicely with her favorite riding habit. When Rose asked how she'd like her hair pinned, that was another easy answer. It seemed silly that such simple choices had ever been cause for concern. It wasn't simply that

Geordie valued what she said—although that delighted Ione—it was being away from London and her parents' expectations, realizing she had more to offer than a pretty face. She felt like a new woman, one who was decisive and confident.

The only blemish on the day was the knowledge that Geordie would not be joining them for their ride. But Ione was determined to enjoy herself regardless. Mr. Rutherford was an amusing sort, and Ione hoped that he might provide some insight into the viscount's intentions, though she would have to be subtle in her efforts. Not that she intended to rush into anything; not that she secretly imagined dancing with Geordie at an elegant affair in London. Silly to suggest that her heart fluttered whenever he called her by her given name. Ione gave herself a once-over in the mirror. Geordie said he could not go riding, but they would be in the Maclaren stables, and perhaps they'd cross paths at some point.

A knock at her door nearly made Ione jump out of her skin. She blushed, feeling foolish for being so easily startled. It wasn't as if she'd been caught doing something wrong. She straightened her shoulders and called out, knowing it must be Tamsin or Rose. "Yes, come in."

It proved to be the former, in a fetching red and black riding habit, with a cunning little hat atop her fair curls. "Have we time to break our fast before Mr. Rutherford arrives?" Tamsin asked, kissing Ione on each cheek.

"Most definitely," Ione said with a resolute nod. "Can't have our stomachs growling and spooking the horses."

Her cousin chuckled. "And I've no wish to make a spectacle of myself on an empty tum." She linked her arm through Ione's and they headed toward the stairs.

"I've been thinking about what you told me about your walk on the beach with Lord Kirkleith. Have you any inkling as to whether he might be considering a courtship, even so soon?"

Ione's steps slowed slightly. Her cousin's question so closely echoed her own thoughts. She didn't know—not for sure—but he was attentive and seemed to enjoy her company as much as she enjoyed his. Perhaps that was simply what she wanted to see. Either way, her time in Scotland and with Geordie was something she would treasure for the rest of her life.

She was aware of Tamsin's scrutiny. "Although," her cousin went on, "I suppose it matters less what he plans to do—for you cannot control that—and more what it is you want him to do. You must be sure not to give him false hope, Ione."

Ione stopped in her tracks, met her cousin's eyes, and responded with absolute sincerity. "Any hope he might have would not be false or in vain." Tamsin hid a smile. "Heaven help me," Ione went on, "I must be mad for considering another courtship." She exhaled, laughing a little. "Still believe I am an example to follow?"

"Most assuredly, dearest." Tamsin patted her hand gently as they maneuvered their way through the dining room's crowded tables and settled at one in the corner.

The meal provided by Mr. Murray and his wife was excellent; this was not surprising, as the kitchen had yet to disappoint. When the last crumb was eaten, the ladies decided the morning was too lovely to waste even a moment waiting in their room. They excused themselves to the back garden and found a comfortable bench with a clear view of the road. The heady scent of the herbs and the warm sunshine made for a pleasant place to pass the time as they waited for Mr. Rutherford to arrive.

He did not keep them waiting long, and soon Ione found herself standing in the large and well-stocked stables of the Maclaren.

Tamsin, having explained her lack of skill, was fondling the nose of an elderly mare to which she seemed to have taken quite a liking. Rutherford's own horse was already saddled and in the stableyard, and he and Ione were contemplating the two hunters set aside for her to choose from.

"It is up to you, Miss Brentwood," Mr. Rutherford said. "Which will you have, the black or the bay?"

Ione eyed the two animals standing before her, noting the fine qualities of each. The bay tossed her head and pranced in place. The animal had spirit, something Ione enjoyed in a mount, but this ride was meant to be a pleasant and relaxing diversion. By contrast, the black mare stood quietly waiting as Ione studied her. Though the creature did not display the same anxious energy as its counterpart, it was no less alert. Head held high, ears swiveling back and forth, the mare looked at Ione with bright, intelligent eyes that seemed to be scrutinizing Ione with interest.

A familiar voice came from the stable door. "She will have the black," announced Geordie authoritatively. He wore a bottle-green riding coat over fawn-colored breeches that fit his muscular thighs to a fare-thee-well. The laird strode toward them, crop tucked under his arm as he tugged on his gloves. "The bay is too prone to wiping a new rider off her back with a handy branch—I've no wish to subject Miss Brentwood to that sort of indignity."

Rutherford looked his friend over. "Are you joining us, then?"

"Indeed I am." The Maclaren bowed. "Burton and I finished our business early, and we thought you would not mind a larger party. He should be—there you are, Ash."

Asher Burton hurried into the stables. "That rascal Ross hid my bree—oh, hello, Lady Tamsin, Miss Brentwood. The grooms will have Goliath and Icarus saddled in a trice and we can be off."

Mr. Rutherford chuckled. "The black it is," he agreed and led the spirited mare off to be saddled.

"I took the liberty of ordering a boxed luncheon for us," Geordie said, his color rising. "Angus will bring it along to the ruins, if that is agreeable. Ross and my sister are already there—Ailsa took it into her head to do some sketching."

"A picnic sounds very agreeable, indeed," Ione replied happily as she watched the horses being led away. Her spirits had soared when the laird walked into the stables; the prospect of spending the afternoon with him filled Ione with delight. But Tamsin's questions regarding the possibility of a courtship echoed in her mind, stilling the flutter of excitement, urging caution lest her heart get ahead of itself.

He met her gaze, his own warm and hopeful. "I am glad to hear it. I hope I was not too presumptuous in choosing the black for you—her name is Kelpie, by the bye."

"Not at all; in fact, I had already decided on the black mare. She has an intelligence in her bearing." Ione assured him. "Though both are beautiful animals, and I do rather enjoy a challenge. I may have to have a go at the bay in the future."

Geordie glanced at the rest of their group; Messrs. Rutherford and Burton were chatting with Tamsin while they waited for the last of the mounts to be saddled. He put a finger to his lips and beckoned to Ione. "I've something to show you."

Ione's interest was instantly piqued. She leaned a little closer to the viscount, curious and full of hope. "Oh? What is it?"

For answer he beckoned her again, and gave her his arm as he led her deeper into the stables. They stopped in front of one of the stalls, and he nodded, indicating that she should look inside.

A diminutive black filly stood there, her legs long and a little unwieldy. She nickered and shook her petite head, trotting up to Ione's outstretched hand. "Kelpie's foal," Geordie explained. "Weaned just a few months; just half a year old. We call her Sprite."

Ione cooed at the little creature, rubbing its silky cheek and neck. "A fitting name, for she is a lovely little sprite, indeed." She glanced up at Geordie. "Thank you for showing me. She'll be a fine mare someday."

"Aye, I think so too. We'll be keeping her when the others go to market." He chuckled. "Ailsa wouldn't hear of anything else anyway. I just thought, since you seem taken with Kelpie, you might like to meet her little one."

Ione gave Sprite one last pat on the nose and pulled her hand away. She glanced toward the yard and then returned her attention to the viscount. "Geordie, there is something I wish to discuss—or ask. Well, a matter I wish to..." Ione took a breath, feeling a bit of the old uncertainty returning. "Oh bother, I'm verging on babbling."

His brows drew together. "Not at all. You can ask me anything, Ione. We're friends, are we not?"

"We are, and I would not bring it up were that not the case," Ione replied, shoulders relaxing. "I want you to know how much our conversation on the beach meant to me—how much our time together has meant."

She paused, smiling despite herself. "And I hope that what I'm about to say is not too forward, but I have resolved to take more initiative in my own fate."

He tilted his head, stormy gaze intent. "Go on."

Ione took another deep breath in a vain attempt to steel her nerves. "When we had tea, you said you were happy that I was free of the encumbrance of my previous engagement." Forcing herself to be bold, Ione met his gaze. "I have been wondering... what you meant by that."

There was a pause; Geordie slowly reached for her hand, turning it palm-side up before peeling back the edge of her riding glove and pressing a kiss to the small heartbeat in her wrist. "Do ye not know, Ione?" he asked quietly, his Scots more evident than usual.

Ione's breath caught in her throat, and she was certain her pulse was racing wildly. "I... hoped, Geordie."

His gaze fastened on her mouth and the air around them seemed charged such as Ione had never experienced; it was tantalizing, even a little frightening, but she could not bring herself to look away.

All at once Rutherford called from the stableyard. "Geordie! Are we going, or shall I go get a good book and put my feet up while you spoon?"

The viscount muttered a litany of creative ways to murder his friend, making Ione laugh a little.

"Perhaps we should rejoin the others," she said, returning his scowl with a brilliant smile of her own. His cheeks flaming, Geordie escorted her to the stable door.

The horses were saddled and the rest of their group already mounted in the stableyard. Geordie took a moment to toss Ione up into Kelpie's saddle, making her feel as though she weighed less than a feather. He swung into his own saddle and the five set off.

They rode for nearly an hour before Ione set eyes upon the ruins where they would take their luncheon. They were little more than a few low and crumbling stone walls, but the view surrounding them was one of extraordinary beauty. Angus had evidently beaten them there with the food.

"We came the long way around," Asher Burton explained, upon Ione's questioning. "Wouldn't have been more than a quarter hour if we'd come straight on." At his words Tamsin vouchsafed him *such* a look that Ione was hard pressed not to laugh aloud.

"I don't mind in the least." Ione reached forward to pat her horse's silky black neck. Kelpie had proven to be a delightful animal with a smooth, steady gait and an eagerness to gallop. If Ione had been back home, she would have found a quiet piece of countryside to run her through her paces, perhaps even attempt a few jumps.

Ailsa and Ross rose to greet them from where they'd set up blankets on the grass. Ross helped the ladies dismount; Ailsa greeted them with a pleased air. "It is a lovely day, is it not? I'm so glad you could join us!"

"Very lovely, indeed." Ione smiled, smoothing her riding clothes. "I'm told you came early to sketch; I would love to see what you've done so far." She looked about to take in their surroundings, sneaking a glance at Geordie as she did. "I'm afraid I have never been very good at sketching anything myself, but it makes me appreciate those who can all the more."

Ailsa blushed, but took her arm. "Here is all I've done. I should have done more, but Dr. McInerny would not sit still and I had to begin again."

"Surely he would not distract such a talented artist at work?" Ione replied, admiring what Ailsa presented. "For shame, Dr. McInerny."

The young Scottish lass threw the doctor a look. "I told him he looked picturesque upon the blanket and he needs must get up and stride about." She was blushing. "Hopeless."

Ross McInerny shrugged. "I would only ruin the loveliness of the landscape, I assure you."

"Perhaps you ought to let the artist decide," Ailsa replied, rather tartly.

His cheeks reddened and he turned to Asher. "Running a bit late, were we?" he asked. "I do hope nothing was amiss."

"No thanks to you," Asher shot a look at the Irishman. "Do stop playing at innocence. It doesn't become you."

Ross laughed. "What is there to eat?" he asked, rummaging through the baskets Angus had delivered. "Anything sweet?"

"May I serve you?" Asher asked Tamsin, including Ailsa in his smile. The blonde colored prettily and acquiesced. Meanwhile, Geordie escorted Ione to a shaded spot by the ruined wall and spread his coat on the grass for her.

She settled on the ground, with a contented sigh. The rolling ocean in the distance, the green hills—dotted with blooming heather, purple and white—and the cloudless cerulean sky created a breathtaking view, giving the day an air of enchantment. The longer Ione was in Scotland, the more she found she enjoyed it. "I cannot say how pleased I am that your business ended early enough for you to join us today, Geordie," Ione admitted, delighting in the way his face lit up when she did.

"My man of business is not happy with me," he confessed, "but I could not miss the opportunity. And what is the point of being clan chief if one can't order people around a bit?"

Ione would have happily continued their conversation, but her response was forestalled by the arrival of Quinn Rutherford. He approached with several plates of food carefully balanced in both hands. "I hope you're hungry, Miss Brentwood," he said jovially. "Mrs. Madden seems to have outdone herself again." He seated himself between Geordie and the open hillside, obscuring the view somewhat.

"You make a better wall than window, my friend," muttered Geordie. Quinn just grinned at him and set to his meal.

"At least he brought plenty to eat. Goodness, Mr. Rutherford, did you leave anything for the rest of our party?" Ione chuckled as she reached for one of the plates.

The picnic proved to be a series of delicious delights; the kitchen seemed to have spared no effort. Ione was particularly fond of the fruit-filled pastries, though it was difficult to eat them without making a terrible mess of it. Given the informality of the setting, she did not bother with a napkin, but licked the sticky filling straight from her fingertips. It was simply too delicious to be wasted. Geordie watched her for a moment contemplatively, then looked away, crimson climbing up his cheeks. He cleared his throat and took a long draught of lemonade, which gave Ione a small sense of satisfaction.

"Mr. Burton tells me that you were all schoolmates." Ione said, delicately dabbing at her mouth to cover the smile that spread across her lips. "I cannot imagine that to have been a quiet time."

"No, indeed," Quinn agreed, though his gaze was on the middle distance. "We shared a room in—"

"Quinn!" Asher barked sharply, pointing down the hill. Something glinted in the thicket at the base of the hill upon which they settled. A second later something else embedded itself in the crumbling wall several feet away from the Maclaren's head: a bolt from a crossbow, buried all the way to the fletching.

Rutherford bit out a curse and leapt on top of Geordie and Ione, pinning them to the wall. "Don't move, if you please."

Asher ran to his horse and tugged a pistol from his saddle, taking aim while Ross pushed the two ladies to the ground. Another bolt sprouted from the wall, just where Geordie's throat had been mere seconds earlier.

Asher took one shot and then another; there was a shout from the underbrush. "Got you, you bastard," he growled, and then grunted as a bolt pierced his hand, causing him to drop the gun.

"Down, damn you!" shouted Quinn over his shoulder. There was a slight whistle, then a dull thud, and Mr. Rutherford flinched, violently.

Ione shifted, reaching for the bolt embedded in the wall near Geordie's head. Her eyes closed as her fingers wrapped around the wicked object. She summoned her magic, tracing along the path of the arrow with her mind's eye. Time seemed to slow; she could see the man crouched in the shrubbery. He was bleeding from a wound on his upper arm, no doubt the result of Mr. Burton's sharpshooting. He'd moved a few paces to the left after the last shot, and was reloading for another shot.

"He's just there!" Ione called out, pointing to the man's precise location. Their assailant cursed and jumped to his feet, apparently giving up on stealth in favor of a speedy retreat.

Tamsin struggled out from under Ross and moved to hide behind a section of wall, dragging Ailsa with her; at her nod the young doctor rolled to his feet and sprinted down the hill, tackling the man before he could make another move.

With their attacker subdued, Ione's attention shifted back to the man shielding her with his own body. Quinn bared his teeth; a thin ribbon of blood trickled from the side of his mouth, and Ione realized with horror that she could hear a strange sucking sound as he collapsed to the side, trying to breathe.

Geordie caught him. "Quinn? Quinn!" he shouted, frantic. "Nononono please, Quinn, don't— ROSS!"

The doctor squinted up at them; Ione could see his expression harden as he seemed to recognize the plight Quinn was in. His lips moved, though whether in prayer or epithet Ione could not tell. The assailant went limp and Ross drew back his fist, slamming the man across the temple.

But Quinn did not have a second to be spared. Ione pushed herself up and ran to her cousin, frantic to buy the stricken man time enough for the doctor to attend him. "Tamsin! Come quickly, Mr. Rutherford has been badly injured!"

Tamsin clambered to her feet, her skirts hampering her greatly, and ran to Quinn's side. Her expression was grim.

"Y—you have to help him." Teeth chattering with fear and tension, Ione could feel tears welling in her eyes. That bolt would have hit her, had it not been for Quinn's selfless protection. She knelt down at Geordie's side, where she remained, the viscount clutching his friend as if he could stave off death itself by doing so.

Tamsin spared her cousin a glance, and then nodded. "Don't let them stop me, then," she murmured. She looked about and grabbed Ione's abandoned napkin, hands flaring anew as she poured a charm into the fabric before pressing it to the wound.

Geordie reared back. "What in God's name—?"

"Geordie, look at me." Ione reached for the laird's hand and squeezed it. "I have been honest with you—please trust me now. My cousin can help Quinn, but you must not interfere." Beside her Tamsin was working quickly, using magic Ione recognized and other techniques she did not. Geordie nodded, eyes wide, then swallowed, gripping her hand tightly as he watched.

Below them, Asher had traded places with Ross and stood guarding the unconscious man, the pistol steady in his uninjured hand. Ailsa had followed Tamsin from the wall and now hovered behind her brother, wringing her hands.

Tamsin's hands were fully alight now, glowing eerily from within as she pressed them to Quinn's wound. Sheer power radiated from her as she forced spell after spell into the now-crimson napkin; Ione could feel magic crackle in the air, like nothing she'd ever experienced from her cousin before. The gout of blood pulsing from the stricken man slowed just as the young doctor arrived at a flat run.

Ross skidded to a stop, nearly slamming into Geordie in his haste to help his friend. This was not the same calm and confident bedside manner he had displayed when Geordie was shot. With one quick tug, he pulled the bolt from Quinn's back and grimaced as he worked over the prone man. Tamsin stumbled away, covered in gore to the elbow, the power that had radiated around her so brightly suddenly extinguished.

All of a sudden Quinn coughed, retched, and took a deep breath. Ross sat back clumsily, slumping slightly. "He'll do," he rasped, his color waning even as Quinn's improved. "Looked worse... worse than it was."

Ione looked from Quinn to Tamsin to Geordie. Her cousin's cheeks were pale, while the expression on the viscount's face was one of astonished skepticism.

Ione quite agreed—the suggestion that Quinn's injury had been anything less than deadly was utterly absurd, but perhaps it was all Dr. McInerny could think to say. Tamsin glanced at Ione, meeting her gaze, and pressed her lips together. Ione gave a slight nod. Whatever it was Ross McInerny was trying to hide—and Ione had a fair idea of what that might be—it was not for them to unmask him.

"Easy, laddie," Geordie was muttering to Quinn, his brogue broad as the Highlands. "Dinna try t'rise. I thought ye dead, Quinn, that arrow—" He broke off, clasping his friend's hands in his own.

Ione tore her gaze from Geordie and Quinn and hurried to Tamsin's side, hooking her arm around her cousin's waist. "Perhaps you should sit. I will see if any of the lemonade survived. You should drink something. It will help you recover." Her cousin nodded and sank to the grass, holding her hands well away from her gown.

Having clearly overheard, Ailsa hurried over with the last of the lemonade, holding it to Tamsin's trembling lips. Ione snatched up one of the nearby blankets and used it to wipe the blood from Tamsin's hands, though there was no hope for the sleeves of her riding habit. When Ione finished with her cousin, she glanced at Geordie. "Are you..." She paused, not entirely sure how to continue. "Are you unharmed, my lord? Dr. McInerny?"

Ross' response was a weak wave of the hand and a slight nod. He was as covered in blood as Tamsin, and looked twice as drained, skin now bearing a distinctly greyish tint, his eyes barely open.

Quinn coughed again and accepted a drink from Ailsa gratefully. "Lady Tamsin..." he rasped, his voice gravelly, "I believe I owe you my life."

Tamsin, leaning against Ione, shook her head exhaustedly. "I assure you—"

Quinn held up a hand. "The bolt pierced my lung—I knew I was dead when it hit. What you did... I've heard things: one does, in my line of work, but I never thought I'd witness it, or be saved by it."

There were tears in Tamsin's blue eyes. "Please, Mr. Rutherford, don't—"

Geordie was looking at each of them with an expression of growing concern. "Be saved by what? What did she do? I don't—I can't—"

"Magic," Quinn supplied. "It was real, honest-to-God magic."

Ione took a breath and spoke up, wishing she could go back to the start of the day, when everything had been full of hope, rather than fear and confusion. "Magic runs in my family." She looked at the laird, her stomach twisting in knots and her fingers beginning to tremble.

Geordie started, stared, swallowed. "Then you— *you*—?"

"Yes, I have magic as well. I cannot do what Tamsin does, but... I possess my own talents." She gestured to the bush where their attacker had laid siege to their picnic. "I used my magic to pinpoint the shooter's position. He might have continued on, if he felt secure in his hiding place." Ione tried to think of something more to offer that might ease the viscount's shock, but there was nothing.

"M-magic," Geordie repeated, flinching backward. "You—you're a—"

Tamsin looked terrified as well as exhausted, tears coursing down her cheeks. "I swear," she managed, "we are not what you think. I—I believe in God, I go to church. This is—a gift, like any other from Heaven."

"It's just as my cousin says: we believe in God; we simply have abilities that others do not. Please, Geordie, we are the same people you met at the inn." Ione swallowed against the lump that was forming in her throat. "I... we would never do anything to harm you. Any of you."

He shook his head and got to his feet. "I need to—to think, to—"

Quinn nodded. "We need to get that ruffian to the magistrate, and to make our statements. I think Asher needs his hand looked at. And Lady Tamsin, at least, needs to rest." He studied the doctor. "You don't look at all well, Ross. Squeamish? Surely Angus is due shortly, to retrieve the—"

Ross shot Quinn a look and pushed himself to his feet. He wobbled a little once he was upright, steadying himself on the wall. After a moment he stumbled to his horse, dug a roll of bandages from the saddlebag, and staggered down the hill to turn his attention to Asher's wounded hand.

Not ten minutes had passed when Angus arrived, leading a small cart. He leapt from his mount at the sight of the chaos that had once been a harmless picnic, and hurried to lend what aid he could. Asher did his best to explain, a carefully expurgated version of events. Angus hogtied the unconscious captive and tossed him in the cart none-too-gently.

The rest mounted, with the notable exception of Tamsin. "I can't—indeed, I *cannot*," she protested. "Let me stay here—I shall walk, when I have rested."

"I will not leave you alone, Tamsin," Ione stated firmly. She shook her head and shifted in the saddle. "If you cannot ride, then you are in no state to walk either. I will wait with you, and when you are rested we will go back together." Ione chanced at glance to Geordie and flinched inwardly at the expression on his face. She wished for all the world that she knew what to say or do to ease his mind.

"No," came Asher's gentle voice. "We cannot leave two ladies alone out here. I will stay, and you, Miss Brentwood, should go back with the others."

"You are wounded, Mr. Burton, and I cannot help you now," Tamsin replied, her voice strained. "I shall be well on my own, I promise you."

Asher shook his head. "My hand will be none the worse for a few hours' delay. I will not leave you alone, my lady."

"Are you comfortable with this arrangement?" Ione asked Tamsin. Leaving her cousin behind felt like running away. "I will only agree to go if you consent to Mr. Burton's suggestion."

"I wish you would all go," came Tamsin's tired reply, "but if someone *must* stay, then I consent."

Ione cast her cousin a doubtful look, but kept to her word and agreed to Mr. Burton's proposal. She blew her cousin a kiss, then turned her horse to follow the cart. She rode in silence, feeling utterly miserable and wishing she had insisted on staying behind with Tamsin.

Geordie said little to anyone on the way back to the castle, and nothing at all to Ione. Ailsa was clearly upset by her brother's breach of manners, looking from one to the other with a bewildered expression; Quinn was tired and clearly uncomfortable, his lips pressed together tightly, and Ross looked as though it was all he could do to stay awake in the saddle. Upon their return to the castle the stablehands took charge of their mounts, and a carriage was ordered without ado to take Ione back to the inn. Still Geordie said nothing, though he cast her a long look before heading into the castle proper.

It was left to Ailsa to observe the pleasantries, such as they were. "I hope you are not too discommoded by today's events," she said quietly, taking Ione's hands. "My brother is..." But it was clear that she did not know *what* her brother was feeling, so she wisely left that alone. "I shall check on you tomorrow. I hope your cousin recovers well from her swoon. Asher will bring her home safely; you need have no fears upon that score." The youngest Maclaren looked as though she wanted to offer more, but simply bid Ione a good day and turned toward the castle doors.

Quinn watched Ailsa follow her brother, then murmured to Ione gently. "Be of stout heart, Miss Brentwood," he said, offering her a small and somewhat strained smile. "True friends, like fine steel, must undergo a tempering process to show their strength. He has never failed yet." With those cryptic words he handed her into the carriage, and she rumbled off toward the inn.

Chapter Eleven

Aftermath

As soon as the carriage stopped Ione tumbled out, not even waiting for someone to offer her a hand as she climbed out. She met Rose upstairs, reassuring her that Tamsin would be arriving shortly, and that a clean dress and hot bath should be made ready. Waving away the maid's offers to help her change, Ione went directly to her room and sat down hard on her bed. She wasn't sure what to feel: hurt, anger, fear; they all thundered through her head like ocean waves during a storm.

She remained alone, not even bothering to change out of her riding habit, despite a second attempt at service from Rose. The day had taken such a devastating turn, and Ione was too shaken to do anything but stare at the door and wait for her cousin to return. When she finally heard Tamsin's arrival, Ione stood, smoothed her hands over her hair and clothes, then stepped into the corridor to see if there was anything she could help with. The distraction would be a welcome break from arguing with herself over how she'd handled things with Geordie. "Do you need me to help you settle?"

Tamsin waved her away. "Let me sleep; tomorrow we shall see what damage we've done, and whether we need to leave."

Ione nodded sadly and returned to her own room without argument. There was no real point to it anyway. Mr. Rutherford would surely have died without the intervention of magic, and Ione could not regret the life saved. But Geordie's feelings had been clear enough: nothing they'd shared in the past days mattered. He hadn't even bid her goodbye when she left the castle. No doubt he felt she'd lied to him—or worse, that she had been using her magic to secure his affections. That thought caused a crack to run down the center of her heart, deep and painful.

To her own surprise, she'd fallen in love with him, and now that love was turning to ash in front of her.

They were not safe here. Geordie—no, Lord Kirkleith now, for surely he no longer counted her among those he trusted—was the leader of his clan. His word was law here. If he called for Tamsin and herself to be taken into custody, it was unlikely the anyone would question the command, nor ask for justification. No, they would have to leave, and leave as soon as possible.

Ione crossed to her trunk and pulled out her traveling desk, selecting a piece of paper and a pen. Though she doubted that Lord Kirkleith would want to hear from her after today, her heart could not abide the idea of disappearing without a word to him. She wanted to explain herself, the magic that ran through her veins, but knew such explanations could be dangerous in the wrong hands. Instead, she settled on short and direct. She told him that she'd enjoyed her time in Balmaclaren—with him—and that she was leaving. She did not say where they would go, for she did not know that herself; only that she would no longer be his concern.

At dinnertime Mrs. Murray brought a tray of food and asked if there was anything else she could do to make the night pass easier. Ione pushed the letter into the older woman's hand and asked that it be delivered to the castle first thing in the morning. She reassured the kindly older woman that all was well, and sat down to the tray of food to prove her words, though she didn't have the stomach to eat. But the charade was enough to convince her hostess, and Ione was left to her misery. Eventually she summoned the wherewithal to change into her nightrail and spent the rest of the evening staring up at the ceiling until she fell into a fitful sleep, long after the clock struck the midnight hour.

Geordie had no better luck with sleeping; instead he sat by his window, nursing a snifter of brandy, lost in thought.

From zenith to nadir in a single day, he mused. At the stables with Ione he'd never been happier, in spite of everything that had gone before; when she'd intimated that her feelings mirrored his own, Geordie'd felt elation on a scale he'd believed lost to him forever after the murder of his father. But this miracle of a woman had saved him once again—or perhaps it was his father's love, working through her. Did it really matter which, so long as both were made happy by it?

And then that disastrous picnic. Geordie shook his head and swallowed another tot of brandy. It had been a moment or two before he realized what Quinn was doing—literally shielding him and Ione from the would-be assassin, taking a near-fatal arrow for his troubles. Had any man ever had such a faithful friend as this?

Near-fatal was a misnomer, he knew. That arrow was meant to kill—would have killed, if not for Lady Tamsin's... Geordie hardly knew what to call it. Well—he did know, but his mind shied away from the word.

Magic.

Geordie shifted in his seat. His catechism had long taught that magic was a myth, tales spun by the uneducated—or unscrupulous—to foster fear and obedience. And yet—and yet. Geordie shook his head again. He could not deny the evidence of his own two eyes. That wound had been fatal; he'd known it, and so had Quinn. Then light had spilled forth from the lady's fingers, had imbued a common napkin with radiance... had kept Quinn alive, Geordie had no doubt. The same sort of light had burst from Ross' hands, though he'd tried to hide it, and then Quinn could breathe again, as though that bolt had not pierced his lung. Magic, indeed. And Geordie was deeply, fervently grateful.

But then Ione had spoken, reminding him that she was there too, and everything had gone wrong again.

He put the glass down with deliberation.

Quinn had nearly died saving not just him, but Ione as well. She could have been killed, and that was what his mind kept replaying. It could as easily have been Ione dying in his arms today: her blood soaking his coat, her eyes closing forever. Geordie knew, with terrifying certainty, that a part of him would have died with her.

He loved her. Loved Ione Brentwood as he had loved no other, as he would never love again. He wanted her to wife, to be the mother of his children; to wake beside him and spend her life with him, now and forevermore. But someone wanted him dead. If he spoke—if he dared—would he be putting her in danger?

The answer was blindingly clear. He could not speak, could never tell her—or could he? If his enemy, whoever it was, had already targeted her, was she not already in danger? And if so, could he not protect her better here, at the castle, as his future wife?

And that, Geordie my lad, is assuming rather a lot after today. Likely she and her cousin would be just as glad to shake the dust of Balmaclaren from their feet and never look back.

Except... was he really assuming so much?

"I hoped, Geordie." Even after everything that had happened, the memory of her sweet voice made him smile.

All right, then—there was still the other thing. Ione had magic too, of some unspecified sort. She'd said it ran in families, which meant her children would likely have it as well. Could he be father to such children—to forever be different from them? Or would his blood remove the gift from future generations—and did he have the right to do that to Ione's bloodline?

The idea doesn't seem to bother her much. He acknowledged the truth of that. She'd said she hoped... and so whether he'd take magic from her children, or father a magical dynasty of some kind, Ione was at peace with it. Perhaps he ought to take his cue from her, since it was a circumstance with which he had no experience whatsoever.

He got up from his chair and stretched as the clock in the hall struck two. He needed to talk with Asher and Quinn, find out their thoughts about the potential dangers now; and there were so many questions he needed to ask Ione—one very important one in particular.

Having decided so much, Geordie yawned as he stripped off his shirt and kilt before climbing into bed. He would sleep a little, and have his answers in the morning.

Despite his midnight musings, Geordie was up at the usual time. He dressed and hurried down to the breakfast table intent on having that discussion with Asher and Quinn, and then he would speak to Ione.

His friends were already settled into breakfast. The mood was subdued, though Asher and Quinn were chatting quietly. Ross was seated a few chairs down from the other two, nudging his scrambled eggs around his plate, unusually quiet, as if trying to go unnoticed.

Quinn looked up when Geordie walked in. "How are you feeling about yesterday?" Whether the question was a professional or personal inquiry, Geordie was unsure.

"I could ask you much the same," he replied easily. "No ill effects?"

Quinn shook his head solemnly. "Miraculously, no. I seem to be good as new." He rolled his shoulders a little tentatively, proving the statement to the room, and perhaps himself.

"I'm relieved to hear it." Geordie filled a plate from the sideboard and took a seat next to Ross, who offered him a slight nod, but seemed to be avoiding eye contact. "For myself, yesterday clarified some things for me, and I've come to a decision. Mostly." He huffed out a laugh at himself. "There are some things I need to know first, though."

Ross glanced up from his uneaten breakfast. "What sort of things do you need to know?" And now he was studying Geordie very carefully indeed.

Geordie turned to the two Queen's agents. "How safe are we, here at the castle?"

Asher answered that one. "As a babe in its mother's arms—as long as she's got a decent grip, anyway. Every attempt on you has been made outside of the castle grounds; Quinn and I walked the perimeter of the grounds again this morning, and the staff is on alert. The walls are solid, every gate is locked. If someone wants to get to you here, they'll have to get past layers of security. Why?"

Geordie considered them. "Would someone be safer here than in town?"

Quinn took a quick sip of coffee, setting the cup back on the table before answering. "They'd certainly be easier to keep an eye on, and the grounds are far more secure than anywhere in Balmaclaren."

The viscount nodded and shoved a piece of toast in his mouth. "That clears everything up nicely, thank you. Or—" He glanced at Ross. "Nearly everything." Geordie waited until his friend was looking at him. "I'm not wrong about what I saw, am I? You have magic too—and that's why you're so pulled this morning?"

Ross' shoulders visibly relaxed before he nodded. "I do. I can heal wounds. It's part of the reason I became a doctor." He glanced at Asher. "Let me see that hand of yours."

Asher held out the bandaged limb obligingly.

Ross pushed his plate aside and carefully unwrapped the hand. Holding Asher's hand, he lifted his free hand over the nasty looking puncture. His fingers lit up with a pale green light, and Geordie watched as the wound shrank and the skin knit back together. When Ross finished, there was not so much as a mark left on Asher's skin.

Asher let out a sigh of relief, twisting his wrist and flexing his fingers. "Thank you. I'd no desire to carry that stigmata any longer than I had to."

"I would have done it last night, but between Geordie's reaction to the ladies' display, and half draining my life-force to pull Quinn from the brink I—I..." Ross stopped and offered Asher an apologetic look.

Galvanized, Quinn pushed out of his chair and reached for Ross' shoulder, turning his friend to look at him. "What did you say?"

"It isn't as bad as it sounds," Ross replied, slowly rising from his chair, hands out in a placating gesture. "Our magic doesn't come from nothing. I have to take from myself to heal others, but I know my limits, Quinn. I wasn't about to sit back and let you die when I could prevent it."

Quinn stared at him for a long moment, then silently pulled his friend in for a hug. "Thank you," he murmured.

The Irishman looked rather taken aback by the gesture for he was slow to respond. After a second of hesitation, Ross relaxed and returned the embrace with a couple affectionate thumps to Quinn's back. "I'd do it again in a heartbeat."

Asher smiled at Ross. "Probably makes things a bit less complicated, now we all know," he observed mildly.

Ross laughed a little. "You have no idea. Wasn't that difficult when we were younger, didn't have access to it. Things got a bit trickier when I turned seventeen and came into my own. Frankly, I'm surprised none of you figured it out before now." He looked at them in turn, settling on Geordie. "You got shot in the shoulder and it was better a day later—that didn't tip you off?"

The Scotsman shrugged. "I was a bit distracted, you know. Surprises me that the rest of you lads didn't twig, though." For answer, Asher held out his hand to Quinn, his fingers beckoning; Quinn muttered an epithet and pulled out his wallet, handing Asher a note. The Englishman glanced at Ross and grinned. Geordie threw back his head and laughed.

Still grinning, Asher put the bank note in his wallet. "You said you'd made a decision," he said, attention shifting back to Geordie. "Are you going to say what it is?"

Geordie shrugged, smiling. "To ask Ione Brentwood t'be my wife. I thought I'd go to town after breakfast." The other three exchanged portentous glances. "What?" Geordie asked.

It was Quinn who spoke up. "A note came for you this morning. From Miss Brentwood." He put a hand on Geordie's shoulder. "I think they've gone."

"WHAT?" Geordie leapt from his seat as though hit by lightning. "Where's this note?"

"I'll go tell the grooms to saddle the horses," Asher said, and ran from the room.

Quinn picked up a folded paper from the sideboard and handed it to the viscount, who scanned it and cursed aloud. "No—NO! I've got to—I need to—" He looked around wildly.

"We're with you, Geordie," Quinn told him, and the three men strode to the stables.

Chapter Twelve

A Hasty Departure

Ione felt hollowed out when she woke. Her dreams had been plagued with nightmare images of angry mobs bearing torches and pitchforks, or Geordie staring at her with anger and contempt, and the terrifying vision of the two men fighting in the field with hatred radiating from them.

She was so tired and downtrodden that she barely spoke as Rose helped her dress and pin up her hair; when at last the maid finished, dropping a curtsey before seeking her own meal, the solitude was a relief. Ione examined herself in the mirror sadly; she looked like the perfect lady, but inside she felt broken beyond repair.

A soft knock on her door heralded a visit from her cousin. Tamsin had clearly been up longer—her clothes and hair were immaculate. The only glaring change was that the smile that usually played about her lips was entirely gone, and her gaze was serious when

Ione ushered her into the room. "I've called for my
coach," Tamsin began, "and I've sent telegrams ahead
to tell my uncle and Tav of our change in plans." She
perched on the edge of the bed. "I think," she went on
slowly, "that we ought to consider a trip to the
Continent."

A mirthless laugh slipped from Ione's lips as she
sat down beside her cousin. "I imagine my father will
agree entirely. When he learns that I disobeyed him to
come here, and then revealed the family magic, I doubt
he'll ever forgive me." She turned away from Tamsin to
stare out the window. "It seems I shall never stop
finding trouble for myself."

"I wish you had not thrown your lot in with
mine," Tamsin replied sadly. "I understand why you
did, but in thinking about it, if Dr. McInerny has not
yet revealed himself after so many years, there must
have been a reason—and we ought not be surprised at
Lord Kirkleith's reaction." She rubbed at her forehead.
"Although for Mr. Rutherford to have been so open
about it... he must have thought it would be all right."
Tamsin sighed. "How very disappointing." She rose to
her feet. "If we are to be unmasked, it would be best to
depart before that should occur. And I do not anticipate
that it will be for long—I have left a letter for his
Lordship; all he need do is touch it and he will forget
all about us both."

Ione closed her eyes, hand lifting to rest at her
heart, as if she could somehow ease the ache there. It
would be best for Geordie to forget her entirely; yet the
idea that she would cease to exist in his mind caused
the few unbroken pieces of her heart to shatter. She
wanted to cry, but couldn't bring herself to do it, for
fear that the tears would wash away the happy
memories of her time here, and leave nothing but the
terrible events of her final afternoon with Geordie. She

took a deep breath and cleared her throat in the hope that her voice wouldn't crack. "That is probably for the best."

"My poor darling." Her cousin's arms slipped around Ione, holding her close. "You truly love him. I am so dreadfully sorry that it should have turned out this way. Nothing is worse than having to let love go before having fairly tasted it."

Ione blinked back tears. "I love the man I thought he was." She paused, throat burning from the effort of holding her voice steady. She cleared it again and hoped that the practicality of her next statement would ease some of the pain. "But if Lord Kirkleith cannot accept me as I am, I love a fantasy. It is better to know that now than to learn it later."

Tamsin kissed her cheek. "Then we had best break our fast and be on our way." She pushed off the bed and held a hand out for Ione.

"I hardly have the stomach for it, but I shall do myself no favor by growing faint for want of food." She took the hand Tamsin offered, and allowed her cousin to lead the way to the common room. At least the noise of the other guests might provide a distraction from her current woes.

Mr. Murray met them at the bottom of the stairs, an unusual encounter when there was a room full of hungry guests to attend to. "If you please, ladies, there is someone in the private parlor for you."

Ione exchanged a worried look with her cousin, but there was little they could do but follow behind the innkeeper and hope for the best. Her mind was a flurry of thoughts and emotions. Perhaps Geordie had come to terms with her abilities—or perhaps he had come to demand they leave his lands immediately. Ione's fingers nervously knotted into the side of her skirt as Murray opened the door. Ione thought she had prepared herself for any possibility, but when the innkeeper stepped aside, she realized just how unprepared she was.

Mr. Murray gave the room a quick nod, and hurried back to attend the needs of his other guests.

Their visitor stretched out both hands. "My dear Ione, I've found you at last!"

Ione stared open-mouthed in utter shock; the air seemed to have been knocked from her body. Of all the faces she'd expected to see, Theodore Gibson's was the last. She stood rooted in place, mind seemingly stalled out by the attempt to reconcile the evidence of her eyes.

Theodore came forward. "I know we parted on terms that were not what I would have liked, but I forgive you, my darling, and I've come to take you home." He eyed Tamsin as she stepped to Ione's side. "Preferably without those influences that urge you to part from your true self."

"Theodore..." Ione wasn't sure how to respond to seeing him here. There was an odd measure of relief in seeing a familiar face, though after the way they had parted company, she was surprised that he had come so far to find her.

Yet she had been of sound mind when she called off their engagement. Her reasons for doing so had not changed, though it seemed wrong to offer an impolite greeting. "It's... good to see you," she added belatedly. The word *good* wasn't quite right, but the polite response was automatic, and in truth, she couldn't think of any other way to respond.

He smiled. "And you, my love. And," he gestured around himself, "in Scotland, no less! We can marry immediately—upon the moment—and begin our lives together, as we planned. I understand your nervousness entirely—to a delicate female, the idea of marriage must be a daunting one indeed, especially one who has been sheltered as you have. But I swear to you, I will care for you, for the rest of our lives. Only give me this chance to show you my love." He wrapped an arm around her shoulder, as if trying to soothe her through a swoon.

Astonished and repulsed by the prospect of becoming Mrs. Gibson, Ione shook his arm away, and took a step back, physically distancing herself from the man. "Mr. Gibson, I appreciate that you have come all this way to find me, but I fear you have done so under mistaken expectations. Should we not speak in private before you begin planning a wedding?"

Undeterred by her response, he took Ione's hand, lifting it to his mouth. "I fail to see why we need discuss anything. You made a mistake and I have forgiven you. There is a chapel down the lane; I have spoken to the vicar already. Maidenly reluctance is to be admired, Ione, but the time for it is past."

Any relief Ione might have felt vanished in an instant. "I did not call off our engagement out of 'maidenly reluctance'. The only regret I have is that I ever accepted your proposal in the first place." Ione jerked her hand away more forcefully. His arrogant demeanor replaced any patience she might have shown with outrage. She was too raw to worry about Theodore Gibson's feelings, especially when he so obviously thought her feelings of little importance. "I do not love you. You may speak to a thousand vicars but my mind will not be changed. I will not marry you, in Scotland nor anywhere else, for that matter."

He sent Tamsin another of those darkling looks. "You loved me well enough until you spoke to a certain party at our rehearsal; it cannot be a coincidence that that same party is in attendance now." Tamsin folded her arms and raised a brow. Theodore returned his gaze to Ione's face. "I suggest you reconsider, my dear. Marriage to me carries so many benefits; foregoing your promise might carry the opposite. Have you realized that?"

"What are you implying?" Now furious, Ione had to work to keep her voice level. Her fingers curled into fists, her teeth ground together.

He shrugged. "I merely wish to make clear to you that you are unlikely to have an offer as good again. You wish for scandal no more than I; but you have so much more to lose." He shook his head and tried again. "I did not make my offer lightly, Ione. I deserve better than to see it dismissed so lightly in return."

Ione bit out her response through a clenched jaw. "I am not so ruined a woman that I would stoop to marry the likes of you!" She was shaking with anger. Her fingers tingled with the urge to slap that condescending smirk right off Theodore's face. "Are you so desperate that you would resort to threats in order to win a wife? You have shown your true nature, Mr. Gibson, and only strengthened my resolve to cast you from my life entirely."

His expression became thunderous, and he took a step toward Ione, leaning forward ominously. "I do not easily give up what is mine, Ione. Reconsider." Mustache bristling, he practically pushed the ladies out of the way and left the room in a flurry of greatcoat.

Ione let out a breath as the door slammed shut behind him. She paced a few laps around the parlor and then lowered herself onto the very settee where Geordie had rested when he was injured. "How I ever convinced myself to accept that man's attentions, I truly cannot recall. I have never been so certain of my course, nor as determined to stick to it." She closed her eyes and rubbed at her temple. She'd thought that Theodore Gibson was a mistake left in London, but here he was, proving that she'd only gone from one problem to the next. Ione opened her eyes and looked at her cousin. "Tamsin, what if he wasn't making empty threats? What if he does something that not only harms my reputation but my family's as well?"

"You cannot be considering acquiescing to his blackmail?" Tamsin shook her head. "He won't expose you, if that's what you mean, for it would mean exposing himself, and censure from our people. Not just censure—he would find himself shunned."

"Of course I will not give in! I would have to have taken complete leave of my senses to consider such a thing," Ione declared vehemently. "But what if he means to cause trouble in some other way? Perhaps I can speak to him, convince him to return to London, put matters off until I can warn my father of this threat."

"I frankly think that is a terrible idea," Tamsin said without hesitation. "This is not England; banns are not required. Nor, in some underhand cases, is the woman's consent. You may find yourself wed without even realizing it." Tamsin paced the room a little too, clearly thinking through this new dilemma "No, I think you must keep your distance from him. It is a good thing we plan to leave today."

"You're right, of course. I made my decision back in London and I shall not risk finding myself wed to that—that weasel parading in a greatcoat. He is more akin to vermin than a man." She got to her feet with a sense of determination unlike anything she had experienced before. She was done allowing the whims of others, or fate, determine her course. She would not have Theodore Gibson, and if Lord Kirkleith could not accept her as she was, then she would not have him either. "There is simply nothing for it, we must leave immediately. I have no desire to see that man again."

"Then come—let us eat that breakfast so far denied us, and we shall leave as soon as may be." Tamsin hooked her arm into the crook of Ione's elbow and ushered them out of the parlor and straight to the breakfast table, head held high, and a look of determination in her eyes. Ione had never been more thankful to have her cousin at her side as she was now.

Though she still felt too aggravated for food to be of much appeal, Ione made a valiant show of eating everything that was presented to her. The meal was a quiet and somewhat hasty one, but it did help Ione clear her mind enough to focus on the task of packing when she returned to her room. With only one maid between them, and time of the essence, Ione was willing to handle the work herself–though it most certainly was not the most orderly affair. Still, she managed well enough, and was waiting by Tamsin's coach a short time later as the luggage was loaded. Mrs. Murray was kind enough to pack them a luncheon so that they need not pause on their journey, and an hour after breakfast they were on their way.

The mood in the carriage was a somber one. "I wish I could have offered Lord Kirkleith a proper farewell." Ione looked out the window as the coach crossed the bridge at the edge of town and started down the road. Their arrival in Balmaclaren had been one of such hope and promise, but their departure could not have been more dismal. "I hate that things have ended so poorly between the two of us."

Rose spoke up hesitantly, her gaze fixed on something outside the window. "Miss?" She pointed down the road. "Someone's followin' us."

Galvanized, Tamsin rolled up the isinglass and poked her head out. She withdrew it a second later and plumped back into her seat across from Ione.

"Dearest," she said to Ione, "I think you may have your chance."

Ione sat up straighter, feeling hope sputter back to life as she poked her head out the window to see for herself. Four riders were pounding furiously toward the carriage, one waving a makeshift flag.

"Ho, the carriage! Stop! Stop!" they cried.

Ione leaned back in her seat, trying not to get ahead of herself, and failing miserably. "It's Geordie! He's come."

Tamsin all but clapped her hands. "Smart man," she said, "I hope. As for you," she turned to her cousin, "do not be too eager, mm? Wait until you hear what he has to say."

"I will, you have my word on it," Ione replied with as much dignity as she could muster with cheeks the color of ripe apples. She hoped Geordie's arrival was an indication that he could accept what she was, but she fully intended to move with caution; her heart could not take another disappointment. These past weeks had taught her a great deal about the cost of making decisions that went against her intuition. Indeed, she felt like a new person, one who was no longer afraid to decide her own fate. She lifted her chin confidently and composed herself, straightening her hair and dress as the sound of galloping hooves drew nearer.

The carriage hove to a stop; scant moments later, booted footsteps on the gravel heralded the approach of one of the riders, and the Maclaren himself threw open the door, his expression as stormy as his grey eyes. "A word, Miss Brentwood, if you please."

"As you like." Ione managed to sound calm and composed, though she wasn't sure how when her heart was pounding so wildly. Thankfully, her skirts and petticoat hid how her knees shook, and helped her to maintain the outward illusion of control.

He handed her out of the carriage and started to walk beside the lane, her hand tucked into his elbow. McInerny, Burton and Rutherford made as if to follow, but they fell back at Geordie's lowering expression.

"Of what do you wish to speak?" Ione asked cautiously as they moved away from the others. The expression on his face was inscrutable, and she dared not venture a guess as to his intentions, for if she was wrong it would be too much to endure after everything else. But waiting for him to answer was too much, and she needed to fill the space between them with words. "I did not expect to see you again, after our parting yesterday."

Geordie slanted her a glance. "I cannot fathom why you would think so. I had thought us friends, and yet here you are, leaving Balmaclaren with only a polite letter between us."

"I thought us friends as well, but your mood at the end of our last meeting did not give me the impression that friendship would continue. You didn't even bid me farewell." Ione answered bluntly, looking into the distance as she struggled to keep her emotions under control. The attack yesterday, and then the meeting with Mr. Gibson this morning, had left her feeling bruised and battered; yet she could not bring herself to resent the man beside her. Perhaps she was a fool after all, for one thing was certain, even now: she loved him, deeply. "As to my sudden departure, there have been other complications that make remaining in Balmaclaren untenable."

"I owe you an apology for that, I know." He pulled her into a small copse of trees, out of sight of the others. Geordie moved to stand before Ione, and took both her hands in his, his expression contrite.

"Yesterday I—" He sighed. "I could not speak to you because I didn't know what to say. You had so nearly lost your life while in my keeping; Quinn would have died, had your cousin not intervened. The revelation of her... skills, and yours... that such skills are hereditary, when my fondest dreams of late—" He broke off, taking a deep breath. "All this is to say that I humbly beg your forgiveness, for ever giving you any reason to think that I value our friendship less today than I did yesterday morning."

"My magic is part of who I am. I can no more change that than the color of my eyes," Ione replied slowly. She needed to be absolutely clear on this point. There could be no future for them otherwise. "It's in my blood, literally. Geordie, Tamsin and I are what my folk call Fae-touched."

"Fae-touched?" Geordie's brows were drawn down in confusion, but he didn't release Ione's hands, nor did his expression show any hint of fear or revulsion. "Do y'mean to say you're one of the Fair Folk?"

"Not entirely." Ione inhaled slowly and considered her next words with great care. "My people, the Fae-touched, are the result of dalliances between the Fae and the mortals. We live and die as mortals, but possess some of the magical abilities of the Fae."

Geordie studied her in silence for what felt like an eternity, then he shook his head. "It matters not t'me how or why you have these gifts. They're a part of you, Ione, and there is nothing of you that I willna' treasure."

A surge of happiness warmed her, but caution still warned against haste. Ione weighed his words before responding and granting the answer he sought. "If you can truly accept who and what I am, then you have my forgiveness." She looked down at her hands, warm and safe, enfolded in his strong grip. But there was still the matter of Theodore Gibson and his threats. Granting Geordie forgiveness did not remove the shadow of her past from the present. "Yet I fear it does little to address the other reason I have to flee."

He lifted her fingers to his lips. "Your forgiveness is more than I deserve; and more, I swear, than I will ever ask you to forgive again. But surely," Geordie released one of her hands and tipped her chin up to face him, "surely there is nothing so fearful we cannot surmount it together?"

The tenderness in his voice nearly stole Ione's breath. For a few precious seconds she all but forgot about her broken engagement and the threats of scandal. She felt comfortable and at peace in a way she couldn't remember experiencing before, and would have been quite happy never to leave the little copse of trees again. But the reality of her situation had to be faced; if one thing was certain, it was that Theodore Gibson was not going to quietly disappear. "The gentlemen I was to marry arrived at the inn this morning." Remembering her meeting with Theodore caused her hands to tremble with fury, and perhaps a little fear. "Geordie, he is threatening to cause a scandal if I do not wed him immediately. He has even gone so far as to make arrangements with the local vicar. If I remain in Balmaclaren he will surely force the matter."

Geordie's mouth drew downward in an awful frown. "The devil he will!" He slipped his arm around her shoulders and drew her close to still her trembling. "Who is this dog? I will trounce him within an inch of his life, for threatening you!"

"His name is Theodore Gibson. And he is the greatest mistake I was ever fool enough to make." Ione settled against him, reveling in the sense of freedom the safety his arms created. "But you already have so much to concern you, I do not wish to add to your burdens."

"There is nothing so important to me at this moment than what is right here, right now." He let out a breath. "It is too soon, I know; and after yesterday's events, I have no right to hope that you could ever consider..."

Ione tilted her head back and looked up slowly, meeting his gaze for the second time. Sensibility urged caution, but the tone of his voice held such sweet promise. "Consider what, Geordie?"

He stroked the backs of his fingers down the side of her face, his gaze very tender indeed. "Do you think, someday, you could ever... love me? For I fear, Ione, that you fill my whole heart, and I... I love you, dearly."

Ione felt her heart swelling with such elation, such warmth and tenderness, that it nearly stole her breath. Tamsin had cautioned against haste, but it all felt so natural, as if she'd always been meant to come to this place, and find this man. Ione's lips curved in a confident, yet intimate smile. "I know I could, for I already do."

It was like watching the sun break through clouds over the sea, seeing the smile bloom across Geordie's face. "Do you now?" His voice was low, a little husky, and it sent a shiver down Ione's spine. "Enough that you might allow me to... kiss you?"

"You would not think me too eager?" Ione answered, knowing she should deny him such a bold request. Even so, she could hardly breathe at the beauty of his face, the sincerity in his eyes. It took every ounce of self-control she possessed to keep from kissing him herself.

He chuckled. "Considering that the next thing I was about to ask was for your hand in marriage, I can hardly criticize." Geordie turned her hand over and pressed a fervent kiss to her palm. "Will you, my darling?"

Ione's eyes widened in surprise. What would Papa think? What would her mother say? What sort of madwoman would break one engagement only to jump into another less than a fortnight later?

But these concerns were fleeting. For the first time in her life Ione knew, without doubt or reservation, exactly what she wanted—*who* she wanted. There was only one answer she could give, and she gave it without a shadow of regret or hesitation. "I will marry you, George Maclaren. Yes, now and always, yes."

His expression was both exultant and exalted. "Bless you, my love," he murmured. He cupped her jaw, tilted her head toward him, and slowly lowered his mouth to hers, giving her plenty of opportunity to back away.

Ione melted into him with the softest of sighs. She'd never kissed anyone before—certainly not Theodore—but embracing Geordie was as natural and wonderful as anything Ione had ever experienced to this point. It woke something inside her, a need and a yearning that overpowered all the rules of etiquette and polite society. The heat of his lips against hers made her knees feel weak, but it hardly mattered, for the ground had turned to clouds beneath her feet.

After a long while he lifted his head, his breathing shaky. "My own love," Geordie whispered. He huffed out a small laugh. "I've no clear idea how we came here, you and I; but I was lost the first time I saw you, I think."

"I was yours from the moment you nearly tripped in surprise at the second inn." Ione laughed softly. Now that she said it, she knew it was true, though it seemed now that her heart had always been in his keeping. "I love you, Geordie. I cannot imagine my life leading me anywhere but to you."

He lifted her hands and kissed them both again. "I will spend my life loving you, Ione. Worshiping you. My own blessing, you are." His grey eyes filled with tears. "'Tis my belief you were sent t'me by the shade of my father, loving me even beyond death."

"Oh, Geordie." Ione cupped his jaw, gently stroking his cheek with her thumb. "Then I shall spend the rest of my days trying to be worthy of the gift he's given us."

Geordie stole another kiss. "I would gladly go to the chapel right now and make you mine in truth; but there are forms to be observed, I suppose. You should contact your family. Tell them, please, that they are welcome to our hospitality during our wedding celebration, which will be whenever you deem it. For now, let you and I pay a visit to Auld Gregor's shop in the village—he often supplied my father with jewelry for my mother. He's bound to have something you can wear for now, at least until we can go to Edinburgh and choose something finer. You will wear my ring, at the least. And then I believe I shall have a chat with Mr. Gibson."

"I don't need fine jewels, I only need you," Ione tucked her arm in his and took a step back in the direction of the carriage. "Shall we share our news with my cousin and your friends? Assuming they won't guess when they see our faces: you, sir, are nearly glowing."

Geordie laughed. "How should I not, when Heaven itself is within my grasp? Here, so that I shan't expire from longing—" He kissed her again, much more lingeringly this time. "There, I feel fortified." They stepped out of the trees and back onto the road, and

Ione was certain that her own joy was as obvious as her new fiancé's.

The other four were making conversation by the waiting carriage: Rose was peering out the window of the coach, fingers pressed to the isinglass. Ione addressed her cousin. "Tamsin, there has been a definitive change in plans. We will be staying in Balmaclaren for a time." She turned back to her betrothed, reveling in the mere sight of him and the knowledge that he saw her not as an oracle, but as the person she truly was. He was hers, and she was his completely. "Do you wish to tell them, or shall I?"

Tamsin looked from one to the other, a smile creeping across her face. "Ione, Ione, will you never be done surprising me?"

Ione smiled impishly. "I certainly hope not! Life would be terribly dull without surprises. Do you not agree, Geordie?"

He kissed her hand. "Indeed I do... my love."

"Well, I'll be damned," expostulated Rutherford, snapping his riding gloves against the palm of his hand. "You did it!"

Geordie laughed. "You may wish us happy."

"And so we do," Ross replied quickly, clapping Geordie on the shoulder with a grin that spread from one ear to the other. "Could not be happier for you, Geordie!"

Asher echoed the others, shaking his friend's hand and thumping him on the back. "Oh, well done, you rascal!"

From inside the coach came the sound of a happy squeal as Rose disappeared behind the curtain briefly and then reappeared, smiling broadly. Chuckling, Tamsin embraced her cousin, then pulled away shaking her head ruefully. "Well, I suppose it was to come out no other way," she murmured.

"I think you knew before I did." Ione laughed, pulling her cousin into another hug. "You will help me with the arrangements, of course?"

"Of course, my dearest—did you doubt it?"

Geordie waited a beat and then presented himself to Tamsin, who looked up at him rather doubtfully. He removed his hat, turning it in his hands. "I hope you can forgive my lapse in manners yesterday, cousin. You have been extraordinarily brave and exceedingly kind, and I pray you will believe that you always have a friend in me."

There was a pause, and just when Ione was beginning to worry, Tamsin grinned up at him. "Thank you, cousin."

"We had best be on our way," Ione said, joy welling up inside of her with such brilliance that she was sure she must be glowing. "I need to write to my family as soon as possible. It's all so new that I fear it will not feel real until they are here to share in our joy."

"Oh!" Tamsin cried all at once, jumping a bit as though startled. Without a word of explanation, she picked up her skirts and hurried back toward the inn, one hand holding her hat in place as she ran.

"Tamsin?" Ione called after her, frowning a little until she realized what her cousin was about: the enchanted letter. She glanced at Geordie, and then her gaze slid to the other three men and the horses waiting nearby. Tamsin would need a few minutes to dispose of the letter—and heaven knew Ione wanted to be sure it was gone. A small diversion seemed to be in order. "Perhaps we could walk back to the inn?" she suggested, offering Geordie a sweet smile. "Rose, would you ride back with the coach so our things are not unattended?" The maid gave an emphatic nod.

"Aye, lads—we'll be here in town for just a little longer," Geordie chimed in, and after a moment's confabulation, Ross and Quinn led the horses toward the stables, while Asher explained the situation to the coachman and then accompanied Geordie and Ione back in the direction Tamsin had bolted. Ione would have preferred a few sweet minutes of solitude with Geordie, but she did not let it trouble her overmuch. They had their whole lives to spend together, and the prospect of that erased any small disappointments in the present.

Chapter Thirteen

A Bit of a Clearing Up

Given the choice, Geordie would have infinitely preferred to have these precious first minutes of his engagement alone with his intended, but with a would-be murderer on the loose, he understood why Asher was following them at a discreet distance. Even so, the walk back through town was one of the finest in Geordie's memory. Somehow, amid so much sorrow and uncertainty, he'd found his way to Ione Brentwood. 'Twas the work of his father's spirit indeed, guiding him to an angel when he needed her the most.

When they finally made it back to the inn they found a rather windblown Lady Tamsin standing by the fire in the common room, a piece of folded parchment crackling merrily atop the roaring blaze. "All sorted," she greeted them with a smile.

Geordie stopped in his tracks and looked from one cousin to the other in confusion. "What's sorted?" he asked Ione.

His future bride's cheeks turned a little pink. She leaned closer to him, her voice pitched for his ears alone. "We believed you might take action against us due to our unique talents. The letter was addressed to you. It would have removed all memory of us as soon as you touched it."

He blanched. "All memory of you?" The idea made Geordie queasy. His hand shifted to cover Ione's where it rested at the crook of his elbow. He looked to her cousin. "Surely—there is no chance of that now, is there?"

Lady Tamsin shook her head. "None whatever, I promise."

The sound of a door opening and closing again was followed by multiple footsteps. Geordie's gaze shifted to the door as the rest of their party joined them. "Here—shall we find somewhere private and have a bit of a clearing-up?"

"Of course, darling," Ione replied, she turned her hand under his and gave his fingers a reassuring squeeze. "It's entirely understandable and long overdue. You've had a great deal to come to terms with of late, and to be engaged on top of it all."

Her understanding and quiet reminder of the joy that awaited them, provided a measure of peace until they could speak without fear of being overheard. Geordie smiled down at Ione and then asked Mrs. Murray to give them a table in the private parlor. She was in transports at the romance of it all, delightedly serving them all tea and fresh biscuits, clearly thrilled by her august company.

When she finished fussing over the details of the table setting and was safely out of hearing, Lady Tamsin reached across the table to touch Geordie's arm. "What worries you?"

Geordie shook his head, feeling his stomach turning again. "I would have just touched the letter and Ione would be... gone, as though she'd never been. The idea is... upsetting. Could *anyone* do this?" Upsetting was putting it mildly, it was deeply disturbing to think that Ione could be taken from him so easily.

"Oh—no, not at all." Lady Tamsin's immediate denial soothed his disordered spirits a little. "This is my gift—to charm items, give them a—a hidden function, if you will. It's not common—though not as rare as Ione's gift."

He rubbed the back of his neck. "Forgive me—it will likely take some time for me to grow used to the idea. I confess myself somewhat in awe." Geordie turned to Ione. "Your gift is rare, Lady Tamsin says. What is it—may I know?"

"Of course. We're to build a life together—you must know of it sooner or later," Ione said, placing her napkin in her lap. It seemed an oddly casual gesture to Geordie, considering the topic of conversation, as if they were discussing something as commonplace as the weather. But then he was still adjusting to the entire concept of magic; it was simply a fact of life to her. "I can see into the future," Ione informed him, tone matter-of-fact. "It is not always clear, and there are limits to what I can do. I cannot see into my own. The visions can be overwhelming at times."

"Wait! Are you saying you're an oracle?" Ross cut in, clearly impressed. It was a reminder that magic had been in Geordie's life far longer than he realized.

Ione glanced at Ross, smiling a little. "I am, Dr. McInerny."

Ross leaned back in his chair, raising his eyebrows and giving a small, slow shake of the head. "I've never met one, nor imagined I would."

"Nor are you likely to again," Lady Tamsin contributed. "It's very rare, highly valued—and a circumstance that's likely at the bottom of our *other* trouble."

"Other trouble?" That was Quinn, frowning. "Sounds ominous."

Ione's cousin lifted her shoulders eloquently. "If you call the specter of forced marriage ominous, then certainly."

Geordie's temper frayed. "Not while I live—I'll not stand for it."

"I never should have entertained Mr. Gibson's courtship," Ione went on, huffing out a frustrated breath. "Even so, I wouldn't have guessed a so-called gentleman of his reputation capable of such wretched behavior." All at once Asher Burton clapped a hand to his forehead and excused himself, hurrying out of the inn without explanation.

Suffused with fury, Geordie forbore to comment on his friend's sudden departure. "What did Gibson say, please?" he asked Ione, careful to keep his tone even, his voice gentle. Through the window he caught sight of Asher legging it down the street.

"He told me that there would be repercussions for rejecting him, that I would have no hope of making a better match or indeed any match if I continued on my course. He accused Tamsin of turning me from him, and threatened to cause a scandal." Ione sat up straighter, lifting her chin defiantly. "He has shown his true colors, if he thinks me so weak-willed and desperate that I would agree to marriage under such circumstances." She paused, and her eyes clouded with worry as they shifted to Geordie. "You should know: he has magic as well."

"Has he, then? What can he do?" Not that it mattered. Geordie would see that Gibson was put in his place, far from Maclaren lands, and from Ione.

"He's an illusionist. That may not sound terribly dangerous, but I assure you, he is skilled at it." Ione replied, the small frown on her face deepening. "Such magic enables him to trick the mind and confound the senses."

Geordie nodded. "I'll be careful," he replied, his accent broadening in his anger. "But I willnae allow his words t'stand—not t'you, nor t'Lady Tamsin."

"A gentleman he is not," Ione's cousin agreed. "He merely looks the part. But a well-formed rind often covers the most noxious cheese," Lady Tamsin said, her expression so puckish that even Geordie had to laugh a bit.

"I'll speak to this noxious cheese," he replied, appropriating Ione's hand, "when once I've put a ring here."

"Do you wish to speak to your mother and sister first?" Ione's fingers laced through his, small and delicate by comparison.

"My mother and sister are very well aware, I expect. For now, I wish to see my ring upon your finger, and to clarify things for Mr. Gibson. Perhaps you and Lady Tamsin would be good enough to join us for dinner this evening, and we can tell them our plans then?" Geordie lifted her hand and kissed the finger in question. What he wanted to do was to remove the ladies to the castle entirely, but one thing at a time—and Gibson was definitely to be dealt with first.

"Of course." Ione shifted in her chair, expression troubled still. "I agree, I'd very much like to have this matter with Mr. Gibson resolved. When I think of how he spoke to me this morning, how he addressed Tamsin..." She broke off and her fingers tightened around Geordie's. "I know you're capable, love, but the reality of magic is new to you. I fear for your safety. I would feel better about this confrontation with him if I knew you were protected."

He nodded again. "Then we must find a way for me to be so."

Asher returned, a smile on his face. "Good news?" Quinn asked him.

"Excellent news," Asher returned. "Your hunch was correct, as usual."

Geordie scowled. "What are we talking about now?"

It was Quinn who replied. "When you told us about your intention to propose to Miss Brentwood," he smiled at Ione, "I thought we should have a look into the man she'd been engaged to, in case of just this sort of complication—we don't need more people trying to kill you. Ash made some inquiries this morning by telephone while the horses were being saddled, and it seems we have our replies."

"And?" Geordie was impatient. "If you know anything about Gibson—"

"More than we did," Asher allowed, with a glance at the two ladies, which Geordie interpreted to mean something unsavory had turned up. "Enough, I think, to convince him to leave you alone."

There was a brief lull in the conversation as Geordie considered his friends' statements. It was Ione herself who broke the silence. "This is an unorthodox suggestion, and I suspect you will not like it, but if I were to be present it would likely stay his hand," she ventured cautiously. "There are no formal rules for how we use our magic. The Fae keep something of a distant eye on things, but rarely intervene, and only in the most serious of cases."

Geordie ran his fingers through his wavy hair. "You're right, I don't like it. Is there no other way?"

Ross cleared his throat and lifted his hand, a soft glow illuminating the palm and fingers. "I can handle the likes of Mr. Gibson. There's no need for you to see the man again, Miss Brentwood."

"But your gift is one of healing." Ione turned to him, shaking her head. "I can see what he'll do before he tries it."

"Never you fear, I have a few tricks up my sleeve that should keep him in his place," Ross replied, the light from his hand brightened for an instant, shifting to a pale green. "And I can be quick with a counterspell if the occasion calls for it." He closed his fingers and the light vanished. "I won't allow any harm to come to Geordie, or anyone else."

"Then that's settled. But first, auld Gregor's shop," Geordie declared. "Not another hour is to go by without my ring on your finger, my lass."

Ione looked from one face to the next, obviously uneasy, but her expression softened when her gaze settled on Geordie. She smiled and pushed her teacup and saucer away. "Then shall we go now?"

"Indeed we shall." He stood, tucking her hand into the crook of his elbow, offered the other arm to Lady Tamsin, and off they went three abreast, the other three men laughing behind.

The shop was not far from the inn, and in mere minutes they were greeted by the tinkling of the bell above the door. Lady Tamsin and the boys took up positions on a bench outside, insisting that the day was far too fine to be spent indoors, and so the newly-engaged couple were granted a measure of privacy.

Auld Gregor's shop consisted of a single front room that was lined with shelves containing a carefully curated collection of antiquities and small marvels from across the globe. Geordie watched Ione peer into Auld Gregor's glass-fronted jewelry counter, a black velvet tray of rings before her. She seemed to be studying each ring, but if he wasn't mistaken, her glance returned more than once to a large opal, surrounded by sapphires. Despite the obvious interest, she indicated a far more modest ring. "Perhaps this one?"

He smiled down at her. "If it's truly your preference. But you're to be the Lady of Clan Maclaren. Our betrothal ring should reflect that." He nodded to the opal ring. "That one, perhaps?"

The sparkle in Ione's eyes was as brilliant as the jewel upon which they landed. "It is far grander than anything I've ever had before." She lifted it gingerly, admiring the ring as she moved it, setting the gem ablaze in a shimmering rainbow of color. "Are you sure, my dearest?"

"My coffers'll run to it. D'you like it, love?" The thought of putting that ring on her finger, to be followed by another, more sacred ring, lit him from within.

"I adore it!" Ione beamed up at him. "It's positively exquisite."

He nodded to Gregor, who discreetly turned his attention to the business of drawing up a receipt. Geordie gently took the ring from Ione and slipped it on her finger reverently. "It's yours. As am I," he whispered, and kissed her knuckle.

With the matter of that ring settled, and a wedding ring safely tucked away in Geordie's pocket, there was yet on more detail to be dealt with. Upon returning to the inn, Quinn and the ladies settled back into the private parlor while Geordie, Asher and Ross sought out Mr. Gibson. It was a simple enough matter—he'd apparently had the temerity to take rooms in the inn as well. *Damn the audacity of the man*, Geordie seethed as he thumped on his door.

When Gibson opened it, Asher and Ross flanked him, each taking an arm as they 'escorted' him backward into the room and planted him in a chair. Geordie kicked the door shut behind him.

"Look here, what is all this?" Gibson protested.

Geordie faced him, arms folded across his chest, feeling every inch of his authority. "You will leave my home and not return, sir."

The Englishman bared his teeth, beady eyes gleaming with indignation. "And who do you think you are, sir?"

"That," Asher calmly informed him, "is the Maclaren of Clan Maclaren. These lands and people are his."

"I fail to see what that has to do with anything. I am here visiting my fiancée, Ione Brentwood—this land and people may be yours, but she belongs to me." Gibson pushed himself out of the chair and adjusted his cuffs. He lifted his chin smugly, and Geordie itched to punch it.

Asher spoke up again. "You have a slippery memory, Mr. Gibson. We are given to understand by the lady herself that your betrothal was ended before Miss Brentwood came to Scotland."

"She is mistaken," was Gibson's cold reply. "Declaring a thing does not make it so, sir. Our betrothal stands." He cast a dismissive glance in Asher's direction

Geordie swallowed the litany of epithets that rose to his lips, instead taking a step closer to the other man. "*You* are mistaken, sir. I am the Maclaren of Clan Maclaren, and when I declare a thing it *is* so. Miss

Brentwood will become *my* wife, and you will return to England, if you are wise."

Gibson snarled, fingers twitching as they lit up; the air took on a strange charge...

Out of the corner of his eye, Geordie saw Ross raise his hand, light flaring from his palm and fingertips. "Geordie, look out—"

All at once Geordie's clothes flared with fire, his skin and hair alight, pain searing through every nerve. He roared aloud, staggering forward before going to one knee, struggling to breathe through the agonizing assault.

Through a haze of searing torment Geordie heard the click of a gun, followed by Asher's voice. "Undo whatever it is you've done to him, Gibson."

Ross placed a hand on Geordie's temple, frantically muttering unintelligible words. The flames subsided, and the burning agony was replaced by a cooling sensation.

Geordie swallowed, wiping the back of his hand across his mouth. "You bastard," he rasped to Gibson. "Ione's well rid of you." The other man made no reply, though his mouth was gaping, his face suffusing purply-red: Asher had his fist twisted into Theodore's collar, cutting off his air. "Stand down, Ash," Geordie muttered. "He's not worth it."

Asher let go—and as he did there was another sudden flare of light. This time Ross was ready for him: his own hands blazed brighter. There was a flash around Gibson's body and he shrieked as though in pain, falling heavily back into the chair. Ross leaned toward him, glowing fists clenched so tightly that they shook. "Don't. Move," he snarled, and his normally dark-brown irises gleamed, the color shifting to a vivid, verdant green. Geordie bridled in surprise, but was distracted by Gibson before he could form a response to the change.

"Bloody hell," Ione's former fiancé wheezed, tugging at his collar. "And this is the sort of person Ione believes she wishes to associate with? It's a good thing I've come for her, to take her from this barbaric place."

"You'll do no such thing," Geordie grated, jaw clenched. "Ione has consented to marry me, and that is what will happen. She has chosen me, Gibson. Not you."

Gibson's eyes narrowed to slits, and he curled his lip. "You know what she is, of course," he said to Geordie.

The looming Scotsman glowered. "Be very careful what you choose to say next, sir."

Gibson shrugged. "It is a matter of fact. She is a practicing witch. A trafficker with demons. How else is she to have such powers?"

Ross growled slightly, glaring at the other man. "You'd best watch what you say, Gibson. Ugly statements like that will see you in a world of misery." He jerked his hand toward the seated man menacingly. "Continue insulting our kind and I assure you, I'll do more than cast a counterspell to shut you up."

Asher spoke up. "Sir, I suggest you leave this place without further ado, and see to your affairs in London. A broken engagement is the least of your concerns, I think."

Gibson rounded on him. "Do you threaten me, sirrah?"

The other man grinned. "Not threaten, but inform, and with pleasure." Ash pushed up his glasses. "I received the most illuminating information just about a half-hour ago." He pulled a piece of paper from his pocket and unfolded it. "Theodore Gibson," he read, "owes a sum of £10,000 to a Mrs. Zouch, of

Clerkenwell—ah, I see you know the name," he went on as Gibson blanched. "A hefty sum, that—and to a well-known Abbess, as well." He leaned in, flicking the paper. "I have more, old chap. The tip of the iceberg, really—and I've had it all forwarded to a friend at the Times for an exclusive to run in Saturday's society column. You're an unsavory lad, and all of London will know it. If I were you," his voice was soft, "I'd be spending my time before then booking passage to India before my creditors came calling."

Theodore looked slightly ill. "You wouldn't."

Asher smiled. "I already have," he replied silkily.

"You're beaten, arsehole. I suggest you leave now," Ross snapped, Irish accent thick.

Gibson rallied, sneering. "You can't do this to me. I have friends in Parliament. I will—"

Geordie leaned down, inches from Gibson's face. "You will leave Scotland, now," he gritted, "and never speak to or of Miss Brentwood again, unless you'd like to become accustomed to passin' yer own teeth with yer shite."

Gibson jumped out of the chair and scrambled around Geordie. "Barbarian," he pronounced, his voice a little shaky. "Very well. I shall go." He turned upon his heel and stalked from the room.

The door shut behind Theodore Gibson with an unimpressive click. Geordie looked at Asher, then caught sight of Ross. The usually calm doctor hadn't moved from his place beside the chair Mr. Gibson had so recently occupied. His shoulders were rigid, his breathing ragged, and there was a wild glint in his now-green eyes.

"Ross?" Geordie's throat was still rough from his ordeal. "All right, there?" He looked at the other man questioningly.

Asher shook his head. "Give him a minute."

Ross didn't answer beyond an abrupt nod. He squeezed his eyes tightly shut, and his breathing seemed to gain a measure of purpose.

Asher laid a gentle hand on his friend's shoulder. "All serene?"

Ross exhaled slowly and opened his eyes, once again brown and tame—if that was the right word—but troubled, Geordie thought. He nodded again. "Aye, I'm not accustomed to using my magic like that." He looked at Geordie and offered a small smile. "It's... Different feel to it, is all."

"I'm grateful to you, Ross," Geordie replied. "That was..." He shuddered. "I thought he'd burn me alive, though I know Ione told me 'twas illusion. Felt real enough."

"I'm only glad it didn't cause the damage real fire would, though the suffering inflicted is bad enough," Ross replied. "Hopefully, that is the last you or Ione ever need see of him."

"We'll make sure of it," Asher interjected, cracking his knuckles.

Geordie nodded. "Just t'be sure," he said, "I'd like Miss Brentwood and Lady Tamsin to remove to the castle. You said it would be safer, correct?"

"So I did," Asher agreed. He paused thoughtfully. "And perhaps it's time to tell her what's going on. She'll be safer if she knows what sort of danger there is."

"Then let's go find them and see if they are willing. The remove should be no trouble, as their coach is already packed," the laird went on. "I confess I'll be relieved when we're all safely home."

Chapter Fourteen

Cake or Death?

Ione nearly paced a rut in the floor of the parlor waiting for Geordie to return from confronting Theodore. She trusted the ability of Geordie's friends, but the wait was difficult to endure regardless. When he finally returned, she threw her arms around him and kissed his cheek, heedless of the others in the room. He laughed and hugged her tightly, assuring her that Theodore Gibson would never trouble her again. He followed that by making the declaration that they would all be returning to Castle Maclaren, where Ione and Tamsin would stay until their safety could be assured.

Less than an hour later the women, their maid, and their belongings were on their way, though the mood of this departure was far brighter than their hasty morning escape. Much to Ione's delight, Geordie tied his horse to the back of the carriage and joined them inside. She spent the entirety of the ride to the castle nestled at his side, admiring the new ring on her finger, and the man who'd given it to her. They passed the time with happy chatter about wedding plans and the festivities of the upcoming ceremonies, and before they knew it, they were pulling to a halt in the courtyard.

Lady Kirkleith herself met them, her daughter at her side. Geordie swung down from the coach and hugged his mother before handing Ione out. She greeted Ione with both hands, kissing each cheek. "I take it, since you are here, that Geordie was successful? Oh, my dears, such happy news! I knew at once you were the one for my Geordie." She took Ione's arm confidingly. "The way he looked at you that fateful evening—I have never seen him so transported. Bless you, my dear. You have made us all very happy."

"I assure you, the happiness is all mine." Ione offered her future mother-in-law a dutiful kiss on the cheek, before holding a hand out to Lady Ailsa. "And I am delighted to be able to call you sister."

"As am I, my dear. I have never seen my brother so happy. Bless you," the younger girl replied, taking Ione's hand and moving closer to give her a gentle hug.

They walked arm-in-arm up the steps of the castle, with Geordie dutifully escorting his mother a few paces ahead. Behind them Asher helped Tamsin and then Rose from the carriage, the latter's face turning beet-red from this unwonted attention.

The doors swung open as soon as Geordie and his mother set foot on the final step. "We've had rooms prepared for you all," the dowager went on as they entered the great hall. "I firmly believe in being as optimistic as possible." She laughed. "Ailsa, my love, will you show your new sister and cousin to their rooms?" Ailsa nodded emphatically, and began pulling Ione toward the grand staircase.

The chambers to which Ailsa led them were far grander than anywhere Ione had ever stayed before. Even Mama's rooms—which Ione had always thought were extraordinarily elegant—paled in comparison. She had her own sitting room, with a table and cushioned chairs of pale pink brocade, vases of fresh-cut flowers, and an assortment of biscuits in the box on the table that stood beside a small, but elegant settee. Long curtains hung from ceiling to floor on two enormous windows that looked out onto the perfectly manicured garden behind the castle, and the rolling sea beyond.

Though impressive and beautiful, the sitting room paled in comparison to the lavish bedroom revealed through a set of double doors at the other side of the room. The enormous four-postered bed took up a good portion of the far wall, with a matching dressing table and large mirror nearby. Ione almost felt the urge to hurry back into the hall, as if she were a little girl who'd snuck into a bedroom too grand for her, and would be scolded were she caught. But this was to be her home, and the rooms she would occupy once she became the lady of the house were sure to be finer still. Ione straightened her shoulders and walked further inside. She moved through the room, tracing her fingers across the patterns intricately woven in gold thread across the deep rose coverlet that adorned the bed.

She nearly jumped out of her skin when she heard the door in the sitting room open and close, to be followed shortly by the sound of one of the servants huffing as they brought her trunk into the room. Rose was a step behind them, fretting over the process. Ione smoothed her hands down her skirts and directed them to put her trunk in the corner. She hoped she sounded more authoritative than she felt. Standing in the midst of all this luxury, the reality of the position she was about to marry into was rather overwhelming.

"Rose, do you know where Lady Tamsin's room is?" Ione asked. No doubt her cousin's appraisal of their new lodgings would be witty, and exactly the thing Ione needed to feel herself again. In a few short hours the course of Ione's life had changed dramatically, and though she was filled with hope and excitement for the future, she felt a need for the comfortable and familiar while she settled into the reality of those changes.

"Yes'm," Rose replied with a curtsey. "Just a few doors down, on the ell." She gestured to indicate where. "My lady said as how she'd leave her door open for you. Shall I unpack for you this time?"

"Yes, please," Ione replied absently, moving past Rose into the sitting room, and the hallway beyond. She found the room without difficulty—it was a lucky thing Tamsin had the forethought to leave her door open, for it would be all too easy to get lost in Castle Maclaren. Ione tapped on the doorframe to alert her cousin to her arrival. "Getting settled?" she asked.

Her cousin turned from supervising the Maclaren maid currently unpacking her trunk. "If that's a word that can be applied in this situation, certainly. Do come in, dearest. I hope you're letting Rose help; it's why I sent her to you, thinking she might seem less overwhelming in all..." Tamsin made an encompassing gesture, "this."

"Oh, indeed. Quaint, is it not?" Ione wiggled a humorous brow at her cousin. She stepped further into the bedroom and examined the painting on the nearest wall for just a moment before returning her attention to Tamsin. "I have a sitting room, and the bed is large enough to sleep a small family. I was glad to leave the unpacking to Rose this time."

Tamsin laughed. "It's breathtaking. As this is your future home, you should expect to have Tav underfoot most of the time. He's like a cat when it comes to luxury, you know." She sat in one of the upholstered chairs by the grate and indicated that Ione should take the other. "But truly, what do you think of it all?"

Ione looked around the room thoughtfully. "I think that there will be much to learn, but that I'm up to the task. And I know Geordie will not let me fail as the Lady of Clan Maclaren. We will face it together, and that makes anything possible."

"I know you're up to the task," Tamsin returned gently. "But are you happy?"

Ione lowered herself into the chair and fixed her attention on her cousin. "I've never been so happy, Tamsin," Ione confessed, knowing the expression on her face was that of an utterly besotted woman. "He is the best man I have ever met. I know it's all very sudden, but I could not be happier."

Tamsin regarded her with a small smile. "There, that is what was missing when I saw you at your rehearsal: true happiness. It suits you, Ione."

"I should thank you, my dear cousin." Ione leaned forward and took Tamsin's hand, giving her a firm but gentle squeeze. "If it had not been for you voicing what I could not that night—how it seems a lifetime ago now!—I might never have met my darling Geordie."

"I have it on good authority that it was fated to be," Tamsin replied, expression warm and playful. "It seems in this matter, your Geordie is as much an oracle as you."

Ione chuckled at that and leaned back into her chair with a contented sigh.

The rest of that afternoon was spent settling in and becoming familiar with the layout of the castle. Lady Ailsa was an enormous help in this, going so far as to draw a map on a piece of foolscap and present it to the cousins with a grin. Tea was sent up to their rooms with a message from the dowager exhorting them to rest until supper.

Ione spent the remainder of the day with Tamsin, carefully selecting her gown for the evening, and fussing over which of her necklaces best suited her new engagement ring. She was utterly determined to embrace her role as the Lady of Clan Maclaren, and wanted to put her best foot forward from the beginning. To that end, she settled on an emerald green gown for her first supper as Geordie's future wife, knowing that it would complement the colors of the Maclaren tartan.

Lady Tamsin chose white, to best set off her cousin's vivid choice, and as the bell rang for the meal the two met in the hallway and headed down the enormous staircase together in a flurry of swishing silk and laughter.

They were directed to the parlor where Ione's future mother and sister-in-law were dressed for dinner and comfortably seated, along with Lady Ailsa's companion. Geordie and the other men were nowhere to be seen.

"Come in, my dears," the dowager greeted them, her bright smile at odds with the black of her mourning gown. "I hope you rested well?"

Ione greeted Lady Kirkleith with a dutiful kiss on either cheek before arranging herself on the settee. Every home had its rhythm, and soon this one would feel as natural and familiar as her family's. But she'd spent little enough time with Lady Kirkleith, and the loss of her husband was still a fresh wound; despite the warm greeting, without Geordie present, it was difficult not to feel more like a guest.

The ladies chatted about inconsequentialities. "...and of course if I can be of any assistance in helping to plan the wedding," Lady Kirkleith was saying, "though as the mere mother of the groom I can remain quietly out of the way if preferred," she finished with a slight laugh.

"Speaking of Geordie," Ione looked around hopefully, "where is he?"

"Primping, I am sure," Ailsa giggled.

"Such behavior," the dowager tsked, though she was smiling at her daughter. "I hope, my dear, you will not hold it against him. He is not usually so late."

As though summoned by his name, Geordie came skidding into the room. "Dreadfully sorry," he began, kissing his mother on the cheek. "Having a bit of a meeting with the boys. They'll be down anon." He took Ione's hands. "How is it you grow more beautiful by the hour?"

"I think it's in the eye of the beholder." Ione teased him, blushing brightly at the compliment.

He kissed both her hands and turned to his mother. "Have I time to show Ione the house before we dine, Mama?"

She nodded indulgently. "Half an hour, my son. Begin with the long gallery, and then show her the west wing. Mind you return on time; Maclaren or no, I shan't hold dinner for you."

He offered Ione his arm, and led her out of the room and away from the others.

"I know it sounds a little foolish, as we have only been parted for a matter of hours and in the same building, but I have missed you." Ione said, squeezing his arm. All the tension of the day faded away, now that she was alone with him.

He grinned, guiding her down the corridor to his left. "I know what you mean. When I saw you just now, I felt as though I could breathe again. God have mercy on me, Ione, I adore you. I am impatient for the day you'll become mine—when shall we wed?"

"Perhaps we need not wait long," Ione answered slowly. An idea was taking shape, one that could both serve her new clan, and her ever-growing sense of impatience to be with Geordie. "After all, it can only strengthen the position of the new Maclaren if he is wed when he officially takes his place as the head of the clan."

Geordie stopped still, then turned to face her, hands moving to her shoulders, his grey eyes intense and smoky. "You'd do that for me?"

Ione offered him a rather sultry smile. "I would. Unless you prefer a longer engagement." She sobered and addressed his question with the gravity it deserved. "I will be the Lady of Clan Maclaren, and I take that seriously. Your clan will be mine and I will do right by them."

After a long moment spent studying her face, Geordie pulled her to him and kissed her with fervor.

Ione leaned into the kiss, returning it with a hunger and heat that surprised even her. When she pulled away again she felt breathless and flushed. "I assume you are in favor of a wedding at the investiture then."

His voice was rough when next he spoke. "I've no idea what I've done to deserve you, my love. Aye, I'm in favor of it. 'Twill be no small thing to the clan."

"Then Sunday it is." She started to lean in for another kiss but thought better of it, knowing that she would lose track of all time and propriety if she let herself. "Perhaps we should tell your family that we've set a date for the wedding. Heaven knows how we'll get everything prepared in so short a time."

He leaned his forehead against hers. "Aye, you're right. Come on, then."

It was a merry group who partook of the dinner, made merrier still by toasts and jesting on the part of Geordie's gang of three. After the meal, Lady Kirkleith retired to her rooms while Ailsa and Miss Anderson returned to the schoolroom Ailsa was so lately out of. The other two ladies rose from the table to leave the men to their post-prandial digestifs.

But her fiancé had other ideas. "I think," said Geordie, pushing his chair away from the table, "we'll dispense with the after-dinner brandies. Lady Tamsin; Ione, my love—will you join us in the library? It's time."

"Time?" Ione exchanged glances with her cousin, completely confused by his sudden proclamation.

He gave her a grin—not the sweet smile she was used to, but the feral grin of a berserker. "For a council of war."

Ione looked at him, then gave a quick nod. "Very well, a war council it is."

They assembled in the library. Ione took a place at Geordie's side on a comfortable bench, waiting until the others were settled before she turned to her betrothed. "It seems we are ready, my love."

"Right." He kissed her hand. "Well, lads, time to come clean."

Quinn nodded. "I'll go first. What you know of us is true, ladies: we are all school friends. What you may not know is that I, in conjunction with my partner, have been tasked to guard Geordie and preserve his life at all costs."

"To guard Geordie? Against what?" Ione looked from Quinn to her fiancé. She'd been witness to not one, but two episodes of violence, and the beginning of this conversation was making her stomach churn uncomfortably. "Just who is it that threatens you?"

Quinn exchanged glances with Asher, of all people. "Three years ago," he began, "an Act in Parliament was passed to give crofters here in Scotland the security of tenure upon their lands, and which allows them to fight for fair rental policies. The previous Lord Kirkleith favored this law, to the displeasure of some of his fellows. The prime minister received an anonymous letter that led us to believe his death was not a simple robbery, as has been put about," he shot Geordie an apologetic look, "but a deliberate act of punishment. The head of our agency, Mr. Melville, had concerns that this might also constitute a threat to the Maclaren that is. Given our long friendship, it seemed expedient to assign us to the job of keeping the new Lord Kirkleith safe until the malefactors could be uncovered and brought to justice."

"But if the act has already been passed, what could they hope to achieve by threatening Geordie?" Ione asked, trying to make sense of the puzzle being laid out before her.

"The late Lord Kirkleith had sponsored legislation that would further amend the Act to allow the crofters access to more land, a facet which was overlooked in the previous legislation. And Geordie has been clear in his intent to continue his father's work." Quinn explained. The current Lord Kirkleith folded his arms and nodded.

"And now they intend to kill Geordie to stop it?" Ione felt the blood draining from her face. Chills skittered down her spine, and she felt the tingle of magic stirring, or rather, the memory of that sensation. "You said that the former Maclaren's death was an act of punishment. What happened to him?"

Geordie's lips thinned; Ross spoke up, though he seemed a little hesitant to do so. "The details don't matter. We were successful in suppressing the circumstances—even Lady Kirkleith doesn't know all, and there is no need to distress you with them."

"That hardly puts my mind at ease, Dr. McInerny," Ione managed, frustrated by his response. She knew there was danger, but this was so much more than she'd imagined and with her fate tied to Geordie's there was no way for her to use her power to gain useful insight. Swallowing her frustration, Ione folded her hands in her lap to maintain an outward appearance of composure. "Mr. Rutherford, you mentioned a partner. Who might this partner be?"

Asher raised his hand. "It's I, Miss Brentwood."

"I suppose that explains the fact that you brought a gun to a picnic," Ione muttered before shaking her head. "I'm sorry gentlemen, this is quite a lot to take in. Is the threat isolated to Geordie, or are there others in danger as well?"

"The scope of their intent is still unclear," Asher said. "But we know that he is on their list—as are you, now."

Ione's mouth dropped open, and she looked around the room as she mentally grappled with the gravity of his statement. "Me? Because I am to be the Lady of the Maclaren clan." She took a deep breath. "Oh, dear," was the most she could manage.

Geordie put a protective arm around her. "I'll not let harm come to you, Ione, I swear it."

"I'd like to see them get to you through me," said Tamsin mildly, and chuckled when they all turned to look at her. "Forgot me, did you? My skills are often improvisational," she added, "but useful in a surprising number of awkward situations."

"Oh!" Asher smacked himself in the forehead and then dug around in his pocket. "Could you tell if an item has been repurposed in just such a way?" He pulled out a group of leather cords, each strung with a strange stone bead, and crossed the room to present them to Tamsin. "Quinn and I found these on Geordie's assailants of the other day; this one," he poked at one of them, "was on the fellow with the crossbow who ruined our picnic. We thought they might be a symbol of some sort of organization, but... perhaps they are more than that?"

Ione leaned forward, realizing that the cords in Asher's hand were identical to the one she'd found on the road the day Geordie was shot. Her jaw tensed, but she held her tongue. If that cord was connected to the plot against Geordie, she might just be able to use it to glean something more.

Tamsin regarded them, then touched one with a glowing fingertip. "There is something here," she agreed, and glanced up at him. "Might I borrow one or two, to see whether I can determine what sort of charm might be in use?"

"Of course." Asher gave them to her, and she placed them in her reticule as he returned to his former seat.

"I can be of help as well," Ross chimed in, pushing off of the wall he'd been leaning against. "My talents may not be as unusual as the ladies here, but I expect they'll come in handy."

"Some oracle I am." Ione muttered, a sense of frustration and helplessness sinking in. Tamsin's charms could do much, and Ross was capable of healing the body, but her own powers seemed frightfully limited in the face of their current predicament. She leaned back in her seat. "I really

don't know what to say to all of this." She looked at
Geordie, her expression strained. "I knew someone was
trying to harm you, but I thought it had to do with your
upcoming investiture and would settle once the oaths
were sworn."

Asher it was who shrugged and answered. "It's a
good opportunity for mischief," he agreed, "since
Geordie will be publicly challenged. But we'll be there
to keep him safe."

Ione noticed a thoughtful expression cross her
cousin's face as well, which gave her some confidence.
Tamsin's solutions were often unusual, but generally
effective. Ione shifted in her seat, feeling as though she
might drown in this tidal wave of information. Even if
she was a target herself, the prevailing thought that
raced through her mind was that she could not abide
losing the man she loved. "What can we do?"

"At the moment, keep our eyes open and protect
you both to the best of our ability." That was Quinn.

Ione considered Quinn's words, wracking her
brain for anything she could offer. Her magic seemed
to shift restlessly, and something nagged at her: a
memory that seemed half-formed, or like a dream... or
a nightmare.

Suddenly the images from her nightmarish
vision rose to the forefront of her thoughts. The vision
of the field, and the two men who struggled violently to
defeat one another. with a rising sense of horror, she
realized one of them was no longer a faceless figure.
Geordie was the man she'd seen struck down. The color
drained from her face again. "I've seen it," she gasped.
"Geordie's enemies will strike at the investiture."

Geordie frowned. "How do you mean? I thought
you couldn't–"

Ione swallowed and tried to put her thoughts in
order. "Sometimes my visions come in the form of

dreams," she glanced at Geordie. "After our meeting at the inn at Thornhill I had a vision. I saw two men fighting in a field or an arena. I couldn't see their faces, but knowing what I do now, I believe you were one of them."

Asher chimed in, attention wholly on Ione. "And the other?"

"Had a knife hidden on his person," Ione stated succinctly, though she knew it was not the answer he hoped for. She closed her eyes and rubbed at her temples, as if the action could summon the details that eluded her. "I wish I could tell you more, but his face was hidden as well. They both had swords, but it was not the claymore that struck the blow."

Quinn nodded slowly, clearly thinking; Tamsin reached over the arm of her chair to squeeze her cousin's hand. "Well done," she murmured. "We'll get this figured out yet."

Ione shook her head, aggravated with the limitations of her gift. Now more than ever she needed details, and they were beyond her reach. "I saw the other man stab Geordie with the dagger, but it was just impressions after that. A sense of loathing and..." she shuddered, remembering the hopelessness and hatred that had seeped across the field and dropped her to her knees. another small detail clarified. "I saw a red cap."

The others exchanged confused glances. "I don't know anyone who wears a cap like that," Geordie offered. "Is it significant?"

"Could it be someone working for another clan?" Ross asked thoughtfully. "Perhaps the red cap is a clue, rather than a literal cap."

Quinn chewed on his lip. "There's a distant bell ringing," he began absently, "but damned if I know why. Something about a red cap... no, it's gone." He shook his head. "Probably not related."

Geordie was shaking his head too. "I've never heard about a clan wearing red caps in particular. Which isn't to say you're wrong, Ross—but I don't know how we'd look into it. I suppose Angus might know."

"It's precious little to go on." Ione hooked her arm through Geordie's, needing to reassure herself as much as him. "The cap could represent something else entirely. A lust for blood, or even that this person has killed before."

Silence descended for a moment, and then Tamsin spoke up. "Perhaps the morning will bring fresh insight?"

"Will you be able to sleep tonight, bonny girl?" Geordie's expression was filled with concern.

Ione could have laughed at that question were she not still reeling from everything that had been revealed. "All things considered, probably not." Ione shook her head emphatically. "Thankfully, magical remedies for a sleepless night are less complicated than our other concerns."

"That they are," Ross said, rubbing his hands together. He glanced around the room. "I have a few options, and enough to go to any who need the help."

"Good to know." Asher pushed himself out of his chair and nodded toward Tamsin. "I think Lady Tamsin is right—we all could use some sleep for now." He looked at the others. "We have time. We'll figure this out."

Chapter Fifteen

Shadows of the Future

For Ione, waking in her lavish bedroom in Castle Maclaren was a rather surreal experience. To open her eyes in a place of such luxury, so intricately woven into who Geordie was, and to know that this was where she would spend the rest of her life, was more like waking into a dream than anything she'd ever dared to hope for. She could not wait to begin her life with Geordie, for everything else seemed little more than a precursor to what that future would bring.

Breakfast was a surprisingly cheerful affair, considering their meeting the night before. Ione spent the rest of the morning in consultation with Lady Kirkleith, Ailsa, and Tamsin over wedding plans—a monumental task given the truncated engagement.

They all met briefly for luncheon, and then the men went off under Angus' direction, "tae make a decent showing on the day, ye tumshie-heided loobies," whatever that meant. The ladies took the curricle into town to see Mrs. Breathnach, the local seamstress, which all parties enjoyed. Upon their return in the later part of the afternoon, Tamsin and Ione went in search of the men.

The ladies found the four stalwart warriors in a fenced-off corner of the yard, squaring off with swords at the ready. "Watch your flank, damn you!" cried Quinn, tapping Ross lightly on the side before dancing back. Asher and Geordie were trading blow for blow, laughing between hard-earned breaths. The heat of the day had begun, now; the ground had warmed and the scent of earth rose about them, coupled with the clang of weapons and the shouts of the men.

Ione had only a moment's warning before she felt the magic beginning to surge within her. The sound of the boys' swords connecting took on a strange echo that seemed to fill her mind and drown out the rustling of the breeze through the nearby trees. She dug her fingers into Tamsin's arm and tried to take control of her magic. "No—no—no, not now!" she managed, before everything swirled and bled white, and her legs gave out.

"What—Ione? Ione!" She could hear Geordie calling her frantically, but could not answer. "What is it, what's happened? Ione!"

The people now surrounding her were like shadows, playing on the edge of the vision: it was the same field she'd seen in her nightmares before, but something was different. The images were clearer, the colors more vivid, the details easier to make out somehow. The sound of fighting was so loud that Ione could feel every blow of the blades vibrating through her. Two men squared off a short distance from where she stood; one face remained obscured by shadow, but the other came into perfect focus.

Ross McInerny raised his sword to meet the attack launched by the other man. The weapons locked and his enemy shifted, pulling a dagger from some hidden place at his belt. Ione tried to call out—to run forward—but she was helpless, rooted to the ground. The dagger flashed in the sunlight and then plunged deep into Ross' midsection. The air grew thick with poison, and somewhere in the distance Ione heard Geordie's anguished cry.

She gasped suddenly, drawing in a deep shaking breath, the first since the vision had taken her. Her eyelids fluttered before she passed out entirely, her mind balking from the horror of what she witnessed.

Ione opened her eyes, still outside. Geordie was sponging her head with cool water; Tamsin was by her side, the other men ranged nearby. "I'm here, love, it's all right," Geordie was murmuring. "Easy, sweetling; I've got you. That's it; come back to me, bonny girl."

Tamsin's blue eyes were worried. "Are you all right, dearest? What happened?"

Ione turned a wide-eyed look to Ross. Her face went numb, but for the stinging of her eyes as tears started to roll down her cheeks. "It changed—my vision changed. I saw..." Ione shuddered, trying to think past the blood and the anguish in Geordie's cry as his friend fell lifeless to the ground.

Tamsin paled. "What did you see, Ione?"

"I saw death, but—it was Dr. McInerny who fell in Geordie's place." Ione shuddered again, burying her head in Geordie's shirt front. Everything ached, from her head to her toes; mind still grappling with the dark and confusing images. Her betrothed wrapped his great arms around her, looking utterly helpless.

Ross drew closer and knelt by her head, fingers aglow. "Here, Miss Brentwood; it's all right, it's all right now. Let me help." Despite the calm reassurance of his word his hand was shaking when it touched her shoulder. Ione felt a wave of magical energy ease muscles rigid with tension, and soothing her aches. "You need to rest, let yourself recover from the shock."

Ione wanted to be helpful, to offer something more than tears and shaking, but she was utterly drained of magic. She put her hand over his. "Thank you, doctor. I will—" she hiccupped, then mastered herself again. "I will read you when my magic is back. I promise you." Ross nodded stoically, but said nothing as he moved away.

Geordie scooped her up, holding her to his broad chest. "Rest you will have, then, my heart." He looked at the men. "Meet me in my study shortly—not a word until I get back. Lady Tamsin, if you would be so good?" She nodded with alacrity and hurried back to the castle before them, buttonholing a passing footman and requesting that Rose be sent to Ione's room at once.

Ione curled her fingers into Geordie's shirtfront as he carried her up the stairs and back to her room. When he laid her on the bed she gripped his hand and held him nearby. "I'm sorry, Geordie. I'll be able to tell you more when I've recovered enough to summon the vision again."

He smoothed her hair back from her forehead and leaned forward to press his lips to it. "We'll work it out, love. Rest now." The breath he let out was shaky. "Is it always like this for you?"

Ione shook her head and took a calming breath. "No, this does not happen often. Telling you about my vision must have changed it. I—I think that's what caused my magic to react this way." She wiped a hand over her face. "I will be recovered after some sleep."

217

Geordie nodded and draped a blanket over her legs. "Your maid will stay with you in case you need anything," he instructed, while Rose nodded emphatically. "Lady Tamsin, will you stay as well?"

Tamsin shook her blonde head. "Not if Ione is to sleep restfully—I should only keep her from it. Rose will fetch me if Ione needs me."

The Scotsman sighed and got to his feet. "As you say. Sleep, then, my love, and mind you dream of nothing but our happy future." He cast a long look back at her, then escorted Tamsin from the room. Ione turned to her side and nestled into the pillows, weariness overcoming distress.

None of them were in the mood for dinner after that, so Geordie and Lady Tamsin made straight for his study after leaving Ione to her rest. Raised voices came through the door; Geordie made a face. "So much for 'not a word until I get back'," he muttered, and opened the door for Lady Tamsin. Quinn was standing in front of Geordie's desk, arms folded across his chest, Asher was pacing in front of the fireplace, and Ross was situated in one of the high-backed chairs with a tumbler in his hands. "Lady present, gents, so mind your language."

"Don't be silly," was the lady's response as Geordie crossed to the decanters and fixed himself a drink. "We've all had a shock, Dr. McInerny more than the rest. I shan't mind if you turn the very air blue, if it helps." She crossed to Ross and laid a hand on his arm. "How are you?"

Ross looked up at her and then raised his half-emptied glass of whiskey. "About this good." He glanced at his friends. "I've delivered news like that to others; quite a different thing on the receiving end. How is your cousin?"

Lady Tamsin lifted a shoulder. "She says she will be well enough with rest, and I believe her. I have only seen her like this once before, and she recovered very quickly that time."

Quinn cleared his throat. "Her vision has given us warning, though." Here he looked at Asher. "And as I was saying, that gives us something to work with."

"And as I was saying," Ross threw back his glass and polished off the rest of the whiskey, "it's not for you lads to decide what I do."

Geordie's expression grew wrathful. "Then you bloody won't be my second. I'll not have your death on my conscience," he told Ross. "I'll cancel the challenges entirely, tradition be damned."

Quinn held up a hand. "Wait a moment, though. Can the vision be changed?"

Geordie frowned. "Aye, it can—I'll cancel the challenges," he repeated.

"That's not what I meant. If the vision can be changed, then I think we should go ahead with them," Quinn clarified. "It's our best chance to flush out the threat, in my view, and without them, we're back at the beginning."

Asher took a step toward Quinn. "You cannot be suggesting we use Ross as bait. That is not what I'm hearing. Because if it is—"

"It's not, and don't be an idiot," Quinn snapped. "But think about it: we know now that Geordie's enemy intends to strike at the challenges, and he doesn't know we know. If we can find a way to keep Ross out of danger, we can end the threat to Geordie at the same time."

Lady Tamsin spoke up. "Ione often says that her visions can be changed. After all, her gift would be spectacularly useless if they could not." Her gaze grew speculative. "The trick, of course, is to keep Dr.

McInerny safe without letting this mysterious enemy know we've twigged."

"No, the trick is keeping me alive without sacrificing anyone else to do it," Ross interjected. He rose from his chair and took up the pacing that Asher had ceased. "Ione said her nightmare changed and I died in Geordie's place." He stopped and looked at each of his friends in turn. "I'll not have you change things at the cost of one of your lives. I intend to fight as planned."

"You bloody *willnae*," Geordie growled, aware that his temper—and his brogue—was getting the better of him and not much caring. "I'll cancel the challenges t'keep you safe—am I the Maclaren or am I not?"

"Technically, not," Quinn reminded him, "until Sunday." He laid a placating hand on Geordie's arm. "We have a few days—we'll work it out. Though as a last resort," he mused, "we'll keep Ross off the field if we must."

Ross shook his head adamantly. "I could not live with myself knowing the cost of it was one of you." His face went a little red. "You will not risk yourselves to save me." He crossed his arms and squared his shoulders.

Asher went to stand in front of his friend, pushing his glasses up his patrician nose. "Watch us," he said quietly.

Tamsin slipped between the two. "Gentlemen," she spoke firmly, "this is the cart before the horse. Ione is resting now. She'll be able to tell us in plenty of time how best to preserve Dr. McInerny—and the rest of you," she added hurriedly, as it looked like Ross was about to protest again. "The beauty of my cousin's gift is that she'll be able to tell us which plans have the best chance of working. Until we can speak with her, I suggest we table the subject for now."

"Lady Tamsin is correct. We're arguing in circles and it's not getting us any closer to a solution," Quinn agreed. The hand on Geordie's shoulder squeezed briefly. "We already knew there was someone looking for blood. The details have changed a bit, but the goal remains the same."

Ross' shoulders seemed to relax slightly, though Geordie could still see the stubborn glint in his friend's eyes. "Just promise me no one will throw themselves in harm's way to keep me here."

"Ross." Geordie waited until his friend was looking at him. "There are no acceptable casualties in this. I've no wish to lose any of you. If we can find no other way out, I *will* cancel the challenges." Ross nodded slowly.

"That's settled then," Quinn added before moving to pour a tumbler of whiskey for himself. "I suggest we keep everyone here at the castle as much as possible, outside of the plans for the investiture. We know our enemy intends to strike there; I see no reason to give him any other opportunities."

Geordie took a fresh bottle of brandy to his bedroom when he retired for the evening; he had a sneaking suspicion that sleep would be elusive, and as the night wore on, he discovered he was right. As he'd no wish to appear the next day like a bear with a sore head, what little brandy he allowed himself didn't help much.

His heart had nearly stopped when he saw Ione collapse like that; and then to learn that the people he cared for most were in deadly danger... His lips thinned. No. They would find a way around this prediction. Ione herself had implied that it wasn't written in stone—after all, her vision had changed once already. Didn't that mean it could be changed again? And if all else failed, Geordie would simply cancel the challenges, or lock Ross in a bedroom or something, although that might simply shift the target to another of his friends.

Fine. He'd lock them all up—toss them in the oubliette and satisfy tradition by himself if he had to. Whatever it took.

He woke with a snort, still in the chair by the window. The early morning sun blazed across his face and Geordie winced, raising a hand to block out the rays while he sorted himself out.

His neck was stiff, no surprise there. But on the whole, he was well enough, and still worried about Ione. When his man came to see to him, Geordie rushed him through shaving and waved him off when he began to fuss about Geordie's hair.

To be fair Geordie did just that more often than not, so the valet took it in stride and merely presented him with his clothes for the day. The young viscount scrambled himself together, held still with an ill grace while his valet made some adjustments, hurried out of his chambers, and as a thumb of the nose to his newly-acquired station, seated himself on the banister of the great staircase and slid down.

Filled with nervous energy, he didn't feel like eating much, instead playing with the silverware until his mother gave him a disapproving look before she left the table with the others, at which point he began to make a tower out of the salt-cellars.

And then Ione arrived, radiant as always, and his world started to right itself again.

Geordie leapt from his seat, toppling the tower, and nearly taking the entire table with him, and came solicitously to Ione's side. "Here, love, let me help you. What would you like to eat? I'll make you a plate."

"I assure you I'm fully recovered." Her smile was bright; his heart turned over. "Please, don't fret over it any longer."

"I shall fret if I choose, my own. Allow me this, if you please." He seated her and made her up a plate, fussing over her napkin and pouring her a drink.

Ione shook her head but graciously allowed him to ease his mind, though how much it helped was up for debate. Of course Geordie said nothing of this. He was pleased to see that she tucked into her meal with enthusiasm; he would have been hard-put to accept anything less and still feel confident in her recovery.

When she had finished and convinced him that she did not need a second helping, nor anything else, she put her napkin on the table and leaned back in her chair. There was a moment of quiet before Ione spoke again. "I really must apologize for any concern I may have caused." She reached for his hand and her touch provided further reassurance. "I assure you, everything will be well. My magic is fully restored and I'm sound in body."

He played with the stem of his glass. "What happened?"

"It is to do with what I am," Ione began slowly. "For the most part, I'm able to control the visions my magic provides. I can summon the ability at will, but..." She shifted in her seat, a small frown on her lips. "There are times when a vision can be so powerful it overwhelms me, and there is nothing for me to do but allow the magic to do as it will."

"It was frightening," he admitted, feeling very vulnerable.

"It is not any more pleasant for me, but this sort of vision is rare." Ione's expression relaxed. "When I was a girl, before I had learned how to control my magic, they happened more frequently. As I have gained more control they come less often. Last night was the first I've had in over a year."

Geordie swallowed nervously, then asked the question that was at the forefront of his mind. "Can the vision be changed?"

Ione nibbled thoughtfully at her lower lip, and Geordie felt his anxiety creeping upward again. Then she fixed her blue eyes on him and Geordie saw hope there. "I believe so, but we must proceed carefully. I need to read Dr. McInerny and summon the vision intentionally, so that I can control it and find the details we need to save him without causing harm to anyone else."

He nodded. "Very well."

"Do you know where the doctor and the others are now?" Ione asked, pushing her chair back. "I think it's best if everyone hears the details at the same time, lest something be missed or mistaken in retelling."

"I'll have some of the staff track them down and we can meet in my study—that way neither my mother nor Ailsa will hear anything they ought not." He held her chair as she rose and then appropriated her hand, kissing her fingers.

Ione's brow furrowed slightly. "I take it you have not told them of my abilities?"

"I have not," he acknowledged. "'Tisn't my secret to share."

"It will hardly be a secret when our children start displaying their own magical gifts," Ione replied. Geordie went very still. Her fingers tensed in his hand; her frown deepening. "I—I assumed you realized our children would be Fae-touched as well." Her face and eyes turned a touch red. "Is that a problem?"

"What? No—no, love. I'd assumed as much. Oh, Ione—" He lifted her chin and pressed his lips to hers tenderly. "'*Doubt thou the stars are fire, doubt that the sun doth move; doubt truth to be a liar, but never doubt I love*,'" he quoted. "No, 'twas only that—you're t'be the mother of my children." Geordie couldn't help the smile he felt creeping across his face. "It's a miraculous thought."

The redness in her cheeks was now obviously a blush. Her lips curved upward in a rather endearingly shy smile. "Yes, I—I suppose it is." She glanced at him and the blush deepened. "The production of an heir will be something of a priority."

At that Geordie shook his head. "Nay, bonny girl. Loving you is the priority. I hope we're blessed with children, but you must know—I'd make no other choice, regardless." His grin widened along with his brogue. "But I fully intend we shall both enjoy the practicin'."

Ione giggled, met Geordie's eyes fleetingly, and then looked away again. When she spoke, it was in a very quiet voice, but with a tantalizing tone Geordie had never heard from her before. "Yes, I believe we will."

There was only one answer to be made to that, and Geordie made it. He glanced about to make sure they were unobserved, and then pulled her close, kissing her the way he'd longed to do for days. Months. No—he'd been waiting for this his entire life, he thought hazily, cupping her cheek as he explored her mouth.

Ione made a soft, small sound of satisfaction, and then her fingers were weaving into the hair at the base of his scalp, holding his lips close to hers and deepening the contact. Her other hand twisted into the collar of his shirt and pulled him closer. The kiss she returned spoke of a longing that equaled his own.

Reluctantly Geordie broke their heated embrace, huffing out a soft laugh as he leaned his forehead to hers. "I can wait a little longer," he whispered. "But not much."

"The impatience is mutual, I promise you," Ione replied breathlessly, and obviously flustered. She squeezed her eyes shut and then opened them as she exhaled slowly. "Other matters to settle first. Have to keep all of you safe and fit for the wedding." She turned and started to walk in the direction of the study, then paused and looked over her shoulder at him. "It's only a few more days of waiting, after all."

Geordie had to clench his fists to keep from reaching for her again. "Right. Meeting. Study," he muttered, and went in search of a footman.

Half an hour later, the six of them found them gathered in Geordie's study. Ione took Ross' hand and closed her eyes. The room grew still and quiet. After a little while, Ione opened her eyes again and laid out the details of her vision. Though she still could not see the face of the man who struck Ross down, the description of the setting confirmed that it was at the challenges. She read Ross a second and third time, until all present were able to get a clear picture of what must be prevented.

Asher had taken copious notes. "Seems clear enough," he murmured, reading over what he'd written. He glanced up at Ione. "As I understand it, you're not able to read 'what if's', is that correct?"

Ione nodded. "Correct, I cannot examine hypothetical possibilities. I can only gain visions from the course we set ourselves on."

"Right." Asher looked up, sliding his glasses up his nose. "Geordie, cancel the challenges."

"D'you think I should?" Geordie was surprised. "All right, then—I'll send out word."

Asher turned to Ione. "Read Ross now, please."

Ross offered his hand to Ione again, though Geordie noted there was a distinct lack of enthusiasm—no doubt the result of listening to the details of his own demise repeatedly.

Ione took his hand and closed her eyes again. There was the same silent pause and then her face went white. "No please no! We cannot cancel the challenges. We mustn't!" She took a few steadying breaths. "It will not stop the assassin; if the challenges don't take place there will be an accident with one of the carriages." Ione looked at Geordie miserably. "Your mother and sister will die as a result of tampering."

"NO!" The cry was ripped from Geordie's throat. "Asher—what have you done?"

Ash was making notes. "Don't cancel the challenges, Geordie. Declare them back on."

A glimmer of his friend's strategy made itself known; Geordie licked his lips. "I willnae cancel the challenges," he said shakily. "They will go on as planned."

"Miss Brentwood?" Asher queried.

Ione looked up, expression resolute. "Yes, Mr. Burton?"

"Read Ross again, if you would be so kind."

She did, and determined that Lady Kirkleith and Ailsa were now safe, but the danger to Ross had returned. This went on for some time, and they were able to eliminate many of the choices they'd thought might help: if, for example, Ross did not attend the challenges, Quinn would die in his stead; or if they changed the day of the challenges, Asher himself was slated for death.

Every combination of events they could think of was exhausted, and so, after several hours, was Ione, and Geordie called a halt. "Enough," he said. "We know more now than we did, but we'll have nothing at all to go on if Miss Brentwood's gifts are used up. We have time yet."

Quinn spoke up, a thoughtful expression on his face. "Are you game for one last query, Miss Brentwood?"

"I believe so," Ione replied, rolling her shoulders as though she'd been engaged in physical labor. "And you, Dr. McInerny?"

Ross looked around the room, eyes settling on Geordie. "Aye, one last time," he answered, voice betraying the toll the process had taken.

"Geordie." Quinn took a breath. "Renounce your title."

Dumfounded, Geordie stared at his friend. The shade of his father rose in his mind's eye; but then he blinked and saw the faces of his friends around him, and knew what he had to do. "I renounce my title and lands, and forfeit my claim to be chief of Clan Maclaren," he said, his voice rough.

"Miss Brentwood," Quinn murmured, "if you please."

Both Ione and Ross seemed to hesitate, and then Ione held her hand out for Ross to take. He merely stared at it, then shook his head and took a step back. He looked at Geordie, face suffusing with color. "No bloody way. I will not let you do this."

"To save your life?" Geordie shook his head. "I'd give it all up, Ross, and never look back."

His friend's eyes narrowed. "Are you sure about that?" He glanced at Ione.

Geordie frowned. "What do you mean?"

"I mean that Mr. and Mrs. Brentwood might be reconciled to their daughter suddenly marrying a peer of the realm," Ross pointed out, "but they're hardly likely to allow her to marry a penniless nobody, regardless of his courage or his gigantic heart."

"I'm not marrying Geordie for his title!" Ione cried indignantly, but Ross held up his hands.

"I've no doubt you love him, Miss Brentwood, as much as he clearly adores you. And seeing how you look at each other I can believe you'd marry him out of hand whether your parents approved or not. But..." He turned to Geordie again. "Is that really the life you would offer her? Poverty and ignominy? And what about Ailsa, and her future? The sister of Lord Kirkleith has her choice of husbands. Take that away..." He let the sentence finish itself.

Geordie wiped a shaking hand over his face. Losing Ross was unthinkable, but losing Ione—or ruining her life, and his sister's... Was this truly the choice set before him?

Ross shook his head, his voice gentle. "No, Geordie. I've never seen you as happy as you are with Miss Brentwood—I won't be the instrument of your misery and regret."

"I—" Geordie opened his mouth and then closed it again. "God help me, then," he replied heavily. "I renounce my renunciation, for what it's worth."

Ross laid a hand on Geordie's shoulder. "We still have time." He waited until Geordie was looking at him again. "Do not give up hope. I haven't. I'm here because you're like a brother to me—all of you are," he included the other men with a look around the room. "We've never failed each other before, and I know we won't start now. I'll see you made clan chief and then I'll play my cello at your wedding after."

Geordie found his voice was wholly suspended for a moment and he cleared his throat. "I hope to God you're right."

Though the meeting in Geordie's study hadn't drained Ione entirely, it was well past dinner before she felt recovered from the exhausting exercise. She'd never encountered a vision that had been so persistent in refusing an acceptable remedy. She tried to put on a brave front for the others, but struggled to hide her preoccupation, and eventually gave up entirely, claiming that she was too tired to join the others in the parlor after the meal.

Yet, once she was alone in her rooms, sleep was the furthest thing from her mind. There had to be a way to avoid death at the investiture. She simply could not accept that their only choice was to exchange one life for another. Ione twisted the end of her braid around her fingers and stared into the fire, replaying the events of the past week in her mind.

Every attempt on Geordie's life had been thwarted to this point, and the culprits taken in, but none would name their employer. It was infuriatingly obvious they all worked for the same person, the beaded cords they wore all but confirmed...

The cords! They were the connection between the ruffians, the strings that connected the puppets to their master, as it were.

Ione jumped out of her chair and crossed to her trunk, frantically tossing digging past the collection of hats and bags that still remained within. She'd tucked the cord in a hat box for safe keeping. She'd used it once before and found the answers she sought, perhaps it would provide the solution once more.

She flung the box open and snatched the cord like a hawk pulling a fish from the sea. Ione held the charmed object between two fingers, considering her options as it swung in the dim light. It seemed like such an unremarkable thing to pin her hope to, but needs must, and she had never needed answers more desperately. Palming the cord, Ione returned to her bed and made herself as comfortable as possible. Considering how things had gone earlier, she suspected it would take more than one attempt.

As it turned out, Ione was correct. She tried every method she could think of, and found little satisfaction in the results. The clock struck half past midnight and apart from being truly exhausted, she was no closer to a solution. Ione yawned and reached to put the bracelet on her nightstand but stopped. The vision had first come in the form of a dream, and when it changed the magic summoned it without warning. Ione wrapped the cord around her wrist and tied it tight. She fluffed her pillow and nestled into her bed. It was time to seek out a nightmare.

Yet again Ione stood in the field, yet again she was helpless to help Ross. She could do nothing but listen to the sounds of combat and watch as the fight grew more and more savage. Their swords locked, and Ione's stomach lurched, knowing what was about to happen. She saw the other man draw his secret dagger, linked in the flash of the metal in the sun. Ross fell to his knees, and suddenly Ione saw a figure behind him.

Tamsin stood opposite Ione, with an expression of astonishment on her face. Ione's eyes locked with her cousin's, and suddenly her feet were suddenly freed from whatever force held her in place. She ran toward Ross and knelt beside him, just as Tamsin approached from the other side. Ione cupped Ross' face, he gasped and his eyes flew open...

The shock of it made Ione sit straight up in bed with a gasp. She looked around the room wildly, her palm against her chest, trying to slow her racing heart. That had never been part of the vision before, but she knew what she'd seen: something had changed, and now, somehow, Dr. McInerny had a chance of survival. Shocking as the results were, the cord around her wrist had served its purpose, but—

A soft knock on her door caught her attention, and then the door opened slightly as a blonde head peeked in. "Ione!" Tamsin hissed. "Are you—oh, you are. Good." She slipped into the room and closed the door behind her. "I've just had the strangest dream—and it seemed so real!"

"What did you dream?" Ione asked, though she thought she had an idea. She flung the blankets aside and swung her legs over the edge of the bed.

For answer her cousin held up one of the strange beaded cords that Asher had given her. "I was examining this—it's definitely got a charm on it—and I must have fallen asleep. Maybe it's to induce nightmares, I don't know, but it seemed like the vision you described before, with the men fighting and Dr. McInerny being stabbed. But—"

Ione lifted her wrist, pushing back the sleeve of her nightrail to reveal the cord there. "But he opened his eyes and started breathing again," she finished for her cousin.

Tamsin moved closer and reached to touch the cord around Ione's wrist, then looked back at the one she held. She glanced up at Ione's face. "I think I know what this charm is for—it connected us, somehow. Those men must have had them so that they could coordinate their efforts." She frowned a bit. "Where did you get that one?"

"The man who tried to take me as a hostage the day Geordie was shot was wearing it. I found it on the road and kept it." Ione untied the leather round her wrist and handed it to Tamsin. "You think it connected Geordie's enemies to one another?" She frowned, considering her cousin's words, and a glimmer of hope appeared. "I have an idea." She outlined her thoughts. "Could it be done?"

A slow smile curved Tamsin's lips. "Yes, I think it could. And I think we should speak to Dr. McInerny."

Ione nodded and reached for her dressing gown. She went straight to the sitting room and then made for the corridor. "I'll need to read him again before we present whatever this plan is." Ione looked down the hallway. "Do you know which room is his?"

Tamsin shook her head. "No, but I can find him." She picked up a small decorative box from one of the tables in the sitting room and whispered to it before setting it on the ground, where it glowed a bit and then rolled out the door. "After you, my dear."

"What on Earth will you come up with next?" Ione murmured, and hurried after it. They tip-toed down the corridor, careful to avoid drawing undue attention.

The box stopped in front of a door some distance from Ione's bedroom. Tamsin looked at Ione and then lightly tapped on the door. They waited, but no answer came. Ione knocked this time, putting a bit more force into it.

There was a pause and then, "Oh, go away Ash, I'm fine." The doctor's voice was somewhat muffled, and unmistakably annoyed.

"Dr. McInerny!" Tamsin said in a stage whisper. "We need to speak with you!"

A weighted silence came from the other room. No doubt they were the last people the good doctor had expected to be knocking on the door in the middle of the night, Ione thought, and nearly laughed at the idea of it. There was shuffling from the other side of the door, and then it opened to reveal a rather disheveled Ross McInerny, hastily tucking in an incorrectly-buttoned shirt. "How can I help?" he asked, pushing hair out of his face. "Are you feeling unwell?"

Tamsin shook her head. "We've thought of a solution to our dilemma," she said, looking up and down the hallway. "May we come in?"

He stared at her, brows rising in surprise. "Into my room? Now?" He looked over his shoulder anxiously, then craned his head out to look down the corridor. "Uh—yes, of course," he whispered, opening the door wider and stepping aside to allow them to enter. Once they were both in the bedroom, he hurried to clear the clothes off the bench at the edge of the bed. "Um, please, make yourselves... comfortable."

Tamsin sat gracefully where he indicated, Ione following suit. "You must know," the former began, "that we have been trying to think of a way around our current situation ever since it arose—and I believe Ione has thought of something that will work."

Ione took up where her cousin left off. "I had the vision again, but this time you seemed to... well, come back, for lack of better description. When I woke, Tamsin was knocking on my door. I believe that the cords that were found on the men who attacked Geordie could be the answer we've been looking for."

"But everything we tried ended with someone else paying the price," he replied, settling on the small chair by the dressing table, rubbing the back of his neck. "How do you know that's not the case this time?"

"We don't *know*, exactly," Tamsin admitted. "But the theory is sound, and the change in Ione's vision gives me hope." She studied him assessingly.

"Tell me, Dr. McInerny, how quickly could you heal a fatal wound, if you knew it was coming?"

He thought about it for a few seconds before responding. "Assuming I knew the type of injury I'd be dealing with, a minute, perhaps a little less, perhaps a little more." He frowned. "That's being optimistic, and I'd have to be in direct contact with the person I was healing."

Tamsin nodded, an expression of concentration on her face that Ione knew well: her cousin was working out a charm. "And what if all you needed to do was to take the wound from something fatal to something less threatening?"

"That would cut the time down," Ross answered thoughtfully. "But I'd still have to be touching the person."

"Last question: if a wound was not fatal but perhaps there was more than one? Would that be faster still, or no?"

Ross looked from Tamsin to Ione, clearly confused. "Might take a bit out of me, but I could do it in a matter of seconds if I had to."

The lady's eyes began to twinkle. "I am delighted to hear it." Tamsin paused, as if to sort her thoughts, and then explained to Ross what they proposed to do. "What do you think?"

Ross exhaled and leaned back in his chair. "Asher and Quinn will do it, but you'll have a battle convincing Geordie."

"One thing at a time," replied Tamsin. "First: let us see whether the plan will work as it stands. Ione?"

Ione held her hand out for Ross, quieting her mind as she closed her eyes. Blood and a casket. Sorrow that should have been joy. Ione's eyes flew open. "Something's wrong, I'm seeing death. I don't understand why this isn't working." She got up and paced, wrapping her arms around herself. "Why did it change? It shouldn't have changed just in the telling."

"Perhaps the magic won't work," Ross replied heavily. "I've never done anything like what you're proposing before."

Tamsin's expression was as close to scathing as it ever got. "The magic *will* work," she told him. She thought for a moment and then snapped her fingers. "You said 'in the telling'—perhaps that's the problem. When we came up with the plan, only you and I knew of it. Obviously Dr. McInerny must know what he's to do; but just before you read him, he said something about the other three men." She assessed her companions. "You seemed to feel, Dr. McInerny, that Mr. Burton and Mr. Rutherford would have no objection, but that Lord Kirkleith would. I propose we do not tell him. Agreed?"

"I don't like keeping this from Geordie," Ione replied, but took Ross' hand again. But putting her reservations aside, she summoned the magic against and the vision she saw returned to images of hope. "That seems to have put things back the way they were."

Tamsin patted her hand. "We must tell him something, so he knows that there is a plan—only keep the particulars to yourself. I would think you can even tell him why, just so long as he doesn't know what will actually happen." Her smile fell away. "It isn't a perfect plan," she admitted. "Something may yet go awry—and in that case, far better that Lord Kirkleith not bear the burden of anticipation. He has enough to cope with at the moment."

"All we know now is that this plan changed your dream and I lived, we don't know whether or not it will bring about someone else's death." Ross pointed out, a hint of stubbornness in his voice.

Ione frowned thoughtfully. This plan had a chance, better than anything else they'd tried before, and she was not going to lose Geordie—or anyone else. "Give me your hand, Dr. McInerny, I'll read you again and see if telling Mr. Burton and Mr. Rutherford changes anything." The doctor complied without argument. The vision unfolded and Ione's shoulders relaxed; she opened her eyes again. "It won't change the outcome."

"But that doesn't—" Ross began, but Ione raised a hand to quiet him.

"I think this is our best option," she stated, hoping she sounded calm and reassuring. "True, I did not see details, but neither did I see any other deaths. I know it's not a guarantee, but it's better than the alternatives."

"And truthfully, Dr. McInerny," Tamsin chimed in, "given the choice between hope of life and certain death... well, there is no choice, is there?"

Chapter Sixteen

A Little Calm

Thankfully, the following day passed without assassination attempts, visits from former fiancés, or unexpected visions. Ross volunteered to present their plan to his friends, and then they all gathered to tell Geordie what they could.

"Well?" he asked, when the door to his study had closed. "Have we a hope?" He looked to Ione as he said it.

"Yes, there is hope, but..." Ione took Geordie's hand in both of hers. "I'm afraid we can't share the details of our plan with you."

He frowned. "I don't understand."

Tamsin spoke up. "The plan is a fragile one," she said carefully, "and we discovered that telling people other than the principals involved alters it, returning the danger."

Geordie considered her, and then looked at the others. "So if you tell me, it won't work."

Ross put a hand on his shoulder and glanced at the ladies. "That seems to be the case. I think this is our best option."

A long pause ensued, and then Geordie sighed. "Very well. Hope is more than we had before, so I shan't quibble." He was quiet again. "I'll not lie; just knowing there's something can be done relieves my mind."

Ione wrapped her arms around Geordie and hugged him gently. "I know it must be difficult to go into this with so little, thank you for trusting us. Thank you for trusting my abilities."

He slipped his arms around her, the corner of his mouth quirking upward. "And who should I trust, if not my own heart? If not my brothers?" Geordie looked at the three men in turn and shook his head. "If you tell me this is best, why then, it's what's best. If you tell me I must not know, then I'll put it from my mind. In fact," he went on, "I propose we all put it from our minds, as much as we can. Tomorrow begins the festivities, and we'll want to put the best face on things. We have one another, and we have hope—let's celebrate that, aye?"

"If the Maclaren deems it so," Ione twinkled up at her husband-to-be. "Then the future lady of the clan can do naught but agree."

By dinner Ione, Tamsin and Ross were all yawning and practically falling asleep in their soup bowls. Tomorrow there was to be a picnic and gathering of the clan, followed by a ball at Castle Maclaren. With so much activity looming, everyone retired early. Ione's sleep was as mercifully peaceful as the day had been.

But when morning dawned, Ione woke in a fit of nerves and restlessness. Today she would be officially presented to Clan Maclaren, and despite Geordie's reassurances, she could not stop fretting over what was to come. Even after a long soak in the tub and a small glass of wine, she remained on edge. Poor Rose nearly ran herself ragged, helping Ione change in and out of more than one dress in the process of choosing one for the picnic. Ione wanted to look perfect for her first public outing as Geordie's fiancée. Now, more than ever, she worried that her past, and the fact that she was English, would make matters worse for him.

At last, Ione settled on a simple white frock, with lace trim, hoping that she'd struck the perfect balance of elegance and warm approachability. She fidgeted with her hair, fussing over this detail and that with little satisfaction in the result. After adjusting the ribbons woven through her hair for the fifth time she stood up and cast a rueful glance at herself in the mirror. She shook her head, giving up on the process. The small clock on the mantle chimed the hour and Ione hurried to the door, knowing she would feel less frazzled when she saw Geordie.

Tamsin met her in the corridor, also in white but with a scarlet sash. "You look lovely, cousin," she smiled.

"As do you!" Ione replied, though she was far from satisfied with her own appearance just now. "I wish my hair would be more cooperative." She tucked a stubborn lock back into place.

"Here." Tamsin pulled a hairpin from her own coiffure and fixed the recalcitrant curl. "Better?"

"Much, and if all else fails, I suppose you could just use your magic to charm it into behaving." Ione laughed a little. "Shall we go see if the men are ready?"

"Yes indeed." Tamsin linked her arm through Ione's as though nothing hung over them, evidently obeying the Maclaren's exhortation to put the best face on things. "They're all in kilts."

Ione did a double-take. "The Englishmen and the doctor too?"

"Mmhm. All the men are wearing them, English and Irish too." Tamsin's blue eyes were twinkling. She leaned close. "Such an assortment of masculine knees! My girlish heart grows faint at the display."

Ione laughed at her cousin's nonsense. "Oh indeed, shall I run back to my room to fetch some fainting salts? A swoon in such circumstances could be quite awkward." For answer Tamsin snapped her fan open and raised a small breeze, sighing theatrically, and then the two of them went downstairs to greet the rest.

Ione was still laughing when they joined the others in the great hall. But when she saw Geordie her laughter faded, and though her lips were still curved in a smile, it was one of appreciation rather than levity. "Hello, my love."

Geordie caught the direction of her glance and grinned broadly. "Hello, my darlin'. You look lovely, as always."

"Thank you," Ione replied, smiling as she took his hand. "You look rather dashing yourself."

"You all look very well, gentlemen," said Tamsin merrily.

Ross and Asher sketched her a bow while Quinn was apparently trying to sort something out behind him, twisting and turning. Ione glanced over at him, hiding a smile under her glove. Then her gaze was back on Geordie. "Where is the picnic to be held?"

"In a pasture by the church," was the reply. "Large enough to hold everyone, and there are trees for shade. I've had it mowed and raked especially." He grinned. "I've ordered the curricle brought 'round, it's such a fine day. Lady Tamsin, I hope you will join the family in it. Ione, my darling," he kissed her hand, "you and I will take a more traditional route, followed at what one hopes will be a discreet distance by my seconds, though one's hopes are likely in vain."

"Oh?" Ione looked at him curiously. "What would that be?"

He laughed softly and preceded them all to the courtyard where the curricle awaited, and behind them... a gorgeous, milky-white stallion, enormous and broad, bearing a saddle clearly meant for two. Geordie led her to the beast. "Ione, this is Starlight. He's to carry us today and tomorrow."

"He's magnificent." Ione looked from the horse to Geordie, affection and excitement removing all traces of her earlier frustration. "As are you, my love."

Geordie looked down at her, his love writ large on his handsome face, before lifting her onto the front of the saddle, which had no pommel, but rather a hooked place for her to sit sidesaddle.

Ione settled into the saddle, hooking her leg over it, feeling a little awkward: the saddle was enormous and not at all what she was used to, being made to accommodate two. However, as soon as Geordie was seated behind her with one arm around her waist, the benefits became abundantly clear. She leaned against him, letting her head rest on his broad shoulder. "Have I mentioned today how very much I love you? These past few days have been like living in a dream."

"No more than I love you, my own heart." He pressed a kiss to her temple and took up the reins. "Now, let's go show you t'my clan, mm?"

They set off at a slow walk; the curricle passed them, Tamsin and Ailsa waving. The three seconds had mounted their own horses and were indeed at a discreet distance: Ione glimpsed them now and again as they went over a rise, and she could hear their horses nicker and snort, but for the most part she had a lovely feeling of solitude with her beloved.

As such, the ride was far too short; but Ione valued it for what it was, an island of calm in what were otherwise stormy seas. And once they had the challenges safely behind them, she had hope that they would find fair winds beyond.

The pasture for the picnic was crowded, all of Clan Maclaren having turned out on a summer's day to celebrate Geordie and remember his father fondly. When Starlight was sighted, a general cry went up, with cheering and the waving of hats and ribbons in the Maclaren colors.

Ione turned to Geordie, surprised and a little unsure. He grinned. "Word's got out. Wave to them, bonny girl. They all want t'love you."

Ione looked from her intended to the assembled group, suddenly understanding in a far more substantial way that she was indeed to be the lady of the clan. She lifted a hand, and waved at them, smiling a little nervously as she did.

Another shout went up, and a thunderous applause, and suddenly rose petals were flying in the air. Ione huffed out a little relieved laugh and waved again as Geordie directed Starlight to the center of the pasture, by a stately old oak. "My friends—my clan," he proclaimed loudly, "I thank you all for your goodness in remembering the Maclaren that was. I hope and pray that I will be half the man, and half the leader, he was." A ripple of approbation. "I gather you all know of my great good fortune in my engagement to Miss Ione Brentwood, and I thank you for all your good wishes as well." He smiled down at Ione. "I have the equally good fortune to tell you all that so eager and dedicated is she to her new role as your lady, Miss Brentwood has consented to wed me this very weekend, that she may be your lady from the first days of my tenure as your chief." He lifted Ione's hand and kissed it. "Though I yet grieve my father, I believe my fiancée is evidence of his blessing. We invite you all to share our joy, in the kirk on Sunday morning."

More clapping, cheers, and rose petals flying; in the midst of it all Geordie dismounted and lifted Ione down from the stallion, after which one of the grooms led the animal away.

"This is all far more than I deserve," she whispered to Geordie, feeling truly humbled by the welcome.

"Not even a drop in the ocean of what you deserve, my heart," he returned in an undertone, and then they were surrounded by well-wishers.

Tamsin, after exchanging glances with Quinn and Asher, took her place near her cousin, with Ailsa on the other side. "Come, Ione," said her sister-in-law to be, "let me introduce you."

Ione cast one last look at Geordie before allowing Ailsa to usher her off through the crowd. She reached out and grabbed hold of Tamsin's hand. "Heaven preserve me, there are a good many people here."

Her cousin nodded. "There are indeed." Her expression was quite serious, for Tamsin.

"It's hardly beneficial, considering certain circumstances," Ione whispered. Even so, she squared her shoulders and smiled as Ailsa began introducing her to one person after the other. She settled into the atmosphere, laughing and talking with those who made themselves known to her, charming them, and being charmed just as often. Occasionally she would catch sight of Geordie and offer him a happy and loving grin.

He'd wink at her, or give her a tender smile, until someone demanded his attention again.

"Ailsa, my dear! It has been far too long. How very grown up you look." A pretty young woman with honey-colored hair floated through the group of people, hands outstretched toward Ione's future sister-in-law, a serene smile across her face. A step behind her were two other women, all three perfectly dressed and groomed.

Ailsa's smile became somewhat forced. "How are you, Morag? Hello, Fiona, Grear. This is Ione, my sister-to-be, and her cousin, Lady Tamsin Claremont." It didn't escape Ione's notice that Ailsa hadn't used the 'in-law' honorific.

"So this is the woman who has our clan so fascinated." Morag's smile grew broader and yet somehow more hostile, though her voice was as sweet as molasses. "Fiona, Grear, this is the lady my aunt was speaking of. How very exciting to meet someone of such notoriety, don't you think?" The two women flanking her agreed with ill-concealed giggles, stepping forward to greet Ione.

"A pleasure." Ione replied, and despite an effort to be gracious, she knew her tone conveyed anything but pleasure. "I'm afraid you have me at a bit of a disadvantage."

"Notoriety?" Ailsa's ruddy brows snapped down. "I can't think what you mean, Morag."

"Oh, the surprise engagement of course," Morag returned, glancing at Ione. "Tell me, just when did you meet Geordie?"

"I—well, in truth, only recently." Ione tried to maintain a confident smile, but every word from the woman's mouth felt like a trap to be avoided. "And how long have you known him?"

At this Fiona and Grear exchanged glances. Morag looked back at them with an expectant air and Grear stepped forward. "Geordie courted Morag for a time."

"Yes," Fiona nodded, her eyes darting to her friends. "More than one person expected her to be standing in your position today."

"Ladies, no need to embarrass the poor dear. We don't want her thinking she's getting one of my cast-offs." Morag waved her hand before fixing her gaze on Ione, a viperous smile spreading across her lips. "Really, darling, Geordie is kind enough, but it was never more than a flirtation on my part."

"Aye, so he did court ye at that," Ailsa interjected tartly. "A long while past, hm? I was only a child at the time, but I remember it well," she added, a not-so-innocent smile on her face. "Twas all just a passing fancy on his side too, seein' as he never did come up to scratch. But it took my brother only days to see that Ione was the one for him."

"Well, then it seems everyone is happier that I am the one standing here today." Ione's own expression lost any reflection of the joy she'd felt minutes before. "How very kind of you to reassure me that there will be no bitter feelings."

Morag's voice turned absolutely icy. "Indeed. I suppose you have more experience with engagements than I do."

The color drained from Ione's face. A scathing remark was on the tip of her tongue, but she managed to cool her temper, instead saying pleasantly, "Yes, I suppose so—and soon, a wedding as well. Of course, as I shall be Lady Kirkleith in just a few days, I am always available to the ladies in the clan—young or old—for advice on these matters, and I would be delighted to advise you on your own engagement, if—I mean when, of course—such a thing should occur." She caught sight of her cousin out of the corner of her eye; Tamsin was wearing a ridiculously broad grin. Morag, on the other hand, looked absolutely furious. Ione simply smiled sweetly, feeling she'd turned the conversation.

"I've heard getting engaged can be something of a sport for London girls," Fiona whispered to Grear, just loud enough to be overheard. "Bagging a bird, they call it."

"Indeed." Morag's smirk returned at her friend's comment, regaining an infuriating look of superiority. "Lovely to meet you, Miss Brentwood, Lady Tamsin. I'll be sure to send your regards to the ladies in London when I'm there." She turned and began to walk away with her cronies in pursuit. When she'd taken a few steps, she glanced over her shoulder and spoke to her friends, though her tone was hardly discreet. "I almost pity Geordie, marrying a clearly grasping Sassenach like that. Though he never was a great judge of character." Her friends giggled and the trio disappeared into the crowd.

Ailsa started after her in hot pursuit, but Tamsin grabbed her arm. "Not now, not here," she hissed. "If you start a scene, she wins."

"It's perfectly fine, ladies." Ione took a deep breath, and forced a smile on her face. It was an expression she'd become so practiced at when she was with Theodore. "I am well aware that not everyone will be thrilled with the idea of the Maclaren marrying an Englishwoman." She lifted her chin, though she could feel her composure wavering. "Now, if you will excuse me, I find I am quite thirsty."

Ione didn't wait for a response before she turned and began to head toward the table with the punch bowl, barely maintaining her smile and exchanging brief greetings as she pushed through the crowd.

Somewhere behind her she heard Ailsa proclaim her intention of finding her brother, but Ione was too flustered to stop.

She reached for a glass of punch and downed it in one go, then reached to refill it, her hands shaking with a combination of anger and horror at what Morag had said. She knew she needed to calm down, to put on a brave face and not let that wretched woman have the satisfaction of seeing how well her words had hit their mark, but the illusion of calm was splintering.

Tamsin grasped her elbow and steered her toward the churchyard garden, making some comment about the herbaceous border. When they were out of sight, she gave her cousin a little hug. "Are you all right?"

"She knew about Theodore, Tamsin!" Ione said, beginning to pace back and forth. "She knew and she used it against me." She turned round, her shoulders slumping. "I fear I will never be rid of that man. I wish I could go back and undo all of it, that I had danced with Geordie the first night he saw me. But Theodore managed to take that from me too."

"Theodore," said Tamsin, her seldom-seen temper in full view, "is a gold-plated arse, and you had a lucky escape. That Morag creature, I guarantee you, has never received a single offer, and you've had two. And *that's* the source of her ire. No one who's seen you look at Geordie can doubt your love for him, nor his for you."

A deep, well-beloved voice interrupted them. "And nor should they."

Tamsin gave Ione's hand a squeeze and made herself scarce while Geordie took her place, looking both worried and rather thunderous. He folded Ione in his arms. "I missed you," he murmured. "Ailsa told me what happened—and that you fired off a few shots of your own." He kissed her nose. "I'm proud of you."

Ione huffed out a frustrated breath. "I should have kept my temper better and not allowed her to bait me." She laid her head on his broad shoulder, trying to find her composure again. "She made a few petty remarks and I behaved like a silly schoolgirl in a tantrum. It's hardly the behavior expected from the future Lady Kirkleith."

A low chuckle rumbled under her ear. "Bonny girl, *you* are the future Lady Kirkleith. There's no other measure, and I'd have you no other way than you are. Besides," he kissed the top of her head, "Morag needs to come down a peg or two. I'll not have my wife disrespected." Geordie tilted her chin up to look into her face. "Come back to the party, hm?"

"So that I can fire off again?" Ione asked, but her temper was cooling, and her tone as close to playful as she could muster. She gave Geordie another squeeze and let her head rest on his chest. "She was awful."

"Aye, and now you know why I never offered for her. Don't let her ruin your day, love. The truth is, you've had two offers, and she none at all. Morag MacRainey can't hold a candle to you, and well she knows it."

"Any woman who would let you get away is a complete fool." Ione blushed, but offered him a genuine smile now. She sighed and released him to take his hand instead. "I can't say my past courtships have been much better than yours. Perhaps someone ought to introduce her to Theodore."

Geordie chuckled. "They'd make a lovely match of it." Ione could have shuddered at the thought of that match, but she chose not to examine the idea in detail.

He led her back to the picnic, where their reappearance was met with mild ribaldry. "Ah, lads," said a grinning Geordie in response to his friends' teasing, "look at her! Can ye blame a man?"

Ione laughed, her face going hot with a brilliant blush. "I assure you, he was the perfect gentleman. We merely got distracted discussing matchmaking possibilities."

"Matchmaking?" Ross held up his hands as if to ward something off. "Not for me, I hope. You're well enough matched for all of us, Geordie."

"No, no." The viscount laughed. "I know better than to expect lightning to strike twice." He tucked Ione's hand securely into the crook of his arm. "Come, bonny girl—let me introduce you around a bit, hm?"

Geordie led her to an older lady presiding over a smaller group, from a pillowed wooden chair. She looked up at their approach, and held out an imperious hand for Geordie's attention. "Lady Ramsay, my aunt," he introduced Ione, "and my cousin Wallace." The young man so named grinned and shook Geordie's hand, getting to his feet with alacrity and bowing to Ione.

"Truly a pleasure." Ione curtsied slightly, putting the episode with Morag from her mind entirely. "I'm very happy to meet more of Geordie's family."

"As are we," replied Wallace.

His mother peered at her through a lorgnette. "A pretty gel, certainly. Where were you educated, child?" she demanded.

"Ivybridge, my lady." Ione replied sweetly.

"An English school, is it?"

"Yes, my lady. My family hails from London." Ione glanced up at Geordie, hoping this response wouldn't be met with disapproval.

Lady Ramsay gave a nod and shot a few more questions at her, rapid-fire, seeming to approve of the answers. At last she looked at her nephew. "A good choice, I believe. Find Wallace one such and I shall be in your debt. Have you a sister, my dear?"

Ione had to stifle a laugh, but was pleased that she'd apparently passed the older woman's examination. "Yes, my lady. She is a year younger than myself."

"And is she out?"

"She is," Ione allowed, "but it is early for her to be thinking of marriage, I believe."

"Pity. A cousin, perhaps?"

"Yes, I do have a cousin." Ione turned to glance back at Tamsin. "As a matter of fact, she is here, but of course I cannot speak for her."

"Wallace," said his mother, "an introduction is in order, I believe." She cast an imperious eyebrow at the Maclaren. "See to it, Geordie."

"Yes, aunt." He was hiding a grin, his lips twitching. Ione nearly lost her composure and had to bite her lip to keep from laughing when she caught Geordie's eye. "Forgive us for now, aunt - I've more of the clan that wants to meet my bride," Geordie said with a bow. "But fear not, I'll introduce Wallace to Lady Tamsin at the dance tonight. Come, love."

Ione managed to hold her laughter in just long enough to avoid offending his aunt. She turned to her future husband with a giggle. "Well, I suppose I met with her approval."

"Indeed you did. Aunt Lorna is a favorite with both Ailsa and me; you'll learn why as you get to know her." He gave her fingers a squeeze and took her to meet the next batch of clansfolk.

Chapter Seventeen

The Ball

Overall, Geordie thought as he tied his four-in-hand for the ball that evening, introducing Ione to the clan had gone well. She'd been absolutely right, bless her, when she'd realized what it would mean to the clan to have a wedding to celebrate after such heartrending sorrow; it was that instinct, more than anything else, that convinced Geordie that she was the right choice to lead the clan at his side.

He studied himself in the mirror. Tidy enough, he thought, to satisfy his mother, and by extension hopefully his bride. He was looking forward to this ball: for he'd be able to dance with his Ione at last, and as often as he liked without exciting untoward gossip. He chuckled. Oh, gossip there would be, no doubt; but as they were to be wed in two days it could do little harm.

The boys were waiting in the great hall at the bottom of the staircase, a decanter at the ready. "Now then, lads," said Asher as Geordie entered. "A toast."

Ross passed a glass to Geordie before taking one for himself. "And high time for it, I say. The first of our group to wed." He looked down at his glass, brows coming together slightly. "Seems like it wasn't all that long ago that we were frightened lads staring at each other on our first day at Farrington."

"Indeed." Asher tapped his glass. "Raise 'em, boys." He cleared his throat. "Here's to Geordie, the best of friends if any man ever had one. He's seen us at our best, he's seen us at our worst, and he still can't tell the difference." His eyes were twinkling behind his spectacles.

Geordie burst out laughing. "To you lot, then: I would rather be here now, with you three, than with the best people in the world." He sipped, still chuckling.

"Excepting of course, the future Lady Kirkleith." Quinn grinned before tipping his drink back. He swallowed, and then raised his glass again. "And not one of us here would begrudge it."

"Always excepting my Ione, of course," Geordie agreed, and finished his drink before a rustle at the top of the staircase caught his attention. He glanced up, then stared, his glass falling from a suddenly nerveless hand.

Ione was standing at the top of the stairs in a gown of lavender silk and delicate snowy-white lace. Sprigs of heather were woven through her dark curls, accentuated by pearls. Soft spirals framed her face, somehow making her eyes seem even larger, bluer. It was the very gown she'd worn on the night Geordie first saw her.

Time seemed to spin backward, except then he'd been struck by her beauty alone, and now he knew and treasured the heart of her.

Ione smiled lovingly at him as she all but floated down the grand staircase. She stopped on the bottom step and her smile grew wider. "Geordie." She dipped her head to him.

He bowed low. "My own love." He would have said more, but his voice seemed to have deserted him in the face of her radiance.

"I found I was feeling rather nostalgic this evening." Ione finished her descent and took a step away from the stairs to turn around slowly. "I hope it is an appropriate choice for the evening."

"Ione," Geordie managed finally, his voice strained. "I—you look—"

"It is not the first time you've seen me in this dress." Ione smoothed her skirts, eyes twinkling.

"No, I—I remember. Believe me." He took her hand and kissed it, reverently.

She leaned closer to him and whispered. "I only wish we'd been able to share a dance the first time I wore it." Her fingers tightened around his. "We've been offered a rare gift, you and I, a second chance. I shall never take that for granted."

"As God is my witness, Ione, I love you," was his soft reply. "We'll dance the rest of our days together."

Guests were arriving now, and Lady Kirkleith requested Geordie to come stand by her to greet them. He took his reluctant leave of Ione and the rest and went to do his duty. After an hour or so, his mother finally set him free to open the dancing.

Eagerly, Geordie hurried into the ballroom to find his beloved; scanning the crowd of familiar faces until at last he spied her. She was happily chatting with her cousin, a glass of punch in her hand and a smile brighter than any other in the room.

His own smile widening, Geordie strode across the marble floor and bowed low before taking her glass and handing it to Quinn. "Will you open the dancing with me, my love?"

Ione's fingers curled around Geordie's as she stepped away from Tamsin. "Of course. We mustn't shirk our duties at our first ball together," she replied. Her response might have been practical, but her smile had turned intimate, and her eyes full of merriment. "Besides, this dance is long overdue."

He kissed her fingers because he couldn't kiss her lips, and led her into the middle of the floor as the small orchestra began to play a Boston waltz. She followed him through the intricate clasping and unclasping of hands, twirling in and out of his arms with graceful ease, and at last they were swooping around the floor, her skirt swinging wide as she lay back in his grasp, leaning back into his grip with an expression of pure trust and adoration when he dipped and lifted her in time with the music.

Ione let loose with a small, breathy laugh as the dance ended. It was a sound of pure bliss and it embedded itself in Geordie's heart, and he knew this would be a memory he cherished for a lifetime. Ione curtsied gracefully. "You are a remarkable dancer, George Maclaren! I hardly felt my feet touch the floor."

"One is only as good as one's partner, my love." Geordie led her back to their friends, passing Lady Tamsin as she was escorted to the floor by his cousin Wallace. 'You owe me', she mouthed before smiling beatifically at her partner, and Geordie laughed aloud.

Quinn was quick to step forward. "And now sir, I do believe I'm next on the lady's dance card." He looked to Geordie with a broad grin as he held his hand out for Ione.

Geordie gave his friend a nod, and watched as Quinn whirled Ione into the crowd of dancers. A tap at his elbow caught his attention and he turned to find one of his brevet aunts with her oldest son in tow. "Aunt Amelia, Calum!" He kissed his father's cousin on both cheeks and shook the young man's hand. "I'm sorry we missed you at the picnic earlier, but delighted to see you now. I hope you're both well?"

It transpired that they were, and professed to be equally pleased to see him. "It's been too long, Geordie, my dear," Mrs. Maclaren said. "I wanted to say how sorry we are about your father."

He sobered, nodding. "It's a loss to us all. Thank you for the flowers you sent to St. Paul's."

"The very least we could do, my boy." She patted his arm kindly. "And you're engaged—and to be wed this very weekend! How proud your father would be. I will confess, I scuttled over here hoping for an introduction." She peered around Geordie, obviously searching for his bride.

Geordie chuckled. "And you shall have one," he replied just as the song ended. "One of my seconds swept her away for a dance, but—ah, here they are."

Ione slipped her hand into the crook of Geordie's elbow even as she thanked Quinn for the dance. She was a little winded, but seemed to be in merry spirits. No doubt Quinn had proven to be a lively partner, with his preference for the more energetic dances. "Mr. Rutherford does enjoy pushing the tempo," she said, fanning herself.

Geordie chuckled—it was such a perfect encapsulation of his friend. "I advise you not to let him polka with you," he replied. "My love, allow me to introduce you to Mrs. Amelia Maclaren and Calum Maclaren. They're cousins of one sort or another, but she is kind enough to let me call her aunt. Aunt Amelia, my intended, Miss Ione Brentwood."

"A pleasure to meet you both," Ione replied, cheeks still flushed from her exertions on the dance floor.

Mrs. Maclaren regarded her with a pleasant air and a faintly assessing gaze. "Welcome to the family, my dear."

"It is an honor that I do not take for granted, I assure you." Ione dipped her head, politely. No doubt the introductions of the day were blurring together by now, Geordie thought; even so, she'd managed to treat each new face with kindness and charm, and he felt himself bursting with pride at every skillful interaction.

The older lady smiled. "For us as well, I assure you. I have never seen Geordie look so happy before, and surely that is due to you."

Calum offered a quick bow to Ione, before turning his attention to Geordie, with a companionable clap on the back. "Ready for the challenges, cousin?"

"Indeed I am," Geordie grinned. "Going to enter the lists?"

His cousin laughed. "Oh, you never know. We'll see who else wants to give the clan a show, hm?"

Geordie saw Ione's smile falter ever-so-slightly. She glanced up at him and then back to Calum before speaking again. "How many challenges are there, typically?"

Calum shrugged. "Oh, two or three, usually. Enough to get the crowd excited, you know. It's all just for show anyway."

"Yes, so I've been told." Ione's voice was soft and thoughtful. Geordie had seen a similar expression on her face when he and the lads had explained the danger of the threats they faced, and she explained her visions concerning the challenges. She blinked and offered an apologetic smile. "All this talk of combat before a wedding tends to make a bride fretful, you know."

Mrs. Maclaren patted her hand. "No reason to fret, my dear. There is no one here who would harm our Maclaren."

"Of course not," Ione smiled at Mrs. Maclaren, but Geordie felt her grip on his arm tighten. She looked up at him, lovingly, though the expression was shadowed by worry. "I'm just anxious for the wedding, I'm sure."

"Of course you are, my dear." Geordie's aunt smiled at her again. "All be well and settled soon." She turned to her son. "Come now, we mustn't monopolize the new Maclaren and his bride." Calum bowed over her hand a second time, and they moved farther into the room.

"All right?" Geordie asked Ione *sotto voce.*

Ione nodded, glance darting around the room, landing on the faces of those nearest before returning to Geordie. "I'm simply ready for the challenges to be past. For a few moments I was able to forget what lies ahead."

He looked around the room too, wondering what she saw. Friends? Enemies? Geordie pressed his lips together. "Here, love. Come with me." He gently tugged her toward one of the doors.

The lines of worry on her face eased slightly, and were replaced by curiosity as she followed his lead. They were waylaid now and again by offers of condolences or congratulations, but escaped the crowds easily enough.

He drew her into an anteroom, kicked the door shut behind him, and pulled her into his arms in the dim light. "It'll be well, Ione. Thanks to you, we know all we must, and whoever wishes us ill knows nothing." He kissed the top of her head, inhaling the heady scent of heather. "I don't know what this plan of yours is, and nor do I need to. I know all will be well."

"Are you the oracle now?" Ione replied, a hint of teasing in her voice, for all of the concern still on her face. She reached up and cupped his jaw. "Not seeing my own fate never bothered me before, but now that it is so intricately woven with yours, I cannot abide this blind spot."

Geordie smiled, then pressed his lips gently to hers. "I willnae leave you, Ione. I would walk away from Heaven itself to stay by your side. Mind you remember that." He sealed that promise with another kiss—no mere touching of lips, but full of heat and love.

The fervor with which Ione returned his embrace was unlike any of their previous kisses. She clung to him, lips parting, a small sound of pleasure—no, *hunger*—was buried in the contact. Her arms wrapped around him, body pressed firmly to his.

He met her passion, nothing loath, claiming her mouth as he longed to claim her body, blood surging south. Geordie indulged himself for a moment or two longer, then pulled his head back, hands shaking. "Day after tomorrow, bonny girl," he managed roughly. "No longer than that."

"It seems an eternity just now." Ione tilted her head and smiled softly. Then—much to Geordie's surprise and delight—she wove her fingers into the fabric of his shirt and pulled him in for another heated kiss.

With that single gesture he was nearly lost. He grunted softly and turned them, pinning her to the paneled wall, hands cupping her head. Geordie hummed his encouragement as he coaxed her to open yet more to his tender siege. "You tempt me beyond bearing, my beloved girl," he murmured, and moved his mouth to the sensitive skin of her neck.

A soft cry escaped Ione's lips, her head tilting to the side, offering him greater access before urging him to meet her gaze. "No more than you do me," she rasped, blue eyes blown dark. Ione pressed her lips to his, tracing a path along his jaw, his neck, and then lightly nipped beneath his ear. There was a desperation in it, a need and longing that Geordie knew well.

He closed his eyes, clenched his teeth, and lifted his head. "Is this what you want, Ione? For I'll deny you nothing." He caught her mouth in another soul-drugging kiss. "I'll come t'you tonight, when the house is quiet, if it's what you want."

She pulled back, fingers tracing the details of his face. Her cheeks flared pink, but her gaze met his. "I want to be yours, Geordie," she whispered. "Our plan is a good one. But the only thing known for certain is that I cannot bear the idea of going forward in this life without being with you. Come to my room, my love."

He let out a shuddering breath. "I'll come," he promised, and kissed her one last time.

Ione slipped from the anteroom to go and repair the damage he'd done to her hair while Geordie paced the room, trying to get his body under control. He was grinning like a lunatic, he felt sure; Quinn—or either of the others—would easily be able to figure out what had happened, and Geordie was having none of that. He found a decanter and a handy bucket of ice, briefly debated just applying the ice directly to the affected area, and then settled for a whiskey and soda.

He was still trying to process the turn his relationship with Ione had just taken. She... *desired* him. He wasn't sure he'd ever been desired before—at least for anything other than his potential inheritance. It was a heady feeling, and in some ways he couldn't believe his luck, but... he hoped she hadn't taken his offer as a sign of disrespect.

But she'd agreed to it, so that boded well. He hadn't even meant to say it, it just sort of came out before he'd thought to stop it.

Well, he would just have to make sure she understood: that he loved her, body and soul, and would do so regardless of what this night brought. And perhaps... Geordie grinned and downed the rest of his whiskey, whistling as he headed back to the ballroom.

His cousins Calum and Hamish were just coming out, in what looked like the middle of a serious conversation. Or at least Hamish was conversing, and Calum listening. It was an odd pairing, to be sure—so far as Geordie knew, they had a last name in common, but no more than that. Still, it was nice to see the usually dour Hamish being sociable for a change. It was, Geordie supposed, kind of young Calum to show an interest in the old man. He greeted both cousins with good humor and made his way into the ballroom.

Ione was with Ailsa, not a hair out of place, or wrinkle in her skirts. Geordie had to wonder if she'd used some magical means to cover their heated encounter. While her physical appearance might not have betrayed their brief tryst, the flash in her eyes when they met his put an end to any doubt he might have harbored.

He smiled to himself and joined them, greeting his sister with high good humor. "Having fun?"

But it was not his sister's voice that answered. "Lady Ailsa—and Miss Brentwood!" Morag was coming toward them.

Ailsa rolled her eyes at her brother. "Well, I was," she muttered, and turned to greet the new arrival with a sickeningly sweet simper. Aware of Morag's earlier treatment of his fiancée, Geordie casually drew Ione's hand into the crook of his arm while giving the other woman a nod.

"Hello, Morag. So glad you could join us," Ailsa murmured. From where he stood Geordie could see her tuck her hand behind her back and cross her fingers, and he quickly turned his laugh into a cough. "My sister and I—forgive me, sister-to-be," she pretended to correct herself, "were just speaking of the London season and how unfair it all is. Do you not think so?"

Morag tilted her head, her smile very 'kind'. "I think it is the most exciting thing in the world," she demurred. "To make your debut and have handsome men in attendance, falling in love with you..." She fluttered her fan and glanced up at Geordie from beneath her lashes. "You'll understand when you're older, my dear," she finished.

Ailsa smiled innocently, her expression rather like the kitchen cat when it's just bagged a mouse, Geordie thought. "I'm sure you're right. I was only thinking—it's always such a tragedy to see a lady go on the shelf after only a few seasons, and received no offers at all. I believe it happens," she eyed Morag, "quite frequently." The other woman bristled visibly.

"Indeed, I have seen more than one lady soured by such things." Ione agreed solemnly, though Geordie caught her exchanging a small glance with his sister. Clearly, she'd picked up on Ailsa's point. Ione lifted her chin even as she reached out to pat Ailsa's hand. "But such worries are hardly worth spoiling such a lovely night. I have every intention of enjoying myself and being thankful for my good fortune. I'm certain you will not face such a fate, my dear."

"Heavens, I hope not—though if I did face such ignominy, I would hope to bear it well and kindly." Ailsa, her gaze on Morag, took Ione's free arm. "Your good fortune is ours, my dear sister. I have never before seen Geordie so entirely satisfied and happy."

"I only hope to bring him even more happiness in the days and years to come." Ione beamed up at Geordie adoringly, as Morag's lips thinned. Geordie was fascinated by this side of the women he loved, watching first one, then another. It was like a deadlier form of tennis.

"Such a romantic story, I always think." Ailsa smiled at her. "Geordie's been chased by many girls since he attained his majority, and never found one to hold his interest. And then he met you. 'Tis enough to make one believe in love at first sight."

"Oh, I certainly believe." Ione replied.

"Love at first sight?" Morag laughed musically. "Oh Ailsa, you always were such a romantic." She cast a dismissive look over Geordie and Ione.

"Aye, I am, 'tis true," the younger woman agreed sweetly. "I've no mind to turn love into more practical matters, as is the habit among fashionable young ladies. Especially those who've been through more than a single season."

"Not all women are willing to settle for the first fellow who glances her way." Morag's eyes narrowed.

Ailsa laughed. "Some women never get the opportunity."

Ione hiccupped softly, then ducked her head behind Geordie's arm. He could hear her chuckling even with the sound muffled in his jacket sleeve. She pretended to cough and looked back at the spectacle, smile barely concealed.

"Of course, I can't expect a child like you to understand the intricacies of romance." Morag's smile was more than a little strained. "How fortunate you will soon have a sister so... experienced."

Ailsa dimpled. "Indeed so. If I am so lucky as to have a suitor, Ione will help me know how to bring him to the point. Some women simply can't, no matter *what* they try, poor dears. And then they are left with nothing but to nip at the heels of those who have found partners in life."

"Oh, I am quite sure Miss Brentwood knows how to bring a man to the point; what else could be gathered by such a hasty engagement?" Morag's smile had turned to a snarl, her lips twitching.

And that was enough. Geordie's brows lowered and he drew himself up, summoning all the authority he could command. "Best rethink yoursel', Morag," he said, his voice deceptively soft. "Surely you're not fool enough to imply what I think you're implying about the woman I intend to wed."

"I'm not implying anything. I was merely agreeing with your sister." Morag glared up at Geordie, clearly seething. "Whatever would make you think otherwise?"

"An unfortunate misunderstanding," he nodded. "I am sure you meant no disrespect to the Lady of Clan Maclaren. Such a thing from an unmarried maid of the clan would be met with no quarter, I assure you. Perhaps you'd like me to reassure your father in person of your support of his laird and lady?"

"Most gracious of you, my lord," Morag bit out through clenched teeth, her eyes darting toward Ione with unveiled contempt.

The levity Ione had been concealing before vanished entirely. She glanced up at Geordie.

"Morag." He snapped out her name. She was well over the mark; he was absolutely livid and he let the woman see it.

Morag visibly flinched, but took a deep breath and a very forced smile spread across her face. "My deepest apologies for any misunderstanding. Let me extend my very best wishes to you, my lord." She swallowed like she'd eaten something bitter, then turned that forced smile to Ione. "My lady."

Geordie went on inexorably. "See that no breath of such rumor meets my ears, Morag, today or any day. And see that you recall your place, especially in relation to my wife." He dismissed her with a lift of his chin.

"Of course, Maclaren." Morag looked like a cat that had just been tossed in water. She dipped her head to him, then to Ione before turning, and all but vanished into the crowd.

Ailsa dusted off her hands, her smile wide. Ione gave Geordie's arm a squeeze, then leaned closer to him. "I truly am the luckiest of women. Thank you for choosing me."

He kissed her fingers, and then laughed aloud at his sister. "You needn't look so smug, Ailsa."

"I cannot help it, Geordie. It's *such* a lovely party." She beamed at them both and went to find their mother.

"Your sister is quite a formidable lady." Ione chuckled. "Remind me not to cross her."

"Considering her defense of you, I suspect it's not something you need to worry about overmuch." Geordie squeezed her fingers. "Come, love. Dance with me again." And as they began their first turn around the floor, Geordie found that it was an entirely different sort of dance that occupied his thoughts.

Chapter Eighteen

Lovers' Vows

Ione paced her private sitting room in her nightrail, dressing gown cinched at the waist. Geordie had offered to come to her room, and she'd said yes. Perhaps it was madness—it certainly wasn't anything anyone would consider proper, and it was nothing she ever would have agreed to in her previous engagement. But everything with Geordie was different. The very air seemed more alive when the man was around. His presence filled her with hope and anticipation, even as the threat of murder hung over them. And that was why she'd told him to come.

Still, she couldn't deny the nervous flutter. Mama had explained what passed between a man and a woman. But being told the practical logistics of such matters hardly gave one a real frame of reference. With Theodore Gibson the idea of it was rather nauseating. But with Geordie... that was a different matter entirely, and the flutter she felt, Ione admitted to herself, was as much excitement as anxiety.

There was a single knock on her door, so quick and soft she might have missed it.

Ione let out a little breath. She rushed to the mirror that hung on a nearby wall and gave herself a once over. Her dark hair was plaited in a long braid, some loose curls twisting around her face. She pinched her cheeks a few times and then hurried to open the door, suddenly realizing the pause might have given her beloved reason to doubt her resolve. "Please, come in," Ione whispered, stepping aside to allow him entrance. "Although this is your home, so I suppose it's a bit silly for me to invite you in."

He had, in fact, stepped back from the threshold and seemed surprised when the door swung open. Geordie waited to speak until the door was closed and latched behind him. "Your home too, now, Ione." He regarded her. "We needn't do this if it worries you."

The offer alone helped Ione relax. She wanted this, but knowing he'd accept it if she changed her mind changed the flutter to a glowing ember. Ione smiled softly and took one of his hands in hers, kissing his palm. "I told you to come, I have not changed my mind." Then she laughed nervously, despite herself. "I'm able to look into the future, and yet I never would have predicted this when I woke today. But Geordie, my dearest, it is what I want."

He cleared his throat, seeming nervous himself, and she took a moment to look at him. He'd changed from the formal outfit he'd worn to the ball, but these were not nightclothes either: a simple woolen kilt, roughly pleated and held in place with a wide belt, and a plain cotton shirt, full-sleeved, that laced up at the neck, where she glimpsed his chest and a smattering of soft, light brown hair. His feet were bare. "Ione," he began, "I want t'say something, first."

"Of course... if you've changed your mind..." Ione stammered a little, then released his hand to anxiously twist the end of her braid. Perhaps she'd been too rash in accepting his offer to come to her room.

"No! No. It's—" He took a breath. "Ater what Morag said earlier, I want you t'know what's true, and it's this: what you and I do here—this is about us, and for us, and no other. There's no viscount in this room, not tonight—just a man desperately in love, and I've come to you like this," he gestured to himself, "to show you—to pledge t'you everything I am. No castle, no title, just me. I swear t'you now, before God and all his angels, that you are my wife and I will love you to my last breath." His gaze was clear, but the line between his brows spoke of some worry.

Seeing such vulnerability from him, made the last of Ione's hesitation vanish. She crossed to him, wrapping her arms around his waist and laid her head against his chest. "I believe you, Geordie, and I trust you." She tilted her head back to gaze up at him. "Whatever vows we exchange on Sunday, this night is our oath to one another."

His brow cleared and he tipped her chin up a little more. "Then let me love you, wife," he murmured, and his mouth descended on hers.

The kiss was heated, and it warmed Ione to the core. Her hands slid up his back, mapping out the curve of the muscles beneath the fabric. This man was hers, and she was utterly, and without the slightest doubt, his. Ione pulled back and took his hand. "Come, let us go to the bedroom," she paused and took a single step toward the door, "husband."

He froze at the word, letting out a breath, and then with an economy of motion scooped her up and held her close to his broad chest as he carried her through the bedroom door.

Ione did not stay idle in his arms. She pressed her lips to his neck, fingers slipping into the laces of his shirt, smoothing over his skin, stroking the soft curls that lightly dusted his chest. His breathing hitched, a response that only served to encourage her exploration, and entice her to bolder action. Ione grinned against his neck, then licked, and tentatively scraped her teeth across his skin.

He groaned—or growled—deep in his chest, and placed her on the bed, rising up long enough to reach behind himself and pull his shirt over his head, throwing it to the ground before leaning over her, mouth upon hers again.

Ione's body arched up toward him, seemingly of its own will, for she'd given it no conscious thought. She simply needed to be closer to him, to feel him against her. It was a longing she'd never experienced before and it was thrilling. The silk of her nightrail, though soft, was an irritant—a barrier that hindered her need for contact.

Geordie pulled at the belt of her dressing gown, spreading the fabric wide while his mouth left scorching trails along the column of her throat. He pushed the silk of both dressing gown and nightrail back from her shoulder and tasted her there, murmuring her name like a supplication.

Yes. This was what she wanted; this was right. They'd always been meant to come to this place, to *this* moment, and Ione didn't need her magic to tell her that. She knew her future, and it was here, now, with *this* man. "I love you," Ione whispered in a voice so breathless and low that she hardly recognized it as her own.

"You're everything to me, Ione. All there is. And I will love you for all of my days," he promised, and then words gave way to a language deeper, older; one of sensation and the joining of two hearts.

Ione sighed, head pillowed on Geordie's bare chest, fingers winnowing idly through the soft hair there. She was spent physically, but had never felt so content. "I believe I see why we're told to wait for marriage, and it is far more practical than mere propriety." She giggled a little.

"Is it, then?" Geordie asked, pressing a kiss to her forehead.

"Yes, indeed." She shifted to prop her chin on his pectoral muscle and grinned at him. "No one would ever leave their beds."

He chuckled. "After Sunday morning, I intend you will not for quite a while," he returned with a grin. "Best be prepared, bonny girl."

"I find myself eager for Sunday afternoon." Ione laughed a little. She leaned her head against his chest again, reveling in the comforting sound of his heartbeat. She could swear her own was beating in tandem with it, and she sighed. "I suppose you will have to leave here before morning."

Geordie caught at the hand on his chest and stretched it across him, pulling her a little closer. "Aye, for appearance's sake. But my heart will remain here, in your keeping, and we have time yet." He kissed her palm. "I want t'love you again, Ione, but I would not want to cause you hurt."

The hour was late and the dawn would bring the challenges, but he was oh, so tempting. Ione scooted up to kiss him. "I would hurt if you left me now," she said with a sultry smile.

He tightened his arm around her middle and turned them both, pinning her underneath him. "Well," he murmured against her skin, "we can't have that."

Even with all the worries and concerns for the challenges to come, Ione slept like a baby after Geordie left her. She woke feeling refreshed and more in love than she'd imagined possible. The birds outside her window were singing sweeter tunes, and the sunshine was so bright and cheerful that Ione thought it almost seemed to sparkle. With Rose's help she was out of bed and dressed early, despite getting considerably less sleep than usual. A short time later she was making her way down to the dining room, brightly humming to herself.

Though Lady Kirkleith, Ailsa and Miss Anderson had yet to make an appearance, Geordie too was already up with the boys, clad in kilts similar to what Geordie had worn the night before, but simpler. Much rougher than the formal, pleated variety, these were more like plaid blankets, buckled around each waist with a wide leather belt. With these the men wore heavy boots and light, loose shirts.

Ione stopped in her tracks and looked her soon-to-be husband up and down. Even if she had wanted to, she would not have easily been able to hide the appreciation on her face. She moved closer to him, hard put to keep her hands to herself, especially with their newfound level of intimacy.

He chuckled and winked. "'Tis mutual, I promise you," he whispered, and began to assemble a plate for her from the sideboard.

Ione cleared her throat and took a seat at the table, turning her attention to the others before she gave herself away entirely. "And how did everyone sleep last night?"

"Well enough, once I went to sleep," Ross replied with a shrug, uncorking a bottle and filling three shot glasses, which he proceeded to pass to each of his friends.

Tamsin looked a bit pulled, with dark circles under her eyes, but allowed that she'd slept well enough once she'd accomplished what she'd intended to do.

Quinn was swishing the murky green liquid in the shot glass, staring at it dubiously. "What is it?"

"Good for you. Drink it," was the only explanation Ross provided.

Geordie eyed it skeptically, then shrugged and downed it, afterward coughing and gagging, making a face. "St. Peter's hairy bawbag, what's in that stuff? It's vile!"

Ross shrugged without looking away from the task of filling his plate. "Oh, the usual, lizard livers, the glands from a sacrificed goat... a bit of blood." He seemed to cough a bit, cleared his throat and looked at his friends. "I said it was good for you. I didn't say it would taste good."

Asher slowly pushed the glass away from himself with the tip of a finger, as though he thought it might explode.

"You might have warned a chap," Geordie remarked as he poured himself a tot from the brandy decanter and washed his mouth out, shuddering.

Quinn tilted his head. "It can't be *that* bad. What's it supposed to do?" he asked Ross.

But Ross had a napkin over his mouth and offered nothing in the way of an answer. Ione shook her head, laughing even as she crossed her arms and tried to look stern. "Shame on you, Dr. McInerny! There are no such things in that brew!"

"Oh, why did you have to go and spoil it?" Ross replied through hiccups of laughter. "They believed every word. I could have had them going all day!" He nudged the potion back toward Asher. "Drink up, then! Don't you like my cooking?"

Asher tossed a piece of toast at Ross' head. "You drink first, you great knob. What *is* it supposed to do?"

"It's a mixture of herbs and incantations that'll make the day less taxing. Greater stamina and whatnot," Ross explained, still chortling, but regaining some semblance of control. He reached into his sporran and pulled out a flask. "Just be glad you don't have to drink what I do. Boosting magic is not a tasty business." All the same, he made a point of pouring a bit of the thick, grainy, yellow liquid into a shot glass and downing it.

Tamsin sat up, looking very interested. "Tasty or not, might I try a little?"

Ross passed the flask to Ione's cousin. "You may wish to have something to wash the taste and... er... grit down."

Tamsin sniffed the mixture delicately while Asher and Quinn drank their potions, the latter making loud retching sounds. She wrinkled her nose and tipped a bit into a spoon, taking the stuff like medicine. "Good heavens," she said, touching her napkin to her lips. "That's upsetting. But," after a moment's further contemplation, "it does seem to do the job."

Ione looked at each of them in turn, then took a dainty sip of her morning tea, quite relieved to be spared the experience of taking a dose of potion herself. She smiled up at Geordie as he set a plate in front of her and settled in the chair beside hers. "And are you feeling rested, love?"

"Aye, I slept well," he replied with a grin. "Exceptionally pleasant dreams."

"How astonishing," Ione answered, gracing him with a warm and intimate smile. She knew she ought to make a better show of discretion, but she wanted to revel in what they'd shared last night. "My dreams were quite delightful as well. It was a wonderful night indeed."

Geordie chuckled and leaned toward her to steal a brief kiss before settling to his breakfast.

The rest of the castle's denizens arrived; the meal was a hearty one and the atmosphere jovial at first, but as it drew to a close there was a noticeable shift in the mood of the group. Ione's stomach knotted with so much worry that she began to regret eating as much as she had. Even with their plan in place she felt helpless, and knowing that there would be little she could contribute once the fighting began gnawed at her nerves.

Her cousin excused herself from the table and met the group in the great hall, her arms full of hardened leather. "These are yours," she told Ross, handing him the first set of bracers, "and these are for you, my lord," giving Geordie a set. "These are the same—choose whichever you like," she said to Asher and Quinn, who sorted themselves out and began to lace up each other's gauntlets.

Geordie looked interested, but seemed to know better than to ask, so he merely held his arms out to Ione in a silent request, while Tamsin laced Ross into the set she'd enchanted for him.

Ione squeezed Geordie's fingers for an instant before turning her attention to securing the gauntlets. When she finished, she traced the intricate patterns emblazoned on the leather, silently praying that their plan would protect him and the others. She released a slow sigh. "Be careful, my Geordie. If I thought it promised a happy outcome I would ride away with you right now, and build a life far from all of this."

He bent his tawny head and kissed the fingers of both her hands. "It'll be well, Ione. We're meant to spend our lives together. I believe that with all my heart." He leaned forward, his lips just brushing the shell of her ear. "Even more so, today." Geordie straightened up and gave her a smile. "The curricle has been ordered for Lady Tamsin, Ailsa, Miss Anderson and Mama. You and I will ride on Starlight just as we did yesterday, and we'll all meet at the challenge grounds."

At the arena, the Maclaren did a proud lap with his bride before lifting her down from the stallion at one end, near where Tamsin and Ailsa and other members of the family had assembled. It boded to be a fine day, and the seats quickly filled.

Ione greeted her future in-laws with a smile that she hoped was convincing, and settled into a chair beside Tamsin. This place was one Ione knew well: she'd seen it before, in nightmares of blood and pain. She envied the spectators who were blissfully ignorant of the very real threats that hung in the air today. For all they knew, this was a social gathering, a time to say goodbye to the Maclaren that was, and to celebrate Geordie's ascension to the position of clan chief.

In need of distraction, Ione turned her attention to the basket at Tamsin's side, noting that Mrs. Madden had filled it with enough food to feed a small army. She reached in and palmed an apple, giving it a little toss before putting it back. "How many people is this basket meant to feed?"

Tamsin smiled briefly, her gaze intent on the field. "Dozens, from the appearance. Look, there's Angus."

Geordie's all-around factotum was striding to the center of the field. The buzz of excited chatter died down and all eyes turned to the man.

"And so it begins," Ione muttered under breath, consciously working to keep her shoulders from hunching upward with tension. She leaned toward Tamsin and lowered her voice. "I know you had a touch of Ross' potion, but if you require more magic, I offer mine freely. Take what you need if the situation calls for it."

"Ladies and gentlemen, freemen and tenants, family, friends, and Clan Maclaren," Angus greeted them loudly. "We gather here to pay tribute to the Maclaren that was, and to welcome and declare loyalty to our new clan chief, George Maclaren!" A cheer went up.

Ione's gaze drifted to Geordie, a small, warm smile spreading across her face. He was an impressive man, tall, brave, and worthy of the position he held. She took a deep breath and scanned the crowd, wondering who among the assembled had darker intent.

Geordie was conversing with his friends as they readied for the challenges. He shucked his shirt over his head, his brawny chest on full view, and strapped the enormous claymore to his back. The others did the same.

Ione cleared her throat and allowed herself a moment of nostalgia, remembering the sensation of his skin against hers. She turned away from him, face burning, and set her focus back on the picnic basket.

Angus was droning on about tradition and so forth, but finally he got to the meat of the matter. "Are there any who would challenge the Maclaren?"

"I would!" Geordie's cousin Wallace strode onto the field, three young men at his back. The general attitude among the group was one of playfulness, and lacked any indication of true malice.

Sensing that this was not the threat that loomed, Ione fixed an amused look on Tamsin. "Did young Wallace speak with you last night? His mother was rather eager for an introduction."

Tamsin chuckled. "He did, indeed. A nice boy."

"Yes, his mother was quite insistent that he meet every available young lady in my family." Ione laughed a little, hefting an apple and rolling it in her hands idly. "She was an intriguing character."

Her cousin nodded. "Yes, I should say so. I met her, too."

Geordie was grinning at Wallace. "All right, then, cousin. All of us, or just me?"

Wallace laughed. "Oh, all of you, I should think. More fun that way."

"As you say," the Maclaren agreed, and they took their stances.

Handsome as Geordie was, this display of sheer size and muscle elevated him into something breathtakingly primal, in Ione's opinion. The sword was nearly as long as he was tall, and he handled it with ease, his muscles bunching and flexing as he swept the claymore around. No finesse here, no parrying or blocking; to Ione it just looked as though they were trying to hack each other's heads off in the name of good fun.

"Not at all the elegant fencing I've seen back in London," she commented.

"Not much elegant about this," Tamsin agreed.

The teams were well matched; as each pair found a victor, the men retired from the field, and eventually only Geordie and Wallace were left, trading friendly barbs as well as the occasional blow. The crowd got into the spirit of it, backing first one, then the other combatant, all in fun.

"Come on, then," said Wallace at the last, with a laugh. "Stop toying with me. I'm getting tired and this thing weighs a ton."

Geordie grinned. "All right, then." He raised his sword and they joined in battle, blow after blow. It became clear rather quickly that Geordie held the upper hand; he drove his cousin back step by step, and then with a twist of his claymore, disarmed him. "Do you yield, Wally?" he asked in a friendly tone, and his cousin nodded.

"I do, and not a moment too soon," he replied. "I'm thirsty." He dropped to one knee. "My arm is yours, Maclaren—such as it is."

Geordie helped him up with a grin, slapping him on the back. He waved to the crowd and went to talk to his companions.

"Is there anyone else who would challenge the Maclaren?" Angus shouted.

"Aye!" called a voice from the crowd, which parted to reveal Calum, his chin high. He pushed through them and came to the edge of the arena, scowling.

Geordie nodded, rolling his shoulders, pacing a bit. "All of us, or just me?" he asked mildly, as he'd done with Wallace.

Calum's lip curled and he pointed his sword at the Maclaren. "Just you."

"As y'like." Geordie raised his sword and Calum came running at him, his own weapon raised high. The viscount sidestepped, pivoting out of the way, bemusement on his face. "Calum?"

His cousin snarled, baring his teeth, and ran at him full bore again, swinging his blade downward in what would have been a deadly arc if Geordie hadn't caught it on his claymore. The crowd murmured uncomfortably. Ione felt a chill shimmy down her spine.

Geordie shoved the other man back, brows drawn; Calum renewed his attack, sword flashing in the sunlight as he drove it toward Geordie's head. The sound of metal clashing against metal rang out over the entirely silent crowd. It seemed to resonate through Ione. She wrapped her fingers around Tamsin's and held on for all she was worth. Something was wrong: this was not the smiling and pleasant man she'd met last night, nor was he the shadowy figure with a blood red cap.

Ione glanced to the bench where Geordie's friends watched, concern evident on their faces. Dr. McInerny's head turned, his eyes locking on Tamsin.

Tamsin spoke to Ione. "Now?"

"This isn't what I saw," Ione replied, hesitating. Yet, the fight between Geordie and Calum raged on before her, and it was obvious that the Maclaren cousin would not be satisfied with anything less than blood. There was no time for self-doubt nor indecision. "Now," Ione said, voice resolute and commanding.

Her cousin nodded and she stripped off one glove, touching a bracelet on her opposite wrist, which sparked briefly. Across the yard Ione saw the three seconds shift in place, adjusting their bracers.

On the field Geordie took advantage of an opening and knocked Calum's sword away. "I'll not fight you anymore," he said, stabbing the claymore into the dirt. "I don't want to hurt you."

The only answer his cousin gave was to launch himself at Geordie bodily, knocking him backward, his hands around Geordie's throat. They fell to the ground, Geordie struggling with Calum's wrists, Calum straddling his cousin's body, pressing forward with his entire body.

Asher shouted and the three ran forward, but Geordie's face was suffusing with blood.

Ione jumped to her feet, upsetting the basket at her side and jostling Wallace, who stood next to her, his full attention on the unexpected battle, the large tankard of ale on the bench beside him evidently forgotten. Ione snatched up the heavy ceramic cup, ignoring the beer sloshing out of it, and did the only thing she could think of: she flung the tankard at him with all the strength she could muster.

The tankard connected hard with the side of Calum's head. The impact stunned him and he broke his grip on Geordie just as the boys reached the pair. Quinn grabbed at Calum none-too-gently and jerked him away from the stricken viscount, who rolled over and began coughing, dragging in air. Ross crouched beside him, blocking Ione's view, though she thought she had a good idea of what he was doing. Sure enough, when he backed away Geordie got to his feet, shaking himself like a wet dog and rolling his shoulders. He held up a hand. "I'm fine," Ione heard. "Who threw that?" Asher pointed to Ione and Geordie looked over at her.

Ione inclined her head primly, suddenly aware that Geordie wasn't the only person looking at her. Every head was turned in her direction, eyes fixed on her. She wiped a hand over her cheek, realizing that Wallace's drink was splashed across her face. "You have a wedding to attend tomorrow, Lord Kirkleith. I would not have you miss it."

A smattering of laughter rippled across the crowd; Geordie laid his fingers on his lips and then his heart before bowing to Ione, his love and gratitude evident in his stormy gaze before he crossed to where Quinn restrained Calum.

Chapter Nineteen

Betrayal

The boys had hustled Calum off to a largish shed on the side of the arena; Geordie stalked in that direction while Angus took the field behind him, blathering on about youthful enthusiasm and wasn't this all great fun or some rot.

The shed, added to the arena for the purposes of first aid, was large enough to fit all five men, a few chairs, a table that dominated the center of the space, and a cot beside. "Would you mind tellin' me," Geordie asked his cousin when he slammed the door behind him, "what in the bloody hell you were tryin' to do out there?"

Calum was struggling between Quinn and Asher, and obviously giving the two of them a go at keeping him still. "I should be clan chief!" he spat in Geordie's direction, winning a forceful shove from Quinn. Calum struggled for another moment and then slumped. He looked at the men holding him and his face crumpled. "Oh, God! Geordie, I..." His words turned to sobs, his head dropping forward.

What in the—? Geordie shook his head. "You're not in line for it, Calum, even if I were—" He paused and swallowed. "Were you trying to *kill* me? I..." He rubbed a hand over his face, unable to grasp the enormity of it. "I thought we were friends, Calum. I thought—"

"No—no!" Calum's sobs turned to wails. "What have I done? I didn't mean—I shouldn't have..." He shuddered. "It hurts! I can't stop it!"

Something was terribly wrong here. "What hurts, Calum?" Geordie looked at his friends. "What's wrong with him?"

Quinn resituated his grip, glancing at Geordie. "He started up like this as soon as we got him off the field."

"I feel it! My head—it's in my head!" Calum lifted his chin, tears streaming down his face, nose bleeding. No—not bleeding, dripping some kind of dark, viscous fluid. He let loose with a yell and then fell into sobbing again. "Sorry, I'm sorry—God it hurts!"

Ross pushed Geordie to the side and leaned close to Calum, frowning.

Outside, Angus was leading the crowd in song at this point. Geordie ran his fingers into his hair. "What is it?" he asked Ross. "This isn't like him—what's happened to him?"

Ross placed a hand on Calum's brow and whispered a phrase Geordie couldn't make sense of, but it calmed his cousin immediately. The doctor reached across Geordie and snatched up a small piece of cotton cloth. He carefully dabbed at the fluid dripping from Calum's nose and held it up to study it carefully.

After a brief examination, Ross' frown deepened. He glanced at each of his friends in turn and when he spoke, it was in a hushed tone. "I don't know what this is, but there's magic in it."

"Can you help him?" Geordie asked.

For answer Ross turned back to Calum and placed his hand on his forehead. "Sleep," the Irishman whispered. Geordie's cousin slumped. "Get him situated on the cot there," Ross instructed. "He'll be out for a few hours at least. I'll see to him when everything is said and done."

Geordie swore and stalked back onto the field, followed by the other three. He held up his hands for silence as the final refrain of 'Annie Laurie' faded. "My cousin is feeling unwell," he said, "and so I think the final challenge will have to go unmet—"

"It bloody willnae, ye English-loving coward!" came a cry from the back of the assembled crowd. "You'll meet my blade or forfeit your title and lands t'me!" Hamish Maclaren pushed his way to the side of the arena, a sword in his hand.

Geordie frowned. "This isn't the time—"

Hamish clambered over the railing surrounding the field and shoved Angus out of the way as the latter tried to block him. "All for show, is it?" Hamish sneered, then spat on Geordie's boots. "I challenge you in truth, boy! Prove your mettle if you can!" Four other men joined him on the field—none of them were faces that Geordie recognized. Hamish swung his sword in a slow circle, then reached out a hand and beckoned.

At the end of the arena, Geordie's mother jumped up. "Stop—stop this!" she cried. "This is wrong—my son is his father's heir! You have no right to contest his inheritance!"

Hamish spat in her general direction, causing a ripple of uneasiness to run through the assembled crowd. "Hey!" Angus shouted. "None o' that, now." He turned to Lady Kirkleith. "Beggin' pardon, my lady, but by Maclaren laws and tradition Hamish has the right to challenge–not that anyone thought him mad enough to do it, the daft bastard."

"I will have my rights," Hamish proclaimed, "or I'll have it known that this *boy,*" he sneered, "is no true Maclaren, and none will pledge their allegiance!"

Scowling, Geordie angrily pulled his claymore from the dirt and paced back a bit. "You're a fool, Hamish Maclaren," he growled. "Lads!" Asher, Quinn, and Ross arrayed themselves on either side of him, blades at the ready.

"Stop!" Another man came running into the arena, unsheathing the sword buckled to his side, and took up a stance by Asher. "I am Dugald Stewart," he cried, "chief of my sept and ally to the Maclaren, now and forever, and I willnae see him challenged on an uneven field!"

Geordie shook his head. "You're a good man, Stewart, but this is not your fight."

Angus stepped in. "This challenge will proceed by the rules," he proclaimed loudly. "You cannae have more than three seconds, Hamish Maclaren. Follow the rules or forfeit."

Hamish glared at each of them in turn, then jerked his chin at the accomplice furthest from him. That man climbed back over the railing, and upon seeing this, the Stewart saluted Geordie and retired from the field. Hamish spat on the ground again. "Satisfied?"

Angus raised his brows at Geordie, who lifted his lip in a snarl. "Aye."

Out of the corner of his eye Geordie saw Quinn swing his blade in a controlled arc. Each of his friends stared down the man standing opposite them.

Whatever happened on this field today, he was not facing it alone. Geordie rolled his shoulders and looked to the stands where his Ione watched. She was worried, that much was obvious, but even from this distance Geordie could see the love in her eyes.

Angus stepped back, and the fight was joined.

Hamish's three spread themselves across the yard, and Geordie's seconds stayed with them; Hamish himself carefully stalked to Geordie's left, sword pointed toward Geordie's chest. Geordie pivoted, keeping the older man in front of him, hands clenching around the hilt of his own weapon. "You're weak," Hamish sneered, "like your father. Whoever took him out did us all a favor."

The shock of his words hit Geordie like a wall of ice. "You *dare*," he began, but Hamish cut him off.

"Aye, he was a weakling and a fool," He took a step closer and swung his blade toward Geordie's right shoulder, as if testing something. When the blow was blocked he continued with another verbal assault. "You're better than he, are you? Are you? Prove it, boy."

There was a dull buzzing in Geordie's ears; his fury mounted to such intensity that the effort of keeping himself in check made his hands shake. "Stop your bloody mouth, Hamish, or I'll stop it for you." Through the haze of anger Geordie could hear the sounds of multiple blades clashing. Quinn gave a shout and there was the sound of impact, followed by a grunt from one of Hamish's men. Geordie vaguely heard Angus call Quinn the victor as the other combatant left the field.

"I could never understand what your ma saw in James Maclaren, but maybe it was all about the money after all," Hamish jeered. "Maybe she was in the pudding club and settled for him, eh? Maybe you're not a Maclaren at all!"

"ENOUGH!" Geordie let out a roar and went for the other man, claymore raised high.

Hamish parried, knocking the blow aside with a look of dark satisfaction. "Touched a nerve, did I?"

Geordie rebounded quickly, and launched another attack. This time Hamish did not parry, but met the downward swing with wild enthusiasm. Steel scraped against steel, and the weapons locked at the hilt.

"Shut your foul mouth!" Geordie let go of his claymore with one hand and backhanded his opponent across the face.

Blood dripped from Hamish's split lip, but he grinned, his saliva pink and dripping. "Maybe your ma's not the only whore," he returned. "Maybe it's that Sassenach wench of yours too, spreadin' her legs for all who'd have her, like all her kind—"

At the mention of Ione, Geordie saw red. "You *bastard*," he snarled, and swung hard, fully intending to—

—kill? Geordie checked his swing and shook his head. He was no murderer, he—

Taking advantage of Geordie's distraction, Hamish pushed in closer, and then... something gleamed in the sun and Geordie staggered back. Pain lanced through his side and he clutched at it, his hand coming away bloody.

An odd sensation broke through the pain. It was a kind of pulling, or knitting together. Ross let out an agonized cry, dropping his sword and going to his knees, arms in front of him. Asher and Quinn suddenly gasped; he looked up to see both his friends' momentum hitch, blood spilling from identical gashes on their sides, exactly where Geordie's own was—but then the wounds disappeared, leaving behind only a smear of gore.

Ross was hunched over on the ground, eyes tightly shut, panting as he pulled his arms close to his chest. His opponent grinned ferally and reared back. "ASH!" Quinn rapped out, but Asher was already there, sword blocking the other man's blow.

"Not bloody likely," Asher growled, and exploded into motion. He kicked the other man in the chest, sending him reeling, then followed up by planting the claymore in the sod and using it to launch himself into the air, wrapping both legs around the man's neck and bearing him to the ground. Ross' assailant struggled to get up but Asher leaned back and in a magnificent show of strength lifted the other man into the air and flipped him over, landing him hard enough to wind him. He clambered onto the man's chest and punched him once in the face. "Yield."

"I will nae—"

Asher bloodied his nose. "Yield."

"Ye cannae—"

One more punch.

"Aye, I yield, I do!"

Meanwhile Quinn was beside Geordie, his sword trained on Hamish. "Drop it," he said, "or I will drop you, I swear it."

Hamish bared his teeth, but after a glance at his second's condition under Asher's furious assault, dropped his sword—and a dagger.

Angus leapt forward, shoving the other man back. "Madman!" he cried. "Did you seek to murder the Maclaren?" Someone was dragging Ross' opponent from the field, moaning; Asher's own adversary quit the field, shaking his head. Angus shoved Hamish back again. "Speak up, man!"

Hamish licked his lips. "I meant him nae true harm," he said, though his eyes narrowed as he studied Geordie. "The boy's fine, look at him." He glanced at the others, his scowl deepening. "I never went near them," Hamish told him, his expression frustrated, his small eyes sparking with anger. "You cannae blame me."

Geordie took a breath to clear his head, looking out across the gathered crowd to find his lodestone: Ione.

She was out of her seat and standing at the fence, worried gaze locked on his face. Geordie inclined his head toward her in reassurance. He saw her shoulders relax and then her attention seemed to drift to Geordie's left, where Ross was still seated on the ground.

His lips thinned. "Keep an eye on that one, Angus," Geordie said with a nod toward Hamish, and went to see to Ross, squatting by him. "What's happened to you?" he asked gently.

Beads of sweat ran down Ross' brow. "I'll be fine," he muttered and offered Geordie a weak smile. "Things got a little... heated." He gingerly moved to push himself off the ground. "You all right?"

"I'm well enough," Geordie admitted. "Head aches a bit, but that'll soon go, I'm sure. Need to take care of something first, and then we can all go home."

He returned to Hamish, eyeing the man as his friends stood behind him. "I can't prove anything, you're right about that," he said, while Hamish listened smugly. "But there is something I can do. Hamish Maclaren, I banish you from my lands and my clan," and now Hamish had gone first white, then red, "for the remainder of your life. If I catch wind of your return—ever—I swear to you now, I will make you regret it."

"You cannae—" Hamish sputtered, but Asher and Quinn flanked Geordie, arms folded across their chests.

"Perhaps you don't quite understand what the Maclaren—the *true* Maclaren—is saying." It was Quinn who spoke, his voice low. "My name," he said, "is Quinn Rutherford, and if you ever learn anything of me, it will be that I have the ear of her Majesty the Queen as well as her prime minister, Lord Salisbury. Leave these lands and these people now, today, and do not return, or I will bring my considerable influence to bear and I will *ruin* you. Do you understand?"

Hamish gaped like a fish, and then flung himself away from Angus, stalking angrily away.

"Send some of the men to watch him, make sure he leaves," Geordie told Angus, suddenly exhausted. He rubbed his eyes as Angus nodded and left.

A hand clasped his shoulder. "Something wrong?" Asher asked.

"My head," Geordie told him. "Aching fit to burst."

Ross stepped up and put a hand on Geordie's other shoulder, and then there was a cooling sensation. The ache in his head eased, though it didn't vanish entirely. "I'll have another go at it once I've rested up a bit," Ross said, offering Geordie a tired smile.

Geordie nodded. "Let's go home." The crowd had already begun to disperse; he took his leave of those he could as politely as he could, but was relieved when his mother took over for him.

There were still far more people around than Geordie would have liked, but a beloved voice rang out over the chatter. Even as Geordie turned in the direction of it, the crowds seemed to part to make room for the future lady of the clan. Ione picked up her skirts and ran toward him, calling his name again.

Relief flooded through him as he swept her into his arms. "It's over, love. It's over, and everyone is all right." Geordie leaned back to look at her. "I don't yet understand everything that happened, but—you're a marvel, Ione. You saved my life, and Ross, and who knows how many others today."

She cupped his face in both of her hands, stroking his cheeks with her thumbs as she looked him over. "You're safe, thank God." She stood on tiptoe and placed a brief and chaste kiss on his lips, seemingly unconcerned with the multitude of onlookers. "It was a group effort, I assure you. All that matters is that it worked."

One of the grooms approached with Starlight. "We can take the curricle, if you'd rather," Geordie offered.

"I'm not the one who spent the day fighting for my life," Ione replied. She stroked his face one last time and stepped away. "We will go home in whatever manner you wish, so long as you're recovered by our wedding."

In the end Ailsa rode Starlight (with much glee) and Geordie and Ione joined his mother and Tamsin in the curricle. Back at the castle he found a hot bath and a hot meal waiting for him, and when once he had availed himself of these, Geordie felt nearly human again, and met the others in his study downstairs for a general clearing-up of mysteries.

Ione settled at his side, fingers lacing through his and clinging tightly. She'd been at his side every moment that was appropriate since returning to the castle. She'd even sat across the table from him and watched with approval as he ate.

"Well, that seemed to work, at least as it was explained to me," Quinn said, clapping his hands together.

Ross looked at him, then to Tamsin. "There were a few surprises, but the burns are almost healed now, never you fear, Lady Tamsin." Across the room the pretty blonde thinned her lips, cheeks going pink, but she gave the doctor a nod.

Geordie felt like a musician given half the score. "If you could perhaps try to recall that it was all a surprise to me—by design—and explain?"

Ione gave his hand a squeeze. "The bracers were charmed. Once they were activated, any injury you received was shared by Mr. Rutherford and Mr. Burton, reducing the severity of the wound. Ross' bracers connected his magic to each of you."

"And pulled it as soon as you needed healing," Ross supplied.

Geordie took some time to think this through. "Are you tellin' me," he began, and Quinn muttered 'uh oh', "that you pair of great oafs took a stabbin' for me?" He turned on Ross. "And you—what happened to you, that you went down? The pullin' of your magic—it harmed you, somehow?"

"In our defense, we didn't know the damned things were going to brand me," Ross answered, avoiding eye contact. "And the lads had my back."

Ione cleared her throat. "It was the only plan that didn't spark a new vision of death." She glanced at Tamsin before returning her attention to Geordie. "We took as many precautions as we could."

Quinn was thoughtful, fingers drumming on the side of his glass. "I still have questions, though." He looked at Ross. "What was wrong with Calum? That black substance," he clarified, side-eyeing the ladies and forbearing to describe further, but Geordie knew what he meant.

The doctor pursed his lips. "Some kind of venom, with a magical element to it. Geordie got a dose as well, though not as large."

"Venom?" Ione looped her arm around Geordie; her eyes darting to his face with unveiled concern. "But it's been treated, yes?"

Ross nodded reassuringly. "I took care of it, I promise you."

"Is that why I–" Geordie broke off, unwilling to admit how close he'd come to doing something unforgivable.

"Went full berserker?" Ross supplied, and nodded again. "As far as I can tell, yes. It seems to be meant to amplify anger and pain–emotional pain, specifically."

Quinn spoke up. "How was it administered? We were all there–we were all paying attention."

Ross rubbed the back of his neck uncomfortably. "As to that, I'm not sure, though with that magical element it could be as simple as a spell cast."

"What I want to know," Asher chimed in, "is what Hamish Maclaren wanted out of all that."

"My title and lands, presumably," Geordie replied mildly.

Asher held up a hand. "Chief of the Maclarens, maybe, but your Kirkleith title is an English one. As to sovereignty over your lands–would his clansmen really cede that to him for killing a very popular laird?"

Geordie thought about that. "You mentioned that Mr. Melville thought my father's death might be connected to the issue of crofters' rights. Hamish," he took a deep breath, "was against them. He came to see me specifically to find out my position on the matter."

The two agents exchanged glances. "I'd very much like to speak to Hamish Maclaren," Asher said, putting down his drink.

"He's already left Maclaren lands," Quinn replied. "Damn." He contemplated his drink. "I'll let the home office know—he's bound to turn up again, and when he does..."

Geordie looked at each of them in turn, at last letting out a huge breath. "Thank you," was all he could think of to say. "I can't—I wish you hadn't had to suffer, but I'm grateful for your care, all of you. I owe you everything."

"You'd have done the same for any one of us, Geordie," Quinn replied first, and the other two men agreed quickly.

"Aye," Geordie admitted. "I would—and I'm no better man than the three of you. As to you ladies," he looked to Ione and Lady Tamsin, "without you, today would have been my last. I've a rough idea of how t'repay one of you," his lips curved a bit, "but my lady Tamsin..." He went to stand before her and took her hand. "From today, I am your most faithful and loving cousin, and if you ever have need of me, I will be at your side."

"The parfit gentil knight." Tamsin smiled. "I ask only two things, my lord: the first," and Geordie raised his brows in inquiry, "is that we drop this lord and lady business, for it is meaningless among family."

"Done," he replied immediately, and grinned. "And the second?"

She considered him. "Only that you care for my cousin to the very best of your ability, every day, for the rest of your life."

Geordie glanced over at Ione, then back to her cousin. "I so swear, Tamsin," he replied solemnly, and they shook on the bargain.

When Geordie returned to his bride's side, she looked up at him with eyes glistening affectionately. "We'll take care of each other. I think we've proven to be a formidable team."

Chapter Twenty

Changes on the Horizon

The house was still and quiet, a sense of contentment in the air, even as change was on the horizon. So much had happened in so short a time that to Ione it seemed another life had passed in the few weeks since she called off her engagement to Mr. Gibson. That night had been so different from this one, Ione mused. She'd been the diamond of the Season, her wedding meticulously planned for months. Now she was simply a woman in love, and the wedding—while sure to be an elegant affair—was only the first step in a life she could not wait to embrace.

Ione had dismissed her maid and insisted on changing into her nightclothes herself. Tomorrow she would become Ione Maclaren, Lady Kirkleith, wife to the chief of the Maclaren clan. For tonight she simply wanted to be Ione. She situated herself at the dressing table and pulled the last few pins from her hair. For the first time in her life, Ione truly liked the reflection that stared back at her. Scotland was meant to be a punishment, but it had tempered her like steel. She'd found her Geordie, but she also found her voice and her strength. She'd found herself, whether her last name was Brentwood, Gibson, or Maclaren.

The sound of her sitting room door opening and then closing pulled Ione from her examination. Geordie had come to her again, propriety be damned, she thought. They belonged together and nothing in the world could be more natural. Once the risk of scandal might have bothered her, but no more.

Geordie tapped once on the bedroom door, stepping inside a moment later. Ione met him halfway, fusing her lips to his. Everyone was safe, the challenges were over, and when morning came, she would bind her life to his. Their meeting tonight was one of joy, of relief, and the promise of things yet to come.

"I oughtn't have come, I know," he growled into her hair, "and I've no expectations. But I needed to see you." A chuckle rumbled deep in his chest. "You've made me a desperate man, Ione Brentwood, and I'll be desperate until you're Brentwood no more, but safely in my keeping. Tomorrow cannot come soon enough for me."

Ione laughed a little herself. "I *am* in your keeping, dearest. The name is merely a formality." She stroked his face, brushing the hair from his forehead. "How is your head?"

"Fine. A little dizzy, perhaps, but only just," he admitted, "and not badly. But the pain is gone."

"From that mysterious venom?" Ione frowned. She studied him carefully, then took his hand and led him to the bed. "Sit. If you're still dizzy you should not overtax yourself."

"Never fear, bonny girl," he replied, using her hand to tug her closer. "I said only just, not completely foxed. I'm a bit lightheaded, is all."

Ione curled into his lap and wrapped her arms around him. "Still," she began, smiling playfully, "I think it would be for the best if you spent a little time in bed." She leaned in and kissed him lightly. "I suspect you'll need your rest these next weeks."

He caught the back of her neck, pressing his forehead to hers. "If it's this bed you mean," Geordie murmured, "rest is not what either of us will be getting. Is that what you want?"

For answer, Ione gently pressed against his chest, urging him back on the bed. "We can rest later."

Geordie left Ione's bed before sunup, which was just as well, since Rose was in Ione's room with the dawn. Ione was rushed out of bed and into a bath, with a breakfast tray warm and waiting when she dried off. She wasn't particularly hungry, but it wouldn't do for her to faint of hunger halfway through the swearing-in. She'd be a wife by then, and expected to stand at her husband's side as he made his oath to the clan, and heard the people's words of fealty in return. In some ways it felt that Ione was marrying the clan as much as the man, and perhaps she was. No matter: she'd found her path in life, and her partner, and they'd more than proven they were equal to the task.

The hallway door opened and closed while Rose was finishing off Ione's hair, studding it with pearls and tiny white flowers. "'Brightly dawns our wedding day'," Tamsin warbled as she waltzed into the room, bringing the bride's bouquet. "'Joyous hour, we give thee greeting!'" Already arrayed in the pale blue gown Ione had chosen for her to wear, she dumped her armful on the bed and went to give Ione a kiss on the cheek. "Good morning, dearest! I hope you slept well?"

As she could not answer truthfully in front of Rose, Ione simply ignored the question. She stood before her wedding dress, as it hung on the door of her wardrobe, brushing the tips of her fingers across the silk. "It really is happening, isn't it? I can hardly say how I came to be here, Tamsin, but I would do it all over again to be with him."

Rose applied fragrant rosewater to Ione's wrists and behind her ears, and then helped her into the lacy white dress, after which Tamsin dismissed her to get ready for the festivities and began to lace up the back of Ione's bodice herself. "It warms my heart to see how he loves you, Ione," she said gently as the maid left the room. When the door had closed behind Rose, Tamsin went on. "I shall take the mantle of oracle for a moment and prophesy: I foresee a long and happy life for you both. And if good wishes and love can make such a thing come to pass, then your future is assured." She turned her cousin to face her, artfully draping the Maclaren plaid across one shoulder, fastening it with a rosette in the same tartan. She kissed Ione's cheek. "Oh, my dear, you look lovely." Tamsin sniffled a bit, smiling mistily.

"Don't cry, cousin, you'll get me started." Ione pulled Tamsin into a tight hug. "I cannot thank you enough."

Tamsin broke the hug and gently turned Ione toward the tall looking glass. "Presenting Ione Maclaren, Lady Kirkleith," she said, a catch in her voice. Ione gingerly touched the Maclaren tartan across her chest, taking in her own reflection. "Oh! That reminds me," Tamsin went on in a return to practicality. "We've had letters from my uncle. He, along with your mama and Elsie, will be arriving tomorrow to meet your new fiancé."

"Oh!" Ione echoed her cousin, meeting her gaze in the mirror with a wide-eyed look of her own. "I entirely forgot to tell them of the change in plans—should I have sent a telegram?" All at once Ione shook her head and smoothed her skirts. "No. It changes nothing. I shall marry Geordie today even if the sky itself should fall. Papa will be disappointed, I am sure, but—" and here she grinned at Tamsin, "it is a feeling he has become used to by now, I am certain." Her cousin laughed aloud; Ione started giggling as well. "They will think we've both gone mad in here."

"It isn't madness, it's joy, and well-deserved after all that's gone before," Tamsin returned.

Ione allowed herself another moment of giddiness before she took herself in hand with a happy sigh. She picked up a pair of lace gloves and her bouquet and pronounced herself ready.

"I'll fetch your escort," Tamsin replied, then hesitated. "Who is it to be?"

Ione stopped midway through the bedroom and stared at her cousin, realizing suddenly, and with a little amusement that in all the excitement she'd forgotten that small, but rather important detail entirely. None of the men in her family were even in Scotland. But was she to be the Lady of Clan Maclaren or not? "Could you ask Angus to come, please?"

Tamsin's brows rose, then she smiled and gave a nod. "See you at the church," she replied, and left the room in a swirl of pale blue silk.

Some time later Angus knocked at Ione's open door. "You sent for me, my lady?"

Ione felt a little thrill at the use of 'my lady'. It was the first time anyone had used the title when addressing her, and it was a delightful precursor to truly becoming Geordie's wife. She smiled at the Scotsman and gestured for him to come inside. "I did, Mr. Maclaren. I wished to make a request of you, a rather important one as it happens."

He immediately stood at parade rest, hands clasped behind his back. "Beggin' your pardon, my lady, but 'twill be seemlier for you to call me Angus, as the rest of the household does. How can I help you?"

"I shall remember that going forward, thank you, Angus," Ione replied, studying him for a moment before she continued. "You've served Lord Kirkleith's family for years, and Geordie speaks of you with great affection." Ione took a step closer to the older man and held a hand out to him. "My family has not yet arrived, and will not until tomorrow. I was hoping you, as the nearest to a father Geordie has, would do me the very great honor of escorting me down the aisle?"

Angus' mouth fell open, and then snapped shut. He blinked a few times, and Ione was pretty sure she saw his chin tremble a bit before he cleared his throat. "I would be honored, my lady." He took her outstretched hand in his and bowed over it, his bristly beard brushing her knuckles.

"Thank you, Angus." Ione's smile broadened. She moved to his side and slipped her hand into the crook of his elbow. "Shall we make our way to the church then?"

He seemed to shake himself. "Yes! Yes, of course. I believe the curricle is waiting for you." He patted her hand where it sat nestled in his elbow and escorted her proudly.

Ione sighed with contentment as he led her out of the room and down the grand staircase. Though she felt a flutter of excitement it was not the sense of dread that she'd experienced with Theodore. It was quite a good thing Angus had her arm, for Ione knew without that tether she'd likely run down the stairs and surely take a tumble in her haste to be Geordie's wife.

The curricle was covered with flowers and white bunting, even to the reins and the cockade in the driver's hat. William the tiger handed her in with a broad smile, taking leave to wish her happy, and when Angus was settled beside her, they set off to the church.

Balmaclaren's main street was lined with well-wishers, waving and throwing petals; they followed behind the curricle, creating a veritable parade of good will that made Ione feel like a queen being welcomed into her kingdom. She smiled and waved back realizing that the feeling she had was that of coming home—but home wasn't a place, it was a person.

Tamsin was waiting for them in the narthex of the Balmaclaren church. She beamed at them both. "Ready? I have it on good authority that Geordie is about to burn down the church, he's chafing so."

"Then let's not keep him waiting any longer." Ione took a little breath to still the excited flutter in her chest. She felt as eager as he, and could not wait to see her beloved and be made his wife in front of God and everyone.

Tamsin gave a nod, the nave doors were flung open, and she sailed down the aisle with a broad smile to take her place at the harp that had been set near the altar for her, next to Ross—who looked notably nervous—and his cello. Geordie stood opposite, flanked as always by Asher and Quinn.

Ione's hand tightened on Angus' arm as the music began and they took their first steps into the church. Her breath caught in her throat when her eyes met Geordie's; everyone else seemed to fade into nothing. She was certain that if Angus had not been holding her arm, she would have lifted right up off the floor, and flown down the aisle to her groom.

Geordie stood transfixed, his lips parted slightly. A shaft of light fell across his head and shoulders, lighting up his coppery hair. She could tell the moment he saw the tartan across her dress: his stormy eyes filled, a single tear slipping free to trail down his cheek, though his mouth curved in a sweet smile.

Ione fixed his image in her mind; she wanted to remember this for as long as this life was hers. She wondered vaguely, if she had indeed begun to fly, for she was hardly aware of her feet touching the ground. Time seemed to slow as the distance between them shrunk and her world centered on Geordie, and the vows they were about to exchange. She smiled up at her beautiful Scottish warrior as Angus released her arm and moved to place her hand in Geordie's.

He brushed at his eyes and took her hand when Angus gave it to him, smiling down at her beatifically. 'I love you,' he mouthed, and they turned to face the celebrant.

Geordie's voice was rough with emotion as he repeated his vows, but loud enough that all present could hear. He took a sprig of white heather from Ione's bouquet and tucked it into his lapel by his heart, as he swore to love, honor and cherish her, to worship her with his body, and lay it down for her if need be. He took her hands in his as the celebrant wrapped a silken length around them, declaring them to be thus bound, hand to hand, heart to heart, forevermore. And then...

"Ye may kiss yer bride, Geordie lad," chuckled the minister.

The look that came over Geordie's face at those words made Ione feel as though her heart had stopped beating. She met him halfway as he leaned down to kiss her, fervently taking his mouth, heedless of those who stood nearby. The only thing that mattered at this moment was that she was his, truly, before God, and there was nothing that could break that bond.

The kiss was tender, heartfelt, and all too brief; then Geordie was leading her back down the aisle amid flying heather blossoms and rose petals. He held her hand tightly in the crook of his elbow and led her back to the narthex. "Ready, wife?" he asked, caressing her cheek.

"I didn't know the word 'wife' could sound so beautiful." She put her hand over his, closing her eyes and leaning her cheek to his palm. "I love you, husband."

Tears started to his grey eyes again. "Thank God for you, Ione Maclaren. Come, let the clan greet their lady." He pushed open the church doors and brought her onto the steps. From the village square arose a clamor of cheering. congratulations, and applause. Geordie held up his hands.

"Friends, family, loved ones all," he cried, voice carrying in the ensuing silence. "I give you your lady and my wife, Ione Maclaren. She is, unequivocally, the best thing that ever happened to me, and I shall love her all of my days." More cheers and laughter, followed by shushing noises. Geordie let out a breath and looked across the people gathered there. "There's but one thing left to do before I'm truly your Maclaren. Will you do it?"

Behind him, the Stewart stepped out of the church and pushed his way through the assembly to stand a step below the viscount, in full view of the crowd. "I will!" he shouted. "I am Dugald Stewart, chief of my sept and ally to Clan Maclaren, and I pledge my fealty to this Maclaren! He will have my sword for as long as I live, God bless him!"

Angus knelt. "You're my chief, just as your father before you," he said, and then louder, "I pledge my life to your service, sure as my name is Angus Maclaren!"

Another voice rose up in tandem with a calloused hand. Donal—he of the missing cow—pushed through the crowd, hat in his other hand. He came before Geordie and Ione. "I, Donal Burns, do so swear my fealty and service to you, chief of Clan Maclaren!" He had a dagger at his belt, and pulled it from its sheath to kiss the blade and hand it to Geordie. "Ye have my loyalty and my arm should ever ye call upon it."

Wallace was the next to step forward, and beside him Calum, looking somewhat the worse for wear but smiling nonetheless. Pledges came fast and furious then, the head of each family swearing their loyalty to Geordie. Ione beamed with pride as she watched her husband's clan come forward, realizing that the support they promised was more than tradition. The people of his clan swore their oaths from the heart, openly and without hesitation.

After a few minutes, the tumult died down, and Geordie held up his hands again. "I thank you all, from the bottom of a very full heart," he said. "And now I've a vow to make to you." From the ripple of surprise, Ione realized this was a departure from tradition. "I swear," Geordie proclaimed, "before God and all of you, that I will serve you to the very best of my ability for as long as I am granted life on this Earth. I know I will fail sometimes, as all men must; but you have my word that I will strive to do all that in me lies. You have pledged your lives to me: I now pledge mine to you."

"You do do a thing thoroughly, Geordie," Quinn observed dryly under cover of the ensuing ballyhoo.

Out of the corner of her eye Ione saw Ross nudge Quinn, then lean over. "Shut it, before he asks any of us to make a speech as well."

"Both of you shut it before you give him any ideas," hissed Asher, but Geordie only laughed.

A private reception was arranged at the castle, though 'private' hardly meant small. Family and the local notables were present, and the ballroom was abuzz with music and happy chatter. It was the beginning of a new chapter for the Maclaren clan, and for Ione. She danced with his friends, smiled and laughed with their guests, but it was Geordie who held her attention and her heart. When it was finally time for them to retire for the night, there was no need for secrecy.

He led her up the grand staircase to the landing, where they bid the rest of their guests goodnight, and then without warning Geordie scooped Ione into his arms and carried her the rest of the way up, much to the crowd's expressed approbation.

He kicked the door to his chambers closed and set her down. "Well, bonny girl?"

"Very well, husband," Ione said with a grin, idly wondering how it was that her cheeks did not ache from a day of smiling. She reached up to tenderly stroke his temple, sobering a little. "Shall we to bed?"

He shucked his jacket and tugged at his tie to loosen it. "Aye, wife. I have it on good authority that I do things thoroughly, so I'd best get started, hm?" All at once his mouth was on hers, though he was smiling too.

They slept little that night, and were slow to wake the next morning; they were slower still in finding the motivation to get out of bed. Ione snuggled against her husband, reveling in the freedom of loving him as much and for as long as she liked. It wasn't until both their stomachs were grumbling that they found the will to dress and go downstairs.

The castle was quiet, all traces of the night's festivities cleaned up and whisked away with remarkable efficiency. Yet even as they approached the dining room, it was apparent they were not the only ones late to rise. The voices of Geordie's friends drifted through the door, happily recounting what seemed to have been an impromptu gathering between Tamsin and the three schoolmates after the reception ended.

Tamsin, when they entered the breakfast room, was buttering a slice of toast. "...never become incapacitated after imbibing, thank you. It's not at all ladylike." She glanced up at Ione and Geordie and smiled. "Good morning, my dears!"

Ione noticed that her cousin was in her traveling suit. "Good morning." She released Geordie's arm and moved to her cousin's side. "Are you leaving us so soon?"

"I'm afraid so. You are well and truly launched—you don't need me underfoot. And my uncle arrives today, so I thought it a good time to retire from the field." Tamsin laughed. "But honestly—Tav is accusing me of abandoning him, so I thought I'd better get back. The duties of being a twin, you know."

Ione kissed her cousin's cheek. She would have liked for Tamsin to stay longer, but this departure was hardly a surprise; her cousin had never been one to linger. "Oh, if I know you, you'll be off on another adventure soon enough." She shook her head and gave Tamsin a playfully put-upon look. "Now that I'm a married woman, I suppose I'm far too dull for you."

"Oh, dearest. Your company is all anyone could desire," Tamsin demurred. "But I've had you all to myself for weeks, and you have better things to do now." She grinned at Geordie, who grinned right back.

"I'm glad you came down—my coach has been waiting for me this past quarter-hour, but I didn't want to leave without a proper goodbye." She rose from her seat.

By unspoken consent they all followed Tamsin out to her coach. Geordie handed her in, and she took merry leave of each; at last they could say goodbye no more, and she tapped on the roof, blowing a kiss to Ione as the coach rumbled away.

When the carriage turned down the road and faded from sight, Ione nestled closer to her husband, resting her head on his arm. As the new lady of the house, she knew it was her responsibility to see that their company was attended to, but all she really wanted was to keep Geordie all to herself.

Quinn eyed them. "Well, I don't know about you fellows," he said to Ross and Asher, "but I plan to take full advantage of the lap of luxury while I'm in it. We'll have to leave soon enough."

"What do you suggest?" asked Asher.

Quinn shrugged. "Billiards and brandy?"

"Or perhaps a ride," Ross supplied. "And then after we can all meet in the parlor. I've something I'd like to share when we've had a chance to settle for the day."

Ione's grip on Geordie's arm tightened as she felt her magic tingle. An odd sort of buzzing began in her head and a shadow seemed to fall over Ross as he and the other two went back into the castle to change into riding clothes. She drew a deep breath, certain that a premonition was about to overwhelm her.

"What is it, love?" Geordie asked, and at the sound of his voice the buzzing in Ione's ears eased away. "Ione, are you unwell?"

"No, I'm—" Ione shook her head. Though no vision had been summoned, she could still feel the magic simmering just beneath the surface. She turned to Geordie. "Something's coming."

He frowned. "You've had a vision?"

Ione shook her head again. "It wasn't a vision, but I..." She stopped and took a deep breath. "It's been a busy few weeks. I'm sure it's just part of adjusting to all of these changes." Hoping that was all there was to it, Ione wrapped her arms around Geordie's waist and stood on tiptoe to kiss him. After a moment he pulled away, and led her into the castle, an intimate smile curving his lips.

ROSS MCINERNY'S STORY
CONTINUES IN *HEALER'S TOUCH*,
COMING SOON!

ABOUT THE AUTHORS

Jennifer learned a love of historical fiction and romance from her mother, but her love for fantasy grew all on its own. Combining the two is one of her favorite pastimes, and one in which she has been indulging since her youth. She has several other novels available, including *Force Majeure, Freeing Fortune,* and *Mr. Pembroke's Ward.* She lives in Pennsylvania with her husband, daughter, and cats.

Christen is an avid reader who enjoys going on adventures whenever she can. Her love of fantasy started at an early age with fairytales and The Hobbit. She lives in Kansas in the home she shared with her late husband. She first discovered a love of storytelling on the stage. In her late teens she began writing, a hobby that helped her through her husband's death. She is the author of the Song of Souls trilogy, and its prequel, *The Twisted Path.* Christen enjoys spending days in her gardens and having adventures with her friends and family.

Seer's Choice is the first book in the Fae-touched Chronicles, and represents the first collaboration between Sanders and Stovall. What began as a birthday gift between authors has truly taken on a life of its own. We hope you enjoy our world.